THE DEATH OF NNANJI

THE SEVENTH SWORD
BOOK FOUR

THE DEATH OF NNANJI

THE SEVENTH SWORD
BOOK FOUR

DAVE DUNCAN

OPEN ROAD
INTEGRATED MEDIA
NEW YORK

Copyright © 2012 by D.J. Duncan

978-1-4976-4032-0

This edition published in 2014 by Open Road Integrated Media, Inc.
345 Hudson Street
New York, NY 10014
www.openroadmedia.com

The Death of Nnanji
is dedicated to

Richard Curtis, who has been my agent for more than twenty years, who carefully recovered all the rights when any of my books went out of print, who pioneered the e-book ahead of almost everyone else, who made all those out-of-print books available once again, who has now become my publisher, and who, in short, has been my steadfast companion in journeys through many strange worlds.

THE DEATH
OF NNANJI

THE SEVENTH SWORD
BOOK FOUR

PREFACE:

ENCORE! ENCORE!

THIS IS A SEQUEL TO *THE DESTINY OF THE SWORD*. It can be read on its own, but if you haven't read the original trilogy, I urge you to start with *The Reluctant Swordsman* and leave this book for last, because otherwise it will spoil the rest for you. If you have read the first three, then welcome back to the World of the Goddess.

This is a book I said I would never write. After every series (eleven so far) fans have asked me for sequels. I always decline, because much of my enjoyment of fantasy comes from exploring an impossible world. Once I have done that, I want to move on and explore another. "The Seventh Sword" was not only the first of my series, it has also been the most successful. Re-issued as e-books, it has again outsold all my other works. Naturally, I have been asked many times for encores.

I refused because I thought that the demigod had sewed everything up at the end of the third book, in an epilogue called, "The Last Miracle". He did hint at later problems, but I couldn't see a story in them. Then one day lightning struck and I saw that, no matter what happened, if a god said it wasn't a miracle, then it wasn't a miracle.

This Volume Four cannot have exactly the same flavor as

the original three, for much of that came from the conflict between Wallie and the World. By now he must have adjusted to its strangeness, but we all encounter new problems as we age, and Wallie is no exception.

(A final note. When names begin with double consonants, both letters should be pronounced. Thus Nnanji sounds like *N'Nanji* and Jja roughly like *Zsa-Zsa*.)

BOOK ONE:

HOW A SWORDSMAN CAME HOME

CHAPTER 1

THE LESSER STARS HAD FADED, BUT THE brightest soldiered on. As a new day approached, the dark eye of the Dream God had set in the southwest; a distant rooster had already begun summoning his wives. Soon the great city of Casr would waken.

Something had wakened Wallie. Something wrong.

There was something very sharp underneath him, digging into his back. The long summer heat still lingered, so he and Jja slept on the balcony outside their bedroom, overlooked by no one. The pallet they lay on was thin, because that let the floor tiles keep them cool on hot nights. No, there was more disturbing him than whatever the sharp thing was. The waist-high parapet around the balcony was armored with downward-pointing spikes on the outside, supposedly making it inaccessible to intruders. Glancing around through half-closed lids and making no unnecessary move, Wallie detected a watcher studying him over the edge: an assassin, on his way in, three floors above the courtyard. His face was blacker than the night behind him. Only the gleam of his eyes gave him away—that, and white teeth holding a knife. Already he was clambering over the parapet, being careful not to catch his legs on the spikes.

Asleep or awake, a swordsman should never be far from his sword, especially if that swordsman happened to be vice-emperor of the World. There had been at least a dozen

assassination attempts against Nnanji since the founding of
the Tryst, and three or four against Wallie, although none
for several years. His sword lay beside the pallet, true, but
it was a king-sized pallet, and he was closer to Jja's side of it
than his own. He would have to lunge to reach it, presenting
his back to the killer. He was also under the bed sheet. If
Jja had her side of the sheet wrapped around her, he would
become entangled. The attacker would be inside his guard
before he could find the sword hilt and sit up to meet the
attack. An assassin skilled enough to climb the wall might
well be skilled enough to throw his knife.

Wallie must be growing careless in his old age.

He did not intend to stop growing older yet, though.

He had a few advantages. He was awake, which the
intruder could not know yet, and he had Shonsu's great
size and strength. The long-dead Wallie Smith, a somewhat
sedentary chemical engineer on another world, would
have had very little chance in this situation, although
assassination had not been an occupational hazard for him
back then. His right arm was under the sheet, the left one
outside, but Shonsu was ambidextrous, and the killer would
have to approach from his left, to avoid wakening Jja.

The intruder swung his feet down to the balcony without
a sound. At once he dropped low, so he was no longer
silhouetted against the sky. He was good! He was now
waiting to learn if he had been detected. Wallie kept his
breathing slow, despite his racing heart. The killer began
creeping closer, although Wallie had no idea how he knew
that, for the man seemed to make no noise at all.

Then the killer's foot nudged the sword, which made a
very faint scraping noise on the stonework, so he was already
within striking distance, and Wallie had not expected that.
He sat up with a howl and swung his pillow to deflect the
knife coming at him. Except it wasn't a knife, it was his
own sword, and that misjudgment very nearly decided the
contest right then there. He deflected the stroke just enough
that he could throw himself flat, underneath it, and grab

the intruder's ankle. Before his hand could be sliced off, he yanked as hard as he could. The man went down.

Judging by his size, he could hardly be more than a boy, but he was *very* good, as lithe as a snake, up on his feet as soon as Wallie was. For a moment they faced off, both crouching slightly, a pillow against a sword and a knife. The killer was wielding the sword with his left hand, so he might well be ambidextrous also. This time the assassin lunged, instead of slashing. The blade went right through the pillow, and Wallie only narrowly escaped being impaled. But he caught his opponent's right wrist and heaved him around, clean off his feet, hoping to slam him against the wall. He had forgotten the ornamental granite column that stood there, supporting a large brass pot. The pot made a resounding clang as it hit the tiles, while the impact of the column was probably felt throughout the building.

That hadn't worked, so Wallie heaved him around in the opposite direction, despite the risk of dropping him on Jja, who was making protesting noises. Again the youth displayed superhuman agility, landing on his feet and yanking the sword free of the pillow in a blizzard of feathers. He might have won the battle at that moment by slashing Wallie's hamstring or Achilles tendon, but Jja sank her teeth in his calf, and that threw his timing off.

Wallie got him by the throat, hauled his arm around his back, and deliberately dislocated his shoulder. The boy screamed and dropped both weapons. Just to make sure, Wallie threw him flat, face down, and knelt on him.

"You all right, darling?" he inquired in the calmest voice he could summon.

"Just a nasty taste in my mouth. You?"

"Perfectly well, thank you. I appreciate the judicious assistance."

At that moment Vixini burst in like an avenging angel. Even before the door at the far end of the bedroom hit the wall, he was out on the balcony, standing over them with his sword in one hand and a flaming torch in the other.

He roared, *"What?"*... and stopped with a gulp when he realized that both his parents were stark naked.

"You're supposed to knock first," Wallie said. "Especially when we have visitors."

"What is going on?"

"We were entertaining an assassin, until your mother tried to chew his leg off."

By that time Jja had managed to free enough of the sheet to pull it up to her chin. "Fetch my robe, will you, Son?"

As Vixini turned to obey, four more swordsmen ran in, led by Adept Sevolno, head of Lord Shonsu's night watch. He showed his teeth in fury at the sight of the intruder—fury mixed with fear, perhaps. When Lord Nnanji heard about this, he might have Sevolno's sword for it, and possibly his head as well. Nnanji was due back in Casr before noon.

"Take him," Wallie said, rising. "Careful of his arm. No, don't maltreat him!" he shouted, as two of the others grabbed the assassin. "Oh, Goddess! *Her* arm, I mean." Displayed in the light of the torches, the captive was both naked and undoubtedly female. "Bring her in here. I want to talk with her." He led the way into the bedroom, leaving Jja with some privacy. The five swordsmen followed, Vixini with his sword still unsheathed.

Wallie grabbed up his kilt from where he had thrown it on the bedand made himself respectable. Then he pulled a sheet from the bed and draped it around the woman, telling the swordsmen to guard the door so she couldn't make a run for it; also the archway to the balcony so she couldn't jump to her death.

Then he took a good look at her. She was young, as was to be expected, and petite, with the elfin figure of a gymnast. She wore her hair short, as did everyone except swordsmen. The People varied in color from light to dark brown, but he had never seen any as dark as she. She had been dyed. Peering closely at her forehead he saw no visible craft marks, which the laws of the Goddess required on every adult, although she was no longer a child. Removing facemarks was an old sorcerer trick, although even hiding them under a coat of dye would be a felony.

"Let me see your eyelids," he said. She just stared up at him in resentful silence.

He smacked her nose—not so hard that it would bleed, but hard enough to make her blink. As far as he could tell from that brief glimpse of her eyelids, she bore no parent marks either, and the skin there, where the dye had worn off, was much paler.

"You're a sorcerer," he said firmly. Only sorcerers could make tattoos disappear, although even the sorcerers officially never did it now, since the Treaty of Casr had brought them into the mainstream of the People's culture. Facemarks were basic to the society of the World.

The prisoner did not speak. Instead she opened her mouth wide, making Wallie recoil in horror. Where her tongue should be was a stump of white scar tissue. She leered at him triumphantly. What sort of fanatic would let her tongue be cut out to prevent her from revealing secrets? Or had she been bribed with a lie that sorcerers could replace missing organs by magic?

"Well, you can still be questioned," he said. "You can write your answers."

She shook her head vigorously.

He smiled. She grimaced as she realized that he had trapped her.

Vixini missed that exchange and put the idea into words. "We can make her talk, my lord! We can play twenty-one questions with her."

"Maybe," Wallie said. "Prisoner, I will promise you your life if you will answer a few questions for me now by nodding or shaking your head. Are you a sorcerer?"

No answer.

"Were you sent by a sorcerer?"

Still none. He did not care much who she was, but he very much wanted to know who had hired her. Most attempts on his life or Nnanji's had been made by dissident swordsmen wanting to return to the old ways of independent city garrisons and roaming bands of free swords. A few had been organized by corrupt rulers or gang leaders who opposed the law and order that the Tryst was seeking to impose on the World. Even religious fanatics had tried, although they had never come this close to success.

Obviously this assassin was not going to cooperate.

"We have the rest of your life to question you," he said. "Adept Sevolno?"

"My lord." The swordsman pulled out his sword and knelt to offer it to Wallie, head bowed in shame.

"Get up, you fool. I want to know how this she-cat got into the grounds and up the wall and past the spikes."

"We'll make her show us," Sevolno said with a menacing smile.

"Not that way! Keep her well locked up, certainly, but find decent clothes for her and call a healer to treat her shoulder. He may give her a potion to ease the pain. You can ask her questions, but no rough stuff, understand?"

One of the first reforms Wallie had imposed on the People had been a complete ban on torture, on the grounds that the information it produced was useless. Sevolno certainly knew that, but a swordsman, and especially one feeling that he had failed in his duty, could easily become overzealous.

"So I want you to go and *look*, to find out how she got in. And if you've gone off duty..." Wallie glanced thoughtfully at young Vixi. He was not a member of the palace night watch and normally wild oxen were needed to get him out of bed in the morning. How had he managed to respond to the disturbance sooner than anyone else? One would get you ten that he had just come home and hadn't been to bed yet. Not his own bed, anyway. He might have taken up wenching, certainly, but more likely he had just been carousing with other low-ranks. "Take Apprentice Vixini around with you and show him what you find. If you've gone off duty before I come down, he can pass on your report. Meanwhile, I'm going to finish my night's sleep. Dismissed."

Wallie strode out to the balcony again, chuckling in silence at the dismayed expression he had seen come over his stepson's face. As one of Wallie's protégés, Vixi must stay in constant attendance on his mentor, and Nnanji's return was certain to keep Wallie on the run every minute until, very likely, past midnight. By then Apprentice Vixini would be regretting his late night.

Jja was under the covers again, but wide-awake. She watched as he retrieved his sword and laid it beside the bed. He dropped his kilt and lay down beside her. The sky was the indefinable, colorless shade it turns just before sunrise.

"It's not worth going to sleep again," she said. She was a big, powerful woman, who had borne four children already and showed no signs of wanting to stop. An invitation like that saved him from making the suggestion. He slid an arm under her and cuddled close. *Ouch!*

Annoyed at the distraction, he felt around and located the sharp object that had wakened him when he had rolled on it earlier, a jagged pebble. He held it up between finger and thumb and whistled in astonishment.

"What's that?" she asked.

"This, my darling, is what saved my life, and probably yours too. It woke me."

"But where did it come from?"

That question had no rational answer.

"Don't ask 'where', ask 'who'."

"What?"

"No, 'who'. Our little friend, remember? You met him once."

Wallie had met him four times. Each time he had appeared as a small, undernourished boy with a gap in his teeth and a big smile, but he was a demigod, a messenger from the maternal deity of the World, known simply as 'the Goddess'. When Wallie had invented the treaty to end the age-old feud between the swordsmen and the sorcerers, the demigod had promised no more miracles. In his own right the demigod was god of jewels, though, and if the appearance of an uncut diamond as big as a thumb joint in a man's bed was not a miracle, then what was it? And if it was, did that mean that events had taken a turn that not even the gods had foreseen?

CHAPTER 2

THE SUN HAD BEEN UP FOR SOME TIME WHEN Liege Lord Shonsu, swordsman of the Seventh, came trotting downstairs to breakfast. He came alone, Jja having been called away to comfort little Budol, who had fallen and banged her head. Wallie felt no guilt at today's tardiness; the World had no time clocks to punch, and he had put in some overtime during the night. He looked forward to a quiet snack by himself on his private terrace, hoping to plan as much as he could of his day. Nnanji was sure to throw a million jobs at him the moment he slid off his horse, or even sooner.

The wonderful summer weather must break soon, but meanwhile the terrace was a shady haven, overhung by trees bearing wonderful fruits: plums the size of grapefruit, blue cherries that tasted like Benedictine liqueur, and something he thought of as chocolate pine cones. Very earthlike pigeons strutted around the paving, muttering and scavenging crumbs.

Today was Masons' Day, which happened to be Nnanji's birthday, meaning that there was little more than two weeks until Healers' Day, celebrated each year to mark his accession as senior liege lord of the Tryst. The previous leaders—Wallie himself, Boariyi, and the late Tivanixi—were conveniently forgotten. This year, although Wallie might be the only one keeping track, would be the fifteenth anniversary.

Two bites into a juicy mango, Wallie's reverie was interrupted. He had forgotten that he had given Vixini a job, and that young man, as both his stepson and protégé, had access to him at any hour of the day or night. He marched out to the terrace carrying a fishing rod, which he laid carefully on the flagstones before whipping out his sword and launching into the formal greeting to a superior:

"I am Vixini, swordsman of the second rank, and it is my deepest and most humble wish that the Goddess Herself will see fit to grant you long life and happiness and induce you to accept my modest and willing service in any way in which I may advance any of your noble purposes."

His normal greeting when there were no outsiders present was a cheeky, "Go, Bear!" which was the local equivalent of "Hi, Dad." This morning, clearly, he had come on business and was enjoying his own importance.

Wallie had risen from his stool and must now draw his own sword to give the formal response before he could resume his meal. Then Vixini took up the fishing rod, except that it wasn't a fishing rod. It was made of spliced canes, like a fishing rod, but the hook dangling at the thin end would have choked a whale.

"We found this. This is how she got in, see?" Rising on tiptoe, Vixini reached up to a window aperture about twenty feet above the ground, and caught the sill with the hook. "It's much stronger than you'd expect," he said cheerfully, lifting himself one-handed, to show that he was, too.

Of course most materials were stronger in tension than compression, but that was not the sort of thought that translated easily into the language of the People. Wallie was more impressed by the assassin's ingenuity and motivation than his son's muscles. "I admire her courage. When she reached the top floor, she must have had to haul herself up with her arms and walk up the wall between the spikes."

"Suppose so." His stepson sat down uninvited and reached

for the cheese basket with one hand and a slice of ham with the other.

"Where did you find it?"

"Hanging on the wall of your balcony, o'course."

Wallie regarded him with the joy and fond envy that parents bestow on dearly loved offspring. Yet Vixi was Jja's son, not Shonsu's. He had been a babe in arms when the late Wallie Smith of Earth became Shonsu, swordsman of the Goddess, so he must be sixteen now. It was a peculiarity of the People that they never counted their ages. They remembered and honored their birthdays, but not the years—and their 343-day year was an inaccurate count anyway, based on religion, not astronomy. The stars ignored it, just as the People did. You were as old as you looked and acted; seniority depended entirely on rank.

The strangest thing about Vixini was that he had grown up to look so like Shonsu, which was undoubtedly another miracle from the demigod. He was already taller than at least ninety-nine percent of the People, dark-haired and brawny, and yet incredibly nimble for his size. Everyone just assumed that they were father and son, and that Vixini would become a swordsman of the seventh rank in due course. Wallie doubted that, because Vixini was so amiable and easygoing. He tried to model himself on the man he believed to be his father, but that man was Wallie Smith. Shonsu, the original Shonsu, had been a vicious psychopathic killer. Vixini had the necessary agility and certainly the strength, but it was very hard to see him clawing his way to the top of the swordsmen's craft. He lacked the arrogance and ambition.

Mouth-full mumble: "Dad... Can I ask a favor?"

"Of course. That doesn't mean I'll grant it."

"Not for me." Vixi swallowed with an effort. "For Addis. He's terrified his dad's going to insist he swear to the craft. He's not cut out to be a swordsman. He's got three feet."

That exaggeration was swordsman slang for a stumblebum. Addis had the normal number of feet. He might not be the superb natural athlete Vixini was, but Wallie had never thought of him as clumsy. It would be in character for

Nnanji to insist that his eldest son swear to his father's craft, for that was the People's tradition. He might not care much whether the Tryst became a hereditary kingdom, but Thana, Addis's mother, was the prototype social climber—Lady Macbeth on steroids.

Until fifteen years ago, the two most prestigious crafts had been the swordsmen and the priesthood, but now, with the Tryst ruling half the World and accepting female recruits, all parents' cherished dreams of their children becoming swordsmen. Since the Tryst could have its choice of any adolescent it wanted, its standards were high, but no swordsman examiner would reject a son of Nnanji if his father wanted him admitted.

He must be fourteen now, Wallie decided. "Is he ready?"

Chewing again, Vixi just grinned and nodded. Children ran around naked. At the first visible signs of puberty they were decently clad and inducted into a craft, and it didn't matter how old they were in years. Initiation was irrevocable. Once a night-soil collector, always a night-soil collector.

"What does he want to be?"

"A sorcerer!" Vixi wrinkled his nose in disgust. To a true swordsman, anyone other than a swordsman was trash, but sorcerers were the lowest of the low. Although the Treaty of Casr had formally ended the age-old feud between the two crafts, neither side trusted the other a hair's-breadth. Wallie could not imagine Nnanji tolerating his firstborn becoming a sorcerer.

Although Vixini and Addis were very different types, they were also lifelong pals. In effect, Nnanji was emperor of the World and Shonsu vice-emperor. They were very different types, too, but the loneliness of power had thrown them and their families together. They had no peers. Anyone else they befriended always wanted something: if not a job, then favors, justice, or revenge. It was rare for both of them to be in town at the same time, so they acted as father substitutes for each other's children. Those children had played together and grown up together. Vixini and Addis were bonded for life.

"What does his mother say?" Nnanji could be as stubborn

as a mountain. Only Thana might budge him when he had
made up his mind about something.

Vixini pouted. "She says he has to be a priest."

What Thana wanted, Thana usually got.

"Why do you have to ask me for miracles at breakfast?"

His stepson grinned, suddenly looking more like a
heavyweight cheeky kid than a potential man-killer. "To
give you the rest of the day to deliver."

"You faith is so touching I feel quite weepy." Wallie
glanced up at the sun. Nnanji had been at Quo last night.
Never one to waste a moment, he was probably halfway to
Casr already. He was quite capable of taking one glance at
his adolescent son and blurting out that he must be sworn
in by nightfall. Or he might just accept Thana's suggestion
without argument. Once he had made a decision, he would
have no way to back down without loss of face, and face
mattered to him much more than it did to Wallie. The most
important thing now was to keep father and son apart
for a couple of days, so Wallie would have time to play
peacemaker.

"Go and find Addis and tell him to... No, *bring* him to
me, at the lodge. I'll find a way to keep him out of sight for
a while."

"Yes, my lord!" Vixi grabbed a couple of bread rolls and
shot away, leaving the assassin's pole hanging forgotten
against the wall.

Wallie regretfully gobbled the rest of his meal and
summoned his bodyguard. Traditionally the swordsmen's
guild had been exclusively male, the only exceptions being
the "water rat" swordsmen of the trading ships, of which
Thana had been one. Almost the only thing on which she
and Wallie agreed was that they disagreed with that policy.
In a sense her thinking came from a different world, just
as his did, because on the trading ships even the civilian
sailors knew how to wield swords. Between them they had
persuaded Nnanji, so the swordsmen's craft was no longer
segregated and a fair number of the younger swordsmen

were female. The same word served for both sexes in the language of the People, although when Wallie thought in English, as he still did sometimes, he had to remember that a swordsman could be a woman. As he walked out the gates of his palace that morning two of the six at his back were. Their leader, Filurz of the Fourth, marching at his side, was male.

The ancient city of Casr had never spread upstream farther than the temple, because the water there was too shallow for ships. When the original lodge building in the town, already in sad disrepair, had proved inadequate to house the Tryst, expansion beyond the temple had been the obvious move, so Wallie had not been surprised to discover that all that land had recently been acquired by Swordsman Katanji, Nnanji's plutocratic brother. The Tryst had been forced to pay a premium price for it, but had done so without argument because Katanji was also its treasurer. Nnanji, blissfully unaware of economics and caring less, had failed to notice any conflict of interest.

Thana ran Katanji a close second in avarice, though, and the next block of land beyond the new lodge grounds had turned out to be in her name, and there she had built the liege's palace, a cross between Versailles and the Taj Mahal. Nnanji never cared where he slept; he was happiest on campaign, in a tent or under a hedge. Wallie himself had built another palace beyond that, a much more modest one, but still a palace. He needed too many servants and guards to get by with a more modest home... had to keep up his status as vice-emperor... entertained a lot.... All true, but he still felt guilty, knowing that the Tryst's enormous wealth came from taxes paid mainly by the poor of the World, as taxes always were in agricultural societies.

And what of all the great reforms he had planned to make? Some had worked, yes. Slaves' babies were born free now, no longer disfigured at birth with slave mark tattoos. Children were not pressured quite so hard into following their fathers' trades. Vacancies among city elders must be filled by election, although the results often verged on chaos.

Trial by jury was being brought in. Other good ideas had failed miserably. Medicine, like every other craft, was frozen by hundreds of sutras handed down from the Goddess a thousand years ago. No sutra mentioned bacteria or asepsis. As for sewage... Almost every city in the World stood on the banks of the River. Where else could you run sewers? The basic creed of the world religion was, *The River is the Goddess and the Goddess is the River.* No sewers.

He had done some good, though, and the People mostly approved when Nnanji or other Sevenths arrived in their town with the Tryst's impeccably honest legions. Swordsmen, being both police and military, had far too often been bullies and crooks as well. Honest kings or elders tyrannized by corrupt swordsmen had welcomed the rescue, and honest garrisons were glad to be relieved of the duty of upholding bad laws. As the Tryst's borders kept expanding, the only serious resistance had come from tyrants and corrupt garrisons in combination, and there the citizens themselves often provided the necessary support.

Crowds parted for the liege, people bowing, saluting, smiling: naked children, scantily clad adolescents, decorous adults, all the way to the ancients robed from head to toe. The colors were common to all crafts, for all had exactly seven ranks: white, yellow, brown, orange, red, green, blue.

Everywhere there were swordsmen. For sixths and sevenths—greens and blues—Shonsu had to stop and accept formal salutes. Salutes from lesser folk he just acknowledged by thumping his chest with his fist.

So he came at last to the lodge, being saluted as he marched through the high gate. The din in the great central quadrangle was deafening. On the well-trampled grass under the shade trees at least two hundred swordsmen were fencing, leaping around, bellowing instruction, banging steel. Their ponytails flapped like banners, they streamed sweat, and they made him feel old. He was old, for a swordsman. Whenever Shonsu had been born, he had seemed about in his mid-twenties when he died and the Goddess gave his body and skills to Wallie Smith. Physically he must be around forty now, and mentally even older. Once he had been the greatest swordsman in the World, but Nnanji had overtaken him, and he knew there were younger men who could beat him now. So far none had been brash enough to do so.

Most days he liked to linger for a while to watch the training, mentally noting newcomers moving up the promotion ladder. Today he had too much on his mind. He carried on around the perimeter to the grandiose edifice that he thought of as the Executive Block. Nnanji called it the Tivanixi Building. To the rank and file it was the Lions' Den. It flaunted pillars, gargoyles, balconies, and turrets in the currently fashionable wedding-cake style. Marble and gilt shone everywhere, for this was a state building, expected to last for centuries.

Just inside the doorway, stood a skinny First, who moved forward to intercept without looking nearly as awed as he should at having to accost the great Lord Shonsu. He was a page on the liege's staff, named… named…

"My lord?"

"Yes, Novice—" *Got it!* "—Gwiddle?"

Gwiddle glowed with pleasure at being remembered. "Master Horkoda sent me to wa— to *inform* you, my lord, that Lady Thana and Chancellor Katanji are both waiting to see you."

"Great Goddess! They're not together, I hope?"

"No, my lord. Master Horkoda is attending her ladyship in your office."

Wallie muttered thanks and turned to the much larger lad hovering in the background. It was Vixini, with a very smug expression on his not-so-innocent young face.

"Where is he?" Wallie demanded.

"In the kitchen, my lord."

"Good man. Keep him there until I send for you. Um, wait…"

Vixi reversed his turn. "My lord?"

Wallie had been thinking about the killer in the night. Had he not wakened in time, he would have died. What would have happened then to Jja and the children? Jja was a highly intelligent and competent woman, but this was still a male-dominated world, and it had no pensions or entitlements. Nnanji might support her, if he thought of it, but chances were that the load would fall on this yellow-kilted kid with the sword on his back. A Second was not paid a living wage and had almost no legal standing, whereas a Third in any craft was an adult citizen, regardless of age.

"I am calling an assembly for Sailors' Day. I am going to put you up for promotion. You are still fifteen sutras short of the requirement for third rank."

Vixini stiffened in astonishment. "But, mentor—"

"I won't have time to coach you myself, I'm afraid. You have my permission to get help from other swordsmen." He turned to Filurz. "Adept, will you see my protégé is fluent in the first 314 sutras by Sailors' Day?"

Filurz looked skeptical but saluted, fist on heart. "My pleasure, my lord."

Vixini looked aghast at the prospect. "But..."

"That's an order, protégé."

"Mentor!" Vixini thumped his chest.

Chuckling to himself, Wallie headed for the guardroom, which offered a private route into his office, bypassing the antechamber where Katanji would be waiting.

"Keep them all here for now," he told Filurz, meaning that he might have to leave the lodge again very shortly. Since he did not need guarding otherwise, Wallie's escort could often spend their days training for their next promotion, which made theirs a very coveted posting.

He crossed the guardroom and stepped through the door into his office. Horkoda of the Fifth looked up with obvious relief, but did not stand up. Horkoda had been a rising star until he was pushed overboard during a fight on a ship. Although he had managed to catch hold of the rail and escape total emersion, by the time he had hauled himself completely out of the water, the piranha had taken all of his left foot and the toes of his right. He spent his days now in a wheelchair—designed by Lord Shonsu, of course—and now much copied in the World.

As Wallie's chief of staff, Horkoda ran the office and kept Wallie sane. Whether Horkoda himself was totally sane was open to question. He had reacted to his personal tragedy by rationalizing that he had been chosen by the Goddess to serve his liege in this way. He had turned into a workaholic, capable of working all night or forgetting to eat.

The office itself was roomy but simple. It was furnished with a table and stools, not chairs, because most visitors wore swords on their backs. A single chest under the window provided adequate filing space, for the World was still very largely illiterate, and the window itself offered a fine view of the riverbank and the mountains of the RegiVul range in the distance.

Lady Thana rose to greet the deputy liege.

CHAPTER 3

THANA WAS ALWAYS A PROBLEM. IN THE EARLY days of the Tryst she had tried sending for Shonsu when she had something to discuss. As a Seventh, he had declined to answer her summons, but that meant that she would not answer his either, so they had reached a tacit understanding that whoever wanted a meeting went to call on the other. In fifteen years Nnanji had never noticed any friction between his wife and his oath brother. She was still a strikingly beautiful woman, if no longer the svelte young goddess whom Nnanji had wooed and won fifteen years ago. Childbearing had thickened her, and in a few years she might be as bulgy as a feather mattress, like her mother, Brota. Nevertheless, Lady Thana was empress of the World, at least in her own eyes, and possessor of unbounded wealth. Nnanji was as honest as an angel; his wife and brother made up for it.

She gestured to make the salute to a superior. "I am Thana, swordsman of the third rank..."

Wallie drew his sword to give the response. Then, "I am glad to see Master Horkoda has been plying you with wine and pastries. I deeply regret keeping you waiting, my lady. I had a disturbed night, and—"

"So I hear. I congratulate you on a very narrow escape."

Just for a moment Wallie wondered if Thana might have sent the mysterious assassin after him, but saw at once that the idea was absurd. Their feud did not run as deep as that. In fact they needed each other, for they were both vital cogs in Nnanji's empire-building machine.

Wallie sat down on the nearest stool. Horkoda reached for his wheels, an offer to leave the two of them alone. Wallie gestured for him to stay.

"So what can I do for you today, my lady?"

"I received your message, of course, that my husband will return. I thought we might drive out together to meet him. I brought my carriage."

They had done that before, so it was not an unreasonable request. Indeed, when she did not invite him along, it was because she had been up to something and wanted to be sure she spoke to Nnanji before Wallie did. He was not aware of anything underhand overhanging at the moment, and Horkoda wasn't sending him signals to warn of something he ought to know and didn't. But Katanji was out in the waiting room, which certainly was unusual. Curious!

And why come in person instead of sending a servant with the invitation?

"That seems like an excellent idea," Wallie said. "The pickets out at the Divide will signal us when his train approaches." He glanced at Horkoda, who nodded to imply that that arrangement had been confirmed. Such signals were sent by pigeon. Nnanji was always pleased to receive a royal welcome when he returned from campaigning, but probably had little idea how much organizing that took. "There has been no further word from Lord Nnanji?"

Horkoda pulled a face. "A brief note, rather cryptic."

"Saying what?"

"Saying only, *Where is Lord Mibullim?*"

Blank looks all round.

"I do not recall any lord Mibullim," Wallie admitted. Nor even an Honorable Mibullim, as he would have been before winning promotion from sixth rank. Nnanji must be referring to a swordsman, or he would have specified the unknown man's craft when he dictated the message. "When did that arrive?"

"Just before dusk last night, late for the bird to fly. I have made extensive inquiries since then, my lord, and no one in the lodge has ever heard of a swordsman named Mibullim." Horkoda's idea of extensive inquiries might have involved staying up all night to question a thousand swordsmen.

Nnanji was at Quo. Casr was on the RegiVul loop, a part of the River very hard to access by boat, so the city's door to the rest of the World was the overland trail to Quo. A swordsman of the seventh rank never went anywhere without an entourage, so if Nnanji had expected to meet this Mibullim in Quo, the man should have been easily located. If Horkoda had found no trace of him, the man did not belong to the Tryst.

"Very peculiar," Wallie said, "but I expect we shall learn more when Nnanji arrives." There was no point sending a query to Quo; he would be well on his way by now. He turned to Thana again. "The moment I hear that Nnanji's party has been sighted, my lady, I shall ride over to your palace and be most happy to ride in your carriage with you."

She rose. "I expect he'll be here shortly. By the way, have you seen Addis anywhere today?"

Was that the real reason she had come here? Probably someone had seen the boy going off with Vixi and she had followed in hot pursuit to their most likely destination.

"Has he run off without his guards again?"

She rolled her eyes. "I suggested last time that we put a ball and chain on him, remember?"

Body guarding an active fourteen-year-old was like trying to glue a snowdrift to a ceiling. Thana had often appealed to Wallie to play the in-loco-parentis role and put the fear of the Goddess into Addis, but he was Nnanji's son: threats just bounced off him.

"If I see him, Thana, I will chain both his balls, I promise you." But Wallie was fairly sure that there must be more behind this visit, so he fed her a cue. "It's about time you found a mentor to handle him."

Cats never really smiled, but some smiles were catlike. "Which craft would you recommend?"

How much she had guessed about Vixini's abduction of her son that morning? Any child balked by one unreasonable parent would at once appeal to the other, and Shonsu was Addis's father substitute until Nnanji returned. Thana was within her maternal rights in not wanting Wallie interfering in the matter of her child's initiation, except that her son's choice of craft might become a matter of geopolitical importance some day.

Wallie had an empire to run, a reception and assembly to organize, a celebration to plan, and here he was, all entangled in the consequences of one boy's hormonal maturation. But that mattered. Of course it mattered! Addis was the eldest son. The World had never know an empire before Thana and Katanji invented that use for the Tryst, but it had umpteen petty kingdoms, and male primogeniture was the commonest means of succession. Vixini had said she wanted Addis sworn in as a priest. That made sense, because kingship was not a craft, and royal heirs were usually sworn to the priesthood. Priests were sacrosanct. Only a swordsman could wear the seventh sword of Chioxin, the sword of the Goddess, but a civilian could own a sword as long as he did not wear it or try to use it. Wallie was not at all sure that she was right, but now he knew how her mind was working, and he could see that the next day or two in the life of Addis, son of Nnanji, might well determine the future history of the World.

Why had there been a diamond in his bed to waken him? Why another assassination attempt just now? Who was Lord Mibullim? On Earth he had distrusted coincidences. In the World he saw them as the handiwork of the gods. All these odd events would turn out to be related, even Addis's coming of age.

"I'm not sure," he said truthfully. "Addis is a clever boy. He has lots of charm. And lately he's been getting very good at using it! He's his father's son when it comes to stubbornness, and probably courage. It's up to you and Nnanji to decide, of course, but don't try to make a fish fly, as they say."

Thana bit her lip and headed for the door. "I shall let you

busy men get on with your labors. See you shortly, Lord Shonsu."

"This way is more private!" Wallie hastily crossed the room and let her out through the guardroom. He did not want her coming face to face with Katanji, or vice versa. Life was complicated enough at the moment without getting any deeper into a family quarrel.

He went back to his stool. "Treasurer Katanji next, of course, please. And, master, why don't you see who else is out there and put off anyone whose business will wait until tomorrow?"

He meant that he wanted no witnesses when he spoke with Katanji, who was usually skirting some law or other on the wrong side. Understanding perfectly, Horkoda wheeled himself over to the door and went out. Wallie opened the hidden liquor cabinet and filled a silver goblet with his best sweet wine. He put a much lesser amount in a second goblet, then turned to hand the first to Katanji as the treasurer strolled in.

Katanji never bothered with formal greetings when he met Shonsu, because he knew Shonsu didn't like them. He had given up carrying a sword years ago. He was dressed very simply, without jewelry or expensive trappings, in a brown robe that would have suited an elderly cobbler or priest, although a sharp eye would note that it was finely cut from first-quality silk and his shoes were crafted from kidskin. This was Katanji posing as a humble state servant. While Nnanji knew nothing of money, Katanji was a financial genius, the richest man in the world. Nnanji lived only for honor and fame. Katanji hadn't an honest corpuscle in his bloodstream. His black curly hair was already receding, exposing the three sword marks on his forehead, only one of which he had come by honestly. His withered arm could have been concealed under his robe, but he carried it in a sling of silk brocade, as evidence of how harmless he was.

He sniffed the air while accepting the drink. "Magnolia scent. Thana's been here. What did she want?"

"The exact opposite of whatever you do, I expect. To the liege's happy return."

"And speedy departure!" They clinked goblets and drank. "Face it, big man, life is more restful when Nanj isn't around. What did she want?"

Wallie waved his visitor to a seat and resumed his own. "You go first."

"My dear nephew, Addis. You seen him lately?"

"Starting to ogle girls, is he?"

"They'll be ogling him soon if we don't hide the evidence. The question is what craft does he swear to? You know what Nnanji will say. What does Thana want?"

"I think she wants him to become a priest."

Katanji pulled a face. "Priests must be able to chant. Have you ever heard Addis singing? He thinks his home key is what locks the house up. And he's no more swordsman material than I was."

Said who? Granted that Addis might well have same of his uncle's trader instincts; that didn't mean he had no other talents.

"He's been working on you, too, has he? What does he have against his father's craft? Just juvenile rebellion?"

"Good sense." No one but Katanji would dare make such a remark, and even he would have to be careful who heard him doing so.

"He'd make a good priest," Wallie said. "He may not sing well, but he can certainly talk." Priests were more than prayer spouters and alms gatherers. They were also roughly the lawyers of the world, dealing with inheritance and civil disputes, just as swordsmen were policemen as well as warriors. There was no craft guild for politicians; priests were the closest.

Katanji sipped his wine. "The boy says he wants to be a sorcerer. I told him that would be over his father's dead body. The trouble is that being a swordsman is likely to be over his own dead body." He chuckled. "Seriously, Shonsu, can you imagine him trying to wear the seventh sword?

He'd be challenged in a minute. Every minute! That thing is a death warrant for anyone except Nanj to wear."

No swordsman could refuse a challenge. If one of the duelists died, the winner could claim his sword. "Or you, of course. Would you wear it now?" Only Katanji would be so brash as to ask that.

Of course Wallie would, and without a second's hesitation. The seventh sword was the Mona Lisa, the papal tiara, the Cullinan diamond. "Perhaps not. But he could own it without wearing it. Remember Arganari?"

"No."

Wallie hadn't thought about the boy for years.

After a moment, Katanji said, "What're you staring at?"

"Oh, just memories..." Why did those memories suddenly seem so pertinent? Because Wallie had seen the hand of the Goddess in that long-forgotten encounter, and he was starting to think Her hand was at work again now. "Arganari was a young prince from Plo who came aboard *Sapphire* briefly, at Tau. His mentor wouldn't let him stay on board, and later they were both murdered by pirates. Remember now? On Nnanji's wedding night? Arganari was just a novice swordsman, but he owned the fourth sword of Chioxin, the topaz. Fragments of others are around, but the topaz is apparently the only other one still usable. He owned it, but didn't wear it."

And the demigod had made some sort of prophecy about the dead Arganari, which Wallie couldn't recall offhand, which might mean that he wasn't supposed to.

Katanji drained his goblet. "Shonsu, when you gave Nnanji the seventh sword, you made it the emblem of the Tryst. Any other swordsman who manages to win it will claim to be liege lord and order all the rest to swear allegiance. But the Tryst isn't a kingdom; it will never accept orders from a priest."

"That's true."

"Addis should be a trader, which is what I am, despite my facemarks. The boy can talk fish out of a pond."

"He does have a way with words."

"Like me, you mean. He looks more like me than I do."

"I wouldn't mention that too loudly if I were you."

Katanji grinned. "It's funny, isn't it? Back in those days, when we were all shipmates on *Sapphire*, I was about the same age Addis is now, but I got it off with every nubile girl in the ship, often two a night. I even talked my way in with a couple of the wives. But not Thana! She was Nanj's. I stayed well away from her. Yet Addis looks more like me than Nanj."

"He's your nephew, not you reborn. He could be a swordsman. Not a great one, but a competent Third."

"A common, journeyman sword banger, whereas he'd be a fantastic trader. Vixini's good, I'm told. You don't have to worry about him not being yours, anyway."

Everyone except Jja and Wallie had forgotten that Vixi wasn't Shonsu's son. Handy things, miracles.

"And it's not an abstract problem," Katanji mused. "Nanj spends about two thirds of his time in the field, campaigning. When he meets a Seventh he doesn't approve of, he challenges him. One of these days his luck will fail him and he'll run into some wunderkind he can't handle. Pardon my plain speech, but you're not getting any younger either. We need a viable plan to hold the Tryst together if anything ever happens to Nnanji. Addis at thirty still in a brown kilt struggling to get promoted to orange just won't do."

Wallie nodded. He knew much more about war and insurrection than any native of the World did. Even Rome had been sacked, and Nnanji's empire was only fifteen years old, not yet armored in tradition and respect. Casr might burn for days if law and order once broke down. No one had more to lose than Swordsman Katanji.

"Have you considered prayer and an offering to the Goddess?"

Katanji gave him a sour look. "Thana came from a trader family. She should see that her son's talents lie more in trading than anything."

"Thana isn't a water rat anymore. She has grandeur now. She's wife of the liege." That was as close as the language

could come to the word Wallie was thinking, which was
empress. "Addis as a priest makes sense. No one kills priests."

"Oh, well. If you won't, you won't. Anything you need?"
Katanji was a great believer in mutual favors.

"Can you get me something to hide parentmarks?"

"Huh?" It was rare to see Katanji at a loss. "You know
the penalty for doing that?"

"I asked first." Wallie smiled. Mention of *Sapphire* had
reminded him of a certain novice swordsman who had
hidden his facemark under a lampblack slave stripe and gone
spying on sorcerers. Katanji had his faults, but cowardice
had never been one of them. Wallie had no reason to believe
that the liege lord's brother ever indulged in such deception
these days, but his hesitation in answering now suggested
that he at least knew people who did.

"I might be able to lay my hands on a sort of makeup that
ladies use to hide moles and so on. It comes off when you
wash your face."

"That will do. I will send a junior over to your hutch to
pick it up. I need it right away. I'll think about the Addis
problem when I have time."

"Don't wait too long." Katanji rose and handed back the
silver goblet, which had been a gift from him in the first
place. When offering wine to Nnanji, Wallie always used an
unglazed earthenware beaker.

CHAPTER 4

A S SOON AS KATANJI HAD LEFT THROUGH THE
waiting room, Wallie went out by the other door. His
guards sprang to their feet, scattering knucklebones and
money, but he spoke only to Filurz. "I need you to come
with me, the rest of you stay. If Master Horkoda comes
looking for me, we'll be down in the kitchen."

Leaving a dozen eyes stretched wide with amazement, he
marched out into the hallway. "I hope you know the way to
the kitchen, because I don't."

"Yes, mentor. Along here."

Swordsmen tended to be short, since agility mattered
more than strength. Filurz was one of the shortest seniors
in the Tryst, a swarthy little man with a high opinion of
his own opinions, which he tended to offer unasked. Wallie
usually overlooked his presumption, because he had a high
opinion of them too. Too many swordsmen were either
dumb jocks or toadyish yes-men.

"This may not be good mentorship," he said as they
started down a long flight of stairs, "but I may be about to
involve you in a major felony."

"In a good cause, I hope?"

"I think so. Adept Sevolno told you about the attempt
on my life last night. Did he tell you where he confined the
prisoner?"

"In the cell in your palace, my lord."

Wallie had a jail in his basement that his guards used as a brig if one of their number came on duty drunk, or otherwise offended. He had excused it to Jja on the grounds that a palace that didn't have everything wouldn't be much of a palace, would it? The children often played in it on rainy days.

"I want you to arrange for her to be taken to the city jail and locked up in the dingiest, smelliest cell they've got. But she must be on her own. The city jail is usually pretty full, as I recall."

"Yes, my lord. I'll have to get a cell emptied for her. Not that they won't do it, or anything."

Not when a swordsman of his rank demanded it.

"And obviously I want her very well guarded. Requisition some swordsmen to keep watch. There may be attempts to rescue her or kill her."

"And in either case we try to take prisoners?"

"Of course. Tomorrow we'll give her some company. Dig up some baby-faced junior who'll cooperate and be discreet about it afterwards. One who can read. We'll paint over his facemark and put him in her cell; see if she'll talk."

"Adept Sevolno said—"

"Yes, I know. She has no tongue. But she can still signal yea or nay." If she were a sorcerer, she would be able to write.

Filurz opened a door, letting Wallie walk through into warm, cozy odors of freshly baked bread. Apprentice Vixini was leaning back against a high worktable, gnawing on half a loaf while chatting up a couple of young slave girls. No doubt the older cooks in the distance disapproved of this, but they were not daring to criticize a swordsman, even a lowly Second. Addis, son of Nnanji, was hunched over, leaning hands and elbows on the worktable, watching but not participating. He was probably fair game for teasing at the moment.

Wallie had not seen the boys together for a while and the contrast startled him. Apart from not growing facial hair, the men of the People went through much the same adolescent metamorphosis as earthly males. Vixini had crossed that divide. He was a young man, close to his final adult height, broad, and piling on muscle, while Addis was still a child, just about to start his growth spurt. His arms and legs were spindly, his face elfin and androgynous. He looked absurdly immature and spindly beside his brawny friend, although there was less than two years between them.

Vixi whipped the bread out of sight. The girls fled. Addis straightened up and gave Wallie the salute to a superior. Wallie responded. He often wondered how much of the day the People wasted in these useless rituals.

"Son, I want you to go straight to Treasurer Katanji at his home. He'll give you a package. Bring it back to the lodge and give it to Master Filurz, who will have some delicious hot sutras waiting for you."

Vixini gave his stepfather mentor a look of a sort that respectful protégés should not, but repeated his orders smartly and departed. Most apprentices would be jumping up and down with excitement at the prospect of an early promotion.

Wallie bent and leaned his forearms on the workbench to put his eyes roughly level with those of Addis, who was now upright. The boy certainly didn't look like a swordsman, or likely to look like one for quite some time. Instead of his father's red hair and pale eyes, he had his Uncle Katanji's jet irises and black curls, and probably his crafty brain as well.

"About that problem you asked Vixi to mention to me." Vixini had not actually said that Addis had asked for Shonsu's help, but that had been the gist.

The boy said cautiously, "Yes, Uncle?" while glancing at Horkoda to decide if he were in on the plot. A conspiracy to frustrate the will of a liege was treason, no matter how thinly one sliced it. Any son of Nnanji and Thana was certain to be as open to argument as a nickel-iron asteroid, and Addis was stubborn in spades. If he wanted to fail the swordsmen's agility tests, he would instantly develop not just three feet, but five or seven. He might even refuse to swear to the code and dare the resulting scandal.

"I'm working on it. Right now I want you to disappear, so I don't know where you are. Where's your escort?"

Addis bit his lip and looked down at the bench. "Seeing that I was going out with Vixi and just coming to the lodge, my lord, I thought I didn't need to interrupt their breakfast."

Terms of address were very important in the World, and by mentioning escort Wallie had just gone from honorary uncle to a lord of the Seventh. Wildness was understandable in a high-spirited adolescent whose friends were all disappearing into the discipline of crafts, but it was also very foolish in his case. Although Casr was unbelievably law-abiding by terrestrial standards, it still had scoundrels, from would-be assassins on down. There would be no limit to the ransom Thana would pay to have her son returned. were he ever kidnapped.

"I have told you a dozen times that Vixini is not an escort. He's only an apprentice and there's only one of him. You're a very *pretty* boy, Addis, son of Nnanji. You have a lovely smile."

Addis looked up with horror, face flaming at the insult. "If any slob tries anything like that with me, I'll rip his balls off."

"Oh, well, that's different. I didn't know you were expert in martial arts! Show me. Put a headlock on Master Filurz."

Master Filurz drew his sword and laid it on the table, out of the way. Then he hunched his shoulders, waiting for the attack.

Addis hung his head again, probably to hide some teeth being ground. "I didn't mean it that way, my lord."

"You didn't? Addis, nasty things can happen to pretty boys, no matter who their fathers are." And here was an excellent opportunity to test the lad's swordsman potential without his realizing. Wallie turned to the frowning Filurz. "Do you know of anyone in the Tryst who's an expert in gutter fighting? Things like choking, eye gouging, finger breaking, biting, fishhooking, kidney punching?" The swordsmen's sutras strictly forbade fighting with any weapon except a sword, but swordsmen were more born than made, and they sprang from all sorts of backgrounds. The Tryst could usually spit forth an expert in almost anything.

Filurz actually laughed. "You have one of the best brawlers right under your nose, my lord—Swordsman Helbringr. Her father runs a tavern on the dockside at Quo. She and her brothers grew up as a rat pack bouncing drunks. And each other, I suspect."

Wallie enjoyed having a bodyguard named Helbringr, although the name did not mean what it would sound like in English, but he hadn't known of her curious background. She would probably achieve promotion to Fourth soon, and there were few women of that rank in the Tryst yet.

He said, "Excellent. If you refuse to accept a bodyguard, Addis son of Nnanji the swordsman, then you'll have to learn how to defend yourself properly. Stay here, and Adept Filurz will send Swordsman Helbringr down to collect you. Adept, I don't want to know where she takes him. I want him taught how to defend himself with his bare hands. And feet, and teeth. I'll collect what's left of him later, probably around sunset. Well, Addis? You man enough to accept some bruises in a good cause?"

The liege's son was unsure how to take this alarming prospect. Behind the bright eyes, a subtle but inexperienced young mind was calculating how best to respond.

"Wrestling with a woman?"

"I'll bet she can wipe the floor with you, and the ceiling as well."

"Puberty, here I come?"

"Oh, you sound just like your Uncle Katanji. Wait here."

Wallie headed back upstairs with Filurz.

Filurz could be quite subtle when he needed to be, which wasn't often. "My lord, the boy seems to think you've just sentenced him to a beating."

"Whatever could have given him that idea? No broken bones, of course, but he's been warned too often."

"I'll tell Helbringr to make sure he won't forget this time."

"Also, adept, please pick out four Thirds to examine

Vixini at the assembly. You willing to tell lies in a good cause?"

"Of course."

"Then you may explain to them in confidence that the boy is far too cocksure of himself and I want him taught a lesson in humility. In other words, I will not be offended however tough they are on him. I don't want the Tryst to think my son is being given special treatment."

"He's still very young to be even a Second, if I may say so, mentor."

No he might not say so! As well as captain of Wallie's bodyguard, Filurz was also his protégé, and by addressing him as mentor, had just reminded him of that fact. He wanted promotion to Fifth, and was hinting that Wallie was neglecting him, too.

"Tell them that too. I don't want you fixing this promotion, understand? Very few Thirds are capable of beating Vixi at fencing now, as you know. I am directing you to make sure that the sutra test is as brutal as possible, so the spectators can't start rumors of favoritism. No easy ones, understand?"

Wallie had been holding Vixi back because he was not mature enough for the responsibilities usually given to Thirds. Yesterday that had seemed right; after the events of the night, it felt wrong, whatever Vixini himself wanted.

Sometimes a despot just had to be despotic.

Horkoda had done a thorough job of weeding the antechamber. Only four swordsmen remained, all needing approval of plans for celebrating the liege's return. The program had become traditional. There must be a big thanksgiving service in the temple, a banquet at which minstrels would sing of deeds of arms—mentioning Lord Nnanji at every excuse—and an assembly of the Tryst, at which missions would be announced, novices admitted, and candidates for promotion would demonstrate their fencing. Any try at promotion was a public event, but the outcome was never certain, and a candidate who failed in front of an assembly made both himself and his mentor look foolish. The betting could be ferocious, which provided opportunities for gain, both legal and illegal. To throw a match was "to do a snail", since snails moved very slowly and coiled up inside their shells when threatened. Some bouts where both fencers were obviously trying to lose had given birth to legends.

None of this could be allowed to interfere with the annual celebration of Healers' Day, two weeks away, although that would include some of the same events.

Wallie did not need long to approve the plans, but the sun was casting very short shadows when he finished. The day was close to noon. Why had there been no word of Nnanji's progress? Neither man put the problem into words, but Wallie could see that Horkoda was as concerned as he was.

"I shall go and call on the wizard," he said. "Send a runner for me as soon as you hear any news."

The sorcerers' tower stood just outside the lodge on the landward side, and normally Wallie would have taken only one or two companions with him on his stroll across the plaza. After last night's episode and Nnanji's strange delay, he took his entire bodyguard. Today every moment must be put to use.

"You also wish to try for promotion, adept?"

Filurz brightened. "If you believe I am ready, mentor."

"Certainly. You only are seven sutras short, as I recall. Here goes. *Number 975, On the Control of Crowds: The Epigram...*"

In most cities the sorcerers built their towers of the darkest stone they could find, but Casr possessed only one building stone, which Wallie identified as a micaceous arkose. It came in attractive shades of pink through gold. Some quarries produced it in fissile slabs that made good roofing tiles, so on sunny days the whole city shone as if it were made of bronze. If the sorcerers felt cheated that their tower could not appear as menacing as they would like, they had never said so. The Casr tower was only a part of a larger complex including several more orthodox buildings. How many people lived and worked there was, like all sorcerous matters, a secret. So was whatever they got up to inside, but whatever it was frequently involved sinister flickering lights and irritating, jagged noises.

No one could doubt that it was the sorcerers' lair, though. Pigeons strutted on the ground outside, looking for grains of the food scattered there for them. The roof of the tower itself sported dovecotes and perching wires. The sorcerers' facemarks were feathers, perhaps because they held birds sacred, or perhaps because they had invented writing and used quill pens to do so.

Out of courtesy, Wallie had sent a herald to announce his coming, and he was ushered at once upstairs and into the presence of Lord Woggan, sorcerer of the Seventh, the wizard of Casr. As usual, Woggan received him in his study, which resembled no other room Wally had seen in the World, in that it featured shelves laden with leather-bound books. Apart from that, the room contained few comforts, all the chairs being hard-backed and upright, the floor tiled, the exposed walls undecorated. He strongly suspected that receiving non-sorcerer visitors was its only purpose and, if so, it contained no secrets or valuables. Even the books might be fakes, for his hints that he would love to borrow some of them had always been ignored. The windows were small and barred, commanding a good view of the lodge grounds.

Lord Woggan bore so little resemblance to Rotanxi, the sorcerer with whom Wallie had negotiated the epoch-making treaty, that they must have been brewed in different cauldrons. He was short and had once been plump, but now his fish-belly-pale face looked as if it had melted, sagging into jowls, bags, and folds, and settling his mouth in an expression of permanent disapproval. Nothing more of him was visible inside his bulky blue brocade gown, and even his hands usually remained hidden in his sleeves.

As the visitor, Wallie saluted first. The sorcerer responded with the customary hand gestures, but using words that differed from the People's standard by invoking the Fire God instead of the Goddess. "Please do be seated, lord swordsman," he added.

No stool being provided to accommodate sword-bearing guests—they never were—Wallie turned a chair sideways and sat.

"I shan't keep you, my lord," he said. "I am sure you are busy. I just wanted to ask about that curious message from Lord Nnanji last night."

He had not truly expected to catch Woggan out, and the old man's reply was the predictable, "Which message was that, my lord?"

Anyone who thought that the wizard of Casr did not read the liege lords' mail ought to have his head bronzed.

The Tryst and its troops in the field had three ways of communicating with one another. The safest was to dictate the message to a couple of third-rank swordsmen with good memories, put them on a ship, and wait the better part of a year for a reply. That was safe because most of the People were still preliterate and their memories were honed like razors; also because no one tampered lightly with two journeyman swordsmen.

The second was to write or dictate a letter and have it delivered by the river folk in relays, from town garrison to town garrison. Letters could be lost or intercepted.

The fast way was pigeon post, but the sorcerers ran the pigeons and charged for their use. Moreover, the birds would only fly homeward and thus had to be physically transported to their point of departure. To carry a word from the farthest reaches of the empire back to Casr would require many flights. That was certainly the least reliable and least secure method.

"It came in late, addressed to me from Lord Nnanji, and said only, 'Where is Lord Mibullim?' As we have no Mibullim of any rank in the Tryst and Lord Nnanji did not stipulate a craft, we assume it must refer to one of your brother sorcerers, my lord."

"If we had a Seventh by that name, I should know him, certainly." Woggan rose stiffly, went to a bookcase, chose a leather-bound volume, and fingered through it until he found what he wanted. He pursed wizened lips, replaced

the book, and returned to his chair. "No, my lord, we have
no record of a Mibullim in the Vul coven in the last century
or so."

"How about other covens, then?"

Doughy smile: "You will have to ask them, I'm afraid.
We sorcerers are not as well unified as you swordsmen."

Wallie could have scripted the entire conversation in
advance. For thousands of years, swordsmen had slain
sorcerers on sight, until he and Rotanxi had made a peace
treaty. Nnanji had accepted it—to everyone's astonishment—
and had persuaded the rest of the Tryst to tolerate it. Anyone
who killed a sorcerer now was charged with murder, anyone
at all.

But the cooperation was threadbare and grudging.
The sorcerers had expected to retain their monopoly on
all forms of literacy. Wallie had bribed them with a few
minor technical advances, such as soap and the basic
door lock, backed up by a threat that he could and would
introduce his own method of writing. So they had taught
him their system, which had turned out to be syllabic,
not alphabetical, but phonetic and easy to learn. He had
taught others. All apprentice swordsmen now had to pass
a literacy test for promotion to Third, although most of
the seniors still scorned such namby-pamby affectations.
Priests, healers, and traders were also taking up this arcane
but useful art.

Woggan leaned back in his chair and tucked his hands
farther into his sleeves. "The most likely explanation, if I
may say so, Lord Shonsu, is that your Mibullim was a free
sword or a guard commander who willingly swore loyalty
to your tryst and was therefore accepted by Lord Nnanji as
a helper. Your practice is to send high-rank recruits back
here to Casr for indoctrination, is it not?"

"I wouldn't use that word, but yes, you are right." Wallie
rose. "And Mibullim either changed his mind on the way
here or met with ill fortune. I should have thought of that
eventually, I suppose."

This pretense of stupidity made Woggan's eyebrows shoot

up like white flags. He didn't underestimate Lord Shonsu any more than Lord Shonsu underestimated him. He might or might not know what had happened to the missing Mibullim; either way he was not about to tell.

CHAPTER 5

MERCIFULLY, THE TRYST'S MARCHING BAND fell silent as soon as it had left the town to begin the long ascent through the surrounding vineyards. In front rode Lady Thana's glittering all-female troop of cavalry, escorting her grandiose carriage, which was drawn by eight of the World's ugly camel-faced horses, all bedecked with bright ribbons and silver bells. Wallie's bodyguards brought up the rear. The pace of the procession was set mainly by the coach, which resembled a large shed on wheels. It rocked and creaked abominably, and Wallie could look forward to at least another two hours of this torment. But he owed it to Nnanji, and even to Thana, to be present when the liege returned.

She sat across from him at one side of the big coach. The window seats on the other side were occupied by her daughter, Nnadaro, and younger son, Tomisolaan, aged around ten and five, respectively. Unlike Addis, both had inherited Nnanji's red hair. So far they were behaving themselves, but their presence made their older brother's absence obvious.

"You still haven't seen Addis anywhere, Shonsu?"

Wallie sighed, tempted to say that he had better things to do than babysit for her. "Thana, I have no idea where your firstborn is, beyond a vague belief that he is somewhere in

Casr." Being bounced up and down on a hard floor, very likely, by a woman larger than himself.

Trader genes detecting the evasion, she frowned at him. "Does Vixini know?"

"No. Addis is usually to be found in Vixini's shadow, but right now Vixini is up to his neck in sutras. Swordsmen in relays are shouting them in both ears. I'm putting him up for promotion at the assembly."

"Vixini? That's ridiculous. Even Nnanji must have been older than that when he reached Third."

"Not much older. When I found him, he was a three-footed Second. The Goddess and I turned him into a hotshot Fourth in two weeks. Vixini is not living up to his potential, so I decided to push him a bit." That was as good an excuse as any. To confess that Wallie himself was suddenly feeling mortal and vulnerable would not be politic.

"Why, for the gods' sake? A Third must be able to lead a troop. Can you imagine any battle tested, likely married, swordsman taking orders from a boy?"

"Easily," Wallie said. "Men don't talk back to someone half a head taller than themselves and half a chest wider." Not even one as amiable and soft-spoken as Vixini.

Thana studied him for a moment, then said, "You had a very narrow escape this morning, didn't you?"

Blast the woman! She sometimes seemed to read minds.

"Yes I did. And I am determined to find out who was behind it."

He didn't mention the inexplicable uncut diamond in his bed, for he considered messages from the gods to be confidential. They were always obscure. The demigod had warned him fifteen years ago that a mere mortal could never understand divine motives, because the multidimensional games the gods played were infinitely more complicated than any human politics and, from some points of view, not games at all.

"I'm worried about Addis," Thana said. "He ran off this morning without his bodyguards. I worry about him when he does that. He's not just the liege's son, he's also a very vulnerable and naive youth. There are predators out there."

More telepathy!

"I saw him soon after I saw you," Wallie admitted. "Yes, he was with Vixini at that time. And I thought exactly what you just said: he's too vulnerable. I sent him off to get some lessons in unarmed combat. He won't need them if he becomes a swordsman, or a priest, but until then they might save his life." Knowing Swordsman Helbringr, Wallie was confident that Addis was already much less vulnerable than he had been when he left home that morning.

Thana was glaring. "You didn't think to ask my permission first? He is my son!"

"And he's the heir to the Tryst, Thana. That makes his safety my concern too."

"And it makes his attendance today to welcome his father home a lot more important than your abominable lessons!"

Not when there were assassins around it didn't. "No. I agree with you that this skipping out by himself has to stop. I would never humiliate an adolescent by having him beaten like a slave, but Addis is not going to forget today's lesson. So it will be doubly valuable."

Thana compressed her lips and said nothing. She never admitted defeat.

In a moment she shouted at the children to be quiet. Her tension was understandable, in that she was on her way to meet a husband she had not seen in almost two years. Restarting their marriage would require tact and adjustment, but she had married Nnanji for his potential, not his sensitivity. Given the primitive state of birth control in the World, she must realistically expect to bear another child within a year.

"Lady Mother?" piped little Tomisolaan. "Why is that mountain on fire?"

The procession was up in the bare brown hills now, good only for rearing cattle and horses. A bend in the road had brought them a fine view over the great bronze city and the wide silver River beyond it. Today the mountains of the

RegiVul range were free of clouds, misty blue ghosts in the fall haze.

Wallie turned to look. "There should be two..."

But there weren't two peaks smoking. One volcano had erupted about the time Lord Tivanixi had summoned the Tryst of Casr in the name of the Goddess. The Tryst had been aimed at the sorcerers, devotees of the Fire God, and the eruption had shown his displeasure. A second eruption had followed soon after Wallie had stepped down in Nnanji's favor, and both peaks had smoldered on and off ever since. They must have had earlier names, but they were known to the swordsmen as Black Top and Red Top— ostensibly from the color of their rocks, but more likely from respective shades of Shonsu's and Nnanji's hair. The peak still smoking was the first, the southern one, Black Top. The other, presumably, was dormant—or extinct.

Wallie glanced back to Thana. She was a practical and hardheaded, almost cynical, woman, but the World ran on superstition. Even Wallie looked for omens in a way he never had before he became Shonsu.

Nevertheless he said, "They stop and start all the time. Don't lose sleep over it."

Thana stopped biting her lip long enough to say, "But when did this happen? We should have been told, or at least you should."

Yes, plenty of people would have told Wallie if they knew of the change: Jja, Vixini, Horkoda, and more. If the news was widely regarded as a significant sending from the gods, he should have heard. Thana seemed to be treating it as such. She looked positively scared, not at all like her usual unshakably confident self. That was not the Thana Wallie knew. Or the change might have just happened today, in which case the gods' message might be urgent.

"They come and go," he said easily. "I expect volcanoes need time off too. By the way, have you ever heard of a high-rank swordsman named Mibullim?"

She shook her head.

"Nnanji sent a message from Quo last night about a

Seventh by that name, and none of us have ever heard of him."

"Falcons?" As usual, Thana had hit upon the most likely explanation. Not all pigeons made it home to their boxes safely.

Some earlier message about Mibullim had undoubtedly gone astray.

Or Mibullim of the Seventh himself had gone astray.

Or the sorcerers who ran the pigeon post were censoring the Tryst's mail, and that was the most worrisome possibility of all.

"If you two don't stop that, I'll tell your father about you!" Thana yelled for the third time in the last two hours.

As before, the threat worked, at least momentarily. Nnadaro could have only vague memories of Nnanji, and Tomisolaan none at all, so Thana was turning him into a bogeyman for them. Then the band struck up again, praise the gods!

"That's my cue," Wallie said thankfully. "Excuse me."

He opened the door and jumped out. The swordsmen all looked tired, dusty, and bad tempered, but he would willing have changed places with any of them to have escaped that carriage ride. He waited for his men to catch up, leading his horse. He took the reins, mounted, and rode forward.

Nnanji's procession was in clear view, but still a mile or so ahead. Wallie urged his horse to a canter, intending to intercept. He soon estimated that Nnanji had about four hundred swordsmen with him, two-thirds of them on foot, which explained why their progress had been so slow. Most of cavalry must be Lord Boariyi's guard from Quo, not Nnanji's. He traveled mainly by ship, and horses were reluctant sailors.

Hearing hooves behind him, he glanced back, to see Adept Filurz spurring after him, uninvited. Having much less of a load to carry, his horse was having little trouble catching up with Wallie's. And Wallie slowed down, because he had just realized what his bodyguard had seen and now proceeded to shout to him.

"My lord! There's too many of them. Who are all those men?"

Far too many. The Quo-Casr road was home ground. Nnanji never took an escort of more than a score when he rode this trail, and usually fewer. Four hundred? If Shonsu's hair had not been tightly clipped in a ponytail it might have stood straight up. This morning he had escaped assassination literally by a miracle. A simultaneous attack on Nnanji would have made perfect sense to whoever was behind it. And a simultaneous attack could never be organized when Nnanji was weeks away, roaming the World; only when he was at either Casr or Quo. That explained the timing.

Filurz drew level and rode alongside. "If those're Lord Boariyi's men, it's the whole Quo guard, my lord. Why? And if they're not, then who by the gods' balls are they?"

"I don't know. Let's work it out. If Nnanji was attacked at the same time I was, and died, then surely Lord Boariyi would have sent a pigeon to tell us, as soon as there was light enough to fly." Unless the sorcerers were behind the plot and were suppressing the mail. If the procession were a cortege it would be flying black flags. Or perhaps not, if Boariyi did not want the assassins to know their attack had succeeded.

One rider had detached himself from the company and was headed to meet him.

"Unless the big man's behind the killing," Filurz growled, still mulling pigeons.

"I can't believe…" Yes, Wallie could believe, if barely. Boariyi had been leader of the Tryst before him. The priests had tricked him into accepting Shonsu's challenge, which he need not have done, and Shonsu had won by the narrowest imaginable margin, in a duel the minstrels still sang about.

Boariyi had accepted that decision. He had been a tower of strength in the early days and ever since. He had extended the Tryst's boundaries almost as much as Nnanji himself had done, until about five years ago, when he had expressed a desire to settle down, and Nnanji had appointed him reeve of Quo. He had served faithfully there, too. But had he nursed a secret resentment all these years? Did he feel that Shonsu had tricked him out of the leadership and then, when he'd decided he didn't want it, given it to his oath brother Nnanji instead of back to the man who'd won it fair and square? That was not how it had looked to Wallie, but Boariyi would not have been human had he not seen it that way sometimes.

If both Nnanji and Shonsu had died in the night, Boariyi would have a very good claim to the leadership now. If Shonsu had died, then Thana would certainly have brought all three of her children along to meet their father and the killer could have made a clean sweep of all other claimants.

"If you're right, adept, then I ought to have been organizing a state funeral instead of a celebration. But that isn't how Lord Boariyi would do it if he were a traitor. He'd have brought his cavalry to Casr at the gallop to take command of the Tryst."

Filurz was shielding his eyes against the sun's glare. "I think that's Lord Boariyi his own self out in front, my lord."

"You're right," Wallie said with a rush of relief. "And that's not the act of a traitor, either. How many people know where Swordsman Helbringr took the boy for his lessons?"

"Just me and Master Horkoda, my lord."

"Remember he's Nnanji's heir. If the liege dies, that kid could claim to own the seventh sword, although his mother would have to hold it in trust until he makes Third. That sword could be a poisoned legacy if ever there was one. If there's more trouble, you may have to race back to Casr and put a wall of steel around Addis."

"Yes, my lord."

The lone rider was indeed Boariyi, now recognizable by his basketball-player height and the way his stirrups almost touched the ground. Although he had filled out since the days of the immortal duel and was even developing the start of an unsightly paunch, he was still a mighty fencer, as Wallie well knew from their last test with foils, some ten or twelve weeks ago. Boariyi was a curious combination of cynic and puritan. He shared Nnanji's obsession with honor and serving the Goddess, and yet he regarded the mundane world with a disparaging eye. Soon Wallie saw with dismay that he was carrying something on the saddle in front of him, a long, thin something rolled up in a rug. A something like a sword.

All three riders reined in. None bothered with salutes.

Boariyi lifted the edge of the rug to show one end of the contents. Yes, the long thin something was a sword in a scabbard of finely tooled leather. The hilt was silver, shaped like a griffin clutching a huge sapphire.

"For you, Shonsu," he said. His oversized mouth twisted in a wry smile. "Our liege ordered me to give you this."

CHAPTER 6

Surely Nnanji would never part with the seventh sword while he lived?

"He's dead?"

"No, he's alive, but he's taken a nasty wound. Very nasty." Boariyi glanced uneasily at Filurz, a middle rank listening to high-rank discussion.

Wallie ignored the hint. If he couldn't trust the chief of his own bodyguard, whom could he trust? "Carry on. What happened?"

"Take this before I change my mind."

With a strange mixture of longing and revulsion, Wallie took the package. Fifteen years... long time... He still dreamt of the days he had worn that most perfect weapon. He didn't draw it, just laid it across his his saddle as Boariyi had carried it, still in its cover.

"What happened?" he repeated.

"He was billeted in the room next to mine. You know it; you've slept there. Middle of the night, I was awakened by a scream. I grabbed up my sword and ran in. The assassin was just scrambling out the window. I got her. I had no choice: it was strike or let her escape."

"Dead?"

"Dead. I ran her through. A woman, hit from behind! Don't tell the minstrels."

The two Sevenths eyed each other for a long moment.

"You want my sword?" Boariyi said, still bitter. "Go ahead: disarm me, take me to Casr for trial. You must have a scapegoat. Of course I had to kill my accomplice so she couldn't testify against me."

"You talk like a shithead. If that was what you'd been up to you'd have given me this trinket sharp end first." Not necessarily! If Boariyi were the traitor, he would not have expected to see Wallie alive. He would be winging it now, trying to find out how much was known, what had happened to the other assassin.

"If not me, then who? These things must take time to prepare. Who outside the Tryst knew he was coming?"

"All Casr did," Wallie said, "so I suppose all Quo did too. He's never been gone so long, so they could have set this up half a year ago. How badly is he hurt? Is he going to live?"

Again the other Seventh glanced uneasily at Filurz, the witness. "I don't think so. She twisted a knife in his guts. He was squirting blood like a fountain. Writhing and screaming. You know how belly wounds hurt."

And kill. The first danger was simply bleeding out, but if Nnanji had already survived some hours, there must be hope that the hemorrhaging had stopped. But even if loss of blood did not kill him, then the punctured intestines would bring on septicemia. The miracle antibiotics of the World were honey and spider web, primitive in the extreme.

"Adept Filurz, go and advise Lady Thana of what has happened. Bring her. Tell Swordsman Tilber to look after the children. She may have to babysit them all the way home."

Filurz thumped his chest with a fist and wheeled his horse.

"And remember," Wallie shouted after him, "what I said earlier about a wall of steel: do it!" Addis must be protected. Only when Filurz was out of hailing distance did Wallie wonder if Vixini, too, should at least be warned. As oath brothers, the two liege lords were equals, and if both were ever put out of commission, some people might see Vixi as a more suitable figurehead for a coup than the even younger Addis.

The two Sevenths began cantering back up the Quo trail.

Nnanji wounded, or Nnanji dying... This had always been a danger, but Wallie had never drawn up contingency plans. Coming from him the suggestion would have seemed self-serving, and no one else had ever dared to raise the issue. He could try to claim the leadership by right, or the council might start quoting sutras and traditions. Past trysts had always chosen their leaders by combat, but past trysts had always been short-lived, ad hoc affairs.

Now the wagons must be circled. There was a major conspiracy here, which would not stop with two bungled stabs at assassination. And Nnanji had put him in charge by giving him the sword.

"Is he conscious?"

"Barely," Boariyi said grimly, staring straight ahead. "When he could stop screaming he insisted we bring him home to Casr. Told me to give you the Chioxin sword. 'For now,' he said! You know the liege. He won't stop fighting until we slide him into the River. The healers washed their hands of him at first glance; didn't dare take his case. I dosed him with some poppy juice to get him into the litter."

Poppy juice was dangerous stuff at the best of times, and especially so to a man weakened by loss of blood. Wallie must give Boariyi the benefit of the doubt for now, but keep him on the list of suspects. He was the only suspect they had, except the ever-distrusted sorcerers.

"How did the killer get into the bedroom?"

The big man glanced at him mockingly. "Nnanji ran up the stairs with her draped her over his shoulder. When Lord Shonsu comes to call, we organize a dinner with senior swordsmen, sorcerers, and the least dull civic officials. When Lord Nnanji comes, we order in the raunchiest juniors and lots of girls. Of course I ordered the arrest of the gentleman who catered the entertainment, but he had not been located before I left Quo."

Wallie shuddered. So far as he knew, Nnanji was always faithful to his wife when she was available. The rest of the time he followed the free swords' belief that any girl he fancied should feel flattered. Only very rarely, if ever, was the all-powerful Lord Nnanji refused. "Thana must not hear of this. Officially the killer climbed in the window. Since she didn't, how did she get a dagger into the liege's bedroom?"

Boariyi flashed his cynical smile again. "That was a puzzle at first. But his aides identified it as his own knife, the one he carried in his boot."

Another shock! Knives and concealed weapons in general were strictly forbidden by the sutras. Wallie had allowed them in the earliest days of the tryst, during the war against the sorcerers, but Nnanji had promptly forbidden them again. News that he had gone back to carrying one was virtually proof that he had encountered sorcerer trouble.

"Then it may not be a conspiracy. She might have been acting alone?"

"That would certainly be a relief," Boariyi said.

Wallie found even that comment grounds for suspicion and wanted to scream and smash something. He would not have described the big man as a close friend, but he had trusted him implicitly and worked with him amicably for fifteen years. Inevitably, though, the least whiff of treason in the air poisoned everyone and everything. No face looked honest, all words were suspect.

To lie to Boariyi now would be futile, for everyone in Casr knew the truth. If he was innocent he would be insulted, and if he was guilty he would be alerted to the fact that he was still a suspect.

"It would, except that a girl climbed up to my balcony not long before dawn. She brought her own knife."

"Great Goddess! Did you catch her?"

"Jja caught her by biting her leg; very effective."

"Then you can question her and get to the bottom of this?"

Damn! Another suspicious question. "I hope so." Then Wallie realized that Boariyi, too, was holding something back. He had not been surprised enough to learn of the second assassin. "Tell me about Lord Mibullim."

That was it. Boariyi nodded slightly in appreciation, as if they were fencing with words. "A friend of my youth. We apprenticed together in Wrou. He joined a band of frees,

I remained and worked my way up to being deputy reeve. Then the Goddess fetched me to Casr for the Tryst. I haven't seen him since the day he made Third."

"But you expected to see him?"

"No. Nnanji expected to. He'd sent Mibullim ahead with two Fourths and a couple of Thirds. They were bringing you orders to muster the largest force possible, but they never reached Quo. There's been major bloodshed in the south. Nnanji narrowly escaped an ambush, several ambushes in fact. This morning his luck ran out."

"Things begin to make more sense, then." Wallie had always been surprised at how little resistance the Tryst had met as it expanded. Nnanji had predicted that a great many swordsmen, perhaps even a majority of them, would welcome it as a cure for the widespread corruption and incompetence in their craft. Mostly he had been right, at least until now. In most places the discipline and the return of honor that the Tryst promised had been welcomed, or at least accepted without a struggle. Now, Wallie had thought that the Tryst had grown too huge and powerful to defy. But bad odds had never stopped wars starting up back on Earth.

"Things look bloody," Boariyi said, "swordsmen being slaughtered wholesale."

"Sorcerers behind it, you mean? I guessed that when you said Nnanji had gone back to carrying a knife." Swordsmen didn't massacre swordsmen. They challenged them to duels, one on one. Only sorcerers would resort to mass violence.

"It looks like sorcerers with swordsmen allies. And thunder weapons again."

Venal swordsmen with sorcerer allies had always been the ultimate nightmare scenario, the dogs ganging up with the cats.

The long procession had halted to await the two Sevenths' arrival. They rode along the column to the litter, near the center. The eight slaves carrying it had been allowed to lay it down. A relief team of eight more bearers stood behind them, and it was clear that the man in charge was a short, thick-shouldered Fifth, whom Wallie remembered leaving

Casr two years ago as a Third. His name was Endrasti, and Nnanji had praised him in dispatches. He saluted, grim-faced.

Wallie returned his salute. "Is he awake?"

"On and off. He insisted he must speak with you when you arrived."

Ignoring the hundreds of watching eyes, Wallie walked over to the litter, which looked as if it had been assembled in a hurry by a gang of shipwrights using the most solid timber in their yards. Endrasti pulled back a drape and stepped aside.

The patient lay on at least a double layer of feather mattresses and was well covered in quilts. The face just barely visible in this foam was an image of Nnanji carved from white wax. His hair had lost none of its startling redness, so rare among the People. Unbound, it framed his head in a scarlet halo and emphasized his corpse pallor, as did the fresh blood around his mouth, for he had chewed his lip until it bled.

Wallie thought of vampires and horror movies. Encumbered by the extra sword he was holding, he did not attempt a formal salute. Just thumping his heart with a fist, he said, "Shonsu, brother, reporting for duty."

Eyes opened, rolled vaguely, and steadied. His oath brother grimaced and managed a gargoyle smile. "Stay away from them, brother. They'll get you in the end." His voice was a painful gasp, forced through a throat raw with screaming.

"Who will?"

"Girls... course!" he groaned at another spasm of pain.

"I've been telling you that for years, you human goat. We'll have you home very soon. Thana'll be here in a moment. Don't worry about anything. Any special instructions?"

The whisper was almost inaudible: "Take care of... kids?"

"Like my own, brother." Clearly Nnanji was in no shape to provide any useful information. Before Wallie could say more, he was jostled aside by Thana, so he backed away.

He was in charge. Boariyi and Endrasti, blue kilt and

red, were waiting for his orders. Four hundred men were watching.

For the benefit of the audience, he smiled and nodded as if he had just exchanged jokes with the patient. He spoke softly. "We'll go on war footing as of now. Adept, you come with me. My lord, bring the liege home, to his palace. I'll have it searched before you get there and post extra guards. Today's password is *Know your enemies* and the rejoinder *Only cats fight in the dark*. We'll hold a meeting of the council when you get to the lodge. I expect you'll want a meal first, and the rest of us would be happier if you bathed, too."

Both men laughed to continue the pretense of lightheartedness.

The council? There were more than two hundred Sevenths in the Tryst now, officially all members of the council, but they were scattered over half the World. Even with Boariyi, the meeting was going to be a pathetically small gathering.

Filurz had gone, racing back to Casr to take care of Addis. Wallie paused at Thana's carriage, to leave the seventh sword in it for safekeeping. When he opened the door, he found Swordsman Tilber cuddling Tomisolaan. She looked guilty and blushed, yet this was the woman who had once challenged a Fourth for making a joke about female swordsmen. Keeping his face straight with an effort, Wallie assured Nnadaro that her mommy would be back soon and she would see Daddy when they got home.

Then he rallied what was left of his personal guard and headed back to Casr to deal with this disaster.

CHAPTER 7

THE HORSES WERE ALREADY TIRED, SO WALLIE set a brisk, but not breakneck, pace. Endrasti rode at his side, waiting for the questions.

"First, then, master. Tell me how you fit into Nnanji's company?" The Tryst had no fixed military structure. Each leader in the field, always a Seventh, made up his own rules as he went along, working with whatever men he had, to deal with whatever conditions he encountered.

"I was his senior aide, my lord. With respect, I believe he relied on me mostly for help with political matters, like things concerning kings or councils of elders or whoever else ran each city."

Nnanji himself was only interested in reforming swordsmen. The need to clean up civic governments as well just annoyed him. It had taken a couple of years and a few nasty accidents before he had been convinced of the necessity.

"He praised you highly in his dispatches."

"Oh. Thank you, my lord."

"He never told you to your face how much he valued your work?"

"Well, yes, he did… But it's nice to hear it confirmed!"

"Nnanji's good at giving praise where it's due, and if you're no good he'll tell you that, too."

"I've heard that happening!" Endrasti smiled to indicate

that the thunderbolts had never been directed at him. He had done extraordinarily well to move up from Third to Fifth in less than two years. He would have had to learn well over six hundred more sutras and raise his fencing to a much higher level. A stickler for regulations, Nnanji would always make sure that his personal favorites received no special treatment.

"So what's all this about rebellion and ambushes? I just need the bare bones now, but the council will want the whole carcass, bones and offal and all. No verbal indelicacies that may escape your lips on this occasion will be held against you, I swear. If Nnanji screwed up, say so."

"Oh, it wasn't his fault, my lord. It happened about half a year ago. We were in the Ulk sector, and the sorcerers of Ulk have never been very cooperative, although they had caused us no trouble. We were working our way upstream toward a very large city named Plo."

"Heard of it." Jja had been born there, and its name had cropped up again later. Wallie had mentioned it to Katanji only a few hours ago.

"We'd heard that Plo was in a different coven's sector, so we knew we might have some trouble. The reeve of a city called Fo swore to the Tryst willingly enough, and ordered his subordinates to do so as well. The elders seemed quite enlightened, so we prepared to move on up to Nolar, the next big town. Then we were told of a land crossing at a loading port called Cross Zek, which was closer. The trail led southward and there were big mountains visible that way. RegiKra, they're called."

That was what Wallie had been trying to remember: a sorcerer city called Kra lying south of Plo. Nnanji would have known that right away. It was rare for two towns or cities to face each other directly across the River, so "Cross Zek" simply meant a minor location opposite Zek.

Endrasti hesitated, moving in rhythm with his horse, staring at the trail ahead.

"So Nnanji had a choice to make," Wallie prompted. "Either go on to Nolar and Plo, where he might need all his men and then some, or go exploring to see if there was access to another reach of the River to the south. Or split his forces and do both. What advice did you offer?" Advice that Nnanji had disregarded, likely.

He received a smile of thanks for the help. "I wasn't happy about the information, my lord, and said so. I hadn't been able to confirm the southern loop story. Cross Zek wasn't a place where people lived, just a dock for loading tin ore. The riverbanks were high and steep there, but a tributary flowed in, so the ships could tie up out of the main flow. There was certainly a trail heading inland, but it might just lead to the tin mines. Winter was coming on; this was southern hemisphere."

Wallie chuckled, a rumble of Shonsu thunder. "I have known my oath brother longer than you have, master. I'll bet he couldn't resist the chance to locate another loop."

"Yes, my lord. He considered sending Lord Mibullim inland to explore, but he wanted him to send him to Casr soon. So he decided to send Master Notukasmo, with a troop of twenty-five. But he was only to reconnoiter, and must be back at Cross Zek by Slaters' Day. The liege himself would take the rest of us over to Zek and then Nolar, but no farther."

"Tell me about Mibullim."

Endrasti frowned at this mention of other trouble. "Mibullim of the Seventh was a free sword, who'd come to meet us in Obla about four weeks before. He had fifteen men in his troop, and they were a very impressive band, my lord. One of them, Master Notukasmo, helped examine me for my promotion and almost shredded my kilt! He gave me the fight of my life, my lord, and I'm fairly sure he threw me the final point out of pity. Lord Nnanji complimented Lord Mibullim on his own fencing. He was eager to enlist, and so were his men."

"Valuable reinforcements." Of course the troop could have been sorcerer agents, but swordsmen took their ferocious oaths seriously, and it would be very hard to assemble such a large group of traitors. The fact that at least two of them were first-class fencers for their ranks was almost certain proof that they were what they claimed to be."Glad to see 'em, we were, sir, because we'd picked up rumors about the king of Plo planning to cause trouble. We knew we might have to wet our blades there. Nolar, which we would come to first, was also large, but I was hoping we might win some support there against Plo. I'd heard of a long-time inter-city rivalry, you see. But we'd smelt blood in the air ever since Arbo."

Over the years the Tryst's expansion had not required as much bloody warfare as Wallie had feared when Nnanji had first suggested that its mission must be to reform the entire swordsman craft. Wallie had imagined the Tryst conquering like an empire, but in fact it had spread more like a religion, by conversion. Its forces had advanced city by city along the River, swearing in the garrisons as they went, collecting and organizing the nomadic free sword troops. Any swordsman who refused to swear allegiance was denounced as a disgrace of the craft and challenged. If he won that bout, he could be challenged again and again, but in practice he would usually accept the inevitable and swear the oath. Since duress was not an admissible excuse for a swordsman, he was just as effectively bound then as if he'd submitted right away. If he later reneged, then he would be challenged again, and this time to the death. The Tryst's commander on the spot— Nnanji, Shonsu, Boariyi, or another—would appoint a new reeve, clean up the guard, and then move on.

In effect, the reeves were police chiefs, kept honest by regular moves to new postings and by Casr's roving inspectors. The inspectors were basically the old free swords, but they now had defined domains and the whole resources of the Tryst behind them; they could investigate even the largest cities and depose rulers if necessary.

Exceptions prove rules, though, and there had been minor battles.

"Cross Zek was a trap?"

"Aye, that it was, my lord. And so was Zek, but we were lucky there. After the Cross Zek scouting party disembarked, the rest of us went over to Zek itself. Wind and current made us detour downstream, but we arrived the following day and were made welcome. The reeve and the mayor had gone goose hunting, we were told, but they'd heard we were coming and left word that we were to be billeted in the shearing barn. We weren't green enough to be caught like that, my lord, so when they sprang their trap, we were ready. They tried to burn the barn down on top of us. That didn't work, but there were a lot of them and there was a battle. We killed every man found with a weapon or seen fighting. We left the women and children in the shearing barn, burned the rest of the town, and scuttled their fishing fleet."

Horrible as that revenge was, Wallie knew that in Nnanji's place he might well have done the same thing, for such blatant treachery must not go unpunished. With thousands of swordsmen scattered over half the World, the Tryst could not allow any to be molested without reprisal. The blood oath that bound it together laid an obligation of vengeance on both parties, so it was now Nnanji's job to see that the dead men were avenged, and any Nnanji oath was automatically Wallie's.

"Did they use thunder weapons?"

"We did not hear or see any, my lord. We guessed then, of course, that the Cross Zek land road was another trap. As soon as possible, Lord Nnanji took us all back there. They'd been ambushed, slaughtered to the last man. Their bodies had been stripped and left for the rats and ravens. If Lord Nnanji had led us all that way, we'd likely all have died."

Clearly Lord Shonsu would be visiting Zek and Cross Zek in the near future.

"Who were these foes, though? Swordsmen or sorcerers?"

"Sorcerers, without a doubt, my lord, so Lord Nnanji said. Or civilians using sorcerers' thunder weapons. No sword cuts, no arrow wounds. They had holes in them, that was all."

So Wallie's old nightmare of swordsmen trying to fight sorcerers armed with guns had come true at last. Even if the Kra coven had nothing better than the Vul coven's smoothbore, short-barrel pistols, this was going to be very ugly.

He reined in and dismounted. "Show me," he said, taking Endrasti's reins. "Pace it out. How far apart were the bodies?"

They were not quite into the vineyards, still in the upland area of dairy farms, where cows slumped on the grass chewing their cud incuriously. Endrasti recreated the scene for him, using fences and even particular cows as landmarks. He conjured up a narrow, steep-sided valley, a deep cut winding through forested hills, with poor visibility ahead and none at all to the sides. Anything, he said, might be hidden in the trees and bushes above. Most of the bodies lay in order of march, as if they had died in a single volley, but a few had tried to storm up the crumbling sides and been shot down from above. Wallie questioned him hard on distance. How far from their victims had the bushwhackers been hiding? The most significant fact that he deduced was that the range had been too great for smoothbore handguns. The bushwhackers had been armed with long guns, so the Kra sorcerers, if they were the culprits, had invented the musket.

"How many wounds per body, could you tell?"

"Well... The crows had been at them, my lord. One or two, was most I saw."

"Were any of them ripped to pieces?" Back when Vul coven had conquered the RegiVul Loop, they had progressed to cannon loaded with grapeshot. The entire garrison of Gor had been wiped out with one such "thunderbolt".

"No, my lord. Lord Nnanji commented on that."

"Our losses?"

"At Cross Zek twenty-six swordsmen, three porters, and a herald; worse than Arbo."

Thirty musket balls could not mow down thirty men. At least twice that many shots would be needed, and that meant either a far greater rate of fire than could be achieved with primitive muskets, or a much larger force. Considering that the enemy could not have known how many swordsmen they would have to deal with, the much larger force theory seemed more likely.

The two men remounted and continued their ride.

"Twice you mentioned somewhere called Arbo."

Endrasti looked at Wallie with dismay. "The massacre at Arbo, on Swordsmen's Day. Honorable Rudere... You didn't receive that dispatch, either?"

The Tryst maintained a picket post at the edge of town. Wallie and Endrasti stopped there to change horses, so they were able to make good speed on the last leg of their journey to the lodge. He went straight to the Executive Block, tossed his reins to a waiting junior, and took the steps at the double. As was to be expected, Master Horkoda was still at his desk.

Wallie barked out the news. "Lord Nnanji was seriously wounded in an assassination attempt last night, in Quo. Have his palace searched from turret to cellar and post double guards. He is coming home with an escort of around four hundred, led by lord Boariyi. His usual quarters must be made ready, and the rest of them will need billeting, feeding, stabling. Inform the lords of the council that we'll meet this evening as soon as Lord Boariyi has had a chance to freshen up. Master Endrasti, here, will attend. Meanwhile, he needs billeting and looking after also."

His aide had heard all this without taking a single note. He could read and write, but still preferred to rely on his childhood memory training.

"You wish a recorder present?"

"Certainly not." Most recorders were sorcerers. "Where can I find the boy Addis?"

Horkoda permitted himself a very faint smile. "In Swordsman Helbringr's quarters in your palace, my lord. Master Filurz arrived less than an hour ago and doubled your guards. Apprentice Vixini is being force-fed sutras as if his life depended on it."

Wallie felt a twist of guilt. The opposite might be closer to the truth. By pushing his stepson into third rank, he would make him eligible for battle, and the war had already started.

* * *

Accompanied by a pickup escort, Wallie rode back to his palace, where he found Adept Filurz newly cleaned up after his ride in, still slightly damp. Addis, he reported, was downstairs, demonstrating his new-found skills.

Sure enough, the swordsmen of Wallie's night watch, and many of his daytime bodyguard as well, were sitting around in the guards' mess, deriding a gladiatorial show. In the center, Addis, son of Nnanji, and Novice Gwiddle, who was shorter but broader, were circling each other warily. Both wore very dirty kilts, originally of first-rank white. Unsworn youths were forbidden clothing except in cold weather, but some protection would be a wise precaution when engaged in Addis's current activity. Swordsman Helbringr was on her feet, being referee and instructor.

"Turtles!" she yelled. "Wake up! Make a fight of it." The rest of her remarks were drowned out in a general chorus of booing, intended as agreement.

Shamed into action, Gwiddle leaped forward, grabbing for his opponent's throat. Addis caught his wrist, extended a leg, and flipped Gwiddle over it, to land face-down on the floor. He dropped his knees on his victim's back and got an arm lock on him.

Yelp of pain from Gwiddle, loud cheers from everyone else.

Addis sprang to his feet, grinning triumphantly.

"Better," Helbringr shouted. "Up! Now, novice, let's see you go for a—my lord!"

Thirty boots hit the floor as the guards sprang upright.

Wallie raised a hand to forestall formal saluting. "I have come to rescue your victim, swordsman. If he can still walk, that is."

Addis was hastily removing his borrowed kilt, a mark of respect that Wallie was still alien enough to find amusing and contradictory. The boy was filthy from top to toe, and well decorated with scrapes and bruises. But his grin looked genuine, as if an all-over beating was a first-rate treat. He had a notable black eye, and so did Swordsman Helbringr.

"I kept trying to call it a day, my lord," she said, "and he insisted on continuing. He wanted to learn every dirty trick you'd mentioned."

"Adept Filurz will demand an explanation of that eye, swordsman."

She smiled, knowing he was joking. "Line of duty, my lord. Boy Addis has put three men in the infirmary and practically ruined Novice Gwiddle." This outrageous statement drew hoots of laughter from the audience and a howl of protest from Gwiddle. Addis's grin grew even wider. He still hadn't realized that he'd been tricked into demonstrating that he had the agility and reflexes a swordsman needed.

Alas, merriment was out of order now.

"Well done, both of you. Addis, come with me, please. Adept Filurz will brief the rest of you."

Wallie took the boy upstairs, to his private quarters. There, amid all the grandeur of silk rugs, travertine paneling, and gilded ceilings, he found his wife spooning mush into Budol, their youngest. Jja, who had once been a slave herself, had innumerable slaves and servants to do that for her if she wished, but insisted that she enjoyed being a mother. She knew at once that Wallie had brought bad news, but her first concern was his companion. She did not even let him finish his salute.

"Gods love us, Addis, what happened to you? We must send for a healer, and a litter to get you home."

"I'm well, Aunt, thank you." He was eyeing Shonsu anxiously.

"Sit," Wallie said. "No, never mind the furniture. Addis, I have grave news for you. Your father has been badly hurt. I'm sure Vixini told you how an assassin tried to kill me last night. I was lucky. Another one went after your dad. He's not dead, but he didn't escape as lightly as I did. I won't lie to you. His wound is very serious."

The childish face paled, making the swellings seem even worse. Budol, who was a very loud baby and knew her rights, bellowed at the interruption in her feeding. Jja obeyed orders.

Addis whispered, "Who did this, Uncle?" Why would anyone want to kill *his* father?

"We don't know. And she can't tell us, because Lord Boariyi killed her. Yes, it was another woman. Your father's on his way back; your mother's with him. They should be home very shortly. I'll take you there."

The boy whispered, "Thank you," but it was a reflex. He had shrunk into a knot of misery and horror. For any child to lose a parent must be Armageddon, but Addis's father was a god. The sun rose and set at his command. Conversely, without him the World would at once become a place of fearful danger. Palaces got sacked. Unwanted heirs could disappear like morning dew.

Jja was staring very hard at Wallie. "Did you have to be so brutal?"

"Addis is not a child any longer, dear. He's about to chose a craft and be sworn. He deserves the truth and he'll get nothing less from me."

After a moment Addis looked up. "They tried to kill you, too. So it's a plot? Who, my lord? Who wants you and Dad both dead?"

"We do not know." Wallie glanced briefly at Jja and then quickly away. "But I just leaned that sorcerers have started killing swordsmen again. About forty men have died in ambushes, somewhere in the far south, near Plo, and most of them were killed by sorcerers' weapons. Jja comes from Plo. I remember her telling me, ages ago, that there was a coven at somewhere called Kra, in the mountains near Plo. It's war. Your father was on his way back to Casr to enlist an army." But today he might have come home to die.

"And now you'll be leading that army?" Jja said coldly.

"I must, dear. It doesn't matter whether they swore the blood oath to me or to Nnanji, he is my oath brother, so his oaths are my oaths, my oaths are his oaths, and they were my vassals. I must avenge them." That was so obviously his duty that he couldn't even hesitate. And he knew that Jja knew it too, even if she didn't want to accept it.

A small voice said, "If I swear to the swordsmen, Uncle, can I come with you?"

Of course not. He would be a novice, a First, and they were never allowed anywhere close to real fighting. But if Addis, son of Nnanji, had seriously entertained ambitions to become a sorcerer, they were forgotten now.

BOOK TWO:

HOW A SWORDSMAN WENT FORTH

CHAPTER 1

ADDIS HAD NEVER KNOWN A DAY AS BAD AS
that one. There could never be a worse. Yet it had
not been all bad. Getting Uncle Shonsu on his side in the
upcoming fight over his swearing had been good. Being
called *pretty* had been extra-putrid, because he knew it was
true. He was pretty, or he had been until Helbringr began
mashing him. Every day he cursed his extra-curly hair.
What sort of swordsman ponytail would that ever make?
He needed a few scars!

Helbringr was taller, wider, and thicker than he was, and
she had treated him like a medicine ball until he got mad
enough to want to hurt her. Then he'd kicked her knee and
chopped at the side of her neck, tricks that Uncle Tomiyano
had taught him when he went voyaging on *Sapphire II*. After
that, the lesson had become more serious, and she'd taught
him all kinds of nasty stuff. Not what a swordsman would
need, but he'd still been planning to be a sorcerer or a sailor
at that time.

Anyone who called him pretty from now on was going to
lose an eye or two.

Then the terrible news about Dad.

Things got patchy after that. He felt blurry and couldn't
think straight. Shonsu probably fed him. And talked a
lot while Addis was eating, but saying nothing he heard.
Couldn't think of anything except Dad. Wounded. Likely

dying. Shonsu wouldn't have hinted at that if it weren't likely. Grandma Brota and Uncle Tomiyano and all the rest of Mom's family were weeks away on *Sapphire II*. They would have to be told. Of course it was two years since he's seen Dad… looking forward to hearing him say how much he'd grown… not looking forward to hearing him say of course he'd have to be a swordsman. Now that wouldn't matter the tiniest bit. He'd happily be anything at all that Dad wanted him to be. Nothing would matter if Dad could even just know him, which Shonsu was hinting he might not.

The fog lifted a bit when he was riding in a carriage, wrapped up in the sort of short, hooded fur cloak that kids were allowed to wear in cold weather. It wasn't cold yet, but Shonsu didn't want anyone to see him yet, for some reason. Mum was home now. And Dad. Going to see Dad. The coach kept bouncing, reminding him of all his bruises. He looked down at his legs, sticking out under the fur, all covered with filth and streaks of blood, scraped and bruised.

"Uncle!" he whispered. "I gotta clean up! Can't let Mom see me like this. She'll erupt, all smoke and lava."

Shonsu chuckled and steadied him with a big hand on his shoulder. "Addis, you're a very brave and very tough lad. You showed that today. I never expected Helbringr to batter you that hard, and she wouldn't have done it if she hadn't seen that you could take it. Would you do a job for me?"

"What sort of job?"

"That's the right answer! A very unpleasant and even dangerous job. Definitely not the sort of thing I would ever dream of asking you to do normally. If you're willing, I'll want you to stay just as horribly dirty as you are now, maybe even worse. But it might help us find out who was behind the attacks on me and your dad. That would be a huge help."

"Really? Me?"

"Really you. It won't be the sort of thing you'll ever want to brag about, but I think you could do it as well as anyone could."

"Then I'll do it."

"Look, we've arrived. Don't mention the job idea to your Dad or your Mom. I'll tell you all about it later, and you can decide then."

"I said I'll do it!" He'd do *anything*!

Someone took the cloak off of him as they went in. The guards and the house slaves all stared at him, but it wasn't any of their business why the young master was muddy and bloody, bruised and battered. Some of them were red-eyed, but he was the liege's son and he wasn't going to weep, not ever. He held his head up as he walked at Shonsu's side across the great hall and up the grand staircase. They had to wait a moment outside the bedroom while one of the guards went in to say that they were there.

Then Mom came out, and there was even more smoke and lava than he'd expected: where had he been, what had he been doing, who had done that? But her caterwauling was really aimed at Shonsu, and the big man just stood there like a rock when the wind blew spray over it. He said nothing until she had run out of breath. Then, "How is he?"

"Breathing. Starting a fever already. Addis, run and get cleaned up at once."

"Let him be," Shonsu said. "He's going to do a job for me, maybe, and I want—"

"What sort of job?"

"Sh! Tell you later." He urged Addis forward.

Addis shook off his hand and Mom's, too, when she tried to take his. He walked in through the door, keeping his chin up. It was dark in there, past sunset now, and with only two lamps burning. A couple of high-rank healers were whispering together in a corner, and some nurses were doing something with jugs and bowls on a table.

He went over to the bed and looked down at the dead-white face on the pillow, framed in red hair. This was *Dad*? He looked so *small*!

"Dad? Dad, it's Addis." He was aware that Shonsu and Mom had followed him in.

The dying man's eyelids flickered. "Addis?"

"Sorry you're hurt, Dad." What else could he say: *Please don't die?*

A word that might have been, "Big."

"Yes, I am big, and I'm going to swear to the code of the swordsmen tomorrow and then I'm going to help find the people who did this to you and kill them. I don't care if it takes me the whole of the rest of my life."

Dad smiled and nodded.

"And you've got to get better, Dad, because we need you: me and Nnadaro and Tomi. And the Tryst needs you. And Mom does."

"I will," Dad whispered.

"Soon! Because I need you to teach me how to fight with a sword."

Mom took his arm. He shook her off again. Shonsu clasped his shoulder and they walked out of the room together. The lamps were all starry.

"Keep looking up at the ceiling," the big man whispered. "That makes eyes behave themselves."

Half way down the staircase, Shonsu stopped him, went down two more steps so their faces were level, and glanced around. There was nobody else near.

"You did that very well, Nephew. What you said to your dad was just exactly right. I'm proud of you. Now, about that job. What I want to do is throw you in jail for a few days. How does that sound?"

This would not be a joke, not tonight. "With the woman who tried to kill you, Uncle?"

"Goddess, you're quick! Very well done! Yes. But think hard before you agree. You'll be shut up in a cell with a murderer, or at least a would-be murderer."

He must have smiled, because his face hurt. "But now I know how to defend myself!"

"That was not why I sent you for those lessons, I swear it wasn't! I didn't think of you for this job until I saw all your scrapes and bruises. She'll be less likely to suspect you in that condition. You don't have to do this, Addis. It's entirely up to you. You'll be sleeping on straw, eating prison food, being chewed up by fleas and lice. It'll be cold, boring, and probably noisy. We'll see that you are watched over, but we can't be too obvious about that, and there is a slight chance that something will go wrong and some rough types will be dumped in the same cell you're in. Then you might get some serious trouble before you're rescued."

If it looks scary, don't stop to think about it, just do it. So Dad had told him often.

"I said I would do it, didn't I? Swordsmen don't go back on their word, do they?"

"No they don't"

Dad wouldn't. He'd said he'd get better.

Shonsu had to go and attend a meeting of the council. He smuggled Addis into the lodge in the fur cloak, then left him in the care of Adept Filurz and Swordsman Helbringr. Filurz was good, a great fencer, even if he was shorter than Helbringr, and Addis trusted her after the day's lessons. They were both officially off-duty after dark, but now there was a war on and that didn't matter.

They looked him over by lamplight.

"She made a very convincing mess of you, boy," Filurz said. "And you don't have a facemark. Your left eye is so swollen that your mothermark doesn't show. We've got some stuff to cover up your fathermark. Now... Oh, you tell him, swordsman."

Helbringr said, "The prisoner is going to be suspicious if we put a boy in with a woman..."

"Not that it never happens," Filurz said, "but you'll pardon my saying this..."

"But I'm not a likely rapist yet? What are you trying to tell me? That you want to dress me up as a girl? Well, I'm not a swordsman yet, so I don't have to challenge you for suggesting it. Shonsu says this will help him and Dad fight the sorcerers, so I'll do whatever it takes. But if you ever tell anyone else I tried to pass as a girl, then I *will* challenge you, both of you! And cut your tripes out." That was one of Dad's favorite threats.

"Son of Nnanji," Filurz said, "I swear by my sword that I will never tell!"

"And I the same," Helbringr said. "I really admire you for doing this. I couldn't believe it when the liege told us to ask you. Here's what we found."

It was a filthy cloth that wrapped around him under his arms and reached to his thighs. It had once, maybe, been white, apprentice color.

"I need tits."

"Can't help you there, son," Filurz said. "Take deep breaths."

"If I'm clothed, why don't I have a facemark?"

"That's good, Shonsu says. Prisoner doesn't have one either. We think she's a sorcerer because of that, and she ought to think the same of you. She can't ask you, 'cos she can't speak, so you don't have to say so. But if you whisper that she's going to be rescued, she might believe you've come to help her."

"Suppose I tell her they're going to cut her head off, or boil her alive?"

Helbringr blinked and looked at Filurz for an answer.

"Might work," he said. "Shonsu said we're not to give you orders about what to do when you're in there. It's your mission, and we don't know how she'll react. But here's what Shonsu suggested: All we know about her is that her tongue has been cut out and she hates swordsmen. If she finds out who you are, she might try to kill you. You can ask questions and she can nod or shake her head. If she knows how to write, she can shape letters with a finger... We want to know who sent her. We want to know if there will be more attempts on the liege's life, or anyone else's. And anything else that comes up in the—I was about to call it a conversation, but it'll be a strange conversation. And it may be days before her nerve breaks and she starts to trust you."

"We have a rescue ready for you," Helbringr said. "Whenever you've had enough or she gets dangerous or you think you've learned enough, shout your brother's name,

Tomisolaan. I know it'll sound funny, yelling for a toddler to come and save you, but you won't forget the password if things have gotten wild. We have three men in the next cell who will take turns listening for you, day and night, and they have keys to the doors. They'll be there in a flash."

Oh, sure. Addis had heard plans like that before and they usually didn't work. Didn't matter. He was doing this for Dad and he knew how to defend himself now.

"You don't have to do—"

"Stop telling me that!"

"What name are you going to use, prisoner?" Filurz asked. "Some woman's name you won't forget."

"Brota," Addis said. "And I've got an idea. Swordsman Helbringr showed me how to fall, didn't you, swordsman? So tell them not to baby me. When they put me in the cell with her, they should throw me in, maybe kick me or spit on me. Be real!"

"Great Goddess!" Adept Filurz said. "He really is Rusty's son, isn't he!"

The jail was a courtyard with cages all the way around it. The walls between cages were made of stone, and the fronts of bronze bars. Most of the cages seemed to be packed tight with living bodies. The stench was awful, and so was the noise, with the inmates screaming at one another, or cursing the "slimes" and "prongs". That was town slang: slimes were jailers and prongs were swordsmen. Dry wood burning in a brazier in the middle of the yard shed some light, but not much, so no one was going to recognize anybody later, after this job was done. Or so a man must hope, anyway. *Dressed as a girl!*

Two slimes marched "her" in, holding "her" arms painfully tight, and another marched ahead with a key and a club. They took "her" to a cell with a single inmate, who was curled up on a heap of straw in the corner but made no effort to escape, so the club wasn't needed. The gate was opened, and the new prisoner was thrown in as "she" himself had suggested. He tried to land as he'd been taught that morning, but Helbringr had never thrown him as hard as that, so he tripped over his own feet and landed a lot harder than he expected, banging an elbow and biting his tongue.

"Filthy stinking shit-eating slimes!" he yelled, meaning it.

The gate clanged shut and the lock clattered.

He sat up, rubbing his elbow. The air was foul, cold, and damp, and the ragged wrap they'd given him was thinner than mist. The assassin was still curled up, but looking at him. She didn't have any clothes on at all. There wasn't enough light to see any details, which was good.

"I'm Brota," he said.

She made a sort of hooting noise.

"What?"

Hoot again.

"Well, if you won't, you won't," he said angrily. "You going to share some of that straw, or do I have to fight you for it?"

She came alive at that, spreading out the meager bedding so there would be room for two—two people very close together. It made sense to sleep like that to keep warm, but how long before she discovered that he wasn't a she? Staying in character, he went across and lay down, turning his back on her. He was shivering, but cold could explain that.

The racket outside was getting worse, not better. The straw stank of sewage. Dad had warned him often that he might not live in a palace all his life. He'd managed not to brood about Dad until then, but now he had nothing else to do or think about. He was very tired, very sore, very frightened. After a while he realized that he was weeping. Didn't matter. Girls did that and there was no one to see him.

Oh, great Goddess, please don't let my dad die!

CHAPTER 2

HAVING RETRIEVED THE SEVENTH SWORD from Swordsman Tilber, Wallie had to decide whether to wear it. The Aye vote said that it was the scepter, the emblem of state, so the sight of it would demonstrate that the work of the Tryst must continue and no one was indispensable. The Nay argued that many people might assume that Nnanji was as good as dead—and if he wasn't, then Shonsu was usurping his authority. Also, Wallie had forced himself to give it up once and did not relish the prospect of ever having to do so again. Feeling guilty at that admission of greed, he compromised by carrying it under his arm when he went upstairs to the council hall.

The hall was a high and spacious chamber that could hold several hundred people. Compared to other buildings in Casr, it was starkly plain, with a high timbered ceiling, walls of flat slate, and horrible acoustics. Windows well above head height shed a poor light even at noon, and Wallie could not complain, for he had designed it himself. To him it was the most interesting place in Casr, perhaps in the World.

Its furnishing varied. Nnanji preferred to hold meetings standing up, so that people would waste less time in what he considered needless chatter. That night it held a single table at the far end, flanked by a dozen stools and lit by seven freestanding bronze candelabras. As he walked forward to join the meeting, the galaxy of twinkling flames illuminated a mere six faces watching his approach, and only four of those belonged to members of the council.

Traditionally, trysts had been led by a band of seven Sevenths, although six of them, like all the lesser ranks, had been bound by the terrible third oath of absolute obedience to the seventh, the liege lord. Nnanji could recite scores of epics about those ancient trysts, yet they had been temporary affairs, summoned by the Goddess to impose order in specific areas. The Tryst of Casr was much more, called to restore the honor of the swordsman craft, and dedicated to extending its rule throughout the entire World. The last time Wallie had inquired, the record clerks had lists of more than two hundred Sevenths, all of them officially members of the council.

Here were four. Many were too old or infirm to attend, some had never been to Casr, and only these few were available there now. The rest were scattered over a large part of the World.

Boariyi, of course, towered over everyone, even Wallie, and especially old Zoariyi, his uncle, standing at his side in a senior's blue robe. He was bent, shrunken and toothless now and did not wear a sword, but age had neither dulled his devious mind nor blunted his extremely sharp tongue. Zoariyi had never quite forgiven Shonsu for stealing the leadership away from his nephew, but he remained loyal and his advice was always worth hearing.

Opposite them stood Lord Joraskinta, a solid, square-faced, young man who had accepted the Tryst more than a season ago when it arrived at the docks of Ashe, the city he ruled, and informed him that the World was changing. From now on all cities would be ruled by civilians, either kings or councils of elders, and swordsmen would be under their direction. Consequently he could accept this new order by swearing absolute obedience to the red-haired Seventh with the deadly smile, or he could refuse; in which case he would be challenged and slain—his choice. As soon as he had sworn, he had been ordered to abdicate his throne in favor of an elected board of elders, and had then been provided with a suitable retinue of senior swordsmen and sent off to Casr, to learn the ways of the Tryst. He had arrived only a couple of weeks ago, and this was his first council meeting. Ultimately, if he seemed reliable, he would be given a worthy job somewhere.

Where was the missing Lord Mibullim, who had been similarly recruited and should have reached Quo before Nnanji?

Lord Dorinkulu, standing alongside Joraskinta and leaning on a cane, had sworn to the Tryst years ago and done great service in extending its borders. Having never properly recovered from a severed hamstring, he served now as supervisor of training in Casr.

A significant couple of paces away from the others stood Katanji, whose withered arm and mere third rank would normally have eliminated him from consideration, but who qualified as an honorary councillor because he was treasurer of the Tryst and Nnanji's brother. Although he had a trader's ability to mask his feelings, he must be more worried than he had ever been in his life. His gaze never left Wallie. Without Nnanji, Katanji's huge personal wealth would make him very vulnerable to whoever led the Tryst.

The sixth man present was Master Endrasti, included so that he could brief the council on what he had told Wallie on their ride in. Tough fighter though he undoubtedly was, he looked overawed at finding himself here, at the center of secular power.

Wallie strode to the end of the table, whose surface was empty except for the candelabras and a small basket containing pieces of soapstone. Without inviting anyone to sit, he tossed the seventh sword in its scabbard down beside them.

"Lord Nnanji is recovering from a wound. To imply otherwise in any way will be regarded as sedition. Does anyone here object to my wearing this sword during his convalescence?"

They all smiled, even Katanji and Endrasti, and Boariyi actually chuckled.

"No, my liege. Lord Nnanji ordered me to give it to you." At that he lifted it from the table, drew it, and went down on one knee. "Live by this, wield it in Her service, die holding it!"

Wallie had overlooked the mystique a sword held for swordsmen. A swordsman must not wear any sword until formally given it by another. Since he had "given" the seventh to Nnanji that way, he must be "given" it back again. He took it with the correct response, "It shall be my honor and my pride."

As he slid it into his own scabbard for now, placing his own sword on the table, he said, "Master Endrasti has much to tell us, and I do not believe he has ever seen our grand map. I suggest we move some lights and stools over there, to the Ulk Sector."

Wallie had designed the hall himself. It was many times larger than it need be for meetings, but the plain slate walls served as a giant chalkboard, on which he tracked the exploration of the World. That would have been impossible before the coming of the Tryst, for the Goddess was the River, liable to alter its geography whenever She wanted. Wallie, by making the treaty with Rotanxi, had loosed the sorcerers' literacy on the World and thus ended the Age of Legends. Endrasti must have seen, and even helped to draw, local charts, but he had never viewed the whole sprawling trace of the River that looped across two walls and was soon going to spread onto a third. Wallie walked him through it with the aid of a weighty candelabra.

"Your reports have helped create this, master, but this is the nearest thing to a complete map of the World that I know of. The sorcerers may have a better, of course; they won't say and certainly won't share it if they do. Here is Casr, on the RegiVul Loop. Fourteen cities, and yet how small it looks!

"The River flows anticlockwise in the Loop, from Ov around to Aus, but south of it lie the Black Lands, where lava flows have made the River unnavigable. We sent an expedition through the upstream rapids, and it found many prosperous settlements. We still have not reached the end of the River in either direction. This green line shows the trail to Quo. You can see the enormous distance you would have to travel to go from Casr to Quo by water."

"It is humbling, my lord. I thought I had seen most of the River already. I never realized how much more of it there is."

"Only the Goddess herself can ever know it all. We call this area the Vul Sector. West of it lies the Zan Sector, but even the sorcerers themselves seem vague about where the boundary lies."

The Zan Coven seemed to be a branch or affiliate of Vul, for it had signed onto the Treaty quite willingly. The Yrt Coven, even farther downstream, had taken little more persuasion. Beyond that, the Tryst had found no more sorcerer cities for several years. If they existed, they kept themselves well hidden, but eventually swordsman missionaries had arrived at Hann, site of the holiest of all the Goddess's temples, and that possibly explained the absence of sorcerers in the area, for sorcerers worshiped the Fire God.

Seen like this, pinned to a wall, the River was actually many Rivers, all seemingly much the same size, but tangled as a fishing line tormented by a litter of kittens. Loops were looped on loops in a gigantic snakes and ladders board, except that the ladders were shortcuts between snakes. It could flow in any direction, dividing and rejoining at random. Very few earthly rivers ever behaved like that, except in deltas, but the Goddess's River never reached a sea or even a major lake. Wallie's engineer training rejected it as an impossible perpetual motion machine, and he had not quite given up hope that, somewhere yet unseen by the Tryst, the World held a mighty mountain range to source all that water and an ocean to receive it. Even so he could not comprehend a stream that sometimes seemed to flow in circles.

The River's major tributaries were branches of itself. It rarely wandered farther north than the RegiVul loop, while Hann lay close to the equator. Lacking chronometers or surveying instruments, Wallie had only a vague idea of longitude, but he suspected that the Tryst now ruled more than half the World. He could not reconcile that with the sorcerers' claim to have thirteen covens, for he only knew of five.

Land roads were rare, but every new one offered another reach of the River to explore. By the time the Tryst had "discovered" Hann, ten years ago, other expeditions had pushed into the southern hemisphere and established cooperation with the Ulk Coven. It was in front of that section of the map that the council now convened, with Zoariyi and Dorinkulu on stools and the others remaining on their feet to demonstrate their manhood.

"Now, Master Endrasti, the last dispatch we had from you and Lord Nnanji, you had just reached a city named Fua. Here." Wallie knelt, laying down the candelabra and accepting a soapstone crayon from Katanji.

"Right bank, my lord. We were sailing upstream, roughly northwest." Going upstream, the right bank would be to the left, but he was too astute to remind his present audience of that elementary truth. "If I may... I think Fua lies farther south than you are placing it. The Dream God was well to the north and clearly showing seven bands, and Lord Nnanji thought he seemed wider than he did from Casr, even."

"You said that in your report. I am worried that you will push the River so far south that I will have to dig up the floor of this hall to fit it in. Fua accepted the Tryst?"

"Quite happily, my lord. They had a band playing to greet us as we docked. But the reeve warned us that we would soon be entering the area influenced by the Kra Coven, and sorcerers had been warning the secular rulers there not to accept the Tryst. That was when Lord Nnanji sent Honorable Quarlaino to Casr with dispatches."

Quarlaino had arrived safely.

"Tell their lordships what happened at Arbo."

"Yes. my lords, after Fua, the next place with swordsmen was Arbo, on the right bank. Quite small, it had a garrison of five. They all swore allegiance, claiming they'd been waiting for years for the Tryst to arrive. And Lord Nnanji didn't blame them for what happened. Some of them were seriously injured trying to rescue our men. They were a varied..."

Testy old Zoariyi barked an impatient cough. Endrasti glanced nervously at his audience and went swiftly to the point.

"The house of joy burned down in the middle of the night. It was the only one in town. We lost eight men in the blaze. One man escaped, an apprentice who had drunk little. The wine was drugged, we're sure. The house girls had either all been warned not to drink it, or been carried out before the fire was lit."

"Lord Nnanji did not retaliate?" Wallie prompted, having been told the answer earlier.

"Not at Arbo, my lord. There was no way of knowing who had set the blaze, and several homes were destroyed, which he thought was a sign to them that the Goddess disapproved. But he did send Adept Rudere and three Thirds back downstream to instruct garrisons to send him reinforcements. The Adept was to continue on to Casr."

"He never arrived. Next town?"

"Ma," Endrasti said. "Quite small, rather quaint. Only two swordsmen there, older men, but very spry still, both brothers."

"We should be surprised if only one of them were," Zoariyi muttered.

Endrasti hastily recounted the near-disaster at Zek and the massacre at Cross Zek, his listeners growling oaths at the news of swordsmen mowed down by gunfire.

Wallie continued writing with his soapstone, extending the map: Fo, Cross Zek, Zek, Nolar, Plo. "That about right?" he asked, rising. He had written in Kra with a query, somewhere in the mountains, farther south.

"Yes, my lord, except that I was told the River flows pretty much due west at Plo and then turns south toward Fex."

That detail could be settled later. "And what happened after Cross Zek?"

"We carried the bodies to the River and sent them back

to Her," Endrasti said. "The liege decided that, as we were clearly in a war and had lost two score men in less than two weeks, we needed reinforcements before approaching Nolar and Plo. Back at Fo, on Shipwrights' Day was when he sent Lord Mibullim and an entourage to Casr with orders to bring you up to date, Lord Shonsu, and ask you to organize a stronger force."

"That seems curious," Zoariyi said. "There are thousands more swordsmen strung along the River itself than there are here. Why come all the way back to Casr to recruit?"

"Probably for gold," Katanji suggested wryly. "Fighting a war would be expensive."

They all looked inquiringly at Endrasti, as if inviting him to change his story, which he did. "As far I recall his exact words, my lords, he said, 'Shonsu knows a lot more about fighting sorcerers than I do, and it's time I went home and gave my wife twins.' My lords."

The remark about twins could not be funny while Nnanji might be on his deathbed, and the suggestion that he did not feel as competent as Wallie to wage this war was so shockingly out of character that for a moment no one said a word. Wallie was less surprised than the rest of them, though. Knowing of Wallie's past life on Earth, which he called his dream world, Nnanji would at least have wanted to consult him on the best way to tackle the crisis.

Knowing there was still more to come, Wallie prompted Endrasti to finish his story. Nnanji had withdrawn downstream with care, warning the city garrisons of potential trouble and in most cases reinforcing them from his diminishing troop. On Slaters' Day he had sent Adept Hazenhik off with dispatches. He and his companions were also missing.

"A week later, on Jewelers' Day, we set off for Casr ourselves. We were down to a mere score of men."

That score of men was the most surprising thing about Nnanji's reaction, though. His usual response to an emergency was to take off like a startled hare, traveling with only one or two companions, because that was much faster. A small group could always sail on the fastest ships, even if they had to sleep on deck, and could almost always acquire horses for the land crossings, buying them outright if necessary. Wallie thought of those madcap junkets as the Nnanji express. Like Julius Caesar, he would often turn up unannounced where he was least expected. This time he had chosen the safe way. Either the danger had seemed extreme, or he was starting to feel his age at last."Thank you," Wallie said. "About a hundred days later, when the liege had reached Quo, he was attacked in his sleep, on the same night I was attacked in Casr. Moreover, three courier parties have failed to arrive and must be presumed lost: Honorable Ruderedispatched from Arbo, Lord Mibullim from Fo, and Adept Hazenhik from... where did you say?"

"Rea, my lord."

"Rea." Wallie folded his arms and looked around the distressed faces. "Add it all up, and we lost three score swordsmen, some of them women. Does anyone deny that we— yes, master?"

Endrasti was fidgeting for attention. "Begging your pardon, liege, but there were two heralds, also. After Lord Nnanji withdrew to Arbo, he sent a herald to the elders of Nolar and another to the king of Plo, proclaiming that he had been attacked and would retaliate in force unless he received submission and compensation."

"What happened to those heralds?" asked Zoariyi.

"Their heads were returned in bags of salt, my lord."

Annoyed that he had not been told of this additional atrocity sooner, Wallie said, "No ambiguity about that answer." Heralds, like priests, were supposed to be inviolable.

"It sounds as if Lord Nnanji was lucky to reach even as far as Quo," Dorinkulu said.

Endrasti glanced at Wallie and received a nod. "I may be able to explain that, my lords. There is an overland shortcut from Rea to Thoy, so the couriers would all go that way. Lord Nnanji still had too many men with him—he couldn't have rented enough mules or horses, so he'd have had to make several trips. Also he'd have had trouble finding adequate shipping at Thoy, whereas we still had two good ones at the Rea end. We came by—"

Wallie cut him off. "Thank you. So he came by a different route. Another possibility would be that the liege's party was simply too strong to attack. Gentlemen, we have an assembly scheduled for Sailors' Day, at which time we must announce our response to these acts of war."

"What will our response be?" Zoariyi snapped.

"Whatever we decide tomorrow. Think about it overnight, and meet again here at the second bell. Just before it, rather. I shall summon Lord Woggan for that hour to explain to us why thunder weapons have returned to the World."

"And if the sorcerer ignores your summons?"

"Then we shall go and get him," Wallie said. "Meeting adjourned."

After the worst day he could remember in years, he was very late getting home. When he did so, he found Thana there, waiting for him in a screaming fury, wanting to know where her son was. Jja's mood was little better, as she had endured two hours of Thana's ranting.

"He is no danger," Wallie insisted. "I have six men watching over him."

"Six men? *If he's in no danger why does he need six men to guard him?*"

"He's in no danger because I have those men there. When you learn what he's been doing, you will be very proud of him."

"*Why should I be proud of him if he's in no danger?*"

"Because he's spending the night in more discomfort than you have ever known in your life, swordsman. He knew what he was getting into and he was eager to help. I am going to let him finish the job he took on and I will not shame him by letting his mother drag him away for bedtime. Addis is growing up, Thana! He will come out of this as a man with achievements to be proud of. Jja will show you out. Goddess be with you."

Jja did so, flashing danger like a looming thunderstorm.

Wallie poured himself a glass of wine and flopped into his favorite chair. She returned and stood over him.

"You treated Thana contemptibly!"

"It's what she needed," he said wearily. "I'm a safe target for her to sharpen her claws on. She's worried sick about Nnanji and she can work it off on me."

That terrestrial logic would have bounced off most of the People like frozen peas, but Jja had lived with him a long time and had a lot of perception of her own. "And Addis? You're letting him prove his manhood?"

"I suppose I am."

"You don't sound too sure."

Wallie drained his goblet and stood up. "Addis is showing his mettle, yes. But whether he's showing it to me or the gods or his father... That I'm not sure. Maybe just to himself. He's being tested. I'm being tested. These are testing times. Let's go to bed."

She slid her arms around him. "Just don't expect me to let you go to sleep for a while yet."

CHAPTER 3

ADDIS WAS CERTAIN THAT HE HADN'T SLEPT all night. The noise, the cold, the stink, the hard stone under a thin layer of straw—not to mention the fact that he was cuddled up with a complete stranger—how could he possibly have been asleep? Yet he seemed to waken with a start when the screaming started.

He remembered where he was. He sat up much too fast, being reminded of all the bruises from yesterday. It was almost dawn; the sky bright, the air cold. The screaming was because men were being dragged out of cells and this was Torturers' Day, which was one of the special days on which criminals were put to death. Nowadays they were just hanged. He'd been told that executions used to be much more entertaining, but Lord Shonsu had stopped the fun years ago.

He'd *lain with a girl*. All night. He knew how the older boys talked about that with longing, mostly just hiding ignorance and apprehension, but all he could remember was the two of them shivering in unison. Nothing else had happened—and wouldn't, according to Vixini, for at least a year yet. Addis wasn't so sure it would take that long. But now a dozen or so men were being hauled away to be hanged. Lucky them. He huddled small against the cold. He was thirsty and he needed to pee. There was a bucket for that. He would have to turn his back and sit on it.

"What time do they serve breakfast in this inn?" he asked.

No answer. He wasn't supposed to know her tongue had been cut out.

"You're not very friendly, are you?"

He decided peeing could wait. When the woman went, he looked away.

He wondered if Dad had made it through the night.

He wondered what would happen to him if Dad hadn't. He'd promised Dad he would swear to the swordsmen and hunt down the —*gulp!*— killers. If Dad died, then Uncle Shonsu would be leader of the Tryst again. The swordsmen didn't like him as well as they liked Dad. It had been right after Addis had made that promise to Dad that Shonsu had sent him on this jail mission. Maybe Shonsu didn't want the son of Nnanji in the Tryst?

No, Shonsu wouldn't leave him here to rot. Shonsu would never do anything so horrible. And Addis had promised to get information out of the prisoner. So the sooner he could, the sooner he could go home to a hot bath and a good meal.

She was a few years older than he was. Pretty face, but very skinny. She did have breasts, not melons, but what Vixi called a nice pair of pears. She ought to be wearing clothes, instead of just an all-over coat of dye, which was streaky and patchy now. Vixi had told him how she'd climbed up the wall of Shonsu's palace. That would take a lot more nerve than most men had.

The shouting was starting up again, inmates yelling insults at the slime, demanding water, or clean buckets, but no mention of food. He was going to die of hunger. Shonsu had warned him it might be days before the girl broke down and began telling him things.

From time to time the slime patrolled, walking past the cage fronts in pairs. Quite often they stopped and jeered at the two "girls", threatening to put a few male drunks in with them, or come in and teach them how to be nice to slime.

Addis decided to try again. "How come you don't have any facemarks?"

She pointed to her forehead and then his, raised her eyebrows. That meant *How come you don't?* At least she was communicating. And he had an answer ready for that.

"My dad wanted me to swear to the courtesans, and I wouldn't. So he and my brothers beat me up and threw me out."

She snorted in disbelief. She pointed at his crotch and wiggled her index finger. *You're a man.*

How did she know that? Better not to ask, or even think about it.

He wiggled his pinkie: *Just a boy.*

She smiled. He grinned back. He decided this honest approach was a lot better than trying to fool her. He wasn't good at lying.

"My name's not really Brota. It's Addis. What's yours?"

Shrug.

"So it's true that somebody cut out your tongue?"

He'd been ready to shudder when she showed him, if she ever did, but he didn't have to fake his horror at all. The white slug of scar tissue in her mouth was much worse than he's expected. He almost retched.

"Ugh! That's horrible. Who did that to you?"

Hand at the back of her head: *Ponytail.*

"A swordsman?

Three. Rape. Cut off tongue.

"I don't believe it!" he said. "Not swordsmen sworn to the Tryst, anyway. My— the liege lord wouldn't allow it. They hang swordsmen for rape, just like other men."

Disbelief, sneer.

"It's true! Liege Lord Nnanji doesn't allow it." Seeing her continued skepticism, he insisted. "Don't you know his story? At about my age he was sworn in to the temple guard in Hann, the men who protect Her most holy temple anywhere, the guard that should be the best swordsmen in the whole World. As soon as he won promotion to Second, he was horrified to discover that they were bad. They took bribes! They stole offerings, bullied pilgrims, even raped them sometimes! When they were supposed to put criminals to death, they took bribes to let them escape. Then the Goddess sent Shonsu of the Seventh to clean them up, and he picked out my—picked out Apprentice Nnanji as the only honest man in the guard, because he needed a second when he killed the reeve. And the two of them fought off the whole guard at an ambush and... Haven't you ever heard the minstrels sing about that battle?"

From the way her eyes rolled, she obviously hadn't and didn't want to.

"Well, it really happened! And then the Goddess called the Tryst and soon Nnanji became a Seventh and the best swordsman, so he became its liege, and ever since then he's been cleaning up the whole craft. So even if the men who, er, abused you were swordsmen, they certainly weren't swordsmen sworn to the Tryst. It didn't happen in Casr?"

Head shake.

"Mm. Could you recognize them again if you saw them?

Hands over eyes.

"Blindfold? Oh... Dark?"

Nod.

Nothing he could promise about finding justice for her, then, but he was making progress. Had she really been raped and mutilated by three swordsmen, or had those been hooligans hired by the sorcerers to make her hate swordsmen?

The one-sided conversation was interrupted then, because the slime came around with food, except it didn't look like food or smell like food. The girl hurried over to the bars, kneeling there with her hands cupped, as if begging, so Addis did the same, and in a moment a jailer appeared with a cart holding two huge pails. Another slime ladled out a double handful of mush for each of the prisoners; then they moved on to the next cage.

It was cold, smelled bad, tasted worse. Addis decided he wasn't hungry enough to eat any of it—not yet and maybe never.

"Here," he said. "You want mine too?"

She shook her head, so he tipped his helping into the

slop bucket and then, reluctantly, wiped his hands on some of the bedding straw. He returned to the back of the cage and sat there, feeling miserable. It wouldn't be so bad if he thought he had any chance of learning anything at all from the assassin. He ought to hate her because of what she had tried to do, but mostly he just felt sorry for her. He could get out of here any time he wanted. Or at least he hoped he could. She was here until they took her away to declare her guilty and hang her.

When she had finished licking her fingers, he said, "Here," and untied his wrap. "You need this more than I do."

She looked surprised, but she took the filthy thing and put it on. He had felt uncomfortable in it, and he was quite used to being naked, but a naked boy locked up with a girl would be unusual. Not all the slime could be in on the plot. Suppose they decided to drag him away to another cell? Or take her away?

Of course all he had to do was shout, "Tomisolaan!" and he would be rescued at once. Wouldn't he? Of course he would! He mustn't worry about that. But telling himself not to worry just made him worry more.

"This isn't much of a chat," he said. "Can you read and write? I can. You could trace out letters to tell me things."

She took her ears in her fingers and wiggled them: *You're a spy.*

He shrugged. "Yes. I was put here to see if you'd let things slip." He certainly hoped that this was *really* why he'd been put here, and that he could *really* get out of the horrible place anytime he wanted to quit. "I know you tried to kill Lord Shonsu. Vixi... That's my friend, apprentice swordsman Vixini, Lord Shonsu's oldest son. He told me how he found the hook you used to climb up the wall. That was really brave of you! I couldn't do that."

She pulled a face and looked away. She didn't want to talk to him any more. He was a swordsman spy. At least she wasn't trying to strangle him.

"One of your friends tried to kill Lord Nnanji the same night," he said.

After a moment she turned back towards him, wanting more.

"She was killed. Lord Boariyi killed her."

Shrug. *We knew the risks.*

"He's very badly hurt. He may not live."

Smile.

"He's my dad," Addis said. "I'm Addis, son of Nnanji the swordsman. That's why I'm here. I wanted to help." Suddenly there was a lump in his throat and a prickling under his eyelids, and he couldn't talk any more.

Jja was very skilled at drawing the poison out of her husband's soul when that was necessary, but even after her expert ministrations, Wallie had slept badly that night. It was not thoughts of more assassins that disturbed him, but the fear that he had been put in Nnanji's place in order to fight a war. Nnanji was a perfect leader for the World's swordsmen. They related to him, almost worshiped him. He believed in honor and the sutras and the will of the Goddess, and with those he had built an empire as large as those of Genghis Khan or Suleiman the Magnificent. He had done it with a bare minimum of bloodshed.

But he had never heard of Iwo Jima, Cannae, or Gettysburg. Nnanji was perfectly capable of lining up a thousand swordsman and charging the sorcerers' guns.

So the war that had so worried Wallie fifteen years ago had now arrived, and the Goddess had put Nnanji out of action. Wallie Smith was no soldier. In truth he was no swordsman, either. His fencing skill had come from the original Shonsu and been given him by a miracle. In the World's terms, Wallie Smith was much more a renegade sorcerer. He had spent the night wondering just what part he was expected to play. To organize the Tryst to cast bronze guns and extract saltpeter for gunpowder would take years, and he did not have years. He must solve the problem quickly, else the Tryst would either fall apart or depose him and go charging bullheaded against the sorcerers' fortress at Kra.

All of this made sense, except that, according to Endrasti,

Nnanji himself had recognized it, and had intended to turn the war over to Wallie anyway. So why had Nnanji been so horribly put out of the game?

What message was the Goddess sending?

Had Wallie made a fearful error in reading Her instructions about Addis? Wallie was the equivalent of godfather to the boy, yet instead of comforting him in his terror, he had locked him up with a would-be killer who had absolutely nothing to lose. The boy's eagerness to take the job was no excuse. Yet Addis could still pass for a girl. He was certainly stronger than the prisoner, and knew just enough about street fighting now to defend himself if she turned vicious. He was supremely motivated, had no facemark yet, and was literate. No one else could possibly have all those qualifications just when they were needed. In the World of the Goddess, coincidences were usually instructions.

He went down to breakfast without waiting for Jja. He was surprised to find Sharon there already, eating a disgustingly juicy mango-type fruit, dribbling down her chin. Sharon was his eldest, if one did not count Vixini, and due to be sworn to a craft very soon. She wanted to be either a midwife or a dancer. Wallie thought midwifery was too stressful and doubted that she had the agility required for dancing, but Jja was arranging for her to be assessed. She was named after Wallie Smith's mother, but "Sharon" was a respectable local name also.

Even more surprising was Vixini on the other side of the table, gnawing on a drumstick. Although the red rims around his eyes suggested that he had not yet caught up on his lost sleep, he was alert enough to notice the sapphire on the sword hilt beside his father's ponytail. He frowned and bit his lip. As soon as informal greetings were finished, he said, "How is Uncle Nnanji?"

"He's recuperating from a wound. Heralds will be announcing this regularly all day in the lodge."

Vixini said, "Mm?" thoughtfully. "Um, mentor?"

Wallie knew what was coming next. "Yes, protégé?"

"You have always instructed me that a man isn't ready for third rank until he's been a swordsman for at least five years."

"That's true as a general rule. A Third exercises the authority of our craft, and kids can't usually manage that. But there isn't a Third in the Tryst who'd have much of a chance against you with foils; you'd even beat some Fourths. I don't want to be accused of creating a sleeper."

Vixini could not hide a glow at such tribute. "Yes, but the sutras…"

"I have given strict orders that you are not to be favored in the sutra tests in any way. I told Filurz to pick out examiners who will not pander to me as liege lord."

Gnaw, chew, swallow… "Don't see this. You want me to fail the sutra test?"

"Certainly not. I very much want you to pass. I will be ashamed and deeply disappointed in you if you fail the sutra test. I am sure Adept Filurz understood. There are plenty of lickspittle swordsmen in the Tryst who would try you with a couple of real easy ones and then declare you qualified. Filurz will do what he's told, choose men who have a grudge against me and will deliberately try to fail you, to get back at me. How many of the sutras are really difficult? I mean long, dull, and non-associative brutes?"

Vixi shrugged broad shoulders. "Six… maybe eight, I suppose."

"Right. Sharon, when are you meeting with the dancers?"

"One on Bronze Casters' Day and two on Sailors' Day. Can you come with us? I mean…" She put on her wounded-fawn expression.

"You mean you want me there to overawe them. No, I'm afraid I've got too many serious problems to deal with while your Uncle Nnanji is sick."

She pouted, but a very broad smile had taken over a certain young swordsman's face. He muttered, "Thanks, Big Bear," and reached for another drumstick.

Recalling his stepson's still-unripened ambition, Wallie decided that two solid days of memorizing sutras might require more motivation in his case. "And besides, there's going to be a war."

"Huh?"

"I'm going to be leading the Tryst to war and I can't take you with me while you're still just a Second."

Vixini's howl of joy sent the pigeons thundering upward.

CHAPTER 4

"LORD NNANJI IS RUNNING A HIGH FEVER. HIS condition is grave, but he is a strong man and very fit. We can only pray and wait. Lord Boariyi, as a former liege, you are the senior member of the council. Should both Nnanji and I ever be out of action at the same time, then you will wear the sapphire sword."

Five swordsmen of the seventh rank and one of third rank sat around the end of the long table in the council hall; no Endrasti now. For once Wallie had ordered pens, ink, and paper supplied, but so far no one had shown any interest in them.

Now to business. He glanced around the faces: hard, determined faces, giving nothing away.

"We have clear evidence of an external attack upon the Tryst at Cross Zek and in the murder of two heralds. We have clear evidence of internal rebellious conspiracy in that three courier squads have vanished, presumably eaten by the fish, and there have been two assassination attempts. We..." He paused at a distant chime.

"Your sorcerer hasn't come," said Zoariyi. "Are you surprised?"

"I'd have been very surprised if he'd been on time. Let's start with you, Lord Boariyi. What action do you propose we should take?"

"Heralds are sacred. Send the strongest force we can

muster against Plo, Kra, and Nolar. Hang the rulers. Fine the cities heavily."

Would anyone expect subtlety from a man of his height, or compassion from a swordsman?

"Lord Zoariyi?"

"Raid the sorcerers' tower here in Casr, and then Vul if necessary."

Better, because possible, but what would happen after that?

"Lord Dorinkulu?"

The old warhorse smiled. "You are asking what I would order, were I in your place. Well, I'd want more information, much more. I'm sure Master Endrasti is very able, but I'd question more of Rust... um, Lord Nnanji's, men. We know Kra's involved, because of the weapons used at Cross Zek. We suspect Plo and Nolar are, because of the heralds. That's less certain, because those two murders could be the work of assassins. The rulers may not have been involved." He turned and pointed his cane at the map. "Your drawing over there... The River flows from Plo to Rea and the Ulk Sector. How does it get to Plo? Lord Nnanji was arriving by the back door. Can we attack downstream, by the front door? Also, I'd certainly want to question that assassin you caught, my lord, tongue or no tongue."

Better still, but the Tryst wanted action *now*. So, probably, did the Goddess.

"Thank you. Lord Joraskinta?"

The youngest Seventh leaned forward, laying brawny forearms on the table. His heavy brows gave him an intense, aggressive stare, which must terrify his juniors. "Like Lord Dorinkulu, I want more information. I want to know what Lord Nnanji's orders were as he withdrew downstream to Rea. He shared out most of his company between the local garrisons. That's good. But I'd want to start farther downstream, and roll men forward, not back. To muster thousands of swordsmen here in Casr and then transport them all to the trouble zone would be... unnecessary." He meant ridiculous, but he was smart enough not to say so before the liege had announced his own decision. "But we could set a snowball going, starting about fifty days' sailing downstream from Plo. Order every garrison to send one quarter of its men forward. We'd have two thousand men long before the wave reached Nolar."

That was good thinking. "Keep talking," Wallie said.

Joraskinta gave him a questing look, as if wondering whether he was being praised or allowed to walk into quicksand. "Like Lord Dorinkulu, I'd certainly inquire where the other route to Plo is. I want to know where on their journeys these couriers disappeared. And I'd warn all our other forces in the field to slow down, perhaps have them join the Plo army, if they are close enough."

"Thank you, all of you," Wallie said. "Lord Treasurer, do you wish to comment at this time?"

Katanji smiled tolerantly at this childish talk of violence. "Finance should be no problem. The Tryst is already employing all its swordsmen, so the only extra cost will be board and transportation. Profits may be quite high, depending on how much damage you cause and what proportion of the population you auction off in the slave markets. Furthermore..." He rose and strolled over to the maps chalked on the slate walls. "Here is Plo, famous for its beautiful women."

"Quite," Wallie said. Jja came from Plo. What was the foxy Katanji up to this time? If Nnanji was as clear as a ray of sunlight, his brother was a fogbank.

"Now, over here," Katanji said, walking several paces westward, "you find the prosperous and salubrious city of Soo, best known for exporting rubies of very high quality." He wandered back to the table. "But the rubies from Soo are known in the jewel trade as Plo rubies."

Trust Katanji to upstage the entire council. The unmarked stretch of wall between Soo and Plo probably meant that the area had not been explored by the Tryst yet, but might mean that it did not exist on the ground.

"You think that Soo and Plo are actually close together?"

"I don't think they're on the same stretch of River,"

Katanji said patiently, "because that would let Plo market its own rubies. Besides, the Soo Reach is well known to us. Plo is almost a backwater. But gems are easily carried, and overland trails are often overlooked or even kept secret. You may not need the front door, my lords. It may be faster to go in by the trading hatch."

Fortunately Wallie was relieved of the immediate need to comment as the doors at the far end swung open. "I will rise," he said. "The rest of you remain seated."

Sorcerers were parading in, six of them. The dumpy blue-robed one in front was Woggan himself. Behind him came two Sixths in Green and three Fifths in Red. All of them had their hoods up and their hands hidden in their sleeves, so almost nothing of the men themselves was visible as they paced solemnly along the hall. Sorcerers were showmen; their gowns were bulky garments with many pockets filled with tricks they used to impress the gullible—lenses, acid, phosphorus, and many others. But if each of these men held two smoothbore pistols, the swordsmen's council could be shot to pieces. Wallie had foreseen the threat, and fifty swordsmen trooped in behind the delegation, taking up position on either side of the doorway.

The first sorcerer Seventh he had known had been old Rotanxi, and they had developed a grudging respect for each other. Since then he had worked with three successive wizards of Casr, each one worse than his predecessor. He especially disliked Woggan, who seemed more devious and obstructive than any.

Wallie rose and saluted with a fist to the heart, while his companions remained on their stools. As a greeting to a visiting Seventh, this was outright insult. A swordsman would have challenged over it. The old sorcerer merely nodded and sat on the stool at the far end of the table. His companions remained standing at his back.

For a moment there was silence, broken only by a few coughs from the swordsmen at the far end of the hall. Wallie had asked for some audible respiratory irritation so that his visitors would know the guards were present.

He dispensed with polite preliminaries. "My lord Wizard, about a season and a half ago, twenty-six swordsmen were ambushed and slain by thunder weapons near the city of Nolar. The Treaty of Casr required that all such weapons be destroyed."

The old man's pouched eyes stared at him for a while, as if waiting to hear if there was more. Then, "I am not familiar with Nolar."

"Near Plo."

"Ah, that would be in the Kra Sector. The Treaty of Casr binds the Tryst and the coven of Vul. We have no control over other covens."

"I understand that. But heralds have been murdered, swordsmen have been drugged and burned alive, couriers have disappeared. In all about three score of my craft brethren have been slain."

"Any of them in Vul's sector?" The wizard's voice was painfully husky. That, combined with his candle-wax pallor, suggested that he was chronically sick, possibly dying. His wits still seemed sharp enough to be dangerous.

"Could be," Wallis said. "We are still tracing the couriers' movements. But you know about the attempted assassinations two nights ago in Casr and Quo. Those were certainly in your sector."

"But nothing to do with my coven. I suggest you question the woman you captured. Disabled or not, she can be forced to provide information." He was well informed, but sorcerers could pick up gossip as well as anyone.

"She is literate? You know this?"

"I am not omnipotent. Literacy was once the most jealously guarded secret of my craft. You—you personally, Lord Shonsu—scattered it everywhere, like rain. Any beggar may turn up learned these days."

"And if she is unable to write her responses, sorcerers can communicate with signs, can they not?"

"So can swordsmen."

This had all been preliminary warm-up. Now Wallie cut to the chase.

"Wizard Woggan, the Tryst has been attacked with thunder weapons in an act of war. We shall retaliate against Kra and any cities allied with it. To do this effectively, we need equivalent weapons. I demand that you supply us with them."

Woggan's doughy face writhed into what might have been intended as a smile. "Impossible. We have none. The Treaty of Casr required that all thunder weapons be destroyed and no more made."

Wallie glanced at the greens and reds behind the Seventh. They were all males, all younger than Woggan. The faces within their hoods, so far as they could be seen at all, were outcrops of granite.

"I have fifty swordsmen behind you, my lord. If I order them to come forward and start strip-searching your retinue, one by one, will I find no thunder weapons in their pockets?"

"You will break the treaty, my lord."

"No, it is you who will break the treaty, by refusing to cooperate. The swordsmen have been attacked. Are you with us or against us?"

"Whatever other covens or secular cities may have done does not concern Vul."

"Yes, it does." Wallie rose and beckoned. With a muffled pad of swordsmen boots, the guard marched forward and surrounded the sorcerers. "Lord Woggan, I asked you if you are with us or against us. You have no other option. Decide now."

"I cannot make that decision. I must refer it to my coven in Vul."

"No time. Decide."

The sorcerer sighed faintly, like an adult dealing with stupid children. "Your terms are too vague. What do you really want?"

"That Vul and other friendly covens force Kra and any allies it has, to sign the Treaty of Casr and abide by it. You will supply us with whatever thunder weapons you have and more as may be agreed later. You will aid us in the war and not aid our enemies."

"Or?"

"Or you and your companions will be held here while my men take over your tower. I have four hundred standing by, waiting for the order. All of you will then be hostage for Vul's cooperation. I have also ordered planning to begin for a full-scale assault on Vul itself." Wallie was bluffing. There were no such attacks pending, and he knew he was violating the treaty he had sworn fifteen years ago. But he was also certain that he would find firearms if he had these men searched.

"You would make war on the whole sorcerers' craft? Just how many swordsman will that take?"

"I cannot tell you how big the Tryst is, because I do not know. The total must change by the hour. Judging by the number of Sevenths we have listed, and excluding the too old and too young, I must command well over 100,000 fighting personnel."

"And how many of those can you assemble in one place and keep fed?"

"Enough. Enough for anything. Your decision, please."

Pause for staring match...

"I will go this far," the wizard said. "We may have a few of the weapons you want in storage in Vul, but the black powder they require to function will certainly have rotted away by now. It will need at least a year to retool to produce more weapons and even longer to supply adequate powder. I will also admit, Lord Shonsu, that I personally agree with your argument that the peace cannot endure unless it applies everywhere, and I am disgusted by what was done the night before last. It had nothing to do with me or Vul coven.

"But it is nothing compared to what will happen if you try any of the mass brutality you are threatening. Go and bluster at Kra. I confirm that Kra is the source of your problems. Further than that I cannot go."

He stood up and turned as if to leave. Fifty swords hissed from their scabbards.

Wallie shouted, "Let them go!"

Fifty swords were sheathed. The sorcerers pushed through

the cordon and headed for the door; the swordsmen trailed them out.

Only after the door closed did Wallie utter a quiet, "Holy shit!"

"You gave up far too easily!" Zoariyi said. "Sutra Twenty-seven, *On Credibility.*"

None of the others was willing to say so, but they were nodding.

"I disagree," Wallie snapped. "Pass it along here, please Katanji."

"Pass what? Where did *that* come from?"

At the far end of the table, where the sorcerers had been, lay a small roll of paper, no larger than a man's index finger.

"Out of Woggan's sleeve," Wallie said. "He dropped it when he stood up and all the swords came out. Everyone else was distracted. He didn't want his companions to see it."

"Be careful how you open it," Katanji said, reaching for the scroll and passing it along. "It probably contains poison spiders."

"Very likely." Wallie untied the thread. Paper was precious in the World, and the outermost sheet was smaller than a postcard. It contained four even smaller scraps, none bigger than a large postage stamp. He began with the big one.

"This appears to be a letter, but the absence of a seal at the bottom shows that it is a copy made for our benefit. Or a total fake, I suppose. 'From the Voice of Zan...' Anyone know who or what the Voice of Zan is?"

After a moment, Joraskinta said, "I would take it to mean that it is an official edict from the Zan coven's ruling council of thirteen, my lord."

Wallie nodded agreement. "From the Voice of Zan to the cryptic Wizard Woggan of Casr... A date that I do not understand." He drew a deep breath as his eyes ran ahead of his voice. "Oh, listen to this! '... introducing Honorable Yarrix from Kra, who journeys to your domain with a covey of four specialists who, er, have cause to hate swordsman. You are required to, um, foster his purpose and eschew hindrance, as mandated by Precept 205 of our conformation.' What say you to that, gentlemen?"

"I'd say you still have two assassins after you," Zoariyi growled.

Certainly. But the language of the People did not always translate exactly into the English of Wallie's thinking. *Have cause* wasn't quite right. An equally valid meaning would be *have been given cause.*

"So much," Katanji said, "for all the crap about the covens being independent. Here you have a sorcerer lord of the Vul coven being ordered by the Zan coven to assist a killer squad from Kra!"

"But Woggan's tipping us off," Joraskinta said. "The sorcerers are split, my lords. We must try to use that."

Cooperation from sorcerers? A sorcerer with *principles?* Truly the World was changing! Wallie unfolded the second sheet. The brevity of the message suggested that the original had been written on a scrap of bird skin and delivered by pigeon. He read it out.

"It begins, 'Warning.' A number that looks like a date, and then, 'Thoy, Arra, 1, 2, 2, 3. Black-white-cat." He glanced around the puzzled faces and explained. "Thoy and Arra are cities on the River. The numbers are written in colored inks. It actually says, 'One blue, two orange, two brown, three yellow.' Either they had no novices with them, or sorcerers don't bother to count those. Black-white-cat must be a coded signature. So what we have here," he added for the benefit of Boariyi and Dorinkulu, who were still lost, "is the obituary of Lord Mibullim. Master Endrasti told us that he was sent off with two Fourths and two Thirds? And three apprentices, I assume, unless those yellows were locals escorting the visitors. The enemy murders boys, too."

The killers had sent a warning to their victims' destination, Casr, to warn the wizard of that city that the Tryst might be asking questions.

"They are efficient," Wallie muttered. "Oh, so efficient!" His hand shook with rage as he picked up the next two sheets. As he expected, they were similar warnings, recording the deaths of the other two missing courier parties, led by Honorable Hazenhik and Adept Rudere respectively. The Black-white-cat signature was the same in each case. It might be a file name.

"I am impressed," Joraskinta said. "These are confessions of murder, my lord. I cannot see why the wizard would forge such documents, and the tally of the dead is apparently genuine. He is trying to win your confidence, whether honestly or falsely."

"And he did not want his subordinates to know what he was doing," Wallie said. He peered at the fifth scrap of paper, whose writing was so crabbed that it was hard to read in the dim light. He expected it to tell him of more swordsmen murdered, disappearances that he had not yet heard about. But it didn't. With a mighty roar, he leaped up so fast that his stool tipped over. He was halfway along the hall before it hit the floor.

The others stared after him in astonishment. It was Joraskinta who picked up the fifth message and read it out: "Men in high places should avoid sweet wine."

CHAPTER 5

VISITORS WERE BRINGING IN EDIBLE FOOD AND other comforts for some of the prisoners. Slime escorted them in and examined everything to make sure there were no knives in the soup or files in the blankets. The slime were probably paid almost nothing for doing their horrible job, but they would live comfortably off what they stole and the bribes they collected. Addis had never been so hungry and cold and scared in his life. The weather had turned. Fall was coming.

"I don't think you were raped by swordsmen," he said. "I think they were sorcerers, or men hired by sorcerers." The girl was sitting with her back to him, but neither of them could leave, and he had nothing better to do than keep trying. He was not going to give up yet. "And I suppose the sorcerers promised you they could cure your tongue?"

No reaction.

"Well, I'm sure they can't do things like that. If they could, they would set up shop and make money at it. They're tricksters."

Still none.

"You're very lucky you got caught by Shonsu and not his guards. They would have roughed you up real bad. And if it weren't for Shonsu, you'd be in some awful torture dungeon. He's the one who stopped torture. You can make anyone say anything, he says, so it's useless."

A little later he tried again. "Shonsu's sort of my uncle.

He and my dad swore the fourth oath together, making them oath brothers, so he's like an 'oath uncle'. I used to call him Uncle, when I was a kid, with Dad being away so much. I'm real glad you didn't manage to kill him."

Nothing.

"And you should be, too. I suppose he'll have to hang you; but that's better than what would have happened to you if you'd succeeded and he weren't around to defend you." What now? "I see I'm wasting my time with you. I never was any good at lying and you don't believe me when I speak the truth, do you? I can get out of here anytime I want, you know. All I have to do is say the password and the men in the next cell will unlock the gate and let me out. Now you know I was put here to spy on you, you're certainly not going to let anything slip."

Stupid, stupid slut, she was!

"What I'd like to know more than anything is whether there are more of you snakes lurking around, and if they're going to try to kill Shonsu again, and maybe finish off my dad if he doesn't die anyway."

She wasn't going to tell him that, not after all she'd done. He had nothing to bribe her with, no authority to try. Didn't mean he couldn't try.

"I can't promise this, because Shonsu didn't say I could, but if you were to promise me that you would answer all his questions truthfully, then I think—this is just my guess, but I know him very well—I think he would agree to spare your life. He's that sort of person."

The girl turned around and looked at him. Then she heaved herself closer without getting up. She started stroking her left palm with her right index finger.

Addis felt a thrill of excitement. She could write! She was probably a sorcerer with her facemark removed. He'd discovered something and his ordeal hadn't been wasted. He spelled out the signs she made: *Addis*!

"Yes, Addis. That's me. What's your name?"

Selina.

"Pleased to meet you, Selina. Pity the surroundings aren't

a bit nicer. You want to ask me something?" More invisible scribbling, letter by letter. "Yes, I would trust him if he swore on his sword. No swordsman ever breaks that oath."

She stared at him with deep dark eyes. They were very big eyes, or perhaps just stretched by fear.

"And I promise I'll try to help if you'll promise to play fair with me, Selina. You give me your word, and I'll show you how I can get out of here. I may need an hour or so to track down Shonsu, but I promise I'll come back and tell you what he says, yes or no."

She offered a hand to shake. He made her spell out the words *I swear I will tell* first, then he shook her hand. He rose and went to the gate, feeling very shaky inside. Suppose this didn't work? Suppose nobody came? It would be like one of those nightmares where your feet won't move.

"Tomisolaan!"

Nothing happened. Oh, horrors! He shouted again, louder, voice going squeaky.

There was a clatter from a lock nearby. A dirty man in a dirty loincloth appeared in front of him, holding a key. Under the grime on his forehead, Addis could just make out three craftmarks, too smudged to be identified, but not swords.

"Let me out, please. I need to report to Lord Shonsu. And you'd better keep a careful watch over this prisoner now, because she wants to talk, and she has dangerous friends."

The anteroom was very large, but when the council was in session all the Sevenths' escorts had to wait there, and Wallie had doubled every Seventh's bodyguard. When he came hurtling out from the hall, he almost fell over swordsmen. They were everywhere, mostly kneeling on the floor playing dice, but some sitting cross-legged in twos or threes, muttering sutras. Immediately to his right was Master Horkoda in his wheelchair, studying papers he was taking from a basket on his lap. To his left stood Adept Filurz, talking with Swordsman Tilber. Wallie beckoned him and withdrew into the hall for privacy.

Filurz followed. "My lord?"

"Very urgent! Send word to my wife and Lady Thana that shipments of wine may be poisoned. Probably only the best quality, but I don't know that for certain. Better warn the lodge commissariat also."

Before Wallie could turn away, Filurz said, "My lord?"

"What?"

"I've just been told that the boy Addis is downstairs and says he 'must' speak to you. He's very excited and says it's urgent, my lord."

Well at least the kid was alive, and maybe he had learned something important. That was what he was supposed to be doing, although Wallie had expected it to take much longer, if it happened at all. "If he's clean, send him in. If not clean him up first." Addis would certainly not have come to the lodge in his female disguise. "Oh, another thing. Tell Master Horkoda we need to question a swordsman, any swordsman, from a city named Soo."

Of course Nnanji, with his perfect memory, would have asked for the man or men he wanted by name. Wallie closed the door on Filurz and walked back to the meeting, still shivering with rage. Five faces watched him approach.

"Well?" he said as he took his seat again. "If poisoned wine turns up, does that mean we can trust Wizard Woggan?"

Boariyi and Dorinkulu nodded, Zoariyi and Joraskinta shook their heads. Katanji just smiled.

"Perhaps," Wallie conceded. "He may, as he says, disapprove of assassinations, either on ethical grounds or because they are counterproductive. He may be capable of poisoning some wine himself to win our trust. But he has given us what seems to be valid information about our missing couriers. What can we do about it?"

The answer, of course, was nothing. Woggan had admitted that the sorcerers had murdered three parties of swordsmen, but he had given away nothing about the identity of the guilty parties.

"Then let's agree on what we do know," Wallie said.

"The thunder weapons used at Cross Zek came from Kra. Agreed?"

The council agreed. Its deliberations were interrupted by the entry of a swordsman of the Third, who came limping along, looking much impressed by being in the presence of the Sevenths. He saluted, giving his name as Umbuti. His long service showed in his graying ponytail and weather-beaten hide, and Wallie could recall seeing him around many times in the past. That Horkoda had found him so quickly meant that he must have been present in the anteroom.

"Master Horkoda says you wanted a man from Soo, my lord."

"We do, and you were one of the original Tryst."

Filurz showed a scant collection of teeth in a grin. "That I was, my lord. Born in Soo, I was, my dad being a horse breaker there. Always wanted to be one of Her swordsman, but Soo's too small to have a reeve. Whenever a ship docked, I would look out for a water rat willing to swear me in and just I was getting desperate I found one—a woman she was, because even in those days there were female swordsmen, but just aboard ships. I didn't care, and she took me on. I was still only a Second when the Goddess summoned her swordsmen to Casr. Me and my mentor was two of the very first to arrive, my lords. Lord Tivanixi himself welcomed us and told us about the sorcerers and all the evil they—"

"Quite. Think back to Soo. How many rings of the Dream God can you see from there?"

The old campaigner had clearly not expected that question. "Why, seven, sir, that being the gods' number, as the priests tell us. Looks just like he does from here, except he's north, not south. Now, farther north from here, when I were up at Num..."

Wallie let him drone for a moment. Although he had no accurate way of measuring longitude, the planetary ring system provided an easy estimate of latitude. At Hann, which was close to the equator, the rings were a single thin band of light across the sky. At Casr the rings were much wider, and a man with good eyes and some religious prejudice could distinguish seven of them. At even higher latitudes, the inner rings were below the horizon.

Umbuti actually paused for breath.

"How far," Wallie asked, "from Soo to Plo?"

Umbuti looked blank. "Plo, my lord? Dunnoit, my lord. Never heard of anyone sailing from Soo to Plo. O' course the Goddess used to move—"

"Well, tell me this, then. Are there mountains near Soo?"

"No, lord. Can't see mountains from Soo. A few hills to the south, the Mule Hills, they're called, where men like my dad and later, I suppose, my brothers catch the horses. Wouldn't call the Mule Hills mountains, though. Not like Snowholme."

"Snowholme?"

"Farther south, my lord. Can't see it from Soo itsel' because of Mule Hills in the way, but an hour's walk inland you get a sight of it, all icy points."

"Is there a trading road across the Mule Hills?"

No there wasn't. By this time Wallie had learned the knack of getting information out of this willing, but not too discerning, witness. Oh, yes, there was a trail the horsemen used, but no traders. Where did it lead? To the other side. And on the other side was the River, at Cross Plo.

Thanked and dismissed, Umbuti, limped away to silent hand clapping by Katanji. The Sevenths frowned at this levity.

"I know some jewel traders in town," the treasurer said. "I'll find out for you. But it sounds like Snowholme must be RegiKra."

Wallie rose and went over to the map. If the journey from Casr to Soo were shorter than the journey to Plo was, then it might be a better jumping-off point for an attack on Kra, but the map could not answer his question, for the River there was just too twisted and too inadequately surveyed. What mattered was travel time. The traders might know, and Horkoda might be able to work it out from the records. The sorcerers would certainly know, but it might be best not to advertise interest in Soo.

He went back to his stool. It was close to noon.

"I suggest we break for the day," he said. "Tomorrow, let's meet again at the same time and draw up plans we can announce the day after at the assembly. Meanwhile, stay vigilant and watch out for poison."

The door of the hall opened and closed, having admitted one boy. Wallie gestured for him to approach. He was less than a third of Umbuti's age, but looked much less overawed by being summoned before the most powerful committee in the World. Most youngsters would be tongue-tied and nervous; not Addis. He had grown up in such company, and even his nudity did not disconcert him, for it was his normal condition. His hair was still wet and his bruises were multicolored, but there was a mischievous glint in his eyes as he drew near, and perhaps a hint of a wink at his uncle. He stopped at the end of the table and proceeded to give the civilian salute to a company: Addis, son of Nnanji the swordsman. Wallie was relieved to see that his eyes were bright with excitement. He was very pleased with himself.

"How's your father?" Katanji snapped.

"Don't know, Uncle. Haven't been home."

"Who's been beating you up?"

"A woman."

Wallie moved to retrieve control of the meeting before the stripling took it over completely. "Many years ago, my lords, on the first day I came before the Tryst of Casr, I presented a boy very little older than Addis to the swordsmen. His name was Novice Katanji. I described him, rightly, as the bravest man in the courtyard. I am happy now to introduce that boy's nephew to you now with the same honor. Addis has spent the night locked up with a murderer. He is worthy of his father. Report, Boy Addis."

"Her name is Selina, my lord. She can write. She swears she will tell all if you will spare her life. I did not promise that you would, my lord," he added quickly, "only that I thought you would and I would pass on her offer."

Boariyi rose and drew his sword to make the salute to a hero. The rest of the Sevenths, including Wallie, quickly

followed suit. Addis knew what the gestures meant, for he
blushed. "Thank you, my lords."

"Very well done," Wallie said. "Go home and comfort
your mother, who must be going crazy worrying about you."

"I promised Selina I would go back and tell her what—"

"No need for that. I'll have her moved to better quarters
immediately. Let no one know where you have been or what
you have been doing!"

"Not even my dad?"

For a moment Wallie had a nightmare vision of Nnanji
blazing into the room, sword in hand, seeking vengeance
on whoever had subjected his son to such a beating, such
mortal danger, and such indignity as a night in jail dressed
as a woman. But Nnanji was in a sickbed or even on his
deathbed, so that wouldn't happen. A boy of Addis's age
might be tempted to brag, but the shame of having dressed
up as a woman would discourage that.

"Of course you may tell your father. And your mother. But
in strict confidence. Warn her you might be put in danger
if the killers learn what you've done. On your way out, tell
Adept Filurz I need him."

As he watched that skinny figure hurrying back along the
hall, almost skipping, understanding came to Wallie like a
thunderclap. Suddenly he saw what his instincts had been
trying to tell him: why he had subjected the kid to such an
ordeal and what the gods were demanding of him.

That boy was the future, the Chosen One.

What Wallie Smith had been to Nnanji, so must he now
be to his son.

CHAPTER 6

WITH A MAZE AS HUGE AS THE LIEGE'S PALACE, you would think a mere boy could slip in without his mother seeing him. But no, the Goddess gave mothers some sort of special noses, to sniff out their offspring. Addis just nodded to the guards on the doors—twice as many as usual—and they saluted him. No hassle! Then he went scampering upstairs, anxious to see how Dad was. At the top stood swordsman of the third rank, Thana, arms akimbo, eyes hot as a furnace.

"And just where have you been?" she demanded.

"Um, how's Dad?"

"He's very sick. Answer my question."

"I was helping out Uncle Shonsu."

"Helping out *how*?"

He didn't like her attitude. The most important men in the whole World had just saluted him as a *hero* and she was still shouting at him like he was a kid. Why did he have to have the Mother from Vul instead of someone more understanding, like Aunt Jja?

"Better not say, Mom. Lord Shonsu says that if the killers find out what I've been doing, they might retali... reti... try to get back at me." He *really* wanted to tell Dad, though, and watch him light up like a sunrise, make him feel better.

"Well you just listen to me, Addis, son of Nnanji the swordsman. Shonsu may be a very important man in the

Tryst, but he's not your father, and while your father is so
sick, you have to obey your mother first. Understand?"

"No." Addis dodged past her and headed for Dad's room.
"Shonsu and Dad are oath brothers, right? So they're equals
in everything and—"

He was at the door when she grabbed his shoulder.
"Don't you backtalk me, boy! Time enough for slippery
priest talk after you're sworn in, and we're going to do that
right away, understand? I've made arrangements with High
Priest Shamoza, and the ceremony will take place first thing
tomorrow morning at the temple."

No, not all right. "I promised Dad I'd be a swordsman.
You heard me!"

"But he didn't, and promises from unsworn children don't
count. Tomorrow morning, Addis! And until then you're
staying here. The house guards have strict orders not to let
you out of their sight for one minute, understand?"

"Yes, Mother, I understand."

He understood that stern measures would be required.
Shivering with anger, he stalked into the sickroom, where
his rage melted instantly to sorrow. The shutters were drawn
on two windows, leaving the room half dark. Near the bed
sat a couple of women in red robes, keeping watch, but he
couldn't make out their facemarks and ignored them. All he
noticed was Dad, lying there like a corpse. And a horrible
smell, like rotting meat or a badly kept latrine.

"Dad? Dad? It's me, Addis."

There was no response, and when he laid his hand on the
bigger hand lying on the sheet, he was appalled by the heat
of it. His father was burning away. His skin was wet, his
face beaded.

He wheeled around to the two women. "Can't you cool
him down? Wipe him with wet cloths or something?"

"Bad idea," said the elder one. "The healers recommend
letting the fever burn itself out. They think he will improve
in a couple of days, if the Goddess wills."

Addis choked down an angry response and gave his

father's hand a squeeze. "I haven't forgotten my promise, Dad," he whispered. "I'll get them for you, I promise."

He strode out of the room.

She was still there. "You listen to me, Addis—"

Still trying to mother him! "No!" he said. "You listen to me. When Dad wakes up, tell him I've just come from making my report to the council. And they stood up and gave me the salute to a hero. Tell him that, swordsman!" He raced off down the grand staircase as she yelled after him.

"Oh, Goddess! *What is Shonsu doing to you?* Now where are you going?"

"To the kitchens," he said without stopping. "I'm real hungry."

He'd just escaped from a real jail and he knew of at least three ways out through the kitchens.

The prisoner had been taken back to Lord Shonsu's palace by Swordsmen Helbringr and Tilber, and there she had been allowed to bathe and eat. She had indicated that she should wear brown, so a wrap of that color had been provided, and now she was sitting in the cell with them, playing a children's tile game that did not require speech. So far the boy's promise had been kept.

Suddenly Lord Shonsu was at the other side of the bars, looming enormous as he always must. The three women rose.

"I am told that your name is Selina," he rumbled.

Selina nodded, trying desperately not to show fear. She had tried to kill this man, and he could kill her with a word to the swordsmen standing behind him.

"And that you will answer all my questions if I promise to spare your life?"

Nod again.

He backed up two paces and drew his sword. "I swear by my sword that I will keep my side of that bargain if you keep yours. If that wording isn't good enough for you, I can summon a gaggle of priests to witness."

She shook her head. No swordsman would perjure himself in front of swordsmen witnesses.

He smiled. "Good. Then let's get down to business."

The gate was unlocked. He came into the cell with her and ordered all the others away, so that the two of them were left sitting across the little table from each other. On the table lay a slate, a stick of chalk, and a rag. Only the orange-kilted leader of Shonsu's bodyguard remained as a witness, sitting in the outer room, holding the key to the gate.

The questions began.

"What is your craft, Selina?"

Dancer, she wrote.

"That helps explain how you managed to reach my balcony. I knew you must be agile. Where are you from?"

Fex.

"That's near Plo, isn't it? The Kingdom of Plo and Fex? You weren't going to cooperate when we first met, and now you are. Why have you changed your mind? You showed extraordinary courage by climbing that wall, so it wasn't from fear."

You not torture.

"The Tryst never tortures, and won't allow civilian rulers to do it either."

Boy cried for father.

That didn't help Wallie's feelings of guilt. "Who brought you to Casr?"

Sorcerers.

"The Honorable Yarrix?"

How did he know that? She nodded. But now she didn't feel so bad about talking, if the swordsmen already knew that much.

Shonsu smiled as if he could read her thoughts. "Yarrix is still at large. He has other assassins with him, Selina. Can you tell me where to find them?"

You pardon them, too?

"No. I remind you that you swore to answer all my questions."

She sat for a few moments with her eyes closed, trying to resolve the conflicting oaths she had sworn, and wrestling with her conscience.

Then she nodded. She wrote: *In a house above a baker's store, opposite a butcher's, on corner, from window could see a statue of man with a bear.*

"Ah! Thank you very much. Adept Filurz, let me out. Bring paper and ink so Dancer Selina can write. She is going to be pardoned as soon as I have approved her confession. Meanwhile she must stay here, but otherwise she is an honored guest in my house. Instruct the guards so. I am going back to the lodge."

I am Selina, dancer of the third rank, she wrote. My father is Ghuri, priest of the Fourth in the temple at Fex, and my mother is Furroa, dancer of the third rank. My mentor was Inpockira of the Fourth. On Slaters' Day a year ago, we sailed from Fex to Plo to dance before the queen. Her Majesty was much pleased with us, and gave Adept Inpockira a purse of gold. But that night a band of men broke into my room in the palace, gagged me and bound me, and carried me away with them. They took me to a place I did not know and raped me many times. Then they cut out my tongue so I couldn't tell anyone about them, and they left me naked in a dark alley. I was rescued by some people I later learned were sorcerers. They treated my injuries and cared for me, but I was too badly hurt to rejoin my dance troupe, and they had gone back to Fex without me.

I was told that the rapists were swordsmen. They wore swords and talked like swordsmen, telling me I should be honored to be pleasured by them. When

*I had mostly recovered from my injuries,
my rescuers asked if I would like to strike
a blow against the swordsmen and I
said I would. They took me up into the
mountains, to a town called Kra, and
trained me in how I could kill the chief
swordsman as revenge for what had been
done to me. I consented to do this. They
promised they would heal my tongue. This
year I was brought to Casr.*

What else would Lord Shonsu want to
know?

*I believed the rapists had been
swordsmen until last night, when I was in
jail. I heard criminals being brought in, and
they were almost all drunk. But the rapists
hadn't been drunk, and they wore hoods
so I couldn't see if they had long hair like
swordsmen. The boy you put in the cell
with me insisted that swordsmen weren't
allowed to do things like that anymore. I
believed what he was saying and knew I
had been lied to.*

Preparations for a punitive expedition were well underway
by mid-afternoon. The Tryst's bureaucracy was primitive,
but so was its style of warfare. Pick out any swordsman
in his kilt, boots, and sword harness, tell him to fetch his
bedroll, and he would be back in a few minutes, ready to
go. The Tryst would need to charter ships and outfit them.
Lord Dorinkulu had been posted to Quo to organize that,
and a steady stream of couriers rode between the two cities.
Wallie was determined to leave before Healers' Day, so he
would not be distracted by the annual celebration. Boariyi
would remain at Casr as acting liege. Joraskinta was to be
Wallie's second-in-command.

Nnanji had needed almost twenty weeks to return from
the war zone to Casr, although he had not spent all that

time in travel. Fortunately Katanji's jewel-trading friends confirmed that there was an overland route between Soo and Cross Plo, and Soo was a lot closer to Casr in terms of travel time. If Shonsu's army could match Nnanji's speed, it ought to reach Soo in early summer. Wallie consoled himself with the thought that Eisenhower had needed years to organize D-Day.

The assassins' hideout had been easily identified from Selina's description. As soon as Wallie reached the lodge, he sent for an eager young Fourth he had his eye on, and told him to, "Go get 'em." Half an hour later, swordsmen swarmed in through doors and windows, no search warrant required. They found Yarrix and his helpers bottling wine, adding a pinch of some white unidentified white powder to every bottle. The only casualty was the promising young Fourth, who took a bullet in his chest and died instantly.

Three pistols were brought back to the liege, and Wallie was relieved to see that the sorcerers had apparently made little progress in gunnery in the last fifteen years. These handguns, at least, had no rifling, percussion cartridges, or automatic weapons. Of course Kra now had muskets, and might have made other progress too. The loot contained some of the other gimcrackery he had seen before, but one item was new to him and very damning evidence: a box of transfers. He had known sorcerers could change facemarks, but not how they managed it. He ordered everything bundled up for him to take with him on the expedition. For years he had kept many of the sorcerers' secrets that he had discovered or guessed at, but now, so far as he was concerned, they had forfeited any right to his silence.

The confirmation of poison roused his ire as nothing else could have done. Everyone drank some wine or beer, sometimes even children, because it was used in cooking and was the easiest way to purify drinking water. The plot to kill him might have taken half his household, including Jja, Vixini, Sharon, Jjon, and little Budol.

Later he went to see the wizard. As usual, he was shown into the library room, lit that evening by oil lamps, but he had to wait a long while before the old man came shuffling in. Wallie snooped along some of the bookshelves, but most of the books seemed to be very dull ledgers that meant nothing without an understanding of the sorcerers' calendar and cryptic file names.

Woggan had come to the lodge with an escort, here he arrived alone, which likely meant that this room was bugged. The secretive way he had passed the scroll strongly suggested that swordsmen were not the only people who did not trust sorcerers.

Wallie's main reason for coming was to express thanks for the help, especially the warning about poisoned wine, but he did not say so directly. Instead he brandished one of the confiscated pistols and crowed how his interrogators had broken the assassin Selina and learned from her of the dastardly poison plot. Although Woggan showed no sign of appreciating the message behind the words, he certainly must.

"And did she say where this rape atrocity took place, my lord?"

"In Plo."

"Then I suggest you direct your complaint to the coven of Kra, not to Vul."

"I intend to," Wallie said. "I shall deliver it in person."

Swordsman Katanji's residence was a modest, four-bedroom house, but its contents would have bought a small city. It stood within the precincts of the swordsmen's lodge, so that no burglar could come closer than the wrong side of the perimeter wall. For added security, Katanji stored the Tryst's bullion in his cellar, forcing Nnanji to keep a permanent guard around the building. Katanji himself could come and go by means of an unlisted tunnel leading to a clothing store he owned on the public plaza, and there he could meet with business associates. Those might be gouty old men trying to buy favors or sweet young ladies selling them, but whichever they were, Katanji regarded their identities as nobody's business but his, and the tunnel as his personal secret. Only the very favored were invited back that way to his residence.

That evening he had brought home an exciting new friend and was just settling down to enjoy an intimate seven-course snack with her. She was a courtesan of the first rank presently going by the name of Swansdown. Her nipples glowed like pink rosebuds through the uppermost edge of an extremely sheer and skimpy white wrap, and her single facemark was not properly healed. In most professions that meant that it had been applied very recently. In hers, nothing necessarily meant anything.

He raised his goblet in a toast. "May the Goddess bless you with a very long and happy career, my dear." After Woggan's warning about wine, Katanji had made sure that tonight's vintages all came from bottles that had been collecting dust in his cellar for years.

Swansdown simpered professionally. "I'm sure it will be happy if all my future clients are as handsome and charming as the first."

He let the lie pass without comment. He was at least her sixth customer in the two weeks since she had been sworn, and her real name was Ritorn. He was not supposed to know any of that, but two of his business associates recommended her highly.

"It always puzzles me that your craft follows the same rank system as the others. You ought to start as blues and descend to white in your old age."

"I expect we get better with practice. I hope I'm not terribly clumsy tonight, this being my first…"

A bell jangled.

Frowning, Katanji set down his goblet. He was certainly not expecting any more visitors that evening, because the days—or nights—when he had entertained more than one such lovely as this were regrettably passed. In any case, it was almost unheard of for anyone to arrive by the tunnel entrance unless he was escorting them himself. Not sure whether he should be more annoyed or alarmed, he muttered an apology, rose, and went through into his study, carefully closing the heavy door behind him. He stepped into a closet and closed that door also before he slid open a panel and looked down to see who had pulled the bell rope. The spy hole gave him a good view of the last ten or so feet of the tunnel, and the visitors could not know that they were being observed from behind.

Surprise, surprise!

Unalarmed now, but annoyed, Katanji headed out to the hall and down a stairway to the secret entrance, a bronze and timber door that would have stopped a charging bull. There was another panel in that. He slid the cover aside.

"Gods' balls!" he said. "What are you doing here?"

"Hiding."

"Hiding from whom?"

"My mom of course. I may be officially a hero, Uncle, but I draw the line at battling mad mothers, especially mine."

Impudent young devil! From there Katanji could see that the rest of the tunnel was empty, so he unbolted the door. "You expect me to stand up to her? I am not a hero, never have been, and never will be."

"Shonsu said you were," Addis said, slipping in before the door was properly open. "Want to hear that story again. She's lined up the high priest to swear me in tomorrow, so I have to lay low until Sailors' Day."

Safely bolted in again, Katanji led the way up to the main floor. "Not just your mother, but mossy old Shamoza too? You're a catch, lad! What craft do you think will dare accept you if the high priest's after you?"

"Swordsmen, 'course. I promised Dad I would track down the people who sent the assassins. You think they're sorcerers?"

"Who told you about the back door into my house?"

"I overheard Dad telling Shonsu about it one night. They were laughing because you thought nobody knew about it. Mm, something smells good." Addis turned aside and strode uninvited into the dining room. "*Devilspit!* Ritorn? Fancy meeting you here!"

Katanji was at his heels. "You two are acquainted?" She

couldn't know his nephew professionally. Addis was growing up, but he hadn't reached that stage yet. And Ritorn was blushing scarlet, which no one in her profession should ever do; also looking as if she would burst into tears any minute, a more conventional tactic.

"We used to play in the park together," Addis said, helping himself to a pickled ptarmigan egg. "And go swimming in the pond. She's younger than me, aren't you, Ritorn? I remember how you'd turn to jelly every time Vixi smiled at you." He glanced at his uncle sadly. "But now I suppose you have to go where the money is?"

The night was no longer young when Wallie got home. He dismissed his guard, accepted salutes from Sevolno and the night watch, and straightaway trudged wearily upstairs towards bed. To his surprise, Jja was still awake, sitting under a blaze of candlelight in the corner, embroidering.

"You'll ruin your eyes," he said, bending to kiss her.

"No, I won't." She laid her work aside and reached for the candle snuffer. "Do you need food? Wine?"

"Just sleep," he said. "It's been quite a day, but it worked out well in the end. We caught them where Selina said we would."

"She's a pleasant girl. Not very intelligent, but well-mannered."

"I don't remember her asking politely if she could stab me."

"Are you going to release her, or send her to jail?"

"Release her. She kept her side of the bargain. Can you help her?"

Jja's smile said that she already had. "She wants to stay here in Casr, and she'll need a mentor. I've arranged for her to meet a couple of Fifths tomorrow."

"Clever girl." He kissed her.

Admitting at last that summer was passé, the weather gods had turned down the outside temperature. The shutters were closed and the bed had been made up inside. As Wallie lay down with a sigh of pleasure, he decided he could probably sleep standing up in a cupboard, if he had to. The last candle flame died. Jja slid in beside him.

"How was your day otherwise?" he asked, cuddling.

"Much as usual. Thana arrived in a rage. Addis has disappeared again. I had to swear to her that he wasn't here."

Wallie chuckled sleepily. "He isn't very much younger than Nnanji was when we first met. And even old Honakura said that Nanj had a head like a coconut. Thana has never been indecisive either, never easily swayed."

"So what is Baby Coconut up to?" Kiss.

"He's going to turn up at the assembly and demand to be sworn in as a swordsman."

"And will you allow that?" Another kiss.

Of course. That was what the gods wanted, obviously.

And obviously Shonsu was what Jja wanted. Sleep could wait.

CHAPTER 7

OVERNIGHT THE WEATHER WENT FROM POOR to horrible, and Bronze Casters' Day brought a steady downpour. That did not bother Apprentice Vixini, who spent it sitting on his butt indoors, listening to and memorizing sutras. As Dad had suggested, he concentrated on the real brutes, like Number 311, *On Exercise*, or 212, *On the Treatment of Wounds*, although the Thirds tutoring him insisted that those were very rarely called for in examinations, simply because they were unfairly difficult and the examiners themselves would have to bone up on them. But they did warn him not to forget the first eighty-nine, the sutras he had needed for promotion to second rank. By the end of the day he was convinced that he was going to make a total idiot of himself in the exam. He didn't care much, because he was far too young to be a Third anyway; all his childhood playmates were still Firsts, in a wide assortment of crafts.

But he would also shame Dad, and he would much rather die than do that.

Sailors' Day dawned cloudy and cold, but not actually raining. By the time the sky was turning from dark to light, Apprentice Vixini had been dragged out of bed, forced fed breakfast like a penned goose—or so it felt—and hauled away to the amphitheater at the lodge.

It was a busy place already. Promotions could be attempted

at any time, but assembly promotions were popular because they were so public, and swordsmen, like most athletes, liked to display their prowess before their friends. The downside risk, of course, was that failures were jeered by a thousand throats or more. This time, with rumors of war boiling through the Tryst, scores of men had begged their mentors for the chance to try for higher rank.

"Here they come," Dad said softly, looking over the throng of heads. "Mean as rat shit, both of them. I blotted one down a rank a couple of years ago, and refused the other one a posting he wanted. Just what you need."

"Thanks, Dad!"

As Vixini's mentor, Dad just stood on the sidelines to witness the sutra test. Vixini himself and the two mingy Thirds sat cross-legged on the damnably cold paving of the stage with their swords in front of them, and the examination began.

"Number 212, *On the Treatment of Wound*s," said Meany Number One.

Vixini got through it, and hoped they could not see how he was sweating by the end. He suspected he'd got pressure bandages and bladder wounds in the wrong order, but they didn't call him on it. He wasn't too surprised then when Meany Number Two asked him for *On Exercise.* He managed that one also, thanks to Dad's backward strategy.

Scowling, Number One tried again. "Number 99."

Vixini hadn't known that he might not be given the title as well as the number, but it must be within the rules, because Dad didn't object. He thought for a moment. "Number 99, *On Diet.*" He was right and the recital felt easy after the two previous horrors.

He thought he had proved himself then, but the Gruesome Twosome were clearly going to try him on the full seven sutras they were allowed. And they'd realized that he'd concentrated on the hard ones.

"Number 95, *The Sanctity of the Sword.*"

Vixini opened his mouth, shut in, racked what few brains he had, and, without daring to look up at Dad, said, "*The Sanctity of the Sword* is Number 15, and Number 95 is *The*

Sanctity of the Fencing Foil. I believe your error credits me with both sutras, Examiner." Except he was sure it hadn't been an error, it had been a trap.

Dad laughed. "He's got you! I have never known an examination continue after an examiner blundered like that."

He was liege lord. No one argued with the liege. The two Thirds rose sour-faced and congratulated Vixini, then stalked away. They would be judging his fencing later, another chance to fail him, but he was looking forward to that.

Dad hugged him. "You've done it, Son! I don't care what Thirds they put up against you in foils, you'll send them back in pieces. Now listen carefully. I've arranged for your match to be in the first round of the fencing. Once you have put your opponents out of their misery, the examiners will go with you to the facemarker, and after that you have to get your new kilt. But then I want you to go straight over to Katanji's house. He has something for you, something very important."

The amphitheater could hold thousands. Wallie had seen it fuller, but never full. Nor had he ever viewed an assembly from anywhere except the Sevenths' box at the back of the stage, which had a cover. On rainy days the Sevenths were dry, but nobody else was. Despite today's ominous sky, so far the rain god was withholding his blessings.

The air crackled with excitement. Many assemblies had been held before expeditions were led out, when men were lambasting the Goddess with prayers that She would cause them to be included, but this was different. Word of the attack on Nnanji and a full-scale war against sorcerers made this the chance of lifetime: fame, promotion, and mention in the epics! How many would Lord Shonsu take? *Goddess, Goddess, make me one of them and I will father a hundred daughters to Your glory!*

It began conventionally enough. The chief herald called for all to rise. The Sevenths entered. The band played. Everyone sang *The Swordsmen in the Morning,* twelve hundred throats in unison. Everyone sat down. Promotions had priority, and the first item was the heralds calling out the names of those who had failed in sutras, so they could be soundly booed. Then the winners came up for their fencing tests. Wallie had been forewarned that there would have to be fifty or sixty matches, which could take all day. The audience might be able to afford the time, and fencing was their sport as well as their profession, so they could never get enough of it; but he couldn't. Once or twice Nnanji had doubled up the fencing. Wallie had decided to make a three-ring circus of it.

There was some surreptitious booing when the herald announced this decision, but soon the fencers were hard at it, leaping back and forth, foils clanging and ponytails flailing. Since every duel required the necessary second examiner, two judges, and a mentor, the stage was packed with dancing competitors and dodging witnesses. Men cannoned off the Sevenths' Box and a couple backed right off the stage and thus out of the competition. Whooping, cheering, and booing became almost continuous. Most of the contestants won both their bouts and were accepted by the judges. Vixini had no trouble.

The final bouts were for promotion to high rank. Each of those had to be allowed the stage to itself, but even a Seventh could enjoy watching fencing at that level, and at the end of it the Tryst had gained two new Sixths and three new Fifths.

But when it was all over and the last sweaty arm had been raised—or not raised—then the liege lord had to walk out from the Sevenths' box and greet each winner. Every name was cheered, and Wallie was relieved to note that Vixini won a cheer as loud as any, because they had all seen that the wunderkind had fenced like a true Third, years older. He wasn't just his daddy's spoiled brat.

Swordsman Vixini strode proudly across the lodge grounds to where his oath-uncle Katanji stored his loot. He wondered what in the World the old rogue had for him that Dad had been so mysterious about. A fancy sword might be one possibility, or a hairclip. There was nothing much else that he would have any use for at the moment. In ten years or so, perhaps a wife and a house, but if he rose to high rank in the Trystand his success today suggested that he couldthen he would qualify for a place in the married quarters. Right now he was an adult and heading off to fight in the first real war in centuries. Life was looking very good!

He was still wondering whom he should ask to be his mentor if Dad didn't want to do that any more when he arrived at the Treasure Chest, as Mom called the place. He trotted up the steps and hauled on the bell. Although Katanji owned at least a dozen slaves, he opened the door himself, which was surprising. Vixini whipped out his sword and took great pleasure in giving him the salute to an equal.

The treasurer responded, then said, "Well done, well done. You'll be as great a swordsman as your dad one day. Come on in here."

He led the way to his living room, past some life-size jade statues, a silver horse, brilliant tapestries, exotic furniture, and four pillars of multi-colored stone. There, sprawled back in a padded chair and scoffing dried dates, was the missing Addis. He had a black eye that was more a rainbow eye, and was wearing a smug, contented expression, but Vixini knew him very well and suspected that he was hiding excitement about something.

"So there you are! Two days ago your mother tracked me down and made me swear on my sword that I didn't know where you were."

"Well? You didn't, did you? I suppose I have to salute you now, do I, *Swordsman* Vixini?"

"You bet your sweet little ass, boy, because if you don't it's going to get well booted."

Addis grinned and jumped up. They exchanged salute and response while Katanji watched with a smirk. Vixini noticed again how very alike uncle and nephew were, but he knew that Aunt Thana hated Katanji so much she could barely stand to be in the same room with him. Addis had no need to worry that his father wasn't who he had been told he was.

Vixini folded his arms. "Well, I have to go back and hear Dad's speech. He promises it'll be a scorcher. He said you had something for me, Uncle."

"Yes. That."

Vixini looked in dismay at all the teeth his young friend was showing. "Oh, no!"

Addis's face fell. He said, "Your..." and stopped.

Oh, shit! "I didn't mean it that way! I would love to have you as a protégé, tadpole, truly I would, but Dad promised me if I got my promotion I could go to the war with him. Firsts are never taken into danger! If I were your mentor, I couldn't go. I couldn't leave you."

But surely Dad would never play a filthy trick like that on either of them?

"Boys, boys!" Katanji said. "I've known Shonsu a long time, and when he talks, wise men listen. He told Addis right here in this room that he could be a swordsman and have you for a mentor. He didn't say Thana could go swim in the River and eat all the piranha, but that's what he meant. He has always been able to guess what the gods want better than anyone I've ever met. If he told you he was going to take you to the war, then he must mean that he's going to take Addis as well."

Vixini looked at Addis. "*Devilspit!* That'll scare the sorcerers shitless, that will! This what you want, maggot?"

"By the time we get to Plo I'll be a Fourth and you'll be saluting me."

It would be great to have a buddy along, someone near his own age.

"Let's go, then. We'll have to run. We gotta pick you out a kilt and boots and a sword... At the double, frog!"

Addis turned to his uncle and thanked him graciously for his hospitality. Then he came running after his mentor.

After the end of the fencing came the postulants, boys and girls joining the craft. Wallie solemnly listened as their mentors swore them in with the words of the code, and then he had to kneel to each one to give each his, or

her, sword. Only then could he return to the Sevenths'
box.

The next item on the agenda, by tradition, was a tribute to
the fallen. There were always two or three, but no assembly
had ever had to mourn more than a half a dozen. This time
there were more than eighty. Two heralds took turns calling
out the names of the dead and the details of their deaths:
the burned brothel in Arbo, the massacre with firearms at
Cross Zek, the murdered couriers. The moans and boos
grew louder and louder. The last death, the Fourth who had
been shot right there in Casr while arresting the poisoners,
provoked a roar that might have been heard in Hann.

Listening to this dread toll, Wallie recalled a suggestion
that he had made years ago but Nnanji and Katanji had
shouted down. Well, they weren't here to shout him down
now, and once he had announced it, they would not be able
to unannounce it.

The Herald glanced around; Wallie nodded. It was his turn.

The great theater fell completely silent as his name was
called and he then walked forward. Lord Shonsu was a stand-
in, the swordsmen felt. The real liege was Lord Nnanji; they
wanted to hear the true story behind his absence. Wallie
intended to give it to them.

"My lords, your honors, masters..." He could never be
as loud as that chief herald, who could have drowned out
a factory steam whistle, but Shonsu had bequeathed him a
fearsome set of lungs. "We all must mourn so many brave
men and women so unfairly struck down. No tears, no
revenge, no compensation, can bring them back. Nothing
can undo the injury of their deaths, but I am happy to
be able to tell you that their families will be cared for by
the Tryst." Applause, starting slowly and building as the
implications sank in. "And this will be true in future for any
swordsman of the Tryst who dies or is disabled in action."
Katanji, wherever he was, would have a dozen concurrent
apoplectic fits.

So Wallie had brought workmen's compensation to the
World. The time was ripe, for he was about to lead the

Tryst into real and present danger for the first time. He must motivate men in large numbers to risk their lifeblood. Nothing held the swordsmen but their oaths, and if the task suddenly felt too dangerous and they decided to cut and run, their liege might find himself fighting alone.

He told them about Nnanji. Thana had sent word that she thought he might be a little better today, but Wallie would not raise hopes yet. There were so many complications that might follow such a wound that the patient would not be out of danger for weeks. Then he told about the attempt on his own life, how he had captured the assassin, and how she had then confessed. That merited a huge cheer, as everyone assumed she had been horribly tortured.

He openly accused the sorcerer coven of Kra of breaking the treaty. Although it had never signed on to that agreement, it had attacked the Tryst with firearms, which was either mass murder or an act of war. He promised that the swordsmen would now march on Kra in all their righteous wrath and raze it.

Wild applause.

"As their liege, I will revenge our brothers!"

Wilder.

He announced the leaders he would take with him.

Some thin clapping. In fact he could not take even a tenth of his hopeful listeners. As Joraskinta had suggested, he must enlist as he went, gather strength from loyal garrisons all along the River. He was fairly certain now that he would go to Plo via Soo, but he did not mention Soo.

"Brothers and sisters, may the Goddess bless our swords!"

That prayer normally signaled the end, triggering a final chorus of the anthem, but Wallie had added one additional item. He hoped that the star had arrived safely.

"There are two young men I will certainly take with me to Kra. The first you have watched win his promotion here today, so he is now qualified to accept a protégé. That protégé you may not recognize."

Wallie stepped back, the herald took his place. "My lords, your honors, masters, adepts, swordsmen, apprentices...

pray honor Swordsman Vixini, and *postulant Addis, son of Nnanji the swordsman...*"

Vixini strode out in his new brown kilt, with a third facemark still oozing blood on his forehead, and a grin as wide as the River. He carried a sheathed sword in his hand, while behind him walked a white-kilted youth, whose eyes shone like stars.

Wallie had expected now to give Addis his sword, as he had the other postulants, but evidently Vixini had not yet made his first protégé repeat the code of the craft, and that had to come first. It was doubtful if either of them had a voice capable of being heard throughout the whole extent of the amphitheater, but they didn't need to, because the code was the first sutra, which everyone present had learned on their own admission day. The audience picked it up and repeated each phrase after Vixini in peals of thunder:

> *I will be evermore true to*
> *the will of the Goddess,*
> *the sutras of the swordsmen,*
> *and the laws of the People.*
> *I will be mighty against the mighty,*
> *gentle to the weak,*
> *generous to the poor,*
> *and merciless to the rapacious.*
> *I will do nothing of which I may be*
> *ashamed,*
> *but avoid no honor.*
> *I will give no less than justice to others,*
> *and seek no more for myself.*
> *I will be valiant in adversity,*
> *and humble in prosperity.*
> *I will live with joy.*
> *I will die bravely.*

When the final promise died away, Shonsu walked forward as his stepson drew the sword from its scabbard. He took it and solemnly knelt to offer it to Addis.

"Live by this. Wield it in Her service. Die holding it."

Well coached, Addis took hold of the hilt and spoke the reply: "It shall be my honor and my pride."

Of course the Tryst applauded. Nnanji's son going forth to fight in his father's stead? This was utterly fitting, even if everyone knew that novices were never allowed anywhere close to real fighting.

That should have been the end of it.

But Addis added a touch of his own. Finding himself holding a sword and being cheered, he turned to face the crowd and made the salute to a company. They loved it. He got the loudest roar of the day. Wallie had not suggested that; neither Vixini or Katanji would ever have thought of it. The boy had flair.

Getting out of the amphitheater turned out to be much harder than getting into it. It seemed as if every man and woman in the Tryst was buddies with Vixini and wanted to congratulate him on his promotion. Perhaps they also wanted to get a look at the Nnanji polliwog, but Firsts were usually ignored, so Addis had nothing to do except stay close to his mentor and try to keep his sword straight on his back. Wearing a kilt felt strange, boots were total weirdness, and his bull-hide harness was already starting to chaff. The scabbard itself was supported by two straps across his back, but the sword was top heavy and the handle kept sliding over to his shoulder, usually his right shoulder, sometimes the other one. He kept his hands away from his facemark, knowing that newly-hatched Firsts were known as "scratchers." But if his life depended on it, he could not keep his sword hilt behind his ear, ready to grab when danger loomed. It was done with a twitch of the shoulder blades, Vixi said, but Addis's shoulder blades seemed to be unusually stupid.

Just short of the lodge gates, Vixi said, "In here!" and stepped behind some bushes.

"Now," he said, counting on his fingers, "you and I have to swear the second oath, so we're properly mentor and protégé. You *must* learn to control that sword hilt, or I'll nail it in place for you. Get busy and grow a ponytail, that's an order. And I have to find a mentor before tomorrow sunset."

"Not your dad?"

"I'll ask him, but I think he's frightened he'll baby me, so he'll say he's too busy. Anything you want to do?"

"I think this sword's too long for me."

Vixi told him to draw it and hold the handle as high as he could to see where the point came on his chest. No, if anything it was too short, put it back. Be careful or you'll cut your ass off. He was amused but not mocking. Vixi never hurt people's feelings.

"Anything else?"

"I'd really like to go home and see how Dad is." He was a swordsman now, and under orders. Only kids ran free and did whatever they pleased.

"Good idea. We'll check on your dad, but it isn't your home any more, kid."

Right! Addis chalked up another adjustment. He would sleep wherever his mentor did now, and that would depend on what *his* mentor said.

So they went to the palace that had been his home until an hour ago. Out in the streets, Vixi had to make a formal salute to every higher rank he met, but they all pretended not to see his First. He was stopped by the guards on the palace gate, of course, who pretended not to recognize this new Third. They certainly knew Addis, and gave the pair of them a lot of ribbing, which Vixi handled by being just as amused as they were.

Maternal instincts working as well as always, Mother accosted them before they even reached the staircase. Vixi pulled his sword and made the salute to an equal. Being unarmed, she gave him the civilian response.

"Congratulations, swordsman," she said. "I don't think Lord Nnanji was any younger than you when he achieved middle rank."

Her eyes wandered at last to Addis. No snow fell, but the temperature dropped appreciably.

"Thank you, Aunt," Vixi said. "And if you want to grab my protégé in a bear hug and give him a huge slobbery kiss, I won't let him challenge you."

"I wouldn't dream of it. Congratulations, son."

"Thank you, Mother."

"I just hope you don't regret this."

"The Tryst cheered him," Vixi said.

"No," she said. "If they cheered, they were cheering his father. Nobody gets cheered until they've done something worth cheering. But his father will be happy to see him. Let's go see if he is awake."

Dad was sort-of awake, not so feverish as he had been two days ago, but still very sick. His head lay on the pillow as if he lacked the strength to move it, and Mom gestured Vixi to go close, into the spot where Dad was looking. He noticed his brown kilt, muttered something complimentary.

Vixi stepped aside and Addis took his place. Dad just stared at him for a while, then blinked a few times. "Makes me feel old, Son," he whispered. "Proud, too. You... mother... something for you."

Mom's lips were clenched so hard they were white, so she obviously didn't approve, but she held out a hand holding a silver hairclip in the shape of a griffon.

"But that's Dad's hairclip!"

"He insists I give it to you. It's very old, and very valuable."

"I've heard the minstrels sing about it," Vixi said. "It belonged to the great hero Arganari, who led the Tryst of Xo. A griffon is the symbol of royalty. You can't wear that, protégé!"

"I'll keep it safe for you," Mom said, her fingers closing.

Addis felt a need to be stubborn. He turned around. "Dad? You want me to wear that hairclip?"

The great Nnanji, liege lord of the Tryst, most powerful man in the World, managed a hint of a nod.

Addis held out his hand for it. "It'll be quite safe on me," he said, "because nobody will see it in my haystack." He never bothered having his hair cut until Mom noticed and ordered the slaves to catch him and hold him down long enough to give him a trim. Mostly it curled up so much that nobody could tell how long it was.

"Swordsmen obey their mentor's orders," Mom said, "and your mentor just told you not to wear this."

"But their mentors obey the liege, Aunt," Vixi said gently. "Put on the hairclip, protégé. As I remember the epic, it came from Plo originally. You can take it back there."

Addis tucked the clip into his hair. Then he stepped close to Mom so she could hug him and kiss his cheek; she wasn't too slobbery.

BOOK THREE:

HOW THE SWORDSMEN PREPARED FOR WAR

CHAPTER 1

"THREE SHIPS?" NOVICE ADDIS GRUMBLED. "A hundred men at most? What sort of an army is this supposed to be?" He was leaning on the rail on a very smelly two-masted trading vessel named *Hyacinth*. Beside his spindly arms on the rail rested his mentor's much thicker arms. They were three days out of Quo, heading for Kra and the war.

A hundred men? Could the sorcerers sleep nights?

"It's not an army, it's an egg," Vixini said. "Two Sevenths, six Sixths, and a whole plague of Fourths and Fifths. Maybe two dozen Thirds altogether, and a handful of low life like you in case food runs short."

Addis was not worried about being eaten. But he did worry that he was the only First included and that the half-dozen Seconds were there only to make his presence not quite so obviously due to personal favoritism. The rest of the Tryst would not be deceived and must resent his special treatment. Apart from that unpleasantness, and the barfy food, this was *life* as it should be. He was a man, almost, among men, doing a man's job. They slept on deck when the nights were dry, because the hold stank, but they told man jokes and did swordsman things like fencing and learning sutras. The River itself was endlessly fascinating, with ships and towns going by all the time.

"There is no point," Vixini continued, imperturbable

as always, "in transporting and feeding thousands of swordsman halfway around the world when the Tryst has many times that many serving closer to the enemy. When we get near to Plo, Dad can start hiring ships and raiding the cities' garrisons. There'll be plenty of eager volunteer Thirds to hatch the egg. But if you're unhappy, there's still time to send you home."

"Piss on that. Sir."

"You can't mean you're actually enjoying yourself?"

"I have trouble not giggling all the time."

"We can help with that," said a new voice behind them.

Novice and Apprentice straightened up and spun around. Master Filurz, formerly captain of Lord Shonsu's bodyguard, had won promotion to Fifth at the assembly, and had accepted Vixini as a protégé. He was a small man, shorter than Addis, but lightning with a foil. And mean, too. He put bruises on Vixi's ribs every day.

"Low life shouldn't waste time giggling," the little man said. "How is your protégé progressing, swordsman?"

"He keeps his sword straight on his back now, mentor. He's doing well with sutras."

That was a hint that Addis wasn't very good with a sword, which was true. The two of them would make a good team, if Vixi did all the fencing and Addis the sutras, but the Tryst wouldn't approve of that sort of sharing.

"Is he? Let's see." Filurz drew his sword. The other two did the same and all three sat down on the deck, with the swords lying between them, in the swordsmen's favored position for sutra chanting. "How many do you know, novice?"

"Eight, master." Since Addis would only need to know eighty-nine to make Second and nobody got to be a Second until he had grown a ponytail, he thought he was doing quite well.

"Is that all? Let's hear number two, then."

Easy one!

2: ON PROTÉGÉS

The Epitome
The protégé shall swear: I, [giving his
name and rank], do take you, [giving his
name and rank], as my master and mentor
and do swear to be faithful, obedient, and
humble, to live upon your word, to learn
by your example, and to be mindful of
your honor, in the name of the Goddess.

Then the mentor shall swear: I, [giving
his name and rank], do accept you, [giving
his name and rank], as my protégé and
pupil, to cherish, protect, and guide in the
ways of honor and the mysteries of our
craft, in the name of the Goddess.

The Epigram
The trunk lifts the branches to the light
and the branches are the glory of the trunk.

"What about the episode?"

"The second sutra does not include an episode, master."

"Quite right. How's your fencing coming?"

Why ask? Filurz could not help but know the answer when they were all cooped up on this poky little ship.

"I am a great disappointment to my mentor, master."

Filurz nodded. "Right answer. You deserve to be beaten."

"This rebuke is justified, master."

"Swordsman, why was your protégé hung over the ship's rail like laundry when you could be teaching him?"

"This rebuke is also justified, mentor."

It wasn't, because there hadn't been any room on deck to fence a moment ago. Now one pair had stopped.

"Then get to work. And two sutras a day from each of you." Filurz lifted his sword, stood up, and was gone.

Addis rose, sighed, and eased his aching shoulder. "Can I try left-handed this time, mentor?"

"No. You're even worse that way around. Go and get some foils. At the double."

"He's right about the beating, you know. Good for morale. Nnanji's son fencing like a duck must have them all in stitches."

"Move!" Vixi roared, aiming a buffet at his ear. It couldn't have been a serious attempt, though, because Addis managed to dodge.

Admiral and General Lord Shonsu was also enjoying the voyage. He had been shut up in Casr far too long. He fenced every day, as he always did, but only his deputy, Joraskinta of the Seventh, could give him a fair match. In fact Joraskinta might even beat him if he really tried, but was tactful enough not to do so in public. Wallie visited the other ships most days. He talked with the high ranks, discussing strategy and tactics. He had demonstrated the pistols and other trickery confiscated from the assassin, Yarrix of the Sixth, so everyone knew about such horrors and wouldn't panic when they were used. He saw Vixini and Addis when he visited *Hyacinth* but made no effort to treat them as special. They were almost always on deck, either fencing or obviously reciting sutras. Filurz was managing to keep Vixini much more industrious than Wallie ever had.

Addis was clearly finding fencing difficult. The contrast between him and his father must be the fires of hell for him. Although he would never be another Nnanji, he was trying very hard and should eventually make a passable Third. If Wallie could get a moment alone with Vixini he could pass on some tips about instructing, which was an art in itself.

Possibly Wallie had erred in manipulating the kid into becoming a swordsman, and erred even more in bringing him into harm's way on this expedition. He didn't think so. The demigod had made a prophecy about Nnanji's firstborn, an ambiguous prophecy, of course, because prophecies were like that. Wallie's memories of it were strangely vague, which his memories were usually not, but gods did not prophesy at all without good reason.

The little flotilla was colorful, with *Hyacinth* flaunting blue hull and white sails, *Speedy* red and gold, and *Rainbow* living up to its name, but most ships were brightly painted. Overall, River traffic was a spray of jewels as varied as the cargoes it carried. Always there seemed to be a thousand ships in sight, both lumbering local traffic transporting the people's food, fuel, and raw materials—such as ore, bricks, tiles, timber, hides, and yarn—and the faster, usually smaller vessels bringing luxuries from far away climes: spices, ivory, amber, gold, and silver. To Wallie's eye it was an artistic delight and a practical nightmare. He watched the hectic jostling as half the ships ran before the wind and half tacked against it, helped or hindered by the serpentine current. Always he wondered about the steam engine.

The principle was so simple that the only reason the sorcerers had not invented it centuries ago must be that they had been shut away in mountain retreats where the need for power was much less. True, perfect cylinders and tight-fitting pistons required very sophisticated metalworking, but the need would soon bring forth the skills. He had released the sorcerers' technology on the World; how much of the Earth's was he supposed to import? The sorcerers were hopeless at theory, probably because their math notation was no more advanced than Roman numerals had been on Earth, but they were supberb experimentalists. He could explain the steam engine to Wizard Woggan in half an hour, the sorcerers would have it working in a year, and in five years every shipyard in the World would be copying it. Paddle boats and stern wheelers would be churning the waters of the River.

What followed then? A huge boost in the quality of life? Or air pollution, forests destroyed, strip-mined coal, and industrial slums?

The weather at the outset had been vile, but it soon improved. The expedition's serpentine course would wander southward overall, reaching semi-tropical territory before real winter set in. If the Goddess willed, it should arrive in the Plo area before the worst heat of summer.

Before they left Casr, Wallie and Horkoda had spent hours in the council hall, comparing the many different routes available. The only way they could make even a rough estimate of distance was to count cities on the map, because large towns tended to develop around three or four days' sailing apart and large cities at about three times that. The spacing might be set by trade factors or social influence or the will of the Goddess, but it was not set by war. Because the swordsmen held a monopoly on violence and were reluctant to kill one another for someone else's benefit, the World was a much more peaceable place than Earth. Once in a while a swordsman might set himself up as a tyrant, although that might involve breaking an oath of obedience and his subordinates would stop him if he offended their personal sense of honor. Only rarely did such upstarts succeed in passing their rule on to their sons, as earthly dictators often did. Whether Nnanji could manage to break this pattern remained to be seen.

Large cities were important because they would be the Tryst's recruiting ground. A hamlet might have a single swordsman, a village constable who could not be taken from his duties. A great metropolis would have hundreds and could certainly spare a few dozen for a season. Since the Tryst's record clerks had notes of over 4,000 settlements of all sizes, Wallie foresaw no difficulty in enlisting a few thousand men to wage war on Kra. He was also certain that Kra was a test. If he could smash Kra, the other covens would fall into line. If he failed, the Tryst would fall apart within a generation and a dream would die.

Every few days, the flotilla tied up to provision, at which time the swordsmen would rush ashore to find enough space for fencing practice. Two weeks after they set out they stopped at the sizable city of Laru, which had a sorcerers' tower and was therefore on the list of mail drops that Wallie had set up with Horkoda. Lord Shonsu summoned his bodyguard and went ashore. First, of course, he had to visit with the reeve, who almost fell on his knees in his eagerness to enlist. When he saw that this would not be allowed, he recommended a couple of quicksilver young Fourths. After watching their fencing for a couple of minutes, Wallie accepted them both, although he had not planned to start recruiting so soon. It was entirely possible that the reeve foresaw these stars outshining him in a few years and was hoping to be permanently rid of them. In that case he was doing them more of a favor than he realized.

Then Wallie was free to call on the wizard, who promised not to report the army's passage to its enemies in Kra, but almost certainly would. At the tower Wallie collected a couple of pigeon-grams and sent one to Horkoda, reporting his progress. Later that day, after the flotilla had sailed, he decided he could now reasonably entertain his stepson and godson-equivalent to dinner. He ordered *Speedy* to draw alongside *Hyacinth* so Prumpt the herald could shout an invitation to them, shouting being beneath a liege's dignity. Vixini nimbly scrambled up on the rail, judged the roll of the ship perfectly, and sprang across, his long legs making light work of the leap.

Addis jumped as a stray gust caught *Speedy*'s sails and delayed her roll. He crossed, but landed hopelessly off balance. For a nightmare moment he stood poised on the rail, arms windmilling madly, eyes wide with horror. Behind him waited instant death, the piranha-infested River. Wallie jumped forward, but Vixi was there before him, grabbing his protégé by his kilt and hauling him forward into his arms. Then he set him down on the deck as if he were a child.

The look Vixini gave Wallie clearly said, "Told you he had three feet," but he didn't put it into words.

Addis said quietly, "Thank you, mentor." And that was the end of the matter.

Speedy had a fairly roomy deck house to serve as the admiral's stateroom, but Addis could only just stand straight in there, while Wallie and Vixini had to crouch. Headroom was always a problem on the River, and the usual solution was to sit on the floor, which is what they did, cross-legged around a cloth spread with a feast. Judging by the visitors' comments and enthusiasm, *Speedy*'s cook was more skilled than *Hyacinth*'s, although Wallie still recalled with nostalgia the magnificent meals he had eaten fifteen years ago, on *Sapphire*.

Both boys were browner and somehow brighter now, he thought. Their facemarks had healed. Even Vixini seemed to have matured and deepened since he donned the brown kilt of manhood and the responsibility of being a mentor. Addis had stopped addressing Wallie as "Uncle," but only his boots and sword showed that he was a swordsman. If there was a hairclip inside that heap of curls, it was a well kept, but ill kempt, secret.

Eventually, after the first pangs had been satisfied, he asked the question that all juniors asked Wallie if they got the chance, because very few mentors could answer it from their own experience. "How does real sword fighting differ from fencing?"

Wallie gave him much the same answer he always gave.

"Lots. It's much more defensive, for one thing. Not many men risk their lives needlessly. I can't speak for women, but I assume that's as true for them. In my great duel to the death with Lord Boariyi, I tried for a quick first blood to rattle him. I was the one who bled, and I admit it rattled me. You'd be amazed at how many highly skilled fencers fall apart when they face a real blade. Some seem to forget their training altogether. That's why we allow betting and minor challenges: to let people fight for real stakes, but money or honor, not blood. The most important thing to remember before the fight starts is to instruct your second carefully. Dueling is exhausting like nothing else. After a very few minutes you may begin to think that a draw would be an acceptable ending after all. Seconds don't have to follow orders, and it's a mistake to try to bind them. When the dance begins, remember that your opponent is feeling just as mortal as you are. After that, I can give you only two pieces of advice about dueling. One, remember your training; and two, try not to do it at all if you possibly can."

But the swordsmen of Plo must know that the Tryst would return to avenge its dead, and that would be all the excuse their reeve needed to swear them by the third oath: *Blood needs be shed, declare your allegiance.* When the two forces met, both sides would be bound to fight to the death.

"I have some good news for you," Wallie explained later. "I'll be passing it around the fleet, but you deserve to hear it first, Addis. Your dad is reported to be on the mend." He passed over the message slip. It said, once the abbreviations were straightened out: *Nnanji sitting up, eating.*

Addis thanked him. "You going to show this to anyone else, my lord?"

"No."

Addis put it away in his pouch. The Tryst in general had never known that Liege Nnanji's injury was so serious that he couldn't sit up or eat, so they must be told only that he was recovering. Not many men or boys would have seen that so quickly.

"Who knows?" Wallie said. "It would be just like him to raise another army and get to Kra before us. Has Master Filurz told you our plans?"

Of course he hadn't.

"Tomorrow, Lord Joraskinta and a few men will be going ashore at a village on the south bank to take an overland trail from there to the next loop. Honorable Quarlaino will go with him, because he knows the Plo area and the best road to it. The rest of us are going on to a city called Soo, which will be a faster journey, if the Goddess wills. Soo is on a different reach from Plo, but it has an overland connection and it should be only a short march for us.

Addis looked puzzled but was too discreet to question.

"You're wondering why I'm splitting my forces. The Soo crossing is not arduous, from what I've been able to discover, but it brings us down to the River at Cross Plo, on the wrong bank. The enemy will try to hinder our crossing, and that's where Joraskinta comes in. The way he is going involves many land crossings before reaching the right stretch of River, so it would be hard to take an army by that route. One ship is easier to hire than hundreds of horses. The way we're going requires only two land trips and we finish up with a long voyage to Soo, sailing between river banks studded with many fine Tryst cities where we can enlist swordsmen."

Addis was smiling.

"Novice?"

"Lord Joraskinta will hire boats for us?"

"Ships. Yes. Well done. We shan't need many just to ferry us over the River, but we do need some. Something else's worrying you. Out with it!"

"Should you be telling everyone your plans, my lord? I don't mean my mentor or I will chatter, but there are sailors who may be in the pay of the sorcerers, and if someone talks too loosely, they'll hear."

"I am quite certain that the sorcerers know everything about us, right down to what we just ate. You two must stay mindful of that. I don't want either of you taken hostage." That was the most important thing he had to tell them, and he waited a moment for the message to sink in.

"What would happen then, Dad?" Vixini asked. Addis could have asked, but hadn't.

"I don't know. Please don't put me in the position of having to decide. This war may be too important to throw away to save some stupid colt who gets himself in trouble.

"What is happening, I believe, is this: Vul made the treaty with the Tryst and the other covens waited to see what would happen. Behold, it worked! The swordsmen stopped killing sorcerers on sight, and the sorcerers are doing very well, manufacturing strange novelties, like soap, locks, and telescopes." The industrial revolution had begun. "Other covens began to join in. There was resistance, of course. There always is. Now the resistance has set up battle lines at Kra. It's probably too late. The Tryst has grown too powerful to stop.

"That doesn't mean that we'll necessarily win this round.

And it isn't as simple as Kra bad, all other covens good. The sorcerers themselves are divided. Not all the Vul coven support us, and likely not all in the Kra group are against us. Treachery may work both ways, but trust no strangers, not even swordsmen."

CHAPTER 2

THE ROYAL PALACE OF PLO WAS A RAMBLING
relict crouched on the craggy hill above the city like a
vulture's nest. A few parts were modern and gaudy, others
had been the quarters of long-dead kings, now used as slave
barracks. Some parts were supposed to be impregnable
fortifications, but looked much like others that had been
designed as royal bordellos. Arganari XIV the Merciful,
holy priest of the seventh rank, king of Plo and Fex, had
never approved of his sprawling residence and often wished
that he had ordered most of it pulled down years ago. The
only reason he hadn't was that it would have cost too much
money, meaning he would have had to raise taxes, and in
those days he had believed that it was his duty to keep taxes
as low as possible.

He would also have lost the respect of his subjects. As priest
as well as king, he knew the importance of appearances, of
the right things being done in the right order and the exactly
right way. Kings who tore down the work of their ancestors
undermined the foundations of their own rule.

Some parts of the pile he did like. On calm days in the
past he had enjoyed wandering along the north gallery,
which commanded a magnificent view of the city below,
the mighty River on whose banks it stood, and the misty,
distant Mule Hills, which were no doubt green with spring
now. Alas, it was years since he had been able to see any of

those things. Moreover, the north gallery was intolerably windy, and he had trouble enough walking at the best of times, without being buffeted by random buffets of gale, every one of which raised a firestorm of pain in his crippled hips and knees. He leaned heavily on his cane and wished that he'd brought two of them.

Old age had stolen most of his sight and today the wind washed away the rest in torrents of tears. To his left the great parade of his ancestors was barely a blur, although children in the streets of the city far below would be able to see them, standing proud against the sky: thirteen gigantic statues of his predecessors looming high on their plinths. The great company began with the over-muscled, near-nude swordsman, Arganari I, and continued with twelve priests to Arganari XIII, his grandfather. The first empty plinth beyond that was reserved for himself, Arganari XIV. Although his line had not been noted for reckless experimentation in nomenclature, each one of them had claimed some special title: the Benevolent, the Shrewd, and so on. Local bird life, with more artistic judgment than respect, decorated them all equally. Some day he, too, would be standing there as a gulls' latrine.

In the past he had often wondered if the Goddess would cause him to be reborn as a palace slave who would gaze on his previous incarnation and pine for lost glory. But She rarely allowed that sort of memory. For all he knew, in a previous life he had been one of these other kings, whose likeness now stared arrogantly out across at the Mule Hills for all eternity. He did look quite like XI, the Sagacious.

It was not the first empty plinth, his plinth, that saddened him, for death was an inevitable and not always unwelcome visitor, certain to coming calling on him in the near future. But he was the last of his line, and the next base after his would not support an Arganari. There would be no Arganari XV. This was the greatest sorrow of his life.

All the kings of Plo and Fex except the swordsman butcher who founded the dynasty had been priests, because the priesthood was a much safer craft. Although kingship had required Arganari to be a skeptical, cynical ruler, as a priest he had always been devout. Ever Her sincere servant, he had performed his sacerdotal duties with faith and diligence. On major festival days he still had himself carried down to the great temple of the Goddess near the River, where all gods were worshiped. All except one, for the Fire God had been cast out millennia ago, and since then had been honored only by the sorcerers.

Yet even a minor and suspect god could summon a king, and that was why the most holy Arganari XIV was enduring his painful progress along the north gallery. Tucked away at the far end of it, spurned and neglected, stood a chapel of the Fire God. Which royal ancestor had built it or why was unknown, but the temple always allocated a priestess to tend it. Once a month she would clean it out and replace the logs stacked on the hearth with fresh. No mortal ever lit that fire, but this morning watchers had reported smoke coming from the chimney. That was how the Fire God announced his presence. When the king answered the summons, the god spoke to him out of the fire.

It was a great regret to Arganari that the Goddess he served had never spoken to him as the Fire God did. She had never granted him a miracle. The closest She had ever come was when She stole his son away to die in a distant land, yet the outcast Fire God honored him with personal messages. Explain that, holy man.

Nigh on half a century ago, when XIII the Benevolent had been visiting his other city, Fex, the chapel chimney had begun to smoke. Terrified half out of his wits, Crown Prince Arganari had answered the summons in the king's stead. The god had informed him that his grandfather had just suffered a stroke and would be dead by sunset, making the younger Arganari King Arganari XIV. It was two days before the news arrived by mortal means.

Twenty or so years later, his son, another Crown Prince Arganari, had sailed off with his bodyguard on a state visit to Fex to let the other half of the kingdom view their future ruler, newly sworn to the swordsman's craft. The Fire God had summoned the king to warn him that his son had been moved by the hand of the Goddess to a distant land. He was currently on his way from Tau to Casr but would be murdered en route by a swordsman, Nnanji of the Fifth. Secular confirmation of the prince's death had arrived about eight weeks later.

There had been two more revelations within the last three years. The news was never good. What dread tidings would he receive this time?

Heart thumping, eyes streaming tears, the king recognized the blur ahead as the chapel. When he reached the door, he found his honor guard of three swordsmen waiting there for him, although he had sent them on to open it. The three blockheads, two yellows and a brown, had been chosen for brawn, not brains, because the entrance was barred by a massive balk of timber that only three strong men together could lift. The young fools, however, had been too frightened to obey their orders before their high priest arrived, as if he could defend them against some monster lurking within. No mortals could imprison a god, so the purpose of barring the door was to keep lay folk out—one did not want irresponsible intruders offering prayers to a suspect god.

"Well?" he wheezed. "Do I have to help you?"

The brown kilt gasped. "No, Sire! On the count of three..."

Nowadays metal workers sold fancy gadgets called locks, which could only be opened by the correct key, but the god might be angered if his privacy were maintained by such newfangled trickery. The three giants managed to lift the monster and even lay it down without crushing their feet. No ogres came bursting forth.

"Dismissed!" the king snapped. "Go and wait at the far end." Their blurred shapes disappeared into the pearly mist of his blindness.

When his lungs had stopped laboring so hard, he hauled the heavy door open, releasing a rush of heat and smoke that made his eyes sting and water even more. He pulled the door shut behind him. He hated and feared this place, haunted by a dread that the guards might return and bar the door again, shutting him in there to die.

The Fire God's shrine was narrow, dim, and austerely empty. From a tiled floor, smooth ashlar walls soared up to a vaulted roof, and the only light came from a small, barred window. The hearth was opposite the door and above it hung a mask of copper and gold. Larger than human, the face itself was quite without expression, for both mouth and eyes were empty holes; but the priestesses kept it polished and as the draft from the fire and wind made it swing on its chains, so the play of light on the metal made it seem alive.

Arganari choked back a smoke-induced cough and leaned his cane against the wall. Then he raised his hands and croaked out the prayer to the Fire God that was contained in the last of the many priestly sutras, as if it had been left in only on sufferance, to be known only to priests of the seventh rank.

> *Lord of hearth and storm, nourisher of crops,*
> *Enrage out hearts against our foes,*
> *Inflame out bodies with lust to breed children,*
> *And give dominion to us who live in high places.*

In Arganari's opinion, that prayer alone was quite enough reason to have driven the Fire God from the Mother's temples.

"*You took your time answering our summons.*" The voice echoed bizarrely in the enclosed space. It issued from the midst of the fire, not from the mask.

"I came as fast as I could. My joints are filled with your holy fire."

"*Beware of insolence, priest. We have news for you.*"

Which is what he had feared. "Good or bad?"

"*Mostly good. We warned you last year against the swordsman tyrant Nnanji who plotted to seize your kingdom and add it to his dominion. Had you followed our instructions more closely, you could have taken him alive and had the pleasure of punishing him for the pitiless*

*murder of your noble son, so long ago. Instead he escaped
back to his lair, planning to raise a larger army and return.
Last Masons' Day, as you count it, it seemed good to us to
have the monster struck down by a woman he had violated."*

"Praise the—praise to you, Dread Lord."

"Quite," said the god, his voice burning with contempt
to show that he knew which deity Arganari had almost
invoked. *"It was our divine decision to cripple him, that he
survive in pain and regret. May he suffer long!"*

"Amen." Arganari had never put much faith in Reeve
Pollex's plans to snare the tyrant alive. No man who had
conquered so much territory so fast could be such a fool as to
let himself be captured. Kra's attacks on the Tryst, at Arbo,
Cross Zek, and elsewhere had admittedly stopped its advance
before it reached Plo's borders, but Nnanji's withdrawal had
been the obviously sensible response. Arganari had never
doubted that he would return with much greater resources,
unless his failure prompted his underlings to start fighting
among themselves.

*"His deputy, the swordsman Shonsu, is on his way here
with an army, also intent on deposing you and your line
and adding your kingdom to their swordsman empire."*

"And this time they will bring a greater force."

"Undoubtedly, but Shonsu is by far the lesser man." The
mask moved in the draft, and the play of light across its
metallic face shaped a brief smile, thin lipped and venomous.
*"Have you forgotten that he was an accomplice in the murder
of your son? It was his sword that Nnanji borrowed to slay
that helpless, wounded child. Tell your reeve to capture that
one, so that you may yet enjoy inflicting an even slower and
more subtle end on him than the one we have decreed for
his master."*

A priest who had named himself the Merciful should not
be tempted by such thoughts, but Arganari was far from
being the only person to have suffered from that brutal child
slaying. The news had killed his wife, and the consequences
for his people must still work themselves out when his
dynasty failed and scavengers made carrion of his ancient

kingdom. It was those loses that cried out for vengeance, far more than his own.

"Listen carefully, little mortal. The fools think to attack you by way of Soo and the trail over the Mule Hills. Order your reeve to muster all the swordsmen he can from up and down the River, and also to empower the largest posse of civilians he can control. Shonsu sailed two weeks ago and expects to arrive by Barbers' Day, although that seems unlikely. We shall send our sorcerers from Kra, armed with fearful weapons and our rage. They will require food, shelter, and ferry transport. Swordsmen cannot comprehend such weapons, so give your reeve explicit orders that he is to obey the instructions of Grand Wizard Krandrak. Do you understand?"

"I hear and obey, Dread Lord."

"And your reeve must make sure that he has taken control of all the traffic on the River, so that even if Shonsu's army reaches it, they cannot cross. Let them starve to death on the left bank."

"The Tryst has enslaved more than half the World already. Can Plo and Fex stop them?"

"Plo, Fex, and Kra, and all freedom-loving cities along the Plo Reach. The Tryst's dominion is founded on smoke. One serious massacre and it will collapse. Followers will slay leaders and in a year the Tryst of Casr will be a legend."

Arganari desperately needed to sit down. Kneeling was out of the question, for he would never be able to stand up again, but his legs trembled and his joints ached. He sagged back against the masonry, feeling its spiteful cold through his silken robe.

"Where am I to find the money? Already my people groan under the taxes you had me impose last year. One season, you promised, and the Tryst would be gone forever. Now you say it is returning in wrath, stronger than ever."

"Ask the fools if they would prefer the tyranny of the swordsmen to the centuries-long benevolent rule of your family. Will you surrender your kingdom to the men who slew your son? If even that crime does not arouse your

righteous anger, then hear this. The ailing Nnanji has sent his own son along on this ill-fated expedition. Does that interest you?"

"His son? The monster's own son?"

"His firstborn, a trainee killer the same age your prince was when Nnanji slew him."

Slew him on the River! For a swordsman to kill a child was most foul murder, but to do so on a boat upon Her holy waters was sacrilege as well. Every day since then Arganari had prayed for justice. Was She about to grant it at last? Could killing children ever be justified? Appalled at the emotions this news raised in him, he dared again to question the god.

"Why are you telling my this, Dread Lord?"

Because if your response to our instructions pleases us, we may just give him to you. You can start to plan something suitable for the brat, to complete his education—fatally! Go and give Pollex his orders. We have spoken."

"Wait!" Arganari shouted, but he was too late. There was no answer. The god had gone from his shrine.

Lord Krandrak, sorcerer of the seventh rank, grand wizard of Kra, watched through the spyhole until the geriatric king had tottered out of the shrine. Only then did he replace the speaking tube on its holder and turn to another spyhole to inspect the public corridor outside. Once he was satisfied that the coast was clear, he slid open the unmarked door of his hidey-hole and emerged into a pantry adjoining a rarely-used banqueting hall. He was happy to escape from the cramped and stuffy little room, one of several secret bolt-holes his craft maintained within the palace. Clad in sandals and plain brown loincloth, carrying his lute, he headed for the queen's quarters.

The coven of Kra had known since its founding, millennia ago, that it was sited dangerously close to the Goddess's city of Plo. The stronger and larger Plo grew, the greater became the peril, for it was only in the last couple of generations that the invention of explosives had evened the odds between Her swordsmen and the Fire God's sorcerers.

Before that deliverance, the God's Voice trick had been one of Kra's methods of controlling the kings of Plo, and clearly it still had its uses. The manual warned that it should not be applied on any particular monarch more than twice, lest he begin to suspect the fake. This was the fifth occasion that the Fire God had summoned Arganari XIV, but Krandrak considered the risk worth taking. The old fool was too far gone in his dotage to notice anything amiss.

The seeming minstrel of the Third was barely forty, which was amazingly young for anyone other than a swordsman to reach seventh rank, and at least twenty years younger than anyone had ever held the post of grand wizard of a major coven. Kra-born, he had been orphaned when young, both his parents having vanished on missions to the lands of the Goddess, presumed murdered by swordsmen. The coven took care of its young and had recognized his brilliance early. For years he had railed against the swordsmen's so-called Tryst—at first alone, and then as leader of a party of rebellious youths. Eventually, and very nearly too late, the antiquities on the council had awakened to their peril and elected him to fill a vacancy. He had refused to accept unless they made him grand wizard, and they had crumbled before his righteous certainty. He had driven the enemy away once, but the second time was going spill a lot more blood; some of it might even have to be sorcerer blood, but the prime strategy must be to make swordsmen kill swordsmen.

Without bothering to knock, he opened an unobtrusive door and walked into the queen's dressing room. That door was reserved for special friends, and the only person who might be behind it at this early hour was the queen herself. Servants were not admitted until after she had risen, which was rarely much before noon.

This morning, though, Daimea was sitting at the table, brushing her hair and studying her own boredom in the mirror. Seeing Krandrak behind her, she came to life, rising and smiling as if they were equals. They were both sworn to the Fire God, but there the resemblance ended.

Maneuvering kings into suitable marriages was another sorcerous technique for controlling the swordsmen of cities such as Plo. King Arganari's third wife had always been statuesque and was now close to monumental, although she had not yet turned thirty. Her skin was smooth as cream, her hair a soft honey shade, a paleness very rare among the People. Her lips were alluring, her breasts breathtaking. She had been born of sorcerer parents in Kra, although this was unknown outside the coven itself. Krandrak remembered her as a cherubic First, because he had been one of the Thirds assigned to train her in the so-called arts of love. Ten minutes into the first lesson, she had been teaching him things. Despite the singers' facemark on her forehead, she was no more a singer than he was a minstrel.

"It went well, my lord?"

"No. The old fool has no fight left in him. You will have to work on him."

She sighed. "Yes, Grand Wizard."

"Fire him up. Raise his spirits!"

"I have had no luck at raising anything else for years."

"We made you, Daimea. We can unmake you. You are very vulnerable to rumors of scandal."

"Forgive my levity, lord." Her humility rang as false as a stone bell.

"Pollex will raise an army, but Arganari has to fund it. Keep working on his worries about the succession and the murder of his son. Frighten him, prey on his fears."

"I'm not certain it is possible to frighten him any more, my lord. He knows he can't last much longer."

"Anyone can be frightened. Tell him about the king of Abae, who left his city to his daughter. She ruled for about a week before a troop of free swords came by and decided to take it over. They impaled her husband and raped the queen to death."

"Yes, my lord." Daimea looked skeptical, so perhaps she had heard the true story. "And while we are on that subject, my lord, I am not quite certain yet, but I believe I may need help disposing of a slight accident."

"Fool!"

"It happens," she said with a shrug.

"Who was it this time?"

"Who knows?"

The queen was a tramp, happy to open for any man she could lay her hands on. The way she looked at Krandrak himself filled him with disgust. He took two quick strides to close with her.

"There is more than one type of accident," he said.

He had a dozen ways to hurt or even kill her, yet she looked up at him with none of the fear his threat should produce. He knew she was not as stupid as she pretended, but he also doubted she was clever enough, or knew enough, to work out for herself how much he needed her for the next half year or so. Her lover must have coached her, and that narrowed the field to one of his own men in the palace. They must both be tolerated now, but after the Tryst had been repelled, they would be expendable.

See that she was not going to answer, he said, "Who is the father?"

"It certainly isn't Old Palsy. If he tried that nowadays you'd hear his bones rattling in Kra. He knows it and everyone in the palace can guess it. The evidence has to go before I start showing."

"I will make arrangements. A woman will ask to show you a topaz brooch, which you will purchase and wear."

Daimea simpered. "Thanks." She sauntered over to a closet and began inspecting gowns.

Krandrak took his lute across to the mirror to check his facemarks. He had journeyed from Kra to Plo as a carter and changed to a minstrel before coming to the palace, but that transformation had been rather hurried. He decided one of the lute shapes was smudged, and opened the hidden compartment in the sound box. With the aid of a small vial of Triple Distillate of Rock Oil and a rag, he wiped the lutes off and reinstalled them with fresh transfers. Minstrel was his favorite persona. Minstrels went anywhere they wanted and swordsmen never hassled them. He had a fine singing voice and performed when he had to.

"Report through the usual channel in three days," he told Daimea. "I want to know your husband's state of mind, and what orders he has given the reeve."

"Yes, my lord. Don't forget what I want, will you?"

"Every man in the city knows what you want."

With confidence born or years of practice, Grand Wizard Krandrak walked out the outer door as if he had every right to be there in the royal palace, but there was no one in the corridor to see him. His next job was to track down Lord Pollex and warn him of the Tryst's approach. Pollex was another sorcerer agent, although controlled by blackmail rather than money or oaths, but still the most important of all for the success or failure of Kra's plans.

Glad to be rid of her obnoxious visitor, Queen Daimea walked through to her bedroom, where Pollex of the Seventh was still stretched out on the bed, stark naked. Just the sight of him made all her internal organs seethe with excitement. He had the sexiest body she knew, and his head on the pillow was framed in a pool of the heavy jet-black hair that fell around her like a tent when he was on top of her. He was also as close to insatiable as any.

"What did he say?" He had a deep, throaty voice.

"He said he would see to it."

"Told you he would. Now come here and stiffen me up again."

CHAPTER 3

ARGANARI'S EYES WERE AWASH AGAIN AS HE hobbled back along the north gallery. The wind still blew in his face, even now, when he was going the other way. He passed the empty plinth that should have been his son's, then the one that waited for him. Thirteen ancestors to go. He knew that if he could see them they would be staring far above his head, not deigning to look down at him. He would not be able to meet their eyes if they did. He had failed them, dropped the torch. The dynasty must end with him.

He had tried. His first wife had died of puerperal fever, and the child with her. His second, Sisila, had been a great joy, the love of his life. She had given him a child, but only one, the boy the swordsmen had murdered. After the shock of Argie's death had killed her, his ministers had begged him to marry a third time, but it been years before he could bring himself to do so. Eventually he had wed Daimea. She had given him a daughter; he would sire no more offspring now. Argair was a sweet child, very quick and intelligent. But what chance did she have in a world of men? Once in a while a king's daughter would try to rule a city, but it never worked for long. Inevitably some swordsman would force her into marriage at sword point and declared himself king. Even then, her children might not succeed her. Often her husband would promote some other son of his from a previous marriage or a casual affair.

So the house of Arganari was ending. But XIV wasn't going to abandon his throne and his cities to the Casr barbarians without a fight.

Exhausted by the struggle and the pain in his hips, he reached the end of the gallery to find the three swordsmen oxen waiting just inside the door. He sent them off to bar the chapel door, while he went in search of a bath, a soothing massage, and his breakfast.

When he was ready to eat, he sent word to Daimea to join him in the state banqueting hall. He ate there from habit, but it might as well have been the porters' mess for all he could see of its opulence. He was informed that her Majesty was sleeping late that morning, and had not yet rung for her tea.

Hating eating alone, he sent for Reeve Pollex to discuss Wizard Krandrak's warnings. He had almost finished his snack when the page returned to say that the reeve could not be found, but he must be somewhere in the palace because his horse was in its stall; the swordsmen were still looking for him. Arganari could imagine a good place to look and suspected that the page could, too.

At that moment Argair came skipping in, bright and fresh as a spring morning. She kissed her father's cheek, sat on the closest chair uninvited, and reached for the sweetmeat dish. She was going to be a great beauty, like her mother.

"Daddy, I want a falcon. Can I have a falcon? For my very own?" Her resemblance to Daimea became even more marked when she wanted something.

"This is not the proper time of year to start training a bird, my dear. But you can start taking lessons, if you want."

She pouted. "Don't like lessons."

She would have to learn to like lessons if she expected to be queen, but she was too young to understand that yet. "I shall be going to the temple this morning. Would you like to come down to the city with me?"

"No. I want to go riding."

"Then have a nice ride. Which pony are you going to take?"

Of course a horse was much more interesting than a father at her age. He was seven times her age and found it almost impossible to hold a conversation with her. After he had refused to give her an all-white pony, a ruby necklace like Mommy's, and four *really cute* pages of her own in a special livery, Arganari was quite glad to see a tall adult figure approaching against the light and hear the pad of a swordsman's boots. He sent Argair off to her nurse, who would be lurking in the mist somewhere.

Pollex whipped out his sword and made the salute to a superior. The king struggled to his feet and gave him the response to an equal, acknowledgment of his rank. He could smell wet hair from the swordsman's ponytail, which was better than the sort of odor he emitted sometimes. Arganari could imagine the gleam of contempt in the man's eyes and thanked the Goddess that he did not have to see it. He had long ago recognized what sort of a woman he had married, but she needed a husband of her own age; he blamed himself for being unable to satisfy her. He had no intention of exposing her or sending her away, as long as she didn't try to slip any strangers into the royal lineage. Daimea was quite smart enough to know that, and smart enough not to stay with any one lover long enough to give him ideas of making the arrangement permanent.

"Sit, reeve. Help yourself to some wine, and food if you're peckish." *After your exertions.* "I had a message from the Fire God this morning."

"What does the Dread Lord want?" asked Pollex with his mouth full already.

"He is confident that the Tryst will come at us from Soo, over the Mule Hills, and we must expect it by Barbers' Day. You are to assemble the largest army and posse you can and prepare to fight on the far bank. The god also insists that Grand Wizard Krandrak have overall command."

"Huh. And what does a sorcerer know about war?"

"I expect his god knows a great deal about it." *And his god provides us with a lot more direct help than the Goddess ever gives us, Goddess forgive me for thinking so.* "Do you feel capable of winning this war without Kra's assistance?"

"Kra didn't need my assistance to start it. Or yours, your Majesty. Did Krandrak ask your permission before he struck down two dozen honest swordsmen with his thunder weapons?"

"He warned me more than a year ago that the Tryst was coming. I agreed that Plo and Kra must join forces to resist it. I discussed it with you and you agreed also. Is burning down brothels better than using thunder weapons?"

"Yes. Only fools get so drunk that they cannot escape from a burning building. I tried to give the Tryst warnings, so that it might back off and find victims elsewhere without losing too much face. Kra forced the issue with its foul sorcery. That is not an honorable way to fight. What does he want of us?"

Arganari told him.

"As your Majesty commands. The god wants us to fight on the left bank? What happens if he is wrong about the Tryst and Lord Whatever-You-Said—"

"Shonsu."

"Shonsu. So what happens if this Shonsu comes upriver from Arbo, instead of overland from Soo, and catches me and your swordsmen on the left bank and you and Plo on the other?"

"You think a god can be deceived? He knows exactly what the Tryst is doing. It sailed two weeks ago. If he doesn't tell us, he will tell his sorcerers. Are you asking to be replaced, Lord Pollex? If you are unwilling to defend me and my cities, as you swore you would when I appointed you, then now is the time to unravel your oath, take up your bedroll, and go." *And no, you can't take my wife with you.*

"Gods' balls, no! I will stake Lord Shonsu and his Sixths out on the north gallery so you can watch the crows eating them. I am merely pointing out that I am a trained fighter and a showoff trickster of a magician is not. I am minded to saddle up Rapier and ride to Kra to consult with Krandrak face to face. Provided your Majesty permits, of course."

Nice of him to ask. "Yes, I will gladly give my permission, provided you do not neglect the necessary war preparations."

"Which will require money, sire, cartloads of gold. A civilian posse must be fed, billeted, paid and trained until the enemy comes. And of course it must be armed, which means buying or making weapons. Other cities will not lend their swordsmen cheaply in such an emergency, nor will sailors hire out their vessels."

"We must explain to the people that paying taxes for defense is cheaper than losing our freedom and possessions to an avaricious invader. Would they rather see their daughters raped and sons murdered?"

"With respect, sire, preach that to them by all means. The last time you decreed a levy and my men went around with the collectors, they were stoned. This will be the third season in a row you have taxed the city. Reeve Ozimshello of Fex told me that some assessors there were clubbed to death."

Arganari sighed, because he knew the truth of what the brute was saying. "How much?"

There was a pause, hopefully while the swordsman considered his tactics and gave the costs due thought. Or he might just be leering and drooling at how much he could rake off for his brothers, sisters, and mistresses. "Three thousand marks."

"No! So much?"

"Not a jot less, if we are to have a chance of winning."

Arganari wondered how much of that he might raise himself. He had already stripped the palace of many of its valuables. What use were they when he couldn't see them?

"Of course it will be easier for me, your Majesty. If the Tryst reaches the city, it will be over my dead body, and I will be safe in the arms of the Goddess. But you will have to witness the rape of your city. They will burn Plo as they burned Zek. Sons will die or be enslaved, daughters will become the playthings of swordsmen."

Arganari shuddered. "Remind me. How much did we raise with the last levy?"

"Nine hundred marks in Plo, six hundred and change in Fex."

"And you want me to extract twice that this time? People will be starving!"

"No money, no defense, sire."

After a sorrowful moment Arganari said, "Very well. If it must be, it must be."

Deciding that he must go to the temple, the king sent for his carrying chair, which was brought in and set down beside him by four large persons wearing the black loincloths of slaves. He had just completed the painful process of climbing aboard when he heard a swish of satin. Daimea leaned in to peck his cheek and let him catch a whiff of her favorite scent.

She gushed, of course. She always did these days, speaking to him as if he was a child. "Darling, I am so sorry I did not join you for breakfast. I was awake half the night worrying about the war, and then, of course, I slept well past my usual hour for rising. I am told you were summoned by the Fire God. That must have been a frightening experience for you. You are so brave…"

And more of the same. Had she just been entertaining Pollex, or had there been another before him? Arganari had long since stopped caring. He liked being fussed over and treated as a human being instead of just a fountain of money and favors. He kissed her again before she left, so he could catch another glimpse of her gorgeous face. Only his wife and daughter ever came close enough for him to see them clearly. Lesser people did not embrace monarchs.

Escorted by a platoon of swordsmen, the king of Plo and Fex descended the steep, zigzag road to the city and then was carried through its winding streets to the temple on the river bank. His grandfather had rarely gone anywhere without a band preceding him, but Arganari had stopped that as soon as he was crowned. At first he had walked on his own two feet with just three or four swordsmen at his heels. The people had cheered him back then, often knelt as he passed, and he had smiled at them and given them blessings. After Argie's death he had taken to going on horseback, but they had still often cheered. Now they hung their heads in silence. He did not know where he had gone wrong. Perhaps he had outstayed his welcome and they were just bored with him. Or they might hate him because he had not given them an heir, so they rightly feared the invasion, insurrection, civil war, and many other horrors that must follow his death.

The temple was large and cold, not yet warmed by the weak spring sunshine. He dismounted at the entrance, under the seven great arches that faced the River. By the time he had tap-tapped his way through the door, a trio of Sixths were there to welcome him, bowing low, praising the Goddess; a couple of sturdy Thirds had moved in close so he could lean on their arms. Even with them taking most of his weight, he needed a long time to hobble the length of the nave. When he drew close to the dais, the other worshipers and priests drew back, so that he might pray alone. His supporters set him down gently on his knees and then withdrew.

"Keep my heart true to Your laws," he began, laying his left hand on the tiles, finding comfort in the ancient words, so familiar to him since he was a child.

The figure of the Goddess was the traditional woman, robed and seated, with her featureless face turned towards her River. It was modeled on the great image in Hann, of course, except that here in Plo it shone with a glorious tiling of lapis lazuli, mined in the Mule Hills across the River. It was one of the great sorrows of Arganari's life that he had never made the pilgrimage to Hann. It had been planned, but his grandfather's sudden death had intervened.

Completing the ritual, he heaved himself as erect as he could manage, sitting on his heels. Now he was allowed a personal prayer. "Great Goddess, your will be done, but I most humbly beseech you to save your people from war and the nightmares of barbarian invasion. Take my life if it will help, but guard the cities you entrusted to me."

What else could he say? *Send me a miracle? The Fire God promised to deliver the son of my enemy into my hands if I do as he bids me. I have obeyed your laws all my life. Cannot you send some word to comfort me in this, my time of troubles, some sign to calm my fears? Must I drive my people into poverty to rescue them from violence? Show me, show me how I can deliver my cities from strife, Great Mother.*

She was just a blue blur, of course, and had been for years. In fact not very much of her would have been visible even had his sight been returned by a miracle, for the dais before the idol was piled high with the offerings of centuries, a great heap of wealth. He ought to have the platform extended yet again, before She vanished altogether from mortal sight. Or, alternatively... *Oh, of course!*

He looked around and gestured urgently to no one in particular. In moments his two bearer priests were at his side, lifting him.

"I will now receive the holy mothers," he said.

As soon as he was out of public gaze, two more low-rank priests appeared with his carrying chair and the four of them carried him upstairs to the throne room. He hadn't sat on the high priests' throne for years. It was damnably hard and cold on his shrunken buttocks, and he wondered if the addition of a simple cushion would be sacrilegious.

The holy mothers of Plo usually numbered about a dozen. Arganari no longer bothered to keep track, and he hadn't summoned them in so long that most of the faces would have been unfamiliar to him even if he could see them. Some of them were carried in and must be as decrepit as he was. When they were ready, one of them nudged the eldest, who cried out in the quavery shout of the very deaf: "You summoned us, Holy One?"

"I did. This morning I was called to the chapel of the Fire God to receive a warning. The Tryst, which was enslaving cities downstream from us last fall and was beaten back, is sending a much greater army against us."

Not one moan of response. Those who could hear him

probably assumed that their status as senior priestesses would shield them from harm.

"We must raise an army of our own to defend the realm and our neighbors. For this we need money, much money."

"More taxes?" called out an ancient voice. Ignoring scandalized hushing noises, she persisted. "In your grandfather's day the imposts were a quarter as much and came only once a year."

This time the background noises were mostly in agreement.

"It's all those swordsmen!" shouted the loudest voice. "Used to be a few hundred of the scum and now he needs thousands."

"People are starving."

"Not a woman is safe from them!"

"I've treated five rape cases in a week, all of them blamed on swordsmen."

"He only needs them to collect taxes so he can afford more swordsmen!"

Never had Arganari ever heard of holy mothers talking back to their high priest in any temple in the World. He screamed, *"Silence!"* and got it.

"No taxes." Now they were listening. "Just minutes ago I was granted a revelation by the Goddess. She did not deny what the Fire God had told me. But She said that She would pay the cost. She told me to raise the money by selling off Her—"

He had to shout for silence again. "Lord Pollex needs three thousand marks as soon as possible. The temple will raise this by selling off Her treasure. Start at the back, with the oldest offerings, so living donors are not offended. *You are dismissed!*" he roared.

He should look into these accusations against the garrison, though.

But later, when the Tryst had been driven off.

CHAPTER 4

THE TOWN OF TRO WAS A LANDMARK ON THE army's journey. Here it would pay off its three ships. They were seriously overcrowded now anyway, because Wallie, like a spoiled brat let loose in a toy store, had been unable to refuse all the good stuff on offer. He had collected thirty-six more middlerank whizzes who were almost pawing the ground in their eagerness to enlist and get some real sorcerer blood on their swords. From Tro the expedition would cross overland to Ki Mer, from where it would have a long downstream run to Soo. At Ki Mer the snowball would truly start to build.

Tro stood right on the equator. At night the Dream God was barely visible at all, a razor-edge line arcing overhead. Missionaries' reports on file in Casr had recorded "Road to Ki Mer" for Tro and "Road to Tro" for Ki Mer, but no account of any swordsman actually making the crossing. At the last few provisioning stops, he had learned that the "road" was a jungle trail, certain to take longer than he had hoped. Moreover he arrived on Minstrels' Day, sixty-seven days after leaving Quo, already a week behind schedule.

Worse still, when Wallie went to disembark, he saw an honor guard lining up on the dock. It was led by a green-kilted Sixth, who presented himself as the Honorable Laruxi, the reeve, and Wallie remembered swearing him into the Tryst eight or ten years ago, when he had been a Fourth

in some other town, far away. He was still the steady-
eyed, competent, quiet-spoken man he had been then, and
once the formal saluting was done, they greeted each other
warmly. Laruxi himself was not the problem, it was how he
came to be there, on the quay. If the local garrison knew
Lord Shonsu was coming, then the sorcerers certainly did,
both here and at Plo.

The wizard had forewarned him of the liege's approach,
Laruxi confirmed, even describing the ship he was on. So
the sorcerers' network was working well, but there was no
mail from Casr waiting for Wallie. Either falcons had eaten
those pigeons or sorcerers had eaten those messages.

He went along to the barracks with Laruxi, inspected the
rest of the garrison, complimented him on running a tight
ship, and then sat down in a shady corner to drink wine
punch and discuss what transportation was available for the
journey to Ki Mer.

"Boots, my lord."

"No mules, no horses?"

Laruxi shook his head. "You might hire half a dozen,
but it would be cheaper to buy them here and eat them
when you get there." He paused in the manner of a man
wondering how to break bad news. The shine of sweat on
his face was due to the steamy tropical heat, but it made
him look frightened. "You will need a week at least, Lord
Shonsu, and you are going to lose men. Half your company
will fall sick, and a third of those will die. The air on the
River is healthy, but jungle air brings on fevers."

"It is not the air," Wallie said. "It is these pests." He
swatted a mosquito on his arm. "They bring the fever.
Those and ticks. Do you know of any other road to the Ki
Mer reach?"

"None, my lord. Tro is as far south as this loop goes, and
Ki Mer is at the north limit of its loop."

"Then the sooner we start the better. One hundred and
thirty men and ten women." Plus six chests of gold. "Tell
me how to get them to Ki Mer."

* * *

As he stalked back to the docks with his bodyguard tramping at his heels, Wallie found himself in a thoroughly bad mood. He really must do something about the Tryst's communications. Had the Goddess forced him out of Casr just to show him how urgent the need had become? For the first time he was seriously considering whether he had made an enormous blunder. He had not known the road to Ki Mer was a death trap. He was halfway to Soo and still had been unable to learn anything about what to expect there. A track that was adequate for a mule carrying a sack of rubies might be impassable for an army of thousands, and that could explain why reports of the Soo-Plo connection had come from Katanji's jeweler friends, not from the Tryst's records.

Nnanji would not have made this error. Nnanji would have remembered Sutra 804, *On Evaluation of Opponents*, and especially its epigram, "Only Cats Fight in the Dark".

Wallie had not merely walked into a swamp, he could not even send word to Joraskinta that he would be late for the rendezvous. The last news of Nnanji had been that he had suffered a setback, and that had been two weeks ago. If he had died in the meantime, Wallie should be hastening back to Casr to organize the choice of a replacement or take over the entire leadership himself.

The real problem, of course, was that the Tryst had become too large to operate efficiently. Unless it could find some better means of communicating than the sorcerers' pigeons, it would collapse altogether. Every great earthly empire—Mongol, Turkish, Roman, and others—had built a fast postal system based on good roads. Roads could not be the answer in the World. To bridge the River even once would be far beyond the technical and financial ability of the People, and a road network would need hundreds of bridges.

Semaphore? The sorcerers had invented the telescope and Wallie had improved it for them, so signals ought to be readable even across the width of the River. Building and manning the thousands of towers needed would be easier than bridging the River even once, but still a staggering burden. Telegraph, then? Simple batteries needed only two metals and some acid, but where to find the miles of copper wire that would be needed? The lines would be vulnerable to sabotage, too, and underwater cables were probably a hundred years away. That left radio telegraphy: batteries, some sort of dot-dash code like Morse, spark gaps, and crystal receivers. The investment need not be great and a ramshackle system like that had worked for decades on Earth until the thermionic tube was invented. He could give them hints on that, even. Yes, once the Kra war had been settled, he would make radio telegraphy his first priority.

When he reached the docks, he found that his army had completely taken them over. This happened every time the flotilla docked. After days of frustration trying to practice fencing in the cramped conditions aboard ship, the swordsmen grabbed every square yard of empty space on which they could set their boots. About fifty couples were clattering about, although he noted with approval that the ships had not been entirely stripped of guards. The crews could not just cut cables and run, taking the army's gear with them. The dockworkers had withdrawn to the nearest shade to watch.

Wallie located Addis being instructed by a Second, which was practically an insult and not likely to help him much. Vixini was being coached by his mentor. Against a Third, Filurz should have, in swordsmen jargon, time to pare his nails, but he clearly didn't. To Shonsu's skilled eye, Vixini was now keeping even the Fifth on his toes. Why in the World was the Goddess pushing the boy on so fast? Was the Tryst going to need another Shonsu in the near future?

They all trusted their liege. He was a hero, he could do no wrong. How was he to break the news to them that they must now cross a fever-ridden jungle?

By the third day of the march, Addis had decided that he would have been much happier as a priest. When he wasn't being rained on he was being steamed and hot water kept dripping off the trees. His boots leaked, his feet and legs ached. He couldn't see his real skin anywhere for insect bites. All he ever did see was Vixi's ass as they climbed steadily upward. He was the smallest, youngest man in the army, and he had to carry Vixi's bedroll and rations as well as his own, because Vixi was carrying Filurz's. The high ranks were all laden with bags of gold, or else driving mules laden with bags of gold, which was probably worse torment. It was beneath a swordsman's honor, he had always been told, to carry anything except his sword. But Shonsu said, "March!" so they marched. Sort-of. Plodded would be more like it, or shuffled: through swamps, under branches, over roots, dead trees, and rocks.

Don't touch anything brightly colored, they'd been told. Little red frogs, for example, were *poison*! Or pretty green-and-yellow snakes, like one he'd passed with its head cut off by somebody up ahead.

They paused to fill canteens at a spring marked by previous travelers as sweet water. It was bubbling out of rocks, and they hadn't waded through a swamp since early morning. The forest canopy was getting patchier, and Shonsu had said they should reach the top of the pass today. Two days going down on the other side.

"Well?" Vixi said as they waited in the lineup to get at the water. "Are you enjoying yourself yet?"

Addis considered the question. "Yes," he admitted. "But I'll be happier when I can look back on this as the good old days."

The big guy grinned. "Right answer, swordsman!"

"There's blue sky up there, see? Let's all laugh."

"And rain clouds over there."

And then something caught Addis's eye.

"*Vixi! Don't move!*" Cautiously he raised his hand to lift his sword from its scabbard. Rocks underfoot didn't mean they were out of the forest, and the snake emerging from the bushes at his mentor's back was as thick as his wrist. It was crawling over a hummock of roots, putting it level with the top of Vixi's boot, within range of exposed calf. It had black eyes and a forked tongue. It was coiling, as if making ready to strike. Addis had his sword out. *Swoosh!* He slashed and cut its head off. Vixi and two other men leaped aside with shouts.

"*Devilspit!*" Vixi said. "Nice one, protégé. Thanks." He looked a lot less fluttery than Addis felt.

"You are welcome, mentor." He wondered if the snake had really meant to bite Vixi, or had just come to complain about the noise.

Master Filurz came back from up the line to see what the excitement was, and told Addis he had done well.

Later, as they waded through the next thorn patch in the next-but-one downpour, Addis thought about oaths. The code was an oath, of course, although the swordsmen didn't count it as such. They spoke of four oaths, numbered in order of severity. The first was a promise of obedience, as when two leaders of equal rank needed to merge their bands for some task. The second was the oath of tuition, which Addis and Vixini would swear together as protégé and mentor. The third was the terrible oath of battle, which all the swordsmen in the tryst had sworn to their mentors, and so, ultimately, to Shonsu and Nnanji, pledging absolute obedience even to death. Only Shonsu and Nnanji were bound by the fourth oath, the oath of brotherhood, for it was limited to two who had saved each other's life in battle.

Now Addis recalled that day many weeks ago when he would have fed the fish had Vixi not caught him and pulled him back aboard. Vixi had certainly saved his life then, more certainly than Addis had saved his today, but they were roughly quits, and it felt good that he hadn't muffed his draw or his slash. A priest would be trained to pray in such situations.

Addis was up to fifty-two sutras now, although he still made mistakes on many of them. Never in his life would he fence well enough to reach high rank, and only Sixths trying for Seventh ever needed to know the last one, Eleven Forty-

four, but he had heard Dad talk of it, and he remembered
the epitome. It said something like:

> *The Oath of Brotherhood*
> *Fortunate is he who saves the life of a*
> *colleague, and greatly blessed are two*
> *who have saved each other's. To them*
> *only is permitted this oath and it shall be*
> *paramount, absolute, and irrevocable.*

Of course a swordsman saving a comrade's life meant
saving in battle, didn't it? The piranha would certainly have
eaten Addis, but the snake might not have been planning
to kill Vixi. Those two little incidents didn't give them the
right to swear the Fourth Oath together, did they?

Or did they?

CHAPTER 5

QUEEN DAIMEA OF PLO AND FEX WAS NOT nearly as good a lay as she thought she was. Pollex preferred a chase before the kill, and resistance aroused him as nothing else did. He found her too disgustingly easy, but she was the queen, so he had to keep her happy for the time being. She was also a sorcerer, as she had whispered to him early in their relationship. There had been a time when swordsmen were expected to kill sorcerers on sight. Those had been the good old days, no doubt.

She wouldn't say what her sorcerer rank was, but it probably wasn't high. Pollex's Kra contact was a bottler in charge of part of the royal wine cellar, and he suspected that Daimea passed her reports to Kra through the same man. For weeks Pollex had been demanding a face-to-face conference with the grand wizard to plan strategy. His entreaties had never even been acknowledged, let alone granted. So one evening he sent for Grundrimp, swordsman of the third rank, but also his cousin and odd-job man. Grundrimp did as he was told and kept his mouth shut.

"You and I are going on a journey," Pollex told him. "Have two good horses ready at dawn; bedrolls and two days' rations, in case we're delayed."

Grundrimp didn't ask where to. He just thumped his chest—which was a large chest, well able to withstand even his outsized fist—and went away.

So next morning Pollex tore himself willingly away from his wife and children, and rode off with Grundrimp to find Kra while the summer sunrise stretched their shadows far ahead of them. There was an ancient law that no one must pass the barrier Rock, which stood beside the only trail heading up into the hills, so nobody ever went visiting Kra. What happened if anyone tried, Pollex intended to find out. Laws didn't trouble him, because he was the one who enforced laws in Plo, and no one was going to enforce any laws on him.

He had only a vague idea of how far away Kra was, but the wagon trail past Barrier Rock headed southwest into the mountains, and he knew that local labor was hired once in a while to maintain it at least that far. It was obviously being used for horse or mule traffic.

Grundrimp did not speak, not a word, not even a good morning. Pollex waited to see how long it would be before he did, but eventually, after a good hour, he was the one to break the silence.

"I was thinking," he said, "that swordsmen used to kill sorcerers on sight." And now he was in league with them. A necessary evil, which many of his craft would regard as betrayal, but justified by his right to self-preservation. "It seems wrong, somehow, that I, a swordsman of the Seventh and commander of the second-largest army of swordsmen in the World, have never killed anyone in my life."

"You've had me kill plenty for you."

"Only because I thought you liked doing it."

Grundrimp didn't argue the point. He never used his sword to do Krandrak's odd jobs. A club for men, usually, or bare hands if the malefactor was a woman. Or a tinderbox, in the case of the Arbo brothel.

The road passed through farmland, paralleling a small river. Fields gave way to pasture, where spring lambs frolicked, and then to woods of beech and oak. About midmorning, as the trees thinned out enough to offer glimpses of snowy peaks ahead, the swordsmen met an empty wagon being drawn by four horses. The driver astride the right lead horse was a comparatively young man wearing brown breeches and a facemark of three wheels. Pollex veered his horse in front of the team, or it would have carried straight on by him. The rider halted his team and stared at Pollex insolently, making no salute at all.

"How far to Kra, carter?"

"If you have to ask, swordsman, you're not supposed to know."

Civilians never spoke to swordsmen like that. Normally Pollex would either have cut off the youth's nose himself or had Grundrimp jelly him. In this case, however, the man was almost certainly a sorcerer, so justice would have to wait.

"Then I'll find out for myself. But be careful in Plo. After today it will be dangerous for you."

"Not as dangerous as Kra will be for you, Pollex. Clear the road."

As soon as they were out of earshot, Pollex said, "If you ever set eyes on that one again, cousin, be sure you get lots of blood on your boots."

In a spacious meadow a stone blockhouse stood beside the trail. There were pigeons on the roof, swallows swooping overhead, and a walled yard with a solid timber gate. Pollex's horse neighed as if catching other horses' scent, but nobody answered his hail or his knock. He rode on, feeling as if eyes were drilling holes in his back.

Snowy peaks moved in on either hand and the river shrank to a large stream. But before the swordsmen reached its source, the forest gave way to fields of grain, with peasants at work in the distance. Sorcerers and their horses must eat, of course. Soon after that they came in sight of the city itself, a sprawl of roofs and towers inside a wall, all built of black stone. A row of thatched cottages some distance away suggested that non-sorcerers were kept outside, but the main trail led straight to the gate.

The wall stood about ten feet high and the top of it, as far as Pollex could see in both directions, was decorated with skulls. Most of them were weathered to a chalky white, as if they had been exposed to the sun for a very long time. The lower jaws were missing, as were a lot of teeth, so he decided these were not battle trophies but some sort of ancestor display. As a rule, the People gave their dead to the Goddess, but that was not an easy option for those who lived in the mountains, far from Her River.

The gate was open, so he rode through, finding himself, in a sizable stable yard, not in a street as he expected. A boy clad in a white cloth beckoned the visitors over to a doorway, from which a man emerged as they dismounted. He wore a brown robe with the hood up to shadow his face, and he had his hands tucked in his sleeves. The boy took the visitors' reins.

The Third did not salute, but Pollex had expected that. Disciplinary action could wait.

"Follow me, swordsmen." He turned and swished back into the darkness within.

Sword hand twitching with fury at such insolence, Pollex followed. The echoes made by his boots and Grundrimp's told him they were walking along a narrow corridor, but he could see very little after the bright spring sunlight, just the dark shape going ahead of him, towards a faint light. He felt a cold draft on his back. They emerged into a wide circular hall with a huge fire crackling merrily on a central hearth.

"Up there," the guide said, gesturing to a staircase. "You are expected."

The stairs, which had no balustrade, wound around the walls, climbing at least twenty feet high before they completed one circuit and arrived at a landing. The walls continued on another two or three stories before reaching unglazed windows and a vaulted roof. Was this a giant's chimney or a temple of the Fire God? Seething at the lack of the courtesy due a lord of the Seventh, Pollex climbed. The air soon became very hot and smoky.

When he had almost completed the circuit, he saw that the reception awaiting him was yet another snub, for it was led by a mere master, accompanied by six apprentices. The six in yellow robes stood in a row, backs against the wall. Red Robe was in the center, blocking a doorway. Like the stairs, the landing had no balustrade. Much aware of the unguarded drop behind him, Pollex walked around to face the Fifth.

"I came to see Wizard Krandrak."

"He is busy," the master said. He looked young enough to be a swordsman; Fifths of other crafts were usually middle-aged or close to it. Only then did Pollex recognize him. He was so accustomed to identifying people by their craft markings that features came second.

"I know you as a minstrel of the Third!"

"Remember where you are, swordsman, and watch your tongue. And you," he said to Grundrimp. "Take off your sword and throw it down there, into the fire."

"Don't!" Pollex snapped.

The roar of thunder made him jump and reach for his sword hilt, but Grundrimp flew backward and was gone. Pollex cried out and leaned over as far as he dared, seeing his cousin lying face up, half on and half off the hearth. His upper body was on the burning logs, the rest of him draped over the curb. There was no visible wound, but he did not move as his hair and kilt began to burn. His eyes stared lifelessly at the roof

Trembling with shock, Pollex turned to face the sorcerers. The six apprentices all had both arms extended, each boy clutching a thunder weapon pointed straight at him. He could not tell which one of them had fired at Grundrimp. The acrid smoke cloud had almost dissipated in the draft. He knew that those deadly little holes in the end of the weapons could spit lead balls at him, for he had heard all about the thirty men who had died at Cross Zek.

"Take off your sword and throw it into the fire," the Fifth said.

Pollex's mouth was so dry he could barely speak. "And if I refuse?"

"Then you will be true to your oaths, for the first and last time."

Pollex unfastened the buckles with shaky fingers and removed his harness.

"Throw it!"

Sword, scabbard, and harness went down to land not far from Grundrimp's head, which had already turned black.

"Squad: safe hold!" the Fifth said. The apprentices all lowered their arms to aim at the floor. "Pollex, you will be allowed to leave here if you do as you are told from now on. You will be only the third member of your craft ever to leave a coven alive. How many civilians have you enrolled in your posse?"

"I wish to speak with Wizard Krandrak."

"You will not, and if you refuse to answer just once more, you will join your friend down there. Grundrimp was human garbage, unworthy to be an offering to our god, and the fact that you tolerated and encouraged him weighs heavily against you also. Do not try my patience further. How many?"

"One thousand, two hundred, fifteen."

"And how many able-bodied swordsman in the garrison of Plo?"

"Two thousand, four hundred, twenty-nine."

The master shook his head in disapproval. "How many when you were appointed reeve?"

A sickening smell of burning meat was drifting up from Grundrimp's funeral pyre.

"I don't... About nine hundred."

"And that was plenty for a city of its size. Small wonder the king's subjects moan about their taxes. You do understand, don't you, swordsman, that you have more to fear from the Tryst than anyone does? Your king is incapable and virtually blind, but not especially evil, so they may well leave him on the throne until he dies, with a regent running the government. But you? You are a prime example of the sort of swordsman trash the Tryst is seeking to drive out. You and your men prey on your city—stealing, extorting, raping as you will. You murder witnesses and intimidate magistrates. You are despicable."

Pollex faked a laugh, a dry laugh, probably not very convincing. "As a murderer whose latest victim is still burning, you could be accused of hypocrisy. You need me to help you stop the Tryst. Casr knows who slaughtered its company at Cross Zek; it will assume that you also set up the mass murder at Arbo and tried again at Zek. The Tryst may blame Arganari for the deaths of the two heralds, but he will deny knowing anything about them, and they may well believe him. If the Tryst sets foot on this bank, it will march on Kra and make the whole town an offering to your god."

"That is possible, but what it will do to you is certain. 'Drain' you? That's how you swordsmen put it, isn't it? And the Tryst is not doing especially well so far. Three weeks ago, Shonsu landed at Tro and promptly led his men into the jungle. He spent a week wandering around there, losing a third of his men to snakebite and fever. He needed another week at Ki Mer to find enough ships to start downstream from there. He can't possibly muster at Soo before Lorimers' Day. He will be fighting in the heat of summer."

"So will we."

"But we will have set up the battlefield at our leisure, and he has to march over the hills to reach us. We will ensure that he has no water and no food. He has messed up so badly that I would not be at all surprised if his men disposed of him for us and went home. Including Fex and the client towns, plus your posse, how many men can you field against the Tryst?"

"Just short of four thousand."

"And how many horses?"

"A thousand, maybe twelve hundred."

"And we shall supply thunder weapons that will tear the enemy to pieces. I think we may look forward to this contest with confidence. You will continue to receive your orders through the normal channels, and will obey them promptly and without question. Is that understood?"

No swordsman of the seventh rank should ever have to take orders from anyone. As reeve of Plo, Pollex could even refuse an order from the king if he felt it impaired his honor. But he had given up his sword, so now was not the time to argue the point.

"Yes, sorcerer."

"Swordsman, you trespassed in coming here without permission. As you said, you may be of use to us in the near future, so your life is spared, but your horse is forfeit. A lusty man like you should manage to reach Plo by midnight. However, before you go you will grovel before me and swear your swordsmen's third oath that you will obey our coven to the death and without reservation."

No! "That oath is sworn only to other swordsmen and on the eve of battle."

"As you wish," the sorcerer said. "But if you refuse, I shall also impound your kilt and boots and make you walk home naked."

No swordsman should ever surrender his sword. That had been Pollex's mistake, and now he must pay the penalty. He stared into the sorcerer's mocking eyes and cursed his own cowardice.

"If you do that, you will have to deal with a new reeve of Plo, because I will be a dead man."

"Ah. This is true. So I shall have to be satisfied with listening to you die. Execution squad, attention! Aim at his legs. On the count of three..." He wasn't bluffing.

Pollex went down on his knees. "I cannot swear the third oath without knowing your name."

"This is true. Swear it, then, to Lord Krandrak, sorcerer of the seventh rank, grand wizard of Kra."

Proxies were not allowed! If that was not this man's name, then the oath would be invalid. Clutching at this feeble straw, Reeve Pollex prostrated himself on the warm stonework and became the first swordsman in history ever to swear allegiance to a sorcerer:

"I, Pollex, do swear by my immortal soul and with no reservation, to be true in all things to you, Krandrak, my liege lord, to serve your cause, to obey your commands, to shed my blood at your word, to die at your side, to bear all pain, and to be faithful to you alone for ever, in the names of all the gods."

Krandrak laughed. "And now you kiss my foot. I didn't feel that. A little more passion, please. Better. I take you, Pollex, as my vassal and liegeman in the names of all the gods."

The very same day that Reeve Pollex was receiving bad news in Kra, Liege Lord Shonsu was meeting with better fortune a couple of thousand miles away, in a city named Gra. Gra was one of the largest settlements on the Soo Reach, perhaps in the World. It sprawled for miles along the left bank—which was now comfortingly on the left-hand side, as *Triumph* headed downstream. The approach of a ship laden with swordsman must have been noticed and reported, because even before the sailors had made fast to the quay, a thunder of hooves announced the arrival of the garrison. That was impressive efficiency. And the blue-kilted Seventh who came charging up the ramp with his men at his heels was almost certainly the reeve himself.

Wallie considered that it was about time his luck changed. The march from Tro to Ki Mer had been the worst disaster of his life. The only chink of light in that darkness had been that most cases of fever had not appeared until after the march was completed, so the victims had been well tended in town and the dead properly returned to the Goddess. The snakebite victims had not fared so well, and those had included one of the mules. Since the mules had been carrying the expedition's treasury, senior swordsmen had completed the trek laden with bags of gold.

Wallie had been among those infected. The World's version of malaria was much like Earth's, making him sicker than he had ever been since he died of encephalitis and awoke elsewhere as Shonsu. The expedition had been forced to linger for over a week in the loathsome tropical pesthole of Ki Mer before it found ships able and willing to transport his army. He had been extremely unimpressed by the quality of the towns, the shipping, and swordsmen he had met since Ki Mer. His plan to enrol an army was starting to look like a pipe dream, with the pipe possibly a sewer pipe. He worried that he might have misunderstood his instructions. Was he being told to turn back?

The gods perform miracles when they please, and never on demand.

But that Seventh who came striding aboard without pausing to ask the captain's permission—that Seventh with the curly hair and the hideous facial scar that dragged his mouth up at the side to give him a perpetual smirk—that Seventh Wallie had met before.

Wallie stepped forward to meet him. He saw the shock of recognition as he reached for his sword. He was the visitor, so he must speak first, giving the salute to an equal. But the newcomer was faster and preempted him.

"I am Yoningu, swordsman of the seventh rank, reeve of Gra, and it is my deepest and most humble…"

That was the salute to a superior, confirming that Yoningu knew who Wallie now was, although even within the Tryst, many Sevenths were reluctant to admit the lieges' higher standing.

As always to a Seventh, Wallie gave the response to an equal. "I am Shonsu, swordsman of the seventh rank, liege lord of the Tryst of Casr; I am honored by your courtesy and do most humbly extend the same felicitations to your noble self."

Then they both roared with laughter and embraced.

"It has been a long time, Lord Yoningu!"

"It has indeed. And you have amply proved me wrong since that day on the jetty at Hann!"

"You have fulfilled your own promise," Wallie said, glancing around the assembly of high ranks, both Tryst and Gra, all waiting to be presented. This would take all day. "But there is another old friend you must meet. Swordsman Vixini?"

There was a disturbance at the back. Vixini's head approached over the rest as he pushed through the tight-packed crowd, looking puzzled and embarrassed. "My lord?"

"Here is someone you have met before."

Even more perplexed, Vixini saluted the reeve.

Yoningu did not respond. His perpetual grin widened. "The last time I met you, swordsman, you badly needed your ass wiped."

"Honorable Yoningu, as he was then," Wallie explained to his scarlet-faced stepson, "denounced me that day and very nearly sent me to the fish."

"Thank the Goddess I did not succeed. my lord, how may I be of service? As loyal swordsmen of the Tryst, the entire garrison of Gra awaits your orders."

"Start with a shady table and some wine," Wallie said.

The efficient Yoningu obliged in spades. The courtyard was delightful, the chair comfortable, the wine delicious, and the serving maid an eye-filling distraction. Only after she had floated away, with a tantalizing backward smile, were the two swordsmen free to start reminiscing. Imperkanni had still been reeve of the temple guard when Wallie and Nnanji returned to Hann with Nnanji some years ago, but by then Yoningu had grown tired of the static life and wandered off to found his own band of frees. When the Tryst found him, he had sworn on eagerly as an inspector, which was basically a free sword with the backing needed to do a proper job of regulating larger garrisons. Later he had agreed to serve as reeve of Gra.

"The stone scabbard gets us all eventually," he explained.

He knew nothing of the revolution at Plo and reacted with outrage to the news.

"How many men do you have here?" Wallie asked, remembering the ferocious resistance he had met when he tried to recruit from Imperkanni's band on that fateful day long ago.

"Not counting juniors, six hundred, forty-two, my lord."

"And how many might be interested in helping me with a brief war?"

"Seven hundred, thirteen, my lord."

Obviously Wallie could not strip the town of swordsmen

altogether. He explained his plan and was relieved to see Yoningu nodding in approval, for the former free sword had traveled far more widely in the World than he had. "Ingenious," he said. "Of course you can't expect every contingent to arrive on the same morning, but as long as you have established a safe bridgehead, a few days' delay should be no problem, or even an advantage."

"I know very little about Soo or the Mule Hills. You don't happen to have any men from there, do you?"

"Men, no," he said, and bellowed, *"Novice!"*

A boy appeared faster than a rabbit could jump out of a hat.

"Fetch swordsman Nostra, at the double," the reeve said, making the lad vanish as fast as he had come. "Are you planning on taking any horses?"

"That will depend on the crossing, about which I know sweet nothing. But I hope to muster about two thousand swordsmen. Outfitting that many with mounts would be a nightmare."

"You'd hope there would be livestock in an area called the Mule Hills. Seriously, hundreds of my lads will be eager to come. How many can you take?"

"How many can you spare? I am well supplied with Fourths and Fifths, and by now we are all pretty much agreed on tactics, signals, and so on. I will leave a few with you to explain to your contingent."

"In that case I can lend you a hundred and a half," Yoningu said. "'Twill do some of my middle ranks no harm to go back to wrestling drunks for a while. If I put on a red kilt, could you pretend not to notice my facemarks?"

Wallie joyfully assured Yoningu that he was more than welcome to join the army. He could, in fact, be second-in-command until they met up with Joraskinta, hopefully outside Plo. The weakness in his plans had always been that he might find himself burdened with castoffs and rejects, but he knew that swordsmen trained and supervised by this Seventh would be outstanding.

Soon after that, Swordsman Nostra arrived, puffing and

heated after running under the midday sun. She was young and attractive; her salute was crisp. Yoningu called for wine for her and told her to bring over a chair. She confirmed that she had come from Soo.

"I was quite young, my lord. When our father died, my mother brought us back to her parents, here in Gra."

So at last Wallie could ask the questions that had been troubling him for weeks. "How big is Soo? How big are the docks? How long will it take us to get there?"

Nostra's answers were concise and carried conviction. About five hundred people, she said, engaged mainly in the horse trade. The men rounded up wild horses, broke them, and exported them, so the quay was well maintained and would take at least two fair-sized vessels. The ruby mines were on the Plo side of the watershed, but the Soo Reach offered better market access. The Mule Hills name was a joke for gently rolling grassland—good horse country, except rather arid in summer. To march an army across to the Soo side? Maybe four days, she thought. Her father had allowed two days on horseback.

"Is there a marked trail?" Wallie asked, thinking about ambushes. He doubted that the sorcerers' chemistry was capable of producing detonators for land mines yet.

Nostra hesitated. "I do not know, my lord. My father used to grumble about water holes."

Wallie noted that he had just been tactfully warned twice of a major problem he might have overlooked. "Worth remembering," he acknowledged. "And how long will it take us to get there?"

"My brother's a sailor..." She thought for a moment. No one would ask about travel time to a place as small as Soo, so she would have to calculate from larger destinations nearby. "About seven weeks, my lord."

Wallie nodded. It was coming together. He turned to Yoningu. "So if I leave a couple of high ranks and a pair of adepts with you, can you organize the hundred-fifty you mentioned and ship out in a week? What's the next large city downstream?"

"Dumo. Two, three days if the wind doesn't shift."

"I'll head straight there. But I'd like you to send someone to recruit at the smaller places in between, to enlist another ten or twenty agile young metal swingers. You can pick them up when you reach Dumo. I'll try to stay five or six days ahead of you. We'll aim for a rendezvous at Soo in eight weeks: Lorimers' Day or Shipwrights'. We'll need each contingent to bring its own rations, plus two canteens per man. I think we should rely on hiring local mounts for our scouts, and the rest of us can hoof it over to Plo. With somewhere between one and two thousand men behind me, I think I can teach the Kra coven not to go murdering swordsmen and heralds."

He noticed the longing in Nostra's eyes and winked to Yoningu.

"Can you cook, swordsman?" he asked her. If he hadn't had seven swords marked on his forehead, she'd have challenged him on the spot. He laughed. "But I dearly need someone with local knowledge. Reeve, can you spare her?"

"Go pack, swordsman," Yoningu told her.

CHAPTER 6

A S THE SORCERER HAD PROMISED, REEVE Pollex received his orders. Try as he might, he could not work out how Kra communicated with the bottler, but it obviously did so. Every evening, the man would appear and tell him what he had to do the next day: buy eight teams of oxen, train the cavalry, enlarge the wharf at Cross Plo, build larger paddocks over there, start moving horses across plus men to guard them, build a larger jetty and derricks to lift heavy cargo, order tents...

Order five thousand colored ribbons so we can tell Plo from Fex and our men from the enemy.

A steady stream of gold from the temple financed all this work, with only a modest fraction of it helping to fund the reeve's retirement. Pollex found himself working harder than he ever had in his life. He barely had time to keep the queen happy, which was important because she had the king's ear and in theory the king could fire him. But soon his spies warned him that he had help from a certain young footman, and that took some of the pressure off.

On Carters' Day, as he left the queen's bedroom, very early in the morning, he found a witness out in the corridor, leaning against the wall and watching him with amusement. No one had any right to be there at that hour. The lute hung on his shoulder identified him instantly. Even a minstrel should not be in that part of the palace, and the king would be outraged if he ever learned that this man was.

"You!"

"Not necessarily," the sorcerer said with all his usual mockery. "I am sometimes me and sometimes not. Underneath it all, however, I am Grand Wizard Krandrak of Kra, and I have come here to lead your army to victory. In case you are tempted to try anything foolish, such as your duty... Show yourselves, lads."

Two sorcerers in brown robes swished into view around the corner. They each had a thunder weapon, held two-handed, pointed downward.

"Please don't think I don't trust you, because I don't," Krandrak said. "This is as good a place to talk as any. The Tryst will arrive at Soo in about two weeks. Today we shall begin active defense. Send out the muster notices to Fex and the minor garrisons. How many horses have you taken across so far?"

"Six hundred, as you ordered."

"Good boy. Today you will lead five hundred fighting men across. Each must carry a canteen and three days' rations. They may bring a blanket, because nights get cold under the Dream God. My helpers and I will require another twelve saddle mounts, ten pack horses, and a light wagon. Bring spares in case any go lame. I intend to reach Soo in two days, so you will have to move."

"And what exactly are five hundred fighting men going to do when they get to Soo?"

"If you have to ask that, Pollex, you are more a fool than I took you for, hard as that is to believe."

Lord Pollex gritted his teeth and said nothing.

By afternoon he was afloat in the lead ship of a small fleet, heading across the River. In practice that meant going either upstream or downstream and then back again, but that day the wind was blowing against the current, which should make the crossing fairly easy. He had chosen his five hundred swordsmen with care, putting them under the command of Lurdako of the Fourth, who was his most favored henchman since the death of Grundrimp. Like him, Lurdako had been born without a conscience.

The sorcerers had loaded some very curious cargo, including a shiny brass cylinder mounted on its own wheeled carriage. Pollex could guess what that was, of course. Remembering what a single shot from a handheld gadget had done to Grundrimp, he could not imagine what use that giant killer would be. A man could only die once, whether he had a finger-sized hole through him or was blown to pieces.

Krandrak, now properly dressed in a blue hooded robe and wearing his correct seven feather facemarks, had chosen to ship out with the cannon, so Pollex boarded right behind him, hoping he might be entrusted with some of the sorcerer's plans. He did not expect to approve of them. For the first hour or so, the wizard conferred in low voices with underlings, but later he settled into a corner of the deck near the bow, shaded by a spinnaker from the blazing midsummer sun, sitting on a comfortable-looking chair that must have been brought along especially for him. There he munched on a packed lunch, sipped wine, and beckoned for Pollex to join him.

"Your men are all bound by the third oath, vassal?" he asked with his customary smirk.

"They are. Every one of them is sworn to obey to the death. They will even jump overboard if I so command. But understand this, sorcerer: if they overhear you calling me what you just did, then it is very unlikely that their oaths will hold. They would turn on me like rabid dogs."

"Rabid dogs are exactly what we shall need, but I do understand your nervousness. There are some gem mines just inland from Cross Plo, and a few temporary horse-hunter camps toward the Soo side, although those are probably not in use at this time of year. If you send a band of men to such a place with orders to kill every living thing present and burn the buildings, will you be obeyed?"

"Including women and children?"

"Including caged song birds and goldfish."

Pollex despised squeamish people, but he had to swallow hard before he said, "Yes. If I specifically order that."

"You will specifically order that. You are to turn the Mule Hills from here to Soo into a desert, is that clear? The Tryst must not find one scrap of food or drinking water on its march. Its swordsmen are to arrive exhausted, weakened by hunger, and crazed by thirst, so that they will stagger up to our guns to die."

As if to emphasize the point, the shadow shifted for a moment, letting the sun blaze down on them.

"Guns? Like that brass thing? Why so big? You expect them to line up like fence posts?"

Krandrak stared at him with open contempt for a moment. "Whatever the queen sees in you certainly can't be your sparkling intelligence. You must have some compensatory facility. That little toy of mine will shoot a ball through a stone wall, but—as you so astutely observed—we do not expect Lord Shonsu to bring stone walls with him. Some of those crates contain cannonballs that will burst into flames when they strike. Just one of them will turn a ship into an inferno, understand? You will also find sealed leather bags full of rusty nails, packed in horse dung. Those burst in flight and arrive like metal hail. They will rip platoons of swordsmen to mincemeat. You know why the horse dung, vassal?"

Pollex just shook his head.

"Because a wound contaminated with horse dung, even a tiny puncture, will lead to death by lockjaw. Our purpose is not just to put the Tryst to flight. We must wipe them out to the last man, no survivors. I expect the news will filter back to Casr in time."

The tiny settlement known as Cross Plo had been transformed. The few permanent inhabitants had disappeared; Pollex did not know how or where to, and certainly did not want to know. The dilapidated jetty had been replaced by a major pier, capable of unloading horses and oxen. A small tent city had sprung up in the background. This side of the Mule Hills lacked running water, and the grass had been scorched to tinder by the summer sun. The danger of wildfire was perfectly obvious to a swordsman—Sutra 423 specifically mentioned it—but apparently sorcerers could see it for themselves, for the ground had been deliberately charred to black for a mile or more back from the shore, and the air stank of burning.

Pollex slept on the ground with his men that night and tried not to think of what must happen when they arrived at Soo the next day.

CHAPTER 7

WALLIE'S BATTLE PLAN COLLAPSED IN RUINS when *Triumph* docked at a small town named Ivo, one day before the army was due to start arriving at Soo.

He called in at Ivo to provision, because a little place like Soo would be unable to feed an invasion of two thousand hungry swordsmen. Food was going to be problem, for whatever the calendar said, the sun was behaving as if this were midsummer. Until the harvest was gathered in, many larders would be bare.

Very few of the swordsmen who had sailed with him from Ki Mer were still aboard. He had unloaded the rest during the last eight weeks to lead and train the various contingents that he had requisitioned. Even the low ranks had gone, because they had accompanied their mentors ashore. The only man aboard below the rank of Third was Novice Addis. Officially he remained because Vixini did, and Vixini because his own mentor, Filurz, did, but Wallie could see the boy was sulky at being singled out, and blamed his parentage for it. He was being paradoxical, because he knew perfectly well that his parentage was the only reason he hadn't been left back home in Casr. Although Wallie could still not quite understand his reasons for bringing the lad along, it still felt weirdly right that Nnanji's son should be present when the Tryst avenged its dead.

The absent middle ranks had been replaced almost entirely

with Thirds, so the ship was now full of strangers. Filurz and a couple of others were trying to shape them into a team, but that was an almost impossible job when they had nowhere to drill or fence. Even learning their names well enough to shout orders in action was no simple task. Wallie was going to land at Soo with an unknown, unorganized force. He hadn't foreseen that weakness in his plan. There were others, as he rapidly discovered.

Ivo was a town of plastered walls and thick, heavy-browed thatch roofs. Its docks showed no special facilities for handling livestock, so it did not compete against Soo in the horse trade. Almost all the vessels in sight were tiny fishing boats, but there was a higher dock for larger ships, and the traders' booths along it all seemed to be offering ceramic ware, so the town might have grown up near a deposit of good clay.

The moment the port official came aboard to extort docking fees from the captain, Wallie went ashore. He should have waited for clearance, but no one argued with a Seventh, especially a swordsman Seventh. He glanced around to see if there might be a swordsman in sight, and was astonished to see three of them striding along the dock towards him, two reds and a blue. A town as small as Ivo couldn't possibly justify having a seventh as reeve. Of course an aging seventh might decide to retire to his birthplace and accept a posting as honorary... no, this man was no geriatric. It was Yoningu, reeve of Gra.

Wallie chuckled. Efficient as ever, Yoningu had overtaken him on the River somewhere and would no doubt complain about wasting time waiting. As they drew closer, he saw the expression on the reeve's face and knew he had been mistaken. Not even the scar dragging up his mouth could make that glower into a smile. Yoningu stamped to a halt and rushed through his salute. He barely gave Wallie time for his response.

"They know we're coming!" he snapped. "They got there first."

"Soo?"

"Soo is gone. The buildings have been burned, the dock

ripped apart, and the people massacred. Vultures are feeding in the street."

Oh, Goddess! About five hundred inhabitants, Swordsman Nostra had guessed. Vultures in the streets meant no survivors to chase them away, and probably no sorcerers lurking in ambush, either, although that must be confirmed. "Go on!"

"We got tipped off by a fishing boat," Yoningu said. "Went close and scouted, but didn't try to land. Could've been a trap. Up to you to make the call. Not even sure we *can* land. The water's low, the bank's high, at least twenty feet. You can still see where they had a long ramp for the horses, but the decking's all gone from the dock, just the piles left. Those'll rip the hull right out of a ship."

Wallie had at least eighteen hundred swordsmen heading for Soo. He had been chewing over as many problems as he could handle even before this news. Now what? Go in with a fleet of small boats, get men ashore, make certain there were no enemy sharpshooters skulking about, rebuild the dock, and only *then* start bringing in the rest of the army? It would take weeks. Fifteen years ago, he had outmaneuvered the sorcerers because they hadn't been trained fighters, just well-armed civilians. That no longer seemed to be the case.

"Our opponents have been studying tactics."

"They have help," said Endrasti, one of the two masters at Yoningu's back. He had been left behind at Gra to brief Yoningu on the whole story. "We've been hearing here about a man named Pollex, reeve of Plo. The king is a historical curiosity and Pollex runs the city like his personal cattle ranch. He's the sort of filth that Lord Nnanji would challenge personally and dispose of."

Wallie stared bleakly into the face of failure. He had been outmaneuvered. His excuse was communications, of course. The sorcerers had known exactly what he was doing, and he had known nothing about them. More than ever, he saw that the Tryst could not survive without better communications.

Passersby were starting to loiter, curious to see such a gathering of high ranks.

"We'd better discuss it with..." He glanced at the other master swordsman, a stranger, who promptly drew his sword to introduce himself as the local reeve."Let's sit down somewhere and talk this over," Wallie said.

"There he goes," Addis said, watching the port official lumber down the gangplank. "Permission to go ashore, mentor?"

"Got any money?"

"Three birds, one spade, a spider, a couple of anchors, several assorted fish, and something that is either a tree or a pregnant heron." Every city on the River issued its own currency, stamped with a variety of symbols. Buying anything usually involved huge arguments about value.

Vixini chuckled. "Sounds like plenty. I'd better come with you to make sure you don't spend it all in the cat house." In fact he had to go, because no First of any craft was legally allowed to own anything. Addis's hoard was all copper mites, close to worthless.

Master Filurz had already grudgingly granted them permission to disembark so that the novice could acquire new boots. Addis had outgrown the pair he had been given when he was sworn, and they would cripple him if he had to march for several days in them. Master Filurz had ordered Vixi to be as quick as possible.

The rest of the army of Thirds lining the rail had not been let loose and raised a terrible chorus of boos as the two ran down the gangplank. Shouts of, "Daddy's little pet!" made Vixi growl and turn red. He looked so like Shonsu that he couldn't deny being his son. Addis sometimes wished they would pick on him the way they did on Vixi, because the only reason they didn't was that he was too insignificant. Hassling someone Vixi's size needed verve. Picking on Addis would be about as sporting as salting slugs.

"This way!" Vixi said, heading to the nearest trader stall. The woman tending it looked understandably surprised that two young sword bangers would be interested in buying her jugs and plates. Cordwainer shops? Ah, if the noble swordsman would go along that way as far as the sausage stall, and then turn left...

Ivo was bigger and hillier than it looked. Vixi had to ask several times before he reached a door marked with a sign in the shape of a shoe. It stood open, for the day was already stiflingly hot, and he ducked inside with Addis at his heels. The cobbler Third was at work, sitting cross-legged on a low table, tapping away at his last. He scrambled up and saluted Vixi.

The news that the First was to be his customer disappointed him. Footwear was normally custom made to fit the buyer's foot and all Firsts wore castoffs. And yet, surprisingly, the cordwainer found a brand new pair in stock that fit. They weren't quite swordsman boots, but they would do until the right thing could be ordered and made. Of course these had been tailor-made for one of the elders of the town and were of superior workmanship, made of the very best Soo leather, and his honor was expecting them that very day. All that went without saying. It was said, but not believed. The boots had been very dusty when first produced.

Addis walked up and down in them, politely asked if he might try them in the street, and did so. He came back—to the cordwainer's obvious relief—and said they were perfect, the most comfortable footwear he had ever worn. That made Vixi grin, because that made them the best of two. Now came the haggling. Vixi pulled some coins from his pouch. The cobbler brought out his scales.

Addis went back out again to look around. He had spent very little time ashore in the last half year, and all-male company was starting to feel inadequate. There was a grocer's shop opposite, a draper's, an apothecary's, a grog shop, a couple of real-eye stopper girls—wow!—and a swordsman.

"Novice, Lord Shonsu wants you."

Addis said, "Huh?" suspiciously. He didn't recognize the man, but that could be because he was a local. He certainly looked like a swordsman: kilt, three swords tattooed on his forehead, sword on his back at the proper angle to draw, proper boots.

"The liege is just around that corner and wants Novice Addis—right now!"

Addis shrugged and went along to the corner to see.

BOOK FOUR:

HOW THE SWORDSMEN FOUGHT THE WAR

CHAPTER 1

VIXINI EMERGED FROM THE CORDWAINER shop with the usual certainty that he had just been rooked out of a year's wages. Even Mom dickered better than he did, and most swordsmen considered their first offer binding. Addis? Left? Right? No Addis. He would *murder* the little turd! He stormed across to a booth where a buxom matron of the Third was selling beakers of watered wine.

"Tapster, have you see my protégé in the last few moments? A First. He was standing right—"

"I seed him," said a customer. "He wend round the corner wit' a Third, a swordsman Third."

"He what?" Oh Goddess! Vixi bulled back across the street, brutally jostling people out of his way. Hadn't Dad told them, *Trust nobody, not even swordsmen?* The alley was narrow and crowded, but he could see over heads and there was no sign of Addis's sword hilt anywhere. A group of women were chatting over the shopping baskets. "Any of you ladies seen a novice swordsman?"

"I saw him," said a bareass youth, one of a pair. "They banged him on the head with a sap; threw him on a cart; covered him with a rug."

"What sort of cart? Which way did they go? Come on!" Vixini grabbed them both and charged down the alley with a spindly arm in each hand. He promised them money, but they seemed eager to help. They might be part of the plot, of course, and be leading him into a trap, but they were the only lead he had. He began yelling at people to get out of his way, but his size did more good than anything else did.

In a few moments the three of them emerged on the dock, back-pedaling to shed speed. The dock was even more crowded than the alley, with the people milling about between wagons, horses, and piles of goods. It was not the big-ship area, where *Triumph* had docked. He could see tall masts and yards there, farther upstream, but here he was at the shabby fishing port, the downstream end. There must be a hundred boats, but no sign of Addis.

"There's the cart!" one of the boys said, pointing with an arm that still bore the marks of Vixini's fingers. All three of them ran. But the cart was empty.

"There!" Vixini caught a glimpse of a sword hilt in a boat just pushing off.

"Yes!" His helpers both shouted at once. "That's them!"

And they had gotten clear away. Already the breeze had caught their sail and the sword hilt had disappeared. There were three men aboard, none of them Addis. Addis might be lying unconscious on the gratings, or might be dead already, but if murder had been the objective, then why bother carrying him off? His death wouldn't help anyone except as an act of revenge, whereas he might be worth a lot on the ransom market.

"Which is the fastest boat?" But that didn't matter. It might take hours to settle that. The thing was to grab a boat, any boat, and get right after them. "Here! Share this." Vixini handed a silver coin to one of his helpers and ran along the jetty, eyeing the boats. He saw one that looked cleaner and sleeker than the rest, with two men in it, doing whatever it was that sailors did in boats.

They looked up in terror as a swordsman boarded.

"Follow that boat! The one with the patch on its sail. My protégé has been kidnapped. I have gold for you and I am on the Goddess's business." *I also have a sword and I am bigger than both of you put together.*

The younger one said, "Aye, swordsman!" and jumped to cast off.

"I'll do that!" Vixini cut the rope with one slash, then the one at the stern. "I'll pay you for them. Here!" He flipped a gold coin to the kid.

The older man was silently pushing off with an oar. Vixini sat down on a thwart, removed his sword and harness so they wouldn't be seen by his quarry, and resisted an urge to bang his head against the mast thirty-two times. What an idiot! Why had he ever let Nnanji's son out of his sight? His protégé! He had sworn a solemn oath, to *take him as protégé and pupil, to cherish, protect, and guide.* And had failed him totally.

Oh, Goddess, forgive me!

The Goddess might, but would Dad? How could he ever face either liege lord again if anything happened to the kid?

He wasn't even certain that he was chasing the right boat, there were so many of them, but the one he had his eye on did have a patched sail and three men in it. He mustn't even get too close. If they saw that they were being pursued, then Addis would go overboard right away. In moments there would be nothing left of him except bones, sinking down to feed the bone worms that lived in the ooze at the bottom. Bodies given to the Goddess could never be produced as evidence.

"I am Ryad, fisherman, of the second rank, and it is...." With many awkward pauses, the older man mumbled his way through the salute to a superior. He was a skeleton packaged in a much-used hide. He looked, in short, as if he ate about once a week and had never owned anything in his life. His hair had been trimmed with a blunt knife; his entire wardrobe comprised a rag tied around his loins.

"I am Vixini, swordsman of the third rank, and am honored to accept your gracious service. I mean you no harm, Ryad. As I said, my protégé has been kidnapped. I think they must be taking him to Soo. Can you take me there?"

Terror, followed by a grudging nod. Vixini tried to

restrain his temper while he worked out the currents flowing here. They feared swordsmen, but he had discovered in the last half year that fear of swordsmen was still much more common in the World outside Casr than it ought to be. He had already given them gold, worth more than they had ever seen in their lives, likely. Were they worried he would take it back? The boat was old and well used; it reeked of fish, but it was still seaworthy; the ropes and sails looked good. Ah! "Is this your boat, Ryad?"

The fisherman shook his head vigorously. Apart from mumbling the words of the salute, he had not spoken. It might not be the swordsman who frightened him so much as whoever did own the boat.

"What's your name?" Vixini asked the boy.

The boy was holding the tiller. He gabbled the words of the salute to a superior without attempting to rise, giving his name as Ryon son of Ryad the fisherman. He bore no facemark but he was no longer a boy. Although he had been naked earlier, he now had a rag draped over his loins for decency in the presence of a stranger Third. It might not go all the way around him if he tried to stand up in it. He was probably older than Vixini himself.

So Ryon could not afford the entry fee that many crafts charged, perhaps not even the necessary payment to the facemarker, and his father had never been able to advance beyond Second. Having been raised in a palace, Vixini found such poverty hard to comprehend. The boat he was following was still in sight, so he had hours to kill yet. He started asking questions, as gently as he could.

He discovered that Ryad was as short of wits as he was of material possessions. His son was a little smarter, but not much. No, the boat was not theirs. Their wages were room and board, meaning a share of the catch and permission to sleep aboard—in reality they were effectively serfs, required to stay aboard all the time, guarding the boat from piracy. The man who owned it would be so enraged when he found it gone that Vixini might well have ruined their lives already. He wondered how best he could handle this without doing even more damage. He wasn't sure how much money he still had in his pouch and was reluctant to take it out to count it, for even what he had left over after paying for his protégé's boots must seem a mighty fortune to these men.

Somewhere back in Ivo his furious father must soon abandon the hunt for the missing children and continue on with his mission, bringing the Tryst to Soo. That would not just be *Triumph*, but a whole fleet of vessels. Did the kidnapers hope they could turn back the invasion by threatening to kill Addis? That seemed utterly crazy. Shonsu would never yield to that sort of blackmail, although he would inflict a terrible vengeance later. And what could Vixini possibly do by himself to rescue his protégé? He was crazy, but madness was all he had left. By failing Addis he had failed a sacred trust, failed every test of manhood as a swordsman saw it.

"Honorable swordsman?" Ryad ventured, greatly daring. Even his silence had alarmed them.

"Call me Vixini. No, call me Vixi, like my protégé does."

Gulp. "Vixi, lord... the money you gave me... it was far too much. I do not even know what it would buy."

And if he tried to spend it, he would be accused of theft.

"How much would be a fair fare to Soo?"

Neither Ryon nor his half-wit father knew, but eventually they suggested two sevenths. What sort of coin was a seventh? Vixini took back the gold and fished out what other money he had.

"How long until we arrive at Soo?"

Ryon asked Ryad. Neither knew. Yes, they had been there and would recognize it, but time was what happened between meals and sleeping. Not today, maybe tomorrow. Mention of meals made Vixini realize that he was hungry.

Wallie headed back to the dock. His next step must be to call a council of war of all the high ranks available in Ivo. Unless an unexpected Napoleon Bonaparte turned up to shine the spotlight of genius on the problem, the meeting would come to the same conclusion that he had reached with Yoningu and Endrasti: they must send a couple of ships

down to Soo and put a landing party ashore to reconnoiter.
It would be wise to take plenty of lumber and tools along
to improvise a dock, and also some dinghies, so that the
ships themselves could stand offshore, out of cannon range.
Dinghies were rare on the River, probably because a ship
was never far from the bank, either to beach or sit out a
storm.

Just when you think things cannot possibly get worse...

Picking his way between the fencers, he came face to face
with Master Filurz looking worried.

"My lord, have you given any special instructions to
Swordsman Vixini?"

"Of course not."

"I let him go ashore to buy boots for his protégé. I told
him to come right back." Shrug. "They should be back by
now, I think."

Devilspit! as Nnanji would say. "Organize a search of the
entire town. There can't be many Firsts with curly hair, and
not one Third as big as Vixini. Have everyone return here
to the ship in an hour, so we don't have to search for the
searchers. Check out all the cordwainers."

When the reports came in, they were much as he had
guessed they would be. There could be no value in killing
either of the boys, and it would take a fair-sized squad of
assassins to damage Vixini. There would be little more
value in taking Addis hostage—Wallie had long ago warned
them that he would pay no ransom—but a sorcerer might
not think that way. And if Addis was taken, Vixini would
inevitably follow to rescue him.

A terrified cordwainer was questioned by eight different
swordsmen and then brought down to the ship by a ninth
to repeat his story to the liege. Stall keepers near his shop
reported seeing the big Third hunting for his protégé. A
couple of dockworkers had seen him commandeer a fishing
boat.

There was nothing more to be done. They were on their
way to Soo—Addis probably, Vixini certainly, for he could

have no reason to go anywhere else, unless he had managed to keep the kidnappers in view, which was unlikely. Their fate was in the hands of the Goddess.

Wallie tried not to imagine returning to Casr without them.

CHAPTER 2

CONCUSSION CAN TAKE MANY FORMS.
They kept throwing him around, hurting him.
Hard boards. Head hurt, oh Goddess did it hurt! Rocking.
Voices. His head, his head! What was happening?
Spinning... why was the World spinning? Dark. Awful
stink. Oh, his head! Spinning. Nausea, need to up-chuck.
Voices. Creaking, splashing. Where was he? What had
happened? Going to buy boots with Vixi. Wet. Pissed in
his kilt? Dark.

He was in a boat. They'd taken his sword. Lying on
boards, smelly boards. Stinking cloth covering him. Voices.
Head throbbing. World spinning, boat rocking. Going to
barf.

"I think it's alive," a man said.

Sunlight exploded as the cover was hauled away. Addis
cried out in protest, screwing his eyes tight shut. In a boat,
rocking a bit. Water rushing.

A sail flapped. The voice said, "Watch that tiller!"

Terrible throb in his head. Gut churning. He shouldn't be
here. He was in trouble.

"Can you talk, Addis?"

He forced his eyes open a little. One of them hurt too
much, but he managed to open the other enough to confirm
that he was in a boat. Could see two men, likely another at

the back, steering. Dirty brown loincloths, hair unkempt. Couldn't make out facemarks.

"Sit up, Addis."

Groan. Would hurt too much.

"Think we hit him too hard, cap'n."

"Naw. Swordsmen have heads of stone."

"If he's going to die we might as well let the little fishes have him now. You going to die on us, Addis?"

I hope so. Just go away and let me do it in peace.

"You want a drink, Addis?"

After some thought, that did seem like a good idea. He'd got a mouth like a hot-weather shit house. He grunted and forced himself to sit up. His head almost burst, the boat spun in circles, his belly turned in the opposite direction. The nearer man dunked a dipper over the side and gave it to him. Holding it with both hands, he managed to take a few sips.

The boat was a one-masted fishing boat, fore-and-aft rigged, making good time in mid-River, going downstream. There were other sails, but too far away to call to for help. Not that he could shout. There might be other boats nearer, behind him, but he mustn't show interest by looking around. Wasn't sure he even could look around.

"Feeling better, Novice Addis?"

"Why'd you keep calling me that? My name's Jjon."

The man in the bow laughed. "Is it? Your parentmarks show mother and father both swordsmen. Were they both men?"

The others laughed. Yes, there were two others.

"Ask Mom that and she'll cut your tripes out." Goddess, even just talking hurt.

"And then there's this." The man held up a small something, too tiny to make out against the glare.

"Huh?"

"It's a message, a sorcerer message. Now why would a boy swordsman be carrying a sorcerer message in his pouch? It says, 'Nnanji sitting up, eating.' Why would a boy called Jjon be carrying that in his pouch?"

Shit.

Fishermen couldn't read. The bastard must be a sorcerer. Double shit.

"Didn't know what it said. I found it. Was going to ask my mentor to read it for me. My name's not whatever you said. It's Jjon."

"Will you swear that on your sword?"

He couldn't, of course. If he forswore his sword, Dad would blot his facemark and throw him out of the Tryst and the craft, both. He'd stay a beggar all his life, a man without a craft.

"Some crook's stolen my sword."

"It's here. I'll let you hold it for long enough to swear that your name is Jjon. That's fair, isn't it, brothers?"

Addis told him what to do with the sword. Then he threw up all over the boat.

He kept hoping he would die, but he didn't. Night came. The boat sailed on, over waters silvered by the light of the Dream God, filling the northern sky. He could probably squirm over the side before they could stop him, do it that way. Might be better than what sorcerers would do to him. Trouble was, River deaths weren't always quick. The piranha sometimes only ate bits of people, spat out the rest.

What a fool! What a sucker! Shonsu had warned him he might get kidnapped. He must have forgotten, must have done something stupid. He couldn't remember, but he had new boots on now, boots he had never seen before. He must have fallen into some trap. And what had happened to Vixi? Vixi wouldn't have let him get taken without defending him. Vixi was probably *dead*!

Oh, Goddess, please be kind to him. Cherish him. Send him back to a good life next time, a longer one. Don't let some stupid idiot like me mess him up next time.

He was a hostage. Shonsu would get a ransom note. Maybe with a piece of Addis attached to show what would happen if he didn't take the army away.

Sometime in the night he realized that Shonsu wouldn't

take the army away. Go back home to Casr and tell Dad? No. Not to happen.

Shonsu would go ahead and conquer Kra and Plo, and he'd find out who had killed Addis and avenge him. Small comfort.

The men took turns steering and watching the prisoner.

It was a very long night.

Morning found Vixini unmurdered. He wasn't too surprised. Any enterprising villains would have killed him while he slept, dropped him overboard, and lived happily ever after on the contents of his pouch and the proceeds from the sale of his sword. Ryad and Ryon were honest because they had been so cowed all their lives that they dared not risk the wrath of anyone above them, which was basically everybody.

A quick scan of the visible traffic showed many boats, but none that he could positively identify as the kidnappers'. Nor did he recognize *Triumph*'s rig anywhere, so all he could do was keep heading for Soo. The reeve there would certainly cooperate in investigating the abduction of a swordsman. It shouldn't even be necessary to mention whose son was asking and whose son had been taken. If Addis was on his way overland to Plo, then Vixini would follow, leaving word for Shonsu when he arrived. Dad might even be there already, for big ships traveled much faster than the little fishing smacks.

Breakfast was dried fish and River water. Yesterday's lunch had been fresh raw fish and River water. When the revered passenger had asked about food, Ryad had dropped the net overboard. Vixini had complained that this might slow the boat and let their prey escape, so it had been pulled up again at once, with four silvery fish thrashing around inside it. Ryad had filleted one and given the hungry passenger a slice to eat, but raw fish was inedible. The rest had been cleaned, split, salted, and laid on the gratings to bake in the sun. By evening it had been quite tasty, or else he had been too hungry to care.

He decided breakfast could wait.

Ryad was still asleep. Ryon was back at the tiller, assuming he had ever left it.

"Are we nearly there yet?" Vixini asked.

"No, er, Vixi."

This was to be ordeal by boredom for Er Vixi, which was his name now. At some time during a very broken night, he had realized how to reward his helpers.

"When we get to Soo, Ryon, I will buy a good loincloth for you and one for your father. I will see you are sworn in as a fisherman and get facemarks. And I will send you back to Ivo with enough money to please the owners." He had almost said "your" owners.

He might as well have offered the man a small city, or a three-masted schooner full of gold. Ryon was so excited that he shouted at his father to wake up and hear the news. Ryad tried to kiss Vixini's boots. Money terrified them, but the prospect that their life of drudgery and hunger might be guaranteed by gaining higher rank was the greatest joy they could imagine.

Why did gratitude always come with a side order of guilt?

By morning Addis could sit up. He was starting to feel a bit better. The spinning had stopped as long as he kept his head still. He could drink, but he refused food and didn't watch while the men ate. There were three of them, all seemingly ordinary working men, smelly and dirty, but the youngest was clearly the leader. The others called him something like Cap'n, which might be his name or a short way of saying "Captain". As Addis's vision improved, he saw that they all wore fishermen's craftmarks, but he was still convinced that the one giving the orders was a sorcerer.

Around noon, with the sun blazing down so that even the sails shed no useful shade, he said, "You really think Lord Shonsu will call off the war just to save me?"

Capn laughed. "Not a hope! You think we're that stupid or you're that important?"

"Oh. Well what do you want with me, then?"

"You're a present."

"A present for who?"

"For the king, old Arganari. You see, your father killed his son. He wants to watch… Well, he can't watch, because he's almost blind, but he wants to listen to you dying."

Addis said, "But…" and then stopped. He knew all about the kid's death. It was in the epic, *Nnanji's Farewell to the Prince*, which Dad always said was the best epic he knew. The prince had been fatally wounded by pirates; he had *asked* Dad to kill him. Dad had borrowed the seventh sword from Shonsu to do it. It had been a Return, a swordsman ritual. A swordsman couldn't refuse to Return another if he asked.

Addis would have to explain that to the blind old king.

When he got to Plo.

Late in the day he managed to eat some stale bread and a piece of salted fish and keep them down.

The men talked about arriving at Soo. This was Lorimers' Day, when Shonsu was planning to start disembarking at Soo. *Triumph* might be right on their heels, or might even have passed them on the way. If Capn and his gang found the Tryst there before them, what would they do with their prisoner? Drop the evidence overboard?

Summer days were long, the nights short. Around sunset, Addis smelt something very bad, the reek of burned houses mixed with something much worse. Soo had been sacked. As the boat drew closer he saw stone walls and chimneys, but no roofs. The docks were gone, leaving nothing but weathered piles standing in the River like petrified herons. The bank was two stories high here and had been faced with masonry, but some of that had been demolished too, so that there were heaps of rock under the surface. Where a narrow ramp had once led down to the water, even that had been half-filled in with burned timbers and bodies. Not just people, but not all dead horses either. It was meat rotting in the summer heat that smelled worst.

The two men working the boat took it in slowly, so as not to crash into the piles and other stuff in the water. Then Capn caught one of the piles with a boat hook and drew the boat in by hand.

"Three four five?" hailed a voice from above.

"Thirteen twelve five," Capn answered, and apparently that was the correct response, for men up above began to lower a very long ladder. They used ropes to steady it, and then made it fast to something at the top of the cliff. There was a menacing gap between the side of the boat and the bottom of the ladder.

"Up you go, Addis," Capn said. "If you fall in we won't try to rescue you."

Normally it would have been an easy long stride from the bow of the boat to the bottom rung of the ladder, but neither his vision nor his balance was back to normal and he kept remembering how he'd have fallen between *Hyacinth* and *Speedy* if Vixi's lightning reactions hadn't saved him. Vixi wasn't here now.

It was all right for a swordsman to be scared, but he mustn't show it, so Addis made the long stride and grabbed the ladder with both hands. He went up a few rungs and turned around. He could kick Capn in the face when he followed, and then there would be one less sorcerer dirtying up the World.

Capn paused. "Just what do you think you're doing, Addis?"

"Wait and see."

Capn produced a sword, Addis's own sword. "I can stick this in your belly from here, you know."

Addis backed up one more rung. "Try now." The throbbing lump on his head was making him even angrier than he would have been without it.

The sorcerer aimed the blade at Addis's kilt. "Don't suppose the king will care whether you've still got balls or not."

The man up above called down, "You mind if I hose down this ladder, master?"

Capn laughed and backed away a pace. "No. You don't mind if I watch?"

Admitting defeat, Addis turned and climbed the ladder before he got peed on.

So Capn was a Fifth, which explained why the other two men had deferred to him. But the two men waiting at the top of the ladder wore swords and swordsman facemarks, and suddenly hope flowered.

"I'm a swordsman," Addis said. "And I've been kidnapped by sorcerers!"

Neither answered.

"What yu' doing, novice?" asked Capn, reaching the top of the ladder. "Trying to foment mutiny?"

"Honorable swordsmen don't take orders from civilians! Especially not to commit crimes against other swordsman."

"Shut your hole, boy," one of the others said. "Honorable swordsman are true to their oaths."

"Move!" Capn gave Addis a shove, so he moved.

But he had just learned what he was up against, or rather what the Tryst was up against. Most swordsmen were bound only to their mentors, who would be bound to their own mentors, but somewhere at the top of a chain there would be a first oath, a promise of obedience, to a civilian. The first oath reserved the oath takers' honor, and the second oath bound protégés to be "mindful" of their mentors' honor, so both allowed swordsmen to refuse evil orders. The exception was the third oath, known as the blood oath, sworn on the eve of battle, which pledged unquestioning obedience to the death, without exception. Only swordsmen bound by the blood oath would take orders from sorcerers, and then only if they had been specifically ordered to do so. Every swordsman in the Tryst was bound by that oath to the two liege lords. Now someone had set up a counter-tryst.

Soo in the low red light of sunset was a gruesome sight, bringing his nausea back with a vengeance. Dead people, dead dogs, dead horses had been left lying in the street. The houses were empty shells. As his captor chivied him

along at sword point, vultures and crows went flapping and
stumbling aside, too full to fly.

Addis should make a run for it, but even walking made
his head hurt, and he knew he couldn't outrun Capn in his
present state. Where would he go if he could? The Tryst
couldn't disembark here without a dock, the banks were too
high. *Triumph* might have come and gone already, slinking
back to Ivo in defeat. Or news of this massacre might
have reached Shonsu back in Ivo, if some passing ship had
discovered it or anyone had escaped alive to carry the news.
Then he just wouldn't come. He would give up Addis as lost.

Had Vixi's body been found?

Capn didn't make him walk farther than one of the
buildings overlooking the dock, which had been a warehouse.
There were still horses in the big paddock behind it. And
there were more swordsmen, one of them a Fourth.

"You got him!" the adept said. "Congratulations, master."

"Not difficult. Get the horses ready. We leave at once."

Addis cringed at the thought of having to ride a horse the
way he felt now.

The adept was shouting to his men to saddle up.
Swordsmen taking orders from a sorcerer? Dad would have
things to say about that if he knew. Another man, a civilian,
came trudging across the miry paddock. He had the stoop
of a clerk, and his facemarks were sorcerer feathers. He gave
no salute.

"No sign of the Tryst?" Capn asked.

"No, master."

"The news is out in Ivo, so they may come tomorrow, or
not at all. You know what to do if any vessels approach."

He leered, showing very crooked teeth. "Kebab 'em on
their swords."

"Try to, but don't overstay your welcome. If you get in
even one hit, I'll be more than happy. As soon as they start
coming ashore, you light the fuses in here and hit the saddle.
I don't want any of you taken prisoner, understand?"

"Yes, master."

"Right," Capn said. "Make sure every rider has two

canteens. The Dream God will light our way." He turned to Addis. "Well, prisoner? Will you give me your parole not to try to escape, or will I have to tie you in the saddle?"

The only bright thing Addis could see about an all-night ride on a horse was that it might very well kill him. The worst thing was that he might pass out and fall on his head, which hurt quite enough already.

"Nothing in the World could make me give you anything except a fatal blow with a sword, sorcerer. Tie me in the saddle if you wish. One day you'll die for this."

Capn backhanded him so hard that he staggered and almost fell. The World spun crazily.

"Smart ass swordsman! I hope the king has you skinned."

He took Addis by the scruff of the neck and pushed him over to where men were attempting to saddle horses made jittery by the mingled odors of fire and carrion.

"You going to mount by yourself or do we tie you on like baggage?"

Addis mounted.

They took off his boots so they could tie his ankles to the stirrups. They tied his hands behind him, which was going to make the journey infinitely worse than it would be if they were tied in front. Soon after that the sorcerer, his prisoner, and the swordsmen rode out of the charnel that had been Soo and up into fresher air in the Mule Hills.

CHAPTER 3

A T SUNSET RYON PROMISED VIXINI THAT THEY would "soon" reach Soo, but the eye of the Dream God had almost reached the top of his arc, meaning midnight, before Vixini began to smell something very bad on the wind. Soon he distinguished the odors of carrion and burnt timber and guessed what he was going to find. He told the fishermen to be as quiet as they could, although he doubted there would be anyone left to meet them. Anyone who sacked a town as badly as Soo had been sacked did not plan on staying long.

They lowered sail and went in on the current, steering with the oars, so the boat moved like a shadow. Ryad caught hold of one of the pilings that marked where the dock had been, and then waited for the passenger's orders while the passenger tried to decide what those should be. Complicating everything was the flat, featureless light of the Dream God, which cast no shadows and ruined a man's depth perception. There were building stone reefs in the water, but even if Vixini dared trying to jump and hop his way over to the actual shore, he would face the problem of climbing the cliff. A cut in the bank that must once have been a ramp for livestock was impossibly plugged with wreckage. Even in daylight this would be a monkey puzzle.

Eventually he saw a place where the climb might be possible. The embankment had originally been faced with a masonry wall, much of which had now been spoiled and thrown down, but parts of it remained, and one edge looked as if it might serve as a ladder for a nimble lad with long arms. He pointed this out to Ryon, who nodded, so they began to maneuver the boat in that direction, using the piles for leverage. Twice they were blocked by debris in the water, but the boat had very little draft, and eventually they brought it up against the slimy stonework. Vixini made the two sailors hold it there by bracing their oars against piles.

Time to go. Below him the piranha, above him maybe human killers. But maybe Addis, whom he had sworn to protect. He scooped half the coins from his pouch and pressed them into Ryon's callused hand.

"Wait for me, please. But if I fall in the water, go back to Ivo and tell a swordsman what happened. He will see you are rewarded, understand?"

Vixini doubted that the fisherman did understand, but it was time for him to go ashore. The embankment was no more than three times his height, but he would have to move a long way to his left to reach the top. His feet rested on rough masonry and his nose was against sand, the former natural river bank, plus much rotted timber that must be the remains of a previous facing. Some of this muck had fallen out, piling up on the remains of the wall to make the footing treacherous; whenever he tried to clear a foothold, naturally more sand came down. Much of the time he had nothing to hold on to. Furthermore, the embankment above him had been leveled with gravel, broken bricks, fragments of tile, and miscellaneous rubbish to make a road, and this now formed the top layer of the cliff. Even a small landslide might drop a rock on his head or sweep his feet out from under him.

He had to take the "steps" sideways, and some of them were more than knee high. The gap in the wall had roughly a W shape, and in the middle he actually had to go back down four or five feet, which was even harder. He went very slowly, dismissing urges to hurry and get it over with, sternly not thinking about falling on rubble and piranha. As he neared the top, his footing became increasingly difficult, for he had larger stuff than sand to clear away, and every pebble seemed to sound like a tattoo of drums as it fell to the River below.

At long last he was able to raise his eyes above the level of the street. The first thing they registered was a ladder lying not two feet in front of him. Of course his sword hilt was slightly higher than his head, so the sorcerer standing to his left had known exactly where he was about to appear, although he might have been following Vixini's progress all the way up. He held a thunder weapon with both hands.

"Prepare to meet your Goddess, swordsman," he said. "Remember to tell Her how sorry you are that you chose such a stupid craft and pray Her to send you back as a sorcerer next time."

Despite a mouth suddenly almost too dry for speech, Vixini said, "You overlook one thing, sorcerer." His right hand plucked a half brick out of the rubble beside him.

"What's that, swordsman?"

Vixini could not miss at that range. He hurled the missile and grabbed wildly for the ladder as the thunder roared. The shot must have missed because he was still alive, and the ladder was just weighty enough to steady him so he didn't overbalance. Then he had both hands on the ladder, left foot on the next step. A heave and his right knee was on the roadway, then he was all up. He leaped to his feet and rushed the sorcerer, who had taken the rock full in the face and dropped his thunder weapon. He was not even upright before Vixini's sword slammed into the side of his neck. He went down in a fountain of blood, not yet dead but as good as. His eyes showed white and his mouth bubbled blood, black in the ring light.

Roaches never came singly; there would be more of them. They could hardly have slept through that thunder. Vixini jumped the ladder and sprinted for the buildings on the far side of road, having to leap over three mangled corpses to get there. He ran into an alley and paused to look back and take stock. Sure enough, in a minute he saw two robed men come running from a doorway just a hundred feet or so from him, and then a third followed. All three rushed over to their dying sentry, which was not the smartest move under the circumstances. If the unknown intruders were armed with weapons like theirs, they would be committing suicide.

Unfortunately Vixini had only his trusty sword, now too bloody to replace in its scabbard. The alley ran north and south, so it was well lit by the Dream God and Vixini was too visible. He hurried through to the back of the buildings, hearing horses even before he reached the corner.

There were four horses in a paddock back there, milling around because the gunshot had upset them. Four saddles hung on the rail, so it was a reasonable, but dangerous, guess that he had only three opponents left to deal with. Odds of three to one were still not good when their weapons were deadlier than his. He ran along to the paddock. If he could jump on a horse, even riding bareback, he could be out of town and out of range of the sorcerers' thunder weapons before they thought to come and safeguard their mounts from exactly that. What stopped him from trying was a boot, lying in the light of the Dream God, just beyond the shadow of the building behind him. In a moment he saw its partner, in the darkness nearby. He knew those boots.

The only reason to remove a man's boots and throw them away in a horse paddock was that you wanted to tie his feet securely to the stirrups. That was both bad news and very good news. Bad, because Addis was a prisoner and likely being maltreated, but good because he was still alive and well enough that his captors expected him to try to escape.

As a child, Vixini had learned that he must never lose his temper because he could hurt people too easily. He had almost taken out a friend's eye once, and he had promised Mom and Dad that he would never get angry again. He almost never had.

But this was different. Addis kidnapped was bad enough, but the wholesale slaughtering of a town was atrocity, not even war. The killers must die for this. No mercy, no scruples!

A faint glow of candlelight showed in a doorway two

buildings along from him, almost certainly the building the sorcerers had come from, because all other doorways were dark. He stepped back into one of the shadowed alcoves just in time. A robed shape emerged from the same alley he had come through and came to the paddock, making soothing noise. One of the horses had already injured itself and was frozen to the spot, unable to move. The sorcerer hurried along the fence, heading closer to that one, and died without knowing there was anyone behind him. This was not the sort of fight where honor counted.

The three mobile horses reacted with more shrill neighs of fright and a thunderous canter around the paddock.

Vixini grabbed the ankles of the man he had just killed and dragged the body into the dark doorway, out of sight. A quick rummage through his gown located the bulk of the thunder weapon, and once he had that in hand, the odds felt a little better. All he had to do now was wait.

Time stopped.

Then: "Adept? You there?"

Nobody answered.

"I don't like this," said another voice. "They must've got the adept."

"I think there's only one of them."

"Fine. Let's just go back to bed then. You may not mind waking up dead, but I do."

"There's no point us staying here. Just two of us can't fire the cannon. Let's mount up and go back to camp and report the barbarians took Soo."

The reply was mumbled. There was a brief argument. Then, "All right. You saddle up, I'll keep watch."

One man strode to the paddock, gown swirling, and climbed in through the rails. The other man stayed where he was, clutching his thunder weapon in both hands, and trying to look in all directions at once. He should have moved out into the lighted paddock, not stayed in the shadows—Dad always said that sorcerers were hopeless fighters.

Minutes dragged by. The man trying to corner the spooked horses had very little success. Once he was bowled over in the filth and scrambled up, cursing, to try again. The one on guard let himself be distracted by the tussle. That was his last mistake.

Vixini left his sword in the body so he had both hands free to hold the thunder weapon as he moved out into the light. The man trying to bridle a horse yelped in terror when he realized that the silhouette he saw against the Dream God was a kilted swordsman where there should be a robed sorcerer.

"Put your hands up! Straight up in the air. Good. Now come here."

When the man reached the rails, Vixini saw that he was younger than he had sounded, although his dark robe indicated third rank. He was also shivering with terror, as well he might, except that there was a difference between three armed enemies and a solitary prisoner with his hands up. Vixini didn't think he could kill this one. He also needed some information.

"You going to cooperate?" he demanded.

"Yes, s-s-swordsman. If you will be merciful."

"You weren't very merciful to the people of Soo."

"That wasn't us! That was swordsmen that killed everyone."

"Never! Swordsmen don't commit massacres."

"They did this one. Reeve Pollex was here himself. Even the children, he told them."

Vixini felt sick. "How many swordsmen?"

"Hundreds."

It was utterly certainly then that Pollex had them sworn by the blood oath, or his orders would have provoked mutiny and challenge. So it was to be a bloody clash of tryst versus counter-tryst. But even so, swordsmen killing children?

"How do you know this if there were no sorcerers present?"

"I didn't say that, swordsman. There were a dozen of us here, but we didn't kill anyone."

Vixini thought for a moment. "If Reeve Pollex commanded the swordsmen, who was in charge of the sorcerers?"

"Grand Wizard Krandrak."

Aha! "And I suppose he gave Pollex his orders?"

The sorcerer agreed reluctantly. "Yes, swordsman."

"My apprentice was kidnapped. He was brought here."

"I know nothing about him. I mean, there was a prisoner. I didn't get a clear look at him. They took him on to Plo, at least that's where they said they were taking him."

"How long ago was this?"

"Around sunset."

"How far is it to Plo?"

"Day and a half on a horse, then a few hours on a boat." The sorcerer's teeth had stopped chattering. He might start getting dangerous again soon.

"You and I will be riding that way together. Turn around." Even an untrustworthy guide would be better than none. The Tryst would here in hours, even if just a reconnaissance party, and to leave this snake with all his evil weapons waiting in ambush was unthinkable.

Vixini made the sorcerer turn around, so his back was to the gun, and then made him strip, which disarmed him. Vixini retrieved his sword and marched his prisoner along to the roaches' nest, where the candles burned.

The building was large, a former warehouse with only its walls remaining. Ashes and other debris had been pushed aside, leaving a big open space, now furnished with what must be the last tables, chairs, and rugs in Soo. Scattered bedding confirmed that this was where the sorcerers had been sleeping, and there had been three asleep, one on watch. A table by the door he had just entered held eight plump canteens and four leather bags. Supposing the bags held rations, why so much water? There must be water in the hills for the livestock.

He would take the sorcerer along as guide. He was no hurry to leave, because the horses had to calm down first.

And there was much to see. The debris heap divided the living quarters from a smaller cleared space at the other end, and that one held a huge brass cannon, gleaming in the light of the Dream God. It pointed at one of the empty window openings and the River beyond. He had never seen a giant thunder weapon, but he'd heard often how Dad and Mom and the others had gone to Sen when the sorcerers ruled it, and how the sorcerers had tried to sink Dad's boat with such monsters. It was a shiny bronze tube as long as a man was tall, resting on a sort of massive cradle. Beside it on the ground were half a dozen balls as big as a child's head, and a heap of leather packets about the same size.

"So! You were planning to sink a few ships, were you?" Vixini went closer to look at the horrible thing. "How do you—"

Right behind him a piece of charred wood cracked underfoot. He spun around in time to deflect the knife thrusting at his kidneys. He kicked the sorcerer's feet out from under him, went down on top of him, and pinned the knife wrist to the floor with his left hand. His right arm was streaming blood, but when that hand closed around the man's throat, there was nothing wrong with its grip. He squeezed, hard and long.

"Snake! Rat!" he said, callously watching the man's eyes and tongue bulge out. "You picked the wrong boy to play those games with."

CHAPTER 4

ON CLEAR NIGHTS HORSES WOULD TRAVEL BY the Dream God's strange, flat light, but they hated it because it did not show up the footing properly. Regrettably, the trail out of Soo was smooth and straight, so Capn's men were able to keep up a fast pace, which was torture for their unwilling passenger. Every hoof beat seemed to crack his spine like a whip and bounce his aching head. Addis had no idea where he was being taken or how long it would take. He was too proud to ask and much too weak, he was sure, to live through it.

How long they went on without taking a break he never knew. He could not even recall later whether he'd still been upright in the saddle when they stopped. He might have collapsed and scared them into thinking he was dying—not that Capn would care about killing a swordsman, but he would want to deliver a live victim to the bloodthirsty king.

So Addis drank greedily and then lay down and stopped thinking for a while. The sun was not yet up when he was shaken awake and told to get on his horse. This time he wasn't tied—but he hadn't given his parole. Not that he had any real hope of escaping, being one half-dead prisoner guarded by ten swordsmen, even trash like this lot. Dad wouldn't tolerate one of them in the Tryst. Of course Addis wasn't exactly a model swordsman himself at the moment.

Stirrups really needed boots, but he'd run barefoot all his

life until about half a year ago, so he still had leather soles of his own. Having his hands free was a big help, and even his horse was happier having a rider who made sense.

The first rays of dawn shone pink and then gold on a line of icy peaks far to the south. Without a doubt that must be RegiKra, the sorcerers' lair.

The sun climbed higher and grew relentlessly hotter. The heat and glare were brutal, with not a single patch of shade anywhere. They ate their rations and emptied their canteens. They passed at least two water holes without stopping. By then both men and mounts were exhausted, all except Capn, who seemed to be made of steel.

He had his reasons, however much the horses complained. He knew where he was heading, and reached it when the sun was halfway up the sky. Once it had been a lonely ranch station or mining camp, located where a steep-sided natural pit held a small, greenish pond, which now contained two bloated mule corpses. The buildings had been recently burned, but might have already been ruined when that happened. One small shed had been left standing, although not quite upright. It might be inhabited by snakes and scorpions, but all that mattered was that it would provide shade. Addis staggered in on his own feet. He was asleep before he hit the floor.

The sun was not very high before Vixini realized why those canteens had been left where they would not be overlooked during a hurried departure. The Mule Hills weren't much more than a gently rolling plain, but there were no signs of people anywhere, and no shade.

Knowing what a cruel load he was for a horse, he had brought a spare; putting the lamed pair back in Soo out of their misery had bothered him more than killing the sorcerers. Although the long gash in his right forearm wasn't deep, it had bled a river, and it kept throbbing. Bandaging it with one hand and some teeth had taken forever, and even then it had still bled for quite a while, although he thought it had stopped now. Blood had soaked both the bandage and his kilt, and some had even run into his boot. Still, bleeding might have been a good thing, if there had been poison on the blade. Damnable sneak sorcerer!

He wondered about Ryad and Ryon. He had looked for them, but they had gone, having most likely fled as soon as the first sorcerer fired his pistol. He hoped the Goddess would reward them for the help they had given him.

The trail was fairly obvious, marked by the passage of many horses not very long ago. He hoped that he might see some houses when he got farther away from Soo. He might even see some wild herds galloping. He liked watching good horses running. Their motion itself was beauty, like good swordsmen fencing.

He drained his first canteen and threw it away. Only later did he realize how foolish that would seem if he did find a place where he might have refilled it.

"It looks like a trap," Lord Yoningu said, lowering his telescope.

Triumph was hove to just off Soo, gently rocking in the current. Three other ships were coming into view behind her and another three were due before evening. The Tryst was a day late in arriving, having lingered at Ivo to load up lumber, tools, and every decent dinghy it could buy.

"You mean the ladder?" Wallie asked. "That's a welcome mat."

"Suspicious!"

"It's so suspicious that I wonder if it may be even be genuine. But I'll grant you that sorcerers do like ambushes and booby traps. Maybe the killers have gone and there are survivors?" But if sorcerers were in possession of the ruins, a landing party would be sitting ducks.

Behind him on the poop deck stood half a dozen middle ranks. The main deck was packed with Thirds, all staring at the remains of Soo and muttering angrily.

"Standing here scratching our armpits won't solve anything," Yoningu said. "Let's lower a boat, send in scouts. I'll lead."

"My privilege."

"With respect, no it isn't, my liege. Lord Nnanji may have died weeks ago. If you get holes shot through you, the whole Tryst will fall apart."

Yoningu was right, of course. However much Wallie felt he ought to be first man up that so-suspicious ladder, it would be a stupid decision. "Then not you, either. We'll pick a good Fourth to captain the boat and specify a junior to go up the ladder first, some kid who deserves promotion and never quite makes it. We'll promote him later under sutra 1139, 'for courage in the face of the enemy.'"

And so it was done. The designated hero scrambled up the ladder and survived. The Fourth and the rest of the swordsmen followed. In a few minutes they signaled the all-clear.

Vixini was virtually asleep in the saddle when his horse began to limp. He reined in and dismounted.

"Need another change, do you, old fellow?" It was a bad sign when a man began to talk to animals. It was a worse sign when he discovered that the poor brute had shed a shoe. He had switched mounts several times, and the other was just as weary as this one. He was so exhausted he could barely stand, and he was lost. The trampled droppings that had marked the trail for him were no longer to be seen on the endless, rolling brown grassland. His last canteen was close to empty.

He hobbled the spare horse, although it wasn't likely to go anywhere. Then he removed the lame one's saddle, led it a short distance away, and ran his sword into its heart. He lay down beside it and constructed the best lean-to shade he could with the saddle and its corpse.

He went to sleep wondering if he would ever wake up.

By the time Wallie clambered up the ladder with Yoningu at his heels, two dozen swordsmen were searching the ruins and others were hard at work improvising a dock out of the surviving piles and the lumber brought from Ivo. At the top he was saluted by Adept Sevolno.

"No one left alive, my lords. Men, women, children, dogs,

cats and a couple of horses, all dead. It must have happened several days ago."

One of the other ships was bringing half a dozen priests and priestesses to care for the dead.

"Any deaths more recent?"

"Yes, lord. Very recent. Did you notice the blood on the ladder? And look at this one." He pointed to a dead sorcerer Third only a few feet away. "Someone came up the ladder and flaking near cut his head off. A swordsman, and a strong one."

He was wrong about the intruder climbing the ladder, because on the way up Wallie had noticed footprints showing that someone—a person with very large feet—had climbed the bank, using the remaining masonry as a staircase. He walked over to the corpse, took up the fallen pistol, and sniffed. It had been fired. So the swordsman had killed the sorcerer, but had himself been wounded. The bloody hand prints on the ladder were his, and the 'he' in question had certainly been Vixini. However much Wallie tried to tell himself that there could be other explanations, he could not believe that. He asked the awful question as casually as he could.

"Any dead swordsmen?"

Sevolno had guessed what he was thinking. "Found three so far, my lord, but all have been dead some days. All Thirds, although there's not much left of them but boots and hair. None of them an especially large man, my lord. The inhabitants may have managed to take a few of the attackers with them, or perhaps these were the reeve and his men."

"Show me."

With Yoningu trailing behind, Wallie followed Sevolno on a grisly tour of the corpse-littered village. Most bodies were so bloated by heat and ravaged by scavengers that it was hard to tell what sort of people they had been in life. In some buildings there had been a last stand, and the packed remains had been burned to blackened bones by the subsequent fire. The swordsmen lay out in the open, recognizable by their trappings. Vixini was not among them.

"I doubt if Soo had more than one resident swordsman," Wallie said, "or none at all. The inhabitants would have been trying to fight back with clubs or pitchforks. Yet look at all the blood, see?" The clay where they lay was black. "All three of them bled to death. I'd like to think that these were members of the attacking force who mutinied rather than slaughter women and children, and were consequently put to death by their less squeamish comrades. See that they are returned to the Most High with military honors."

"Aye, my lord. Now over here..." Sevolno led the way to one of the frontage buildings. "One of those canons you described, my lord. Glad they weren't alive to shoot at us with that! And a fourth dead sorcerer, dressed for his funeral. See the marks on his throat? He's been throttled, my lord. I can't find any wounds on him to account for the blood. Lot of blood."

But there was a smear of blood on the blade of the dagger lying half underneath him. So had whoever had lowered the ladder been wounded here, and by that dagger, not the pistol? Seriously worried now, Wallie prowled around. He soon identified the cartridges of gunpowder, and the fuses leading to them. At that point he ordered everyone else out and explored the building by himself. He had not been at all surprised to discover that it had been mined. Back before the treaty, the sorcerers had used electrostatic generators as burglar alarms: touch the door handle and you got fried. In this case they had used gunpowder.

He wondered why the cannonballs had holes in them, like bowling balls. Then he found tongs, and a jar full of water with some lumps of pasty stuff in the bottom. He knew at once that it was phosphorous, which the sorcerers had formerly used to do party tricks. Pack a lump of that into a hole in the side of a cannonball, then shoot it into a wooden ship, and you'd have a cozy blaze going in no time.

The plan had been for the gun squad to fire a few shots at the incoming fleet. At that range they would have almost certainly set some of them ablaze. As soon as any survivors came ashore, though, the defenders would have lit the fuses, jumped on their horses, and ridden for the hills. An hour or so later—bang. Wallie defused the mine.

Bedding for three on the floor. Five full water bottles and three bags of food on a door at the rear. And two boots, not swordsman boots, filthy and badly crushed. How to explain those?

Once he was satisfied that the building was reasonably safe, he went out and beckoned for Sevolno to order a guard placed on the gunpowder. Fortunately the curse of cigarettes had not yet been loosed upon the World, so he did not need to warn about the dangers of smoking there. Yoningu and others gathered around.

"What else have you found?"

"Horses out back," Sevolno said, leading the way there. "Two killed with a sword. One of them obviously damaged a leg, so maybe both of them did, and they had to be put down. Three saddles left on the rail. Maybe there were more horses, and the swordsmen who killed the sorcerers took them and rode away with them, you think?" He pointed. "Two more recently dead sorcerers over there. We may find some more if we keep looking."

Wallie stared at the gentle brown hills behind the little town. Five canteens, three saddles, two dead horses, four bodies. It was hard to make the numbers fit. On Earth good horse country usually meant limestone, to provide calcium for strong bones, but limestone was often porous and poor at retaining water. Somewhere out there, he hoped, Addis was still alive in the hands of his kidnappers. Vixini might be only a few hours behind them, if he was still functioning. The only way to cross that griddle in midsummer would be to travel by night.

"Have you looked in the wells?" he asked.

Sevolno scowled at being found wanting. "Not yet, my lord." He dispatched a Third with a gesture. The man ran over to the nearest well, whose windlass had been removed and, presumably, burned. Horses drank like whales and it would be easier to have wells close to these paddocks than drag water from the River. He peered down the shaft, which couldn't be very deep, for the water table would be level with the River.

He came running back with his face almost green. "There's something down there, my lords. I think… It may be dead children!"

Wallie nodded. River water was drinkable, but the poisoned wells would make it harder to assemble an army here, and Plo was a long way away. Every watering hole would have been treated the same way.

"How long will it take us to round up enough horses to send out a scouting party?" he asked Yoningu, who had rejoined the group. "And get them here? We'll have to rig a derrick to hoist them out of the ships, or else clean out that ramp."

"A week?" the Seventh said grumpily. "Four days minimum."

"You have one day maximum. At least three horses, six better, by sunset tomorrow."

"Aye, my lord. Who d'you think were the swordsmen who killed all these sorcerers?"

"Just one swordsman," Wallie said. The boots were the message. He had a lump in his throat.

"One swordsman against four sorcerers armed with thunder weapons?"

"Vixini. He was enough. Funny, I used to think he was too easygoing to be a swordsman."

"With respect my lord," Yoningu said, "I don't know why you bothered to collect an army. That son of yours seems capable of handling the whole war by himself. And I congratulate you wholeheartedly on his courage."

The listeners chorused their agreement, for that was the greatest of compliments to a swordsman. Courage could only be taught by example.

Courage was not necessarily enough. Vixini had cut down two men, shot a third, and throttled a fourth. Then he had ridden off, still searching for his stolen protégé. But there was a hostile army ahead of him and he had lost a lot of blood.

* * *

By evening, Soo was almost habitable again. The priests had tidied up the bodies, giving them to the River and returning their souls to the Goddess. Swordsmen had dragged the dead animals to the river bank and disposed of those corpses too. They had also cleaned out some of the buildings well enough to make them usable as long as the weather stayed dry.

Liege Lord Shonsu was sitting on a keg outside the sorcerers' now-deserted lair, staring glumly at the River and contemplating failure. He had begun this war in the belief that the gods were appointing him their general because he would do a better job than Nnanji. Assuming that gods did not make mistakes—while not denying that they might get outwitted or outbid by other gods—then he had either misread their message or he had just proved that he was a complete idiot. Or both. Nnanji would have gone by the sutras. While he might have lost battles against sorcerer firearms, he would not have dug himself into the bottomless pit that Wallie had.

Oh, Wallie had known enough to avoid a few minor mistakes, but what did he do now? Ships had gone back to Ivo to collect as many horses as the garrison there had been able to assemble and could be loaded aboard. So in a day or two he would be able ride out with a mounted patrol. Every well in town had been poisoned with corpses, mostly children, who would not jam in the shafts. The obvious conclusion was that the sorcerers had also poisoned all the water between here and Plo. An enemy ruthless enough to wipe out a village would have no scruples about letting wild horses die of thirst. It was midsummer. An army could not march far without water, certainly not if it might have to fight at the other end. Water was heavy.

What galled him most was that he had no one to blame except himself. He had been in too much of a hurry, and he had tried to fight an enemy who knew his every move and whose communications moved fifty times as fast as he could. Had he known about the jungle between Tro and Ki Mer, he would not have come that way. Had he known more about the Mule Hills he would have seen how easily the sorcerers could block his access. He could see no alternative now except to call off his attack and start over, using another approach, and that would advertise to the entire Tryst that he had been outwitted.

A pair of crows started a screaming match over some tasty morsel that one of them had found. If there had been ravens, they had left, leaving the leftovers to lesser vermin like crows. There were scores of crows in Soo at the moment, cleaning up the last traces of the massacre. They were strutting around everywhere...

"Begging your pardon most humbly, my liege," Yoningu said, looking out the window, "but you seem to be sitting on the high-ranks' supply of beer."

Wallie jumped. "What? Oh, I was just keeping the sun off it so it didn't get too hot."

He rose and stared once again at the crows. They were his answer. Now—at last!—he read the message the gods had been trying to send him. At last, and perhaps too late.

CHAPTER 5

CLOSE TO SUNSET, ADDIS WAS PRODDED AWAKE, given a meager drink of water, and told to saddle his horse. He felt he ought to refuse, but he was too weak and befuddled to try. The fact that his escort seemed in little better shape than he was did nothing to comfort him. The horses, now revived by drinking from the poisoned pool, might sicken and die later, but Addis might not have much "later" to look forward to, so he was tempted to scramble down the slope and drink his fill. Perhaps fortunately, Capn ordered him to mount up before he could decide.

The last thing the swordsmen did was set the hut on fire. No doubt they wanted to deny even that tiny scrap of shade to the Tryst when it came this way, but they were also denying it to the sorcerers they had left behind in Soo.

"Move!" Capn barked. "We've got a long way to go yet."

Vixini awoke as the sun was setting, emptied his last canteen, saddled up, and set off on the last leg of his journey. He was well aware now that his carcass was more likely to feed vultures than piranha; he just hoped that he would not be able to notice the difference. He had certainly lost the trail, so the best he could do was keep the Dream God at his back and head south.

As twilight began to fade, he saw smoke—far away and well to west of his route—but there had been no thunderstorms, so fire meant people. Whether good people or bad people didn't matter now. He turned in that direction. The brighter stars were appearing, and he could use the Southern Triangle as a better marker than the Dream God.

It took his horse an hour to take him close enough to smell the smoke and see that it came from a grass fire, little flames creeping northward as a southerly breeze urged them on. He followed the trail back to its source and found a burned-out shed, whose embers still glowed. The rest of the ruins had been destroyed much earlier, and he dared hope that he had stumbled on traces of Addis's kidnappers. They could not be many hours ahead of him.

Each on his own feet, man and horse slithered eagerly down to the water. The horse drank greedily. Vixini balked at the sight of the mules' ballooned corpses floating there like grotesque fish. Knowing he must have water or die, he used his sword to dig himself a tiny well in the sand a foot or so from the pool edge. As muddy water seeped into the hole, he sent a brief appeal to the Goddess that She would keep it free of poison, then began scooping it up with his hands. Nothing had ever tasted better.

Now... How many hours was he behind Addis, and which way had he gone? The ground was much drier here than it had been around Soo, and he couldn't afford to wait for daylight to hunt for tracks.

Just when Addis was certain he must go to sleep and fall off, horses whinnied. Capn called for his men to halt as a band of horsemen came galloping out of the night. Swordsmen! Addis saw ponytails and sword hilts and his heart leaped with joy.

A voice rang out in challenge. "Thirteen twelve five?"

"Twenty-four, seven, twenty-five." Capn had halted his horse right next to Addis's. "We don't want any nasty accidents, hostage."

One of his flunkies moved in on the other side. Between them they stuffed a rag in Addis's mouth, wrapped another around his head to hold the gag in place, and then pulled a bag over his head. They must have had those ready to hand.

Capn spoke briefly with whoever was in charge of the guard, but Addis could not make out what was said. The journey resumed, up a gentle slope, down another. Addis heard muffled voices, smelled latrines, wood smoke, and cooking odors. A good swordsman being led through the enemy's camp ought to take note of everything so he could report it all when he escaped and returned to his mentor, but this one couldn't see anything, and nothing he heard made sense. Besides, he had very little hope of ever returning to Soo, let alone Ivo. He could still not remember what had happened there, but he knew that Vixi had almost certainly died trying to defend him. If Shonsu had any sense he would have turned around and set off for home by now.

There was no point in keeping his eyes open inside the bag. It was easier to let them stay shut and rely on the motion of the saddle to keep him awake, or almost awake.

He was told to dismount. Then his hands were tied in front of him and a noose put around his neck so he couldn't run away—hot chance of that happening! He was loaded into a cart, where there was straw for him to lie on. Bliss...

Some time in the night he was shaken awake, and marched along a jetty to a ship. The bare deck was less comfortable than the straw, but with his ankle tied to a rail, that was where he had to stay. He went back to sleep.

As dawn prepared to make its appearance, Vixini's horse stumbled and stopped. He had been riding in a stupor. Shaken awake by the sudden cessation of motion, he realized what was happening and slid from the saddle. His own legs almost buckled under him, while the horse sighed heavily, as if to indicate that he should have done that long ago. Then it lay down and died.

He knelt, cut an artery and sucked out as much blood as he could. At least it removed the awful taste in his mouth, although the replacement was not much better. Now he was bloody outside and in.

Where was he? The ground looked much the same in every direction, but dawn was going to emerge to his left, so he had still been heading more or less south. He couldn't last much longer unless he found water soon.

There being no further reason to linger, he started walking. Or stumbling. Or even staggering. After a while he saw that he had a shadow. Swiftly the World grew brighter, and a lark began to sing overhead. The grass all around here had been burned, and soon he was dusted all over by soot blowing in the wind. The ragged peak of RegiKra stood majestic along the horizon.

He wondered how long he could keep walking. This was definitely the final lap. If he lay down, he would never rise again.

The sun was above his left shoulder. Off to his right, roughly southwest, brilliant fires flamed along the horizon. Huh? Whatever was happening there was manmade, and human life meant water, so he turned and dragged his boots in that direction. Before long he realized that he was seeing sunlight reflected off bronze cannons. Furthermore, he had been noticed and eight horsemen were galloping in his direction.

He wasn't alone any more.

There was a proverb about buying a lion to get rid of the mice.

CHAPTER 6

VIXINI STOPPED AND WAITED, AND IN A FEW moments he could make out seven brown kilts and one red. In a few more there were horsemen all around him.

"Your name and allegiance, swordsman?" the Fifth demanded. He was young for his rank and had a hard smartness about him that Vixini found encouraging. As long as everything was done by the sutras, he should not be in much trouble. On the other hand, if these were the sorcerer allies who had massacred Soo, then he had fallen in the midden.

He tried to speak and produced only a croak.

The Fifth smiled sympathetically and handed over his own canteen. Vixini drained it, then handed it back, wiping his mouth with his right hand. His bandage reminded him that he was covered in dried blood. That could not look good. He reached for his sword.

"Leave that! Just answer my question."

"My name is Vixini, protégé of Filurz of the Fifth, and I am sworn to the Tryst of Casr."

The Thirds exchanged glances.

"I am Malaharo of the garrison of Fex. Whose blood is that, Swordsman Vixini?"

"Mine, Master Malaharo."

"How did you get here and why did you come?"

"My horse died under me some hours ago. I rode there

from Soo and am now walking, as you see. My protégé was kidnapped by some sorcerers and I am looking for him."

This time all eight exchanged glances. They did not look happy.

"Alone?

"Quite alone."

"Aren't there sorcerers at Soo?"

"There were. They attacked me, so I killed them."

"All of them?"

"Four. That was all I could find."

His captors did not seem happy to hear this, either, which was odd. Vixini was quite proud of it.

"I will treat you as a witness," Malaharo said, "if you swear to abide by Sutra 243."

That was generous indeed. Vixini would not be blindfolded and could keep his sword, although he mustn't draw it without permission. "I so swear. Thank you, master."

Malaharo told his two smallest men to double up and provide Witness Vixini with a mount. He was so weak that he needed help to mount. They closed in around him and escorted him up the slope toward the cannons.

The makeup of the squad was interesting. Malaharo wore two ribbons on his right shoulder strap, one violet and one green, plus a blue one on his left, meaning he was sworn to a mentor who was sworn to a Seventh. His own protégés would wear violet, green, blue on the right, but only two of the Thirds did. The others wore an assortment of colors, although the highest rank was always either violet or red. Two Thirds also had a colored flash on the left shoulder to show that they had sworn protégés of their own. The Tryst of Casr used the same ribbon system, but would assign a patrol duty like Malaharo's to one man and expect him to use his own followers, making up any shortfall by borrowing from one or more other seniors. That Pollex was doing otherwise suggested that he had doubts about his counter-tryst's loyalty.

As Dad often said, a swordsman bound by the blood oath

must obey orders, but he didn't have to enjoy doing so, and that could make a big difference to how well he performed his duties—designating Vixini a witness and not a prisoner, for example, might be a form of protest.

Nothing in Sutra 243 said a witness couldn't look. Vixini looked. He saw plenty. The line of eight bronze canons along the crest of the rise was terrifying. An army on foot could not possibly maneuver around them for a flank attack as fast as they could be turned to counter it. Even cavalry might not be mobile enough.

From that slight ridge the land sloped gently down to the River, a mile or so away, with the faint smudge on its far bank likely Plo itself. Between guns and river bank stood the camp of the counter-tryst: rows and rows of tents, hundreds of them, with flags, latrine pits, and smoking cook fires. A camp that size must billet thousands of men. Dad had expected to bring seventeen or eighteen hundred with him, but unless those tents were bluff, Kra had assembled many more than that, without even counting the cannons. The inhabitants were eating breakfast, scores of men lined up to receive sizzling plates of ribs and loaves of fresh bread. Vixini realized that he was starving.

He was taken before a Sixth who looked very much like Filurz—short, wiry, and mean. He was sitting outside his tent, gnawing meat and quaffing beer, while scowling at having his feast interrupted. His shoulder flashes showed that he was Malaharo's mentor, and Malaharo addressed him as Honorable Impendoro. He told Malaharo to interrogate the "spy" and listened without interrupting his meal.

Vixini repeated what he had said earlier. He claimed that he had a duty to come to his protégé's rescue, and hinted that all honorable swordsman had a duty to aid him in this. There was some sutra to that effect, but it was higher on the list than he knew so far, and he could see the hints bouncing off the Sixth like hailstones.

He refused to answer questions about Dad or the Tryst, citing Sutra 175, "On Secrecy". This did not go down well. A lot of middle ranks had gathered around to listen, and the Sixth seemed to become aware of them at that point. Perhaps sutras were about to become embarrassing. He drank beer, wiped his mouth on his arm, and stood up.

"Bring him," he said. "Have the rest of you got nothing better to do?"

Vixini had. He needed to eat two large breakfasts, drink two buckets of beer, and sleep for a week. And then find Addis.

The headquarters of the counter-tryst was marked by a line of three larger tents, each flying a colored flag: violet, red, and black. Soon the senior officers assembled on chairs and stools to inspect the witness, or prisoner: two Sevenths and five Sixths for the swordsmen, a Seventh and two Sixths for the sorcerers. No one offered Vixini a seat.

An even larger audience than before had collected behind him to audit the proceedings. Perhaps they were all bored, waiting for the war to start, but Dad wouldn't have tolerated such slackness. He would have set them all to work—unless, of course, they were to be shown something important, like how to interrogate a spy.

The only ones who mattered were the three Sevenths. It took very little talk before Vixini had worked out that the red-ribbon swordsman was Pollex, reeve of Plo, and the violet was Ozimshello, reeve of the twin city of Fex. The sorcerer must be the grand wizard of Kra. Vixini was undoubtedly prejudiced against Pollex already, but he found something repellent about the man, and every time he opened his mouth he seemed worse. He was well built, but he had coarse features and a contemptuous manner. Ozimshello was older and quiet-spoken. Any love lost between the two of them was unlikely to turn up soon.

Pollex listened with a sneer to Vixini's third telling of his story.

At the end he said, "You're a spy. And if you weren't when you were brought in, you know far too much now to be allowed to leave. Who fancies a little sword practice to start the day?"

"Wait!" said the grand wizard, if that was who the

sorcerer Seventh was. "Tell us, spy, what is the name of this protégé you are chasing so diligently?"

Sutra 175 forbade a protégé to discuss his mentor or his mentor's business, but it did not restrict a mentor's rights to say anything he liked about his protégé.

"With respect, my lords, that is immaterial. I would do the same whoever he was."

The sorcerer chuckled. "But I want to know his name." Obviously he already knew the answer.

"Do your men kidnap many novices without even asking their names?"

"Insolence?" the sorcerer purred. "Defiant to the end? How touching! This boy's protégé, my lords, is Addis, son of Nnanji, who is currently on his way to Plo as a personal gift from our god to King Arganari."

Pollex scowled at being this upstaged before an audience. Regardless of crafts, putting three Sevenths together was just asking for trouble. "What would his Majesty want with a novice swordsman?"

"Revenge for his own son's murder, many years ago. But what matters more at the moment, my lord, is that this boy, his mentor, your prisoner, is Shonsu's son."

"What? You sure of that?"

"I am always sure."

"Then we must send his head back to Soo in a barrel of salt," Pollex said. "Or should we first torture him for a day or two to see what we can learn from him?"

The silence that followed was poisonous. It was one of Ozimshello's protégés, Impendoro, who spoke up. "With respect, my lords, Master Malaharo, my protégé who apprehended this man, granted him the status of witness under Sutra 243. It was an error of judgment, but it does concede the prisoner certain rights."

Vixini didn't think it was an error of judgment at all. It might have been a minor act of mutiny, but he was comforted to learn that the army of Plo and Fex, while it might have massacred the defenseless civilian population of Soo, had not totally lost its dedication to the ways of honor. He was also starting to suspect that the Fex portion was much less enthusiastic about this war than the Plo contingent.

"See that he is punished," Pollex snapped. "Shonsu's son? Now we know how he got three facemarks before his milk teeth fell out. Swordsmen, we are gathered here to slaughter the Tryst of Casr. Who volunteers to begin the butchery by killing this Daddy's pet?"

Vixini turned to look over the crowd behind him, which comprised many hundred swordsmen, but also many short-haired civilians and a scattering of hooded sorcerers. After a moment a hand went up, and then a dozen or so more: the toadies, the thrill seekers. Vixini could have mentioned that he was bound to the Tryst of Casr by the third oath, which carried an onus of vengeance, so anyone who killed him would be marked for death, but that would have sounded like begging for mercy.

"Adept Morgo!" Pollex announced.

A lanky young Fourth squirmed his way out of the crowd and saluted. A single red tag on each shoulder showed that he was a direct protégé of Pollex and mentor to at least one junior.

"Challenge this man and kill him. If asks for the grace, refuse."

Morgo smiled. "Aye, my lord! And if he offers the abasement?"

"Refuse, of course. I want his head."

Some spectators muttered angrily. A man challenged by a higher rank had the right to offer the abasement, which involved horrible things like cutting off his own ponytail, breaking his sword, and publicly eating dirt. Vixini would never consider it a preferable alternative to death.

Morgo smiled again. He turned to Vixini and made the sign of public challenge, so simple even a civilian would guess what it meant: two index fingers crossed like engaged swords. He was probably ten years older than Vixini; Pollex would not have chosen him unless he was a superb fencer.

Vixini mirrored the gesture back to him in acceptance. "I don't want the grace," he snapped. Hunger always made him irritable, and if he was going to be challenged to death, then he would much rather it begin now than three days from now. "Who will be my second?"

He was bone weary, dried out, and desperately hungry, but he was not going to try to weasel out of this. He didn't want to die. Life was one long romp, every day a fresh joy, but his duty to Dad, to himself, and to all his friends, demanded that he stay true to his oaths. He would show these renegades how an honorable swordsman died.

Silence. They all knew that they were about to witness an execution, and to counter the will of one's liege lord was outright folly.

"Looks like you will have to manage without one," Pollex said.

Malaharo stepped forward. "I will be Swordsman Vixini's second." He handed Vixini his canteen again. It had been refilled.

"You are true to the code, master," Vixini said loudly, as he pulled out the cork.

"Then I will second Swordsman Morgo," Reeve Pollex announced, rising.

The duties of seconds were listed in Sutra 517, the most important being that together they could declare a draw or call off the match, but there would be no mercy here today.

Reeve Ozimshello stood also. "You appear to have been wounded, Swordsman." He was offering Vixini an out, for the grace could not be denied to a wounded man.

"Nothing serious, my lord." With a flick of his shoulder blade, Vixini flipped his sword hilt over to the left.

"Ambidextrous, like your father? Many times I have enjoyed hearing the famous epic, *How Shonsu of the Seventh fought Boariyi of the Seventh for Leadership of the Tryst of Casr.*"

"I always strive to be like my father, sir, yes." Dad detested that epic. Doggerel, he called it.

"Good luck," the reeve said loudly. "See fair play, Master Malaharo."

The spectators had been busy in the meantime, urged

on by the middle ranks. The crowd had been pushed back to clear a larger killing ground, which was being roughly outlined by a border of tables, chairs, pillows, and even spare boots. It seemed the entire army had gathered to watch a swordsman die.

The duelists and their seconds stood in the center. Vixini handed the canteen back to Malaharo and drew his sword. Morgo drew his. He had a narrow, hungry face with a sourly twisted mouth, but his eyes were shining joyfully. Some men enjoyed killing, even craved it, as if it had become an addiction for them, and it was a safe bet that Pollex had chosen Morgo so that there would be no scruples at the end, after Vixini began to bleed. Only very rarely was a single wound enough kill a man in a duel.

Administering the coup de grace even to a horse was bad enough.

The fencers saluted. Normally Vixini would not be overly worried at the prospect of fighting a Fourth. Even sour old Filurz admitted that he was a very good Third. On the ships coming from Casr, he had won at least one point against every Fourth aboard and had been able to beat a few of them consistently. Normally he would rank his chances of drawing first blood against an unknown Fourth at better than even. Normally. The last three days had left him a physical wreck, and first blood would mean nothing in this match.

That didn't mean he was ready to give up.

Vixini said, "Now!" *Let's get it over with.*

They approached cautiously.

Morgo was right-handed. Vixini's right arm was throbbing and swollen, his fingers no longer working as they should, but he was just as nimble with his left. Dad had always insisted that he practice equally both ways.

Normally he would play an older man for his endurance, because wind was the first thing to go, but he was so close to collapse himself that he must gain a quick victory if he were to have any chance at all. Fortunately lefties always had a slight advantage against right-handed opponents, because they got more practice fighting cross-wise than the orthodox did. Morgo was bound to be cautious at first, another reason to try for a quick decision.

Morgo lunged, Vixini parried at quarte, but did not riposte. Morgo lunged again, a little more confidently. Vixini parried again, retreated a pace. And again. The next time he parried recklessly at tierce and cut at Morgo's arm. He felt the contact even before he saw the blood. Morgo jumped back, staring in outrage at the cut. It would not disable him, but it would shake his confidence.

"Yield?" Malaharo called.

"Refused!" Pollex retorted, predictably.

"Oh, take him away and bring me a fighter!" Vixini yelled. "Is this capon the best thing you can find? I'm a rank lower and dead on my feet and he can't do any better than that? I've known grandmothers who could—"

The audience was supposed to think he was rousing Morgo to attack, and in this case Morgo himself was definitely part of the audience. But an instant before he began to move, Vixini lunged *passata-sotto*, full length, using his whole height and reach, trying to breaking his fall by hitting the ground with his right hand. Morgo could not have expected a strike from such a distance, and Vixini's blade stabbed into his liver. He cried out and crumpled, dropping his sword, hands clutching at his belly as blood jetted from the wound.

Someone started a cheer, and many voices echoed it. Vixini scrambled to his feet, but the World spun around him.

"Yield?" Malaharo called again.

Pollex stared at his fallen champion for a moment before he said, "Refused."

Morgo was beyond hearing, let alone resuming the fight. Although Vixini was upright, his abused right arm throbbed wildly and was probably bleeding again. He sheathed his sword and went back to Malaharo, holding out a hand for the canteen.

"The fight is not over, swordsman," Pollex shouted.

"Yes it is."

"Are you afraid to kill him?"

"I already did. If he asks me for the Return, then I will oblige him."

But Morgo was unconscious. Four Thirds wearing twin red flashes came forward to carry the dying man away.

Cheering began again. Vixini had the impression that it had been started by Reeve Ozimshello. It certainly was loudest around him, where his violet-tagged supporters were now concentrated. Pollex was scowling and his red-tags weren't joining in. He raised a hand for silence

"So you aren't just your Daddy's pet, Swordsman Vixini! That was impressive fencing."

"Thank you, my lord."

"We'll have to try you a little harder. Master Malaharo, this nonsense is your fault, for invoking Sutra 243. Challenge this man and kill him."

Half the spectators laughed and half booed. The laughs were loud and the boos guarded.

The Fifth lost color. He glanced appealingly to his mentor, who just shrugged. Vixini gave up any hope that he could possibly come out of this alive without somehow managing to kill every man of the counter-tryst, up to and including Pollex himself. The onus of vengeance alone determined that. He was especially reluctant to hurt Malaharo, who had spared him the indignity of being bound, disarmed, and blindfold.

"And who will be my second this time?" He knew who would second his opponent.

"I will." Reeve Ozimshello walked into the ring.

Vixini saluted, fist on heart. "You honor me, my lord." Morgo had been one of the Plo crowd but Malaharo was a Fex man. The split in the counter-tryst was becoming clearer every minute.

Pollex had flushed bright red with anger, and that was very interesting. If Ozimshello had sworn the blood oath to Pollex, Pollex could tell him to withdraw his offer to be Vixini's second. Since he wasn't doing so, it would seem that there were two counter-trysts, not one. The division between red tags on one side and violet on the other was quite obvious now. The crowd was shrinking as the civilians of the posse made themselves scarce.

"We are ready!" Pollex shouted.

But Vixini wasn't. He had been lucky against Morgo. At the best of times he would have almost no chance against a Fifth like Malaharo, and these were the worst of times. He could barely stand, let alone fight. In a normal match he would yield right away, or do a snail, but Pollex would merely give his man a direct order to kill him, so snail was out.

For him at least.

He caught Malaharo's eye and unobtrusively moved one finger in a spiral. Did the swordsmen in this part of the World use the same jargon as the Tryst in Casr did? Would his signal be understood? Malaharo blinked, looked away, then subtly nodded, moving one finger in a spiral.

"We are ready!" Pollex shouted again.

Had Malaharo really understood what Vixini was suggesting? For a Third to beat a Fifth was not unheard-of, but it was not going to happen today. Not honestly.

"Are you ready, principal?" Ozimshello inquired.

"Ready, my lord."

"Your principal has not yet challenged, Lord Pollex."

Malaharo made the sign of challenge.

Vixini responded. He strolled forward, drawing his sword.

Blades clattered. Feet danced forward and back, with Malaharo not pressing Vixini nearly as hard as one of his rank should. Even if he had interpreted Vixini's cryptic signals correctly, could he trust his life to a man he did not know?

Yes! Just for an instant, the Fifth left himself open. Vixini nicked his shoulder. Malaharo lowered his blade and examined his cut, which was barely bleeding.

"Yield!" Ozimshello shouted.

"Offer refused," Pollex responded. "Fight on!"

Vixini slammed his sword against the side of Malaharo's head. Although he did not put anything like his full strength into the blow, it was quite hard enough to cut into the man's brain—had he used the edge instead of just the flat. Malaharo dropped and lay still. He might have a nasty bruise, but he was faking his coma.

Total silence. No one quite knew what to make of that performance. Vixini shrugged. Too weary even to sheath his sword, he dragged himself over to the Fex spectators in search of water. The laughter and jeering began.

"Yield now?" the reeve of Fex inquired.

"Refused," replied the reeve of Plo. "Master Malaharo, get up and kill that man, or I will sentence you to death for cowardice."

"You," Vixini shouted, "are a bloody turd! No one else here can tell you so, but I can, and do. As a swordsman, you aren't fit to clean out a barracks latrine. Murderer and child killer!" Gasping for breath, he sagged down on one of the stools that marked the boundary between spectators and fencers. The World was spinning, and he knew he was very close to his limits. He could not possibly expect to win a serious sword bout now. Any First could thrash him.

"This is becoming interesting!" Reeve Pollex announced, his face scarlet with rage. "Somebody drag that carrion away, and we'll deal with him later. A Third, now a Fifth! How high can Babyface the Terrible go? Honorable Impendoro, are you willing to obey my orders and kill that brat?"

"Are you scared to try it yourself?" called out a familiar voice practically at Vixini's back.

Pollex spun around to glare across at the speaker, who was the sorcerer Seventh, undoubtedly the grand wizard of Kra. "That would spoil the fun, my lord. If you aren't enjoying this, go away."

Vixini struggled to his feet, although it felt like bench-pressing an ox. He had just had a better idea. Why should he wait until the detestable Pollex found a willing executioner? While he had the chance, why not avenge Addis's kidnaping and the atrocity at Soo? Why not die to some purpose? With the last of his strength and one mighty backhand slash, he cut off the sorcerer's head.

CHAPTER 7

KRANDRAK'S HEAD DROPPED AND ROLLED.
For a moment the rest of his corpse stood there, spouting
blood high from the severed arteries, spraying everyone near.
Then it collapsed.

Pollex cried, "Krandrak!" and ran forward a few steps. "That
was murder!" The rest of the company was shocked into silence.

Well, yes, but it had felt good. What now?

"Justice, I'd say," roared the other reeve. "Not murder.
Good riddance. Swordsman Vixini, we'll give you a fair
trial and acquit you on the best excuse we can think of."

"You'll do no such thing!" Pollex roared. "That killer has
to die now."

Ozimshello whipped out his sword.

Pollex drew his.

"You dare to draw against your liege?" Pollex shouted.

"You are not my liege," Ozimshello shouted back. He
might be older, but he was equally loud. They were bellowing
across the killing ground, like challenging bulls. "I gave you
only the first oath, and that reserves my honor. My honor
was vomiting at what you were doing to Shonsu's son. I
withdraw from your command and your war, and I take all
the men of Fex with me."

The men of Fex roared their approval at the top of their
lungs.

The men of Plo jeered uncertainly.

"Treason!" Pollex said.

"Swordsman Vixini," Ozimshello said without turning to look at him, "son of Shonsu, will the Tryst of Casr accept my allegiance and that of my liegemen in the garrison of Fex?"

Vixini had no ready answer for that. In his wildest dreams he could never have imagined such a question ever being put to him and he was too tired to think straight.

"Who massacred the people of Soo, my lord? Who slaughtered the men of the Tryst at Cross Zek? Who killed the two heralds? Who had our courier swordsmen killed, and who burned eight swordsmen alive in Arbo?"

"Not me and none of my men. Reeve Pollex and his sorcerer friends."

"Then," Vixini said in what he suspected must be the most outrageous usurpation of authority in the history of the World, "I accept your allegiance to the Tryst of Casr in the name of my father, Liege Lord Shonsu, swordsman of the seventh rank."

With a roar of anger a sorcerer Third emerged from the crowd about eight feet along from Vixini and aimed a pistol at him with both hands. Before Vixini had time to accept that he was about to die, three swords came slashing down and another sorcerer died. His gun fired a shot into the ground.

That noise seemed to break the spell. Suddenly it was sorcerer-killing time again. Yells, shots, and screams of terror drowned out the seniors' shouts for order. Even among the men of Plo, men and women in hooded robes were being struck down. Honorable Impendoro grabbed Vixini and dragged him into the crowd.

"Keep your head down, you great numbskull. You want it shot off?"

Silence fell when there were no more sorcerers to kill, quickly followed by a great yell of triumph.

Pollux bellowed, "To me!" His men flooded forward.

Ozimshello began barking orders to his own forces. Then the fight was on. Vixini lacked the strength even to draw his

sword again, let alone fight anyone, but his arm was seized
again by Impendoro, Malaharo's mentor. "Come with us!
You've done enough fighting for one day."

Staggering wildly, Vixini tried to run with him, being
dragged along in a mob of about a hundred swordsmen.
Another hand gripped his other arm, and between them
they rushed him forward.

"Great sword work, lad," said his second supporter, a Third
much older than himself. "Saw your dad years ago. Knew
you the moment I set eyes on you. You fight like him, too."

Vixini lacked the breath to reply. The moment they were
clear of the tents, he realized that they were heading for
the picket lines where the horses were tethered. The fastest
runners were there already, starting to untie them. There
would be no time for saddles.

"Stay out, you hear?" the Sixth repeated, releasing him.
"That's an order."

Vixini was sworn to the Tryst, so it was doubtful that he
had to take orders from anyone who wasn't, except he had
just claimed to swear all these men in... The truth was that he
had no choice. He found a rail to drape himself on, accepting
the fact that he was almost out on his feet. He was young and
strong and, he believed, tough, but every man has limits.

Horses were rampaging everywhere. The men of Fex were
scrambling aboard bareback, sometimes falling right off
again. Already Plo men were arriving to dispute possession,
swords clashing. No shots rang out, for any sorcerers left
alive must be frantically seeking cover. If the gun crews
managed to turn their canons around, of course, they could
do enormous damage, but how would they tell friends from
foes? How did anyone? Only by shoulder tags and Vixini
didn't have any. His bloodstains and bandaged arm made
him conspicuous; Pollex's men would kill him on sight.

Even without saddle or stirrups, a swordsman on a horse
had a slight advantage over one on foot, but the men of Fex
were outnumbered. The civilians had all fled in the direction
of the River. There was a lot of dust and shouting: Plo! Fex!
Plo! Fex! Plo! Fex!...

Dad had always said that the epics made it sound simple, but real battles would be very confusing places. Fortunately Ozimshello had been the first to see the importance of the horses, so he had more cavalry while the cavalry lasted. Now he was trying to make a fighting withdrawal to the dock. Vixini doubted that there would be many left alive to board ships, even assuming there were any ships left to board. Smart captains would have cast off the moment the fight broke out. But he had better stay ahead of the fighting, so he heaved himself off the rail and began dragging his feet down the slope, struggling to stay upright. If he lay down he would pass out cold, and then what?

Then... Surely a hallucination? Men singing? Yes! They were singing the anthem of the Tryst at double time:

> *The swordsmen in the morning come with*
> *glory on their brows,*
> > *With justice on their shoulders borne,*
> > *And honor in their vows.*
> *Evil they will overcome and righteousness*
> *espouse.*
> > *Her swords go marching on!*

Several hundred swordsmen were running toward him, and Vixini knew the burly, beetle-browed Seventh in the lead. He stopped and stared as the Seventh detoured to reach him.

"Vixini!"

"Lord Joraskinta!"

"Goddess! What is going on?"

"Violet tabs good, red ones bad. Tryst and counter-tryst."

"Right. Healer! Come and take this man. Violet shoulder tabs are our lot, men... Pass it on."

For a moment longer Vixini just stood there, resisting the efforts of a healer to pull him away, acknowledging waves and grins from the army running past him. Poor Dad! After all the work he had done in the last half year, it looked like he had missed the war.

BOOK FIVE:

HOW SOME SWORDSMEN FAILED TO RETURN

CHAPTER 1

AT ABOUT THE SAME HOUR OF THE MORNING as Adept Malaharo and his men were taking his mentor into custody, Novice Addis was standing on the deck of a smelly little freighter, anchored just offshore of Plo. His ankle was still tethered, his hands tied behind him, his arms badly cramped. He was staring up at the city and the great mountains behind it.

Plo was a very big city. Addis had not lived all his life just in Casr. He'd already traveled more than most men did in all their days. For the last two summers he'd worked as a sailor on Grandma Brota's *Sapphire II*, going all the way around the RegiVul Loop as far as Ov. In the last half year he'd seen many great cities on the journey here, but Plo topped every one of them. The docks went on forever, all full of ships. The temple near the waterfront was humongously big, and its seven spires were plated with gold. That enormous castle on the hill must be where the king lived, the king who wanted to listen to him dying. That did not feel like a good idea at all.

His head had stopped aching and life would be good again if he could just escape from the sorcerers.

"Hungry?" Capn asked, appearing with a basket and a large beaker. There were sausages and fruit in the basket.

"Starving, thank you for asking." Hard to speak when his mouth was watering so much.

"You can have this if you'll swear not to make any trouble or try to escape."

The part about not making trouble was all right. But not trying to escape was not.

"Stuff it." Addis went back to admiring the view.

"You're a stupid, stubborn brat."

"You're an asshole."

Capn laid down the food and drink and untied the prisoner's hands.

"No promises," Addis said, flexing his arms at last.

"No promises at the moment, but you're going to find the trip up to the palace a lot less comfortable without them." The sorcerer leaned back against the rail to watch the prisoner eat, as if he thought Addis might untie his tether and leap overboard.

Addis sat. He ate greedily, being careful not to look at the nail. It was a large, rusty nail, almost a spike, but not so big that he couldn't hide it in his fist if he got the chance. It was bent. Someone had thrown it away in disgust and it lay in a corner of the deck, out of reach as long as his ankle was tethered. If he could get that, he would have a weapon—not much of a weapon, but better than bare hands.

He ate everything, which wasn't very much. Capn tied his hands behind him again before removing the basket and mug. Sly assholes were the worst sort.

A man in a dinghy hailed the ship and then came alongside. He bore sailor facemarks, but the way he and Capn spoke to each other suggested that they were well acquainted. There was no use asking him for help, but when Capn dropped him a rope ladder and he climbed up, he left the boat tied but unattended. That looked promising.

Capn went below. Another of his gang came to untie Addis. He was a big man, probably more blubber than muscle, but the bigger they are, the harder they fall. It was a long time since Swordsman Helbringr's martial arts lesson, so Addis didn't try anything fancy. He rammed two fingers at the man's eyes and kicked the back of his knee. The man went down with a crash, but he caught hold of Addis's ankle as he tried to run. Addis fell headlong. He tried to bring a foot around to kick his opponent's nose in, but the man was too strong for him, and no stranger to roughhousing. He dragged Addis to him and slammed a fist in his face, knocking all the fight out of him.

"Stop that!" Capn said, coming up the ladder.

"Little slug tried to get away from me."

"Of course he did. Put this on him." He had brought a white sorcerer robe.

Addis didn't try to resist as they dressed him up as a novice sorcerer. He didn't have to open his hand, though—the one now clasping the nail.

"Look down there," Capn said, pointing at the dinghy.

Addis looked. "What about it?" But he could guess that he was supposed to see the barrel in it.

"That's how you're going to travel unless you promise to behave yourself. We'll gag you, bind you, and nail you up like salt fish. And when we get you to the palace we'll roll the barrel down off of the cart, just as if that's what you are, understand?"

"What do I have to promise?"

"Swear on your honor as a swordsman that you won't cause any trouble."

Addis thought about it. "On my honor, I so swear," he said reluctantly. Escape hadn't been mentioned this time. What the sorcerer thought of as making trouble, he would consider to be getting out of trouble, so they disagreed on what had just been agreed. And if Capn was so worried that he might escape, then there must be a reasonable chance that he could.

He was a good little boy after that, obeying orders. He made no protest as they gagged him and pulled his hood forward so the gag didn't show. He climbed down into the dinghy and sat there, enjoying the view as it was rowed to a jetty. He climbed up on the dock and went where he was told, never straining at the tether that Capn held.

He waited obediently until the horses arrived, and then

mounted the one provided without fuss. He let them tie his wrists to the pommel of his saddle and his ankles to his stirrups. The floppy, oversized robe with its oversized sleeves hid all the bonds. They set off with him surrounded by six sorcerer Thirds, led by Capn in red.

After last night's sleep and a good breakfast he was feeling much better today, whichever day this was. The hood annoyed him as they rode through the city and up the long hill to the palace, because it limited what he could see. He was awed by the beautiful buildings and wide streets. The big plazas sported gigantic trees, marble fountains, and laughing children. The adults all seemed healthy and busy, and beggars were rare.

He kept looking for swordsmen but couldn't see any. Probably they were all across the River in the army he'd seen yesterday. Had that been yesterday? Didn't matter. It felt like a week since he'd been snatched in Ivo. He found no chance of escape before the little procession reached the top of the great rock and approached the castle gate. There were plenty of people going in and coming out, and at last he saw swordsmen. About six Thirds were supposedly guarding the door, but they weren't paying much attention to who went in or out, being more interested in chattering to one another or pretty girls.

As his horse neared the archway, Addis stuck the nail into its back and scratched it as deep and far as his bonds allowed. The horse screamed in pain and reared, jerking its reins out of Capn's hands. Addis ripped it again, so it tried to bite him. It bucked and broke free, kicking and protesting. People scattered.

He hoped the guards were watching now. He couldn't look to see, for it was as much as he could do to stop having his neck broken in all the bouncing. It was more than he could do to stay in the saddle. He slid. He couldn't fall to the ground, but he did fall sideways, one leg bent beneath him, one straight out, and his hands still tied to the pommel, where the horse was pouring blood.

Men rallied around and calmed the horse. They went to lift Addis upright and discovered the problem.

"What's all this?" said a guard, coming to see. He saw the facemark, and that was all that was necessary.

He pushed Addis's hood back. No ponytail, but a lot more hair than any other craft allowed. He untied the gag.

"Help me! I'm a swordsman and I've been kidnapped!"

Nothing wrong with his lungs. Should have been a herald.

More guards came running. One of them blew a whistle. Capn tried to bull his way through with the horses, and that was an even worse idea, because out came the swords.

"Down!" roared the swordsman who had his sword point at Capn's ribs. "Dismount!"

The sorcerers were forced to dismount. Addis was untied, but stayed where he was, astride his trembling, hard-done-by horse.

A swordsmen Fifth arrived, an older man almost as big as Shonsu, with a grizzled ponytail. A master swordsman wouldn't take any crap from a sorcerer of any rank. He said, "What's all this?"

Looking down at him from his perch, Addis said, "I am Novice Addis and I was kidnapped by these civilians. They took my sword and brought me here against my will."

"What's the bruise on your face?"

"They hit me when I try to escape."

"Wait!" Capn shouted. "This boy is wanted by King Arganari himself. He ordered Grand Wizard Lord Krandrak to bring this boy to him."

The sorcerers were now so outnumbered that each one was standing on tiptoe with a drawn sword under his chin and another at his back. Beautiful!

"Did he now? Well you're not wearing enough facemarks to be the grand wizard, so which shit heap are you?"

Growling the words, Capn made the salute to an equal.

The swordsman acknowledged, using hand signals because there wasn't room to swing his sword around properly. His name was Alacrimo. "Now, then. First of all, this complainant isn't a *boy*, he's a swordsman. Only swordsmen arrest people and that specially goes for other swordsmen. So if the novice is summoned to the king, then the palace guard will take him there."

"This is no honorable swordsman. He swore on his honor that he wouldn't try to escape."

"*I did not!*" Addis yelled. "I swore I wouldn't make any trouble. I've not *been* making trouble, I'm trying to get *out* of trouble!"

Master Alacrimo seemed to have trouble controlling his smiling muscles. "Makes sense to me."

"You are making a big mistake, swordsman!"

To address a master by the name of his craft was as good as spitting on him. Alacrimo swelled even larger. "No, *sorcerer*, you have made a mistake. You are under arrest on suspicion of kidnaping. Put your hands on your heads, all of you!"

He turned to look up at Addis. "Tell me briefly how you came to be there, novice."

"I was in Ivo, about three days ago, maybe four, I've lost count. I went with my mentor to buy new boots. The next thing I remember, I was a prisoner in a boat with Master Capn and other men, and I had the grandad of all headaches. I'm afraid they must have killed my mentor, because he wouldn't have let them take me. They took me to Soo and brought me here on a horse and across the River."

"And what did you see on the other bank from here?" Alacrimo asked narrowly.

"A big army camp. They're waiting to repel the Tryst. They've killed everyone in Soo and left the bodies for the scavengers."

"Didn't know about Soo, but the camp is right."

"And I saw swordsmen taking orders from sorcerers!"

The listening swordsmen growled like angry dogs. One muttered, "That damned Pollex!"

"None of that!" the big man said. He held out a hand to help Addis dismount. "Freckles, take these suspects to the charge room, strip those gowns off them and lock them up. You come with me, Novice Addis."

Life was improving by the minute. As Addis walked away with Alacrimo, he heard Capn's protests turn into the sort of noise a man makes when punched in the kidneys. It was very pleasant not to be tied up, and even to feel the old familiar feeling of walking over horse dung in bare feet. The entrance to the palace was huge and bustling with people. They ought to have clouds under those ceilings.

"Now you tell me just why his Majesty would want a novice swordsman abducted?"

Addis had already decided to trust Master Alacrimo, if only because they had much in common, specifically a strong dislike of sorcerers.

"The king had a son who died many years ago. He was killed by my father."

The swordsman stopped dead, causing several other people to veer hastily. "Your father?"

"Nnanji of the Seventh, liege lord of the Tryst of Casr." That rolled off the tongue very nicely.

"But that was... I've heard that epic sung a thousand times."

"It was a Return," Addis agreed. "Dad borrowed the seventh sword from Uncle Shonsu. Well, he's not really my uncle, but he's Dad's oath brother, so that makes him my oath uncle."

Alacrimo swallowed hard and glanced around as if checking that no one was listening, but everybody was giving him a wide berth. "Describe the seventh sword, then."

"It's just gorgeous. The hilt is a silver griffon holding a sapphire this big. And all down one side of the blade there are bare-assed heroes fighting monsters, and on the other side girls with nothing on either are playing with the same monsters. The balance is superb."

Alacrimo let out a long breath. "Like the Fourth! Right. You're still making sense. Great Goddess! The son of Lord Nnanji!"

"Eldest son. I have a sister, Nnadaro, and a brother, Tomisolaan."

"The eldest son of Lord Nnanji. And where is the Tryst?"

"I can't tell you that, master."

"No, of course you can't. I shouldn't have asked."

Addis looked up at the big man's very wide eyes. "The sorcerers said the king wants to kill me because my dad killed his son. Does he do that sort of thing often?"

"Ah." Alacrimo's weathered face closed like a castle door. "Well, lad, his Majesty is old and not in good health. But he will not be doing anything like that when I'm around. I'm acting head of the palace guard at the moment and it would offend my honor very much to see an innocent boy punished for something his father did, especially when that something was a mercy, not a crime."

Much better!

"But," the big man continued. "I'm not sure where the reeve is. Lord Pollex might not feel the same way, and he said he would be coming back today. We'd better get this over with quickly."

That sounded like a good idea.

CHAPTER 2

NOBODY ASKED ADDIS FOR HIS PAROLE AND certainly nobody suggested that he was a prisoner, but.

He was put in the care of a Third and twoSeconds. They took him to the guards' bathhouse which had hot water on tap like all good palaces should, although even Dad's didn't have it for anyone except family. They gave him a fresh white kilt, a shiny pair of boots that fit him, and a swordsman's harness. Couldn't do anything about a ponytail, because only the Goddess made those and the quartermaster was right out of them. Pity his sword had been stolen, but no doubt Master Alacrimo would issue him one. Afterwards, they meant, so Addis was still a prisoner.

A message arrived saying that King Arganari was going to receive the novice in a full court, and that would take some time to organize.

They asked if he was hungry.

About an hour later they said he couldn't possibly still be hungry, could he?

And half an hour after that he said, no, he wasn't, thank you, not any more. By then he'd learned enough to know that Reeve Pollex and his cronies were the sort of swordsmen Dad called vermin.

Most of Dad's palace would fit inside the throne room. Well, maybe not, but it was very huge and shivery-splendid, all colors, carvings, columns, and curlicues, with pictures in tiles on the floor and more pictures on the ceiling and gold statues everywhere. There were a lot of people around too, but they were barely noticeable in so much space.

Addis stood beside Master Alacrimo at the main door and stared along the great hall to where the king and queen perched on golden thrones at the far end. He glanced at the flunkies near him and then up at the big swordsman. All of them were looking grim.

Queasy moment... Too much lunch.

Addis said, "This is going to be all right, isn't it, Master?"

"It may be unpleasant, lad. The old gentleman may shout at you or call you names, but nobody's going to punish you for something you didn't do."

The king said something to somebody. That somebody said something to a herald. The herald called out, "Summon the son of Nnanji!"

Another herald halfway along the hall repeated the cry, "Summon the son of Nnanji!"

A third herald, right by the door, glanced at Alacrimo, got a nod, and bellowed, "The son of Nnanji!"

The two swordsmen set off across the plain. When they passed the herald in the middle he bawled out, "The son of Nnanji!" Addis felt offended by being presented as the son of Dad. He was a person in his own right and he had been maltreated. A little justice was what was required here.

The king was obviously very old, huddled and shrunken inside his blue robe, with a gold coronet perched askew on a bald head sticking forward like a turtle's on a neck as wattled as a turkey's. He was a priest, the seven wavy lines on his forehead made much wavier by his wrinkles. His mouth kept working as if he were chewing something, but the way his face had shrunk suggested that he had no teeth. The hands gripping the arms of his throne were skeletal and knobbly.

The queen on the other hand, was only a fraction of his age and had plenty of flesh, a lot of which was visible. Her jewels were splendid, her hair a funny fawn color. She was regarding her husband with a very disapproving expression.

Alacrimo halted about three paces from the thrones. "Your Majesty, I have the honor to present Novice Addis, swordsman of the first rank."

He thumped his chest, turned smartly, and marched off to the left.

The king was peering in the general direction of Addis with his eyes half closed and his head wavering like a corn stalk in the wind. "Is he there?" he asked in what was probably meant to be a whisper.

The queen's reply was not audible, but she was nodding as she said it.

Addis wondered if he ought to salute.

"Beloved subjects!" the old man proclaimed, in a high, shrill, voice like an axle in need of greasing. "Many years ago a great crime was committed, a great injustice was done—to me, to you—a great loss was inflicted on all of us." A priest must know how to make himself heard. "Argie... my son, Prince Arganari, who would have succeeded me as Arganari XV had he lived, was struck down most foully. He was a swordsman, a First. The Goddess had summoned him to the tryst she had called in Casr, he and members of the palace guard, including his mentor, Master Polini. They never arrived at Casr. They were despicably slaughtered by a swordsman named Nnanji. A swordsman of the Fifth murdering a mere novice, a child! For all these years I have prayed to the Mother of us all that She would one day grant me justice—grant all of all of us justice—and now behold! The son of Nnanji has been delivered into my hands. Is this not Her doing?"

He leered toothlessly around his court, as if acknowledging cheers, ignoring the icy silence that greeted his words.

"What say you to that, son of Nnanji?"

Addis was no priest but he had a good pair of lungs and he intended to defend himself from this old maniac's nonsense.

"With the greatest respect, your Majesty, the facts as I

have heard them were not quite as you imply. To start with, my father was not then a Fifth, but only a Fourth."

The king seemed surprised by that, sitting with his toothless jaw dangling.

Addis galloped ahead. "I know that's not what the epic says, but I have heard the story from Dad, and my mother, and also Lord Shonsu, all of whom were there. Apart from a few details like that, my dad says that *Nnanji's Farewell to the Prince* is the most accurate epic he's ever heard, so... Sire?" The old loon was drooling. Was he going to have a fit?

The king roused himself. "Go on! Go on!"

"Well, Sire. It was my parents' wedding night, Wheelwrights' Day." He knew that day because it always meant a family visit to the temple to give the Goddess an offering. Even if Dad wasn't in town, Mom would take them.

"Bah! It was long after that, because the sorcerers didn't prophesy it to me until Masons' Day. You're just parroting the wicked epic. It's all lies."

"*Sire!*" Just in time Addis remembered he was addressing a king who could order his head cut off, and he only had Master Alacrimo's word for it that he would not let anyone carry out the sentence. "Sire, sorcerers cannot prophesy! They send messages by pigeon, so they get to know things much sooner than anyone else does. I'm surprised it took them until Masons' Day to get the news here, to Plo."

"Go on!" The old imbecile seemed to be hanging on every word Addis spoke, so he plunged ahead.

"Well, Sire, the night was very still. And they had just completed their marriage vows when they heard swords clashing and cries coming from a boat nearby. It was the pirates who killed Polini. And they wounded your son so badly that he asked my dad to give him the Return. They'd met earlier, in a town called Tau, and he thought my dad was a hero, which he was, and—"

Brainwave!

Why hadn't he remembered this sooner?

"Before your son asked my dad to, um, Release him, he gave

him this. And when I left Casr two seasons ago to come here, my father gave it to me to return to you, because it belonged to your great ancestor Arganari, so it is rightfully yours."

No doubt the sorcerers would have stolen the silver hairclip if they had noticed it, just as they'd taken everything else except his kilt, but it had been invisible in his mop all the time, and it was still hanging in there. He brought it out and took one step toward the throne. At once swordsmen with drawn swords appeared alongside the twin thrones as if they'd sprung out of the ground. Addis froze.

A footman stepped forward to present a silver tray. Addis laid the hairclip on it, and watched as it was borne in state to the king and proffered with a bow. Arganari fumbled for it, found it, and held it up to his nose. He made a strangled noise, causing the queen to lay a hand on his arm and lean closer, looking worried.

"A token! A token of Her special blessing... Come here!"

"Sire?" Addis said.

"Come here, boy, come here so I can see you."

Addis glanced at the swordsmen nearest the king and received a grudging nod. So he went up to the throne.

"Closer!"

The king grabbed his head and almost hauled him off his feet, pulling their faces nose-to-nose close. Eyes as yellow as pee peered at Addis, scanning every pore and eyelash of him. "Yesh... yesh..." The dotard was drooling again, barely able to make words. "Yes! Knew the voice. The voice exactly. Face very like. Up! Up! Help me up, boy!"

He winced horribly at the pain as the bewildered Novice Addis helped him rise. Everyone else in the hall promptly went down on their knees, all except the swordsmen guards and the queen. Addis almost did, because Arganari was leaning so heavily on him.

"My people, let us give thanks! I have prayed diligently to the Most High that She send me a miracle, and behold, She has done so! A most wonderful miracle! A miracle to inspire minstrels for a thousand years! When were you reborn, Argie?" He thrust his right eye almost into Addis' left.

Oh, Goddess! "I was born on Shepherds' Day, your Majesty."

"Wheelwrights' Day they were married and you were born on Shepherds' Day? That fits doesn't it, my dear?"

Addis staggered as the king leaned forward to peer at his wife.

"Exactly forty weeks, I think, Sire. Yes, it fits." She looked amused, pleased. Shouldn't a wife be alarmed when her husband goes screaming wet-hen bonkers?

All the courtiers started shouting in a great storm-surge of noise, in which only a few words like "Yes" and "Right!" and "Glorify the Mother!" were distinguishable. Apparently everyone humored the senile nitwit when he had these attacks. The priest-king raised his free hand for silence.

"My people, let us praise Her!" He began to chant a hymn in a strong, if quavery, voice. Everyone else seemed to know the words. Addis did, so he joined in too, even if he did seem to be describing himself as a *manifest blessing.* His mom would not agree with that, most of the time. But his mom had nothing to do with him any more, since he was sworn, and he was beginning to think he might not see her for a very long time, if ever. He would need a new mentor... *Oh, Vixi! Why couldn't Vixi have lived to see this?*

The king demanded to be put down, and Addis managed that quite gently, he thought. Everyone else was now free to stand up. Funny, but from what he could see, just about everyone was either pleased with all this madness, or else very skilled at hiding their real feelings.

"You never could carry a tune," the king muttered, "but you're not as bad as you were last time. Come and stand at my right hand, son. Push that stupid swordsman out of the way. Beloved subjects, tomorrow we shall hold a service of thanksgiving in the temple, and adopt Novice, um..."

"Addis, Sire."

"Adopt Novice Addis as our son, with the name of Arganari."

Gods' balls! Things were moving too fast for Addis. A free gift of a kingdom was a nice thought—especially such a gloriously rich city as Plo—but to agree to things like adoption he would need permission from his mentor and his father... Except that his father was half a world away and his mentor was dead. He should certainly play along to stay out of the hands of sorcerers and Reeve Pollex. In a few weeks he could sell a few gold plates and sneak away to buy passage on the River, back home to Casr...

"But Argair, my love?" the queen murmured.

The king cackled to indicate the arrival of another Good Idea. "Oh, why yes, of course! Tomorrow we shall adopt Novice Oddis as our *heir* with the name of Arganari, and we shall betroth our beloved daughter Argair to this Eddis son of Nnanji, as a token of the friendship between him and ourselves, and a pledge of our acceptance of the Tryst as guarantor of peace to our domain of Plo and Fex. You father will accept that?" he asked, peering up at what he must be seeing as the Addis Blur.

If you can ride a pony you can ride a horse, Mom always said.

"Truly, Sire, my father, Nnanji, swordsman of the Seventh, liege lord of the Tryst of Casr, will be overjoyed to hear of this joining of his house with that of the ancient lineage of the legendary Arganari I, leader of the tryst of Xo, and he will gladly guarantee to the people of the great domain of Plo and Fex, as he does to all peoples dwelling under the protection of the Tryst of Casr, honest government and all their historic liberties."

How was that, Dad? Mom would shit sideways at the thought of any son of hers sitting on a real throne. Was it just possible that any of this might be *real*?

"Nobody," Addis concluded, "need fear the Tryst except corrupt swordsmen."

Apparently that was what they wanted to hear. The beloved subjects roared their approval. Who were all these people? Officials? Aristocratic parasites? Palace flunkies? Rich landowners or merchants? Whoever they were, there seemed to be a lot more of them than there had been at first, and they loved that last bit.

Were they going to be *his* beloved subjects, one day soon?

"The only part my father would not approve of, Sire," the heir whispered, in his first attempt to influence government policy, "is that you say you welcome the Tryst, but you have deployed an army on the far bank to repel it. Perhaps that army could be disbanded—as a token of good faith, that is?"

The king mumbled and drooled. "Pollex wanted it," he quavered.

"But, Majesty, if I may presume to make a personal comment, it may be that your subjects do not approve of Lord Pollex."

The old relic looked up at him sharply, and for a horrible moment Addis thought he had overreached himself and burst the bubble.

"Are you sure of that?"

Swordsmen taking orders from sorcerers, poisoned wells, the massacre at Soo, and all the things he had been told by the swordsmen right here in the palace—Addis was utterly certain, but people who spoke up against corrupt reeves had a very short life expectancy. That was why Dad had been trying to stamp them out, and if he could risk his life day after day for years in the quest, how could Addis do less? "I believe that he is a very evil man, Sire."

The king glanced the other way. "What do you say to that, my dear?"

The queen looked at Addis.

Addis looked at the queen. He wasn't sure how to signal *Which side are you on?* with his eyebrows, but he did his best.

She said, "I think Prince Arganari is absolutely correct, love, and very brave to speak up. Pollex is a horror, a sub-human brute. He makes my flesh creep every time I look at him. If the prince were not a very clever and upright young man, the Goddess would not have sent him to you in your time of need."

Addis couldn't have said it better himself.

Tears welled up in the tired old eyes. "Oh, Argie, Argie! How I have missed you all these years! Long, long I have waited for someone I could trust to give me honest counsel. Where is that Fifth who brought you in?"

"Master Alacrimo... um, Sire." Addis was horrified to realize that he was starting to talk like Dad already. He had spoken the name like a summons.

It was taken that way. The acting reeve marched in from the side and saluted the throne. But he was looking at Addis as he did so, and there was a gleam in his eyes that might mean... might mean several things.

"Sire?"

"Um, I am advised that Lord Pollex is not a good reeve. I hereby dismiss him. If he shows up, put him under arrest. Who is that fellow at Fex?"

"Lord Ozimshello, sire?"

"That one. Get him here and tell him he's to be reeve of Plo as well until we can, um, think about it."

Without doubt the king had just made a popular decision. The subjects roared louder than ever. The old man gaped for a moment, and then just sat there and grinned, once in a while glancing up at Addis as if to share the enjoyment. He wasn't quite the dimwit Addis had first taken him for, apart from the weird obsession that his dead son had been returned to him, and perhaps a priest could believe in prayers being answered with miracles more easily than a swordsman could.

The queen caught her husband's sleeve and whispered something. He nodded, and raised a hand for silence. "Announce her," he said.

"Her Highness Princess Argair!" boomed the herald.

Oh, all gods! In all this busy governing business, Addis had forgotten that there was a marriage involved. There's bound to be a hitch, Vixi would have said. But Old Drone, one of their tutors, had explained that royal marriages were usually diplomatic arrangements, and Addis was being treated as royalty in this madhouse. He did not want to get married yet, though, not for ten years at least. How old would she be, if she were ancient Arganari's daughter? Old as Mom? Older?

But the girl who walked in and curtseyed to the king was about the same age as Nnadaro. That was better, especially when he recalled that his sister had no interest in boys at all. Rough, smelly, and loud, she called them. Argair was a lot prettier than Nnadaro and was going to be a beauty like the queen. Maybe even have, um, a bosom like hers! At the moment she looked terrified, listening to her father explain that she was to be betrothed to this novice swordsman, this one here...

Argair looked at the new Prince Arganari in horror.

Addis winked.

Her chin shot up indignantly, then she hastily lowered her gaze and seemed to fight back a smile. He stepped forward, took up her hand, and kissed it. She blushed scarlet, the courtiers applauded. Ten years might be a bit too long to wait for the real thing. Five, maybe?

"So I win the fairest jewel in the kingdom," he exclaimed, hamming a little.

Even redder. "And I the handsomest swordsman."

"It's my eyelashes," he whispered.

She liked that.

"You have no sword!" the king exclaimed. "We can't have a swordsman without a sword! Where's that reeve?"

Master Alacrimo came forward again.

"Fetch the sword!" the king demanded. "Get it down. And you give it to him."

This was too much! First escape from death, then a mighty kingdom, a very promising fiancée, and now... *What sword did he mean?* Not...

Yes he did. Alacrimo was snapping orders to swordsmen: a gangling Third, a very brawny Second, and a wisp of a First. All three went behind the thrones. The two big ones hoisted the novice to sit on their shoulders, and then up to stand there, so he could lift the fourth sword of Chioxin free of its peg. A moment later, Master Alacrimo was down on one knee before Addis, proffering him the priceless fourth sword of Chioxin in the ritual that must be even older than Chioxin.

"Live by this. Wield it in her service. Die holding it."

"It shall be my honor and my pride." Addis took it, remembering Shonsu giving him his first sword at the assembly, half a year ago.

It was glorious, as beautiful as Dad's seventh. The guard was a gold basilisk holding a huge orange stone, but the decoration on the blade was very similar, monsters and heroes on one side, maidens and monsters on the other. There were only a couple of nicks on the edge, and the leather of the grip seemed as good as new. Stunned, he just held it and marveled for a moment.

Then Alacrimo said softly, "No honorable swordsman challenges a First, prince."

Meaning: *You can wear it safely as long as the palace guard is around.*

"Thank you, Reeve." Addis turned his back on the beloved subjects to face the thrones and salute his new adoptive parents and his fiancée.

This was turning out to be a very interesting day.

CHAPTER 3

AS ALWAYS, YONINGU HAD DONE WHAT WAS required of him. By evening, six horses had been delivered at Soo, and two of them were already laden with water skins to supply a scouting expedition. Wallie was determined to lead it in person, so he would see the ground firsthand and establish whether there was any practical way to move his army over the Mule Hills. Taking Adept Sevolno and a couple of Thirds along, he set out as the sun was setting.

Witnesses in Ivo had reported that the trail to Cross Plo ran almost directly south. If he reached the River anywhere else, he could just follow the bank northward, because Plo lay at the extreme north of a very large loop. That was assuming he didn't blunder into an opposing army first, of course.

They made good time, barely stopping, but by dawn it was obvious that there was no shade, no safe water, and virtually no cover anywhere. The Mule Hills, in fact, were not unlike the prairie of his boyhood, but they did not make him homesick for Weyback, Saskatchewan. As scenery, they suddenly became more interesting when a stray beam from the rising sun caught something shiny. Out came the telescopes. Southwest of him, three horsemen were riding northward, and the reflection had come from a sword hilt.

That was an easy decision.

After a while the Soo party's approach was noted, and

the others turned to meet them. To Wallie's astonishment, their leader was Honorable Quarlaino, whom he had last seen half a year ago, going off with Lord Joraskinta to arrange for ferry boats to transport the army over to Plo. He was accompanied by a Fifth and a Fourth, both strangers to Wallie. Smiling, Quarlaino, made the salute to a superior, sadistically drawing it out as long as he could. Wallie responded at a dignified pace.

"Well met, your honor," he said. "You have news for us?"

"Sad, sad news, my lord. I regret to inform you that you are too late. The war has been won; it is all over."

"Won by Lord Joraskinta and his gallant companions?"

"Well, we did help, but the real hero was someone else. It might perhaps—" he glanced inquiringly at his companions. "Might perhaps be an exaggeration to say he won it singlehanded?"

They shook their heads. "It would be an injustice to say otherwise," the Fifth remarked.

Wallie lowered his head like a threatening bull. "Some details, if you would be so kind?"

"I did not see personally." Quarlaino gestured for the Fifth to take up the tale.

"One of your own men, my lord. He arrived yesterday morning in a condition of extreme physical distress, tracking a missing protégé. Lord Pollex, the late reeve of Plo, declared him a spy and sent a Fourth to challenge and kill him. It was manifestly unfair, considering your, um, man's condition. Fortunately your man won in a fair fight, killing the Fourth in a memorable feat of arms.

"Pollex then sent a Fifth up against him. This was such a gross injustice that the Fifth faked a knockout rather than hurt the youngster. At that point Vi—your man, my lord, denounced Lord Pollex as unfit to shovel barracks night soil, and cut off the grand wizard's head… my lord."

"*Is he alive?*"

The Fifth grinned. "Oh, yes, my lord. Alive and well. He shamed us all! He showed us how a true, honorable swordsman should behave. A sorcerer tried to shoot him, so the swordsmen turned on the sorcerers and slaughtered them. Lord Ozimshello, reeve of Fex, then withdrew his men from Lord Pollex's command and declared his allegiance to the Tryst of Casr, which your son accepted in your name, my lord."

"The hell he did!"

"Yes, my lord. And the fight broke out. Lord Joraskinta arrived just in time to turn the tide, my lord, but the honor belongs entirely to Swordsman Vixini. Lord Joraskinta has promised to promote him to adept for his performance."

Wallie looked around the circle of grinning faces but could not see them for tears. *Vixi?* "He was always such a polite, gentle, well-mannered boy... Is there any word of Novice Addis, his protégé?"

"Not yet, my lord. We believe the sorcerers took him on to Plo or Kra, but we have no details, as yet."

Vixini a hero... But if anything bad had happened to Addis, how could Wallie ever face Thana and Nnanji?

Being summoned into the presence of two Sevenths when one had a murder charge hanging over one's head was a disquieting start to a day, and Vixini had been feeling fragile even before the message came. He ached all over and his arm hurt, trying to swell under the bandages and showing nasty red patches outside it. He was led to where the high ranks were sitting on the grass, eating standard camp rations, with only the wide gap that the rest of the army left around them showing that they were in any way special. All they wanted, they said, was to have Vixini share their breakfast, forget about formality.

There was no doubt that Lord Joraskinta was in charge. The former ruler of Ashe who had sworn to the Tryst of Casr little over a year ago, had turned yesterday's rout into victory by arriving with seven hundred fresh swordsmen. He was looking more than a little pleased with himself. Nobody else had much to be proud of. The death toll was going to be about eight hundred, when the seriously wounded died.

Lord Ozimshello, reeve of Fex, seemed older than he had

the previous day. He must be worrying about his change of allegiance and how King Arganari would react to the news. His honor might be called into question, and that could mean death for a swordsman. After the battle he had formally sworn the third oath to Joraskinta on behalf of the Tryst, so Vixini's outrageous presumption in accepting it earlier could be quietly forgotten. The survivors of the Plo contingent had waived their onus of vengeance and sworn loyalty to the Tryst instead. None of them could be held guilty for crimes they might have committed, because they had been acting under orders, but something would have to be done about their broken oaths. The priests would find a way.

Nobody need care what Lord Pollex would say to all this, because Lord Pollex was extremely dead, and just who had put so many holes in him would never be known, or even discussed. Grand Wizard Krandrak was no longer a problem either, thanks to Vixini, but that had been murder in front of thousands of witnesses.

"Between mouthfuls," Joraskinta told Vixini, "tell us where Lord Shonsu is and what happened at Soo."

Soo was not a good topic for mealtime conversation, but Vixini told his story. He was certain that Dad would be at Soo by now, and had been saved from a sorcerer ambush there by the actions of Vixini's own strong right arm. He described his journey briefly, and how he was concerned about the lack of water in the Mule Hills.

"I heard that the springs were being poisoned," Ozimshello said. "It was a despicable crime. I don't think he can risk bringing his army across the hills on foot in midsummer."

"Last night I sent Honorable Quarlaino to tell him our news," Joraskinta said. "I wanted someone he knows and will trust. He will explain that the war is won." Under his ferocious brows he actually smirked.

"What will you do about Kra?" the reeve asked.

"How serious a fight will they put up?"

"I don't know, my lord. No outsiders are ever allowed in Kra or even within sight of it. We don't know what manpower it has or what defenses."

"I haven't seen a single sorcerer since I got here."

Vixini, too, had been wondering where the sorcerers had all gone. Possibly they had been favored targets and killed out of hand, but the army had included civilians. He risked offering an unsolicited opinion.

"You could look among those priests, my lord, or the healers. All the civilians, in fact."

"Brilliant!" Joraskinta thumped a fist approvingly on his own knee. Then he explained to Ozimshello, who was looking blank, how Lord Shonsu had found facemark transfers in the assassins' gear back in Casr. "You have your father's insight as well as his fencing skills, swordsman... I should say 'Adept' because Lord Ozimshello and I have agreed to promote you one rank under Sutra 1139. Congratulations."

"Well deserved," Ozimshello agreed. "Something wrong?"

"My lords, my—I am five years too young to be even a Third. A Fourth? The men will think my father has favored me obscenely."

"Not when the minstrels have done with you, they won't!"

Oh, no! "Minstrels?"

"*How Swordsman Vixini Smote the Sorcerers in Soo,*" Ozimshello suggested.

Joraskinta chuckled ominously. "*How Vixini of the Third Avenged the Ambush at Cross Zek!*"

"*How Swordsman Vixini Ended the War of Plo with One Stroke of his Sword!* The whole gang of minstrels has been hunting for you, so we said they could have you on the boat. You do want to come across to Plo with us?"

Vixini shuddered. How in the World was he going to hold his head up in Casr if all this got around? "My lords, I *murdered* Krandrak!"

"What you did was justice for the massacres at Cross Zek and Soo. The Tryst needs a hero after this, and you are he, Adept Vixini. Lord Pollex thought to bring a facemarker. You will see her and find an orange kilt before we leave. That's an order. "

"You ended the war, Lord Joraskinta, not me!"

"That's not true," Ozimshello said. "It was your courage

and honor in facing up to Pollex that shamed us all. I realized, and so did almost everyone watching, that you were being true to the code and the rest of us were not. And yet we were standing there watching Pollex torture you. That was why I switched, and why the Fex garrison followed my lead. Many of the Plo men did, too."

"See?" said Joraskinta. "So stop being modest! That's another order."

Ozimshello laughed. "Something more is bothering you, adept?"

"Just..." Vixini said gratefully. The reeve was a perceptive leader. "Just that I owe my life to the mercy and courage of Master Malaharo. I have been looking for him to give my sincere..." No?

"I regret to tell you that he is among the fallen," Joraskinta said. The two Sevenths concentrated on eating.

After a moment Vixini worked out what was not being said—that in a sense Malaharo might be considered fortunate. Had he survived, he would certainly have had to face trial as a traitor for disobeying a direct order from his liege. Scores or even hundreds of swordsmen must have switched allegiance in the battle, but few could had turned their coats quite so blatantly as Malaharo had in throwing that fight with Vixini. The rest might escape judgment for lack of clear evidence against them. Likely it would be up to Dad to decide whether to admit such renegades into the Tryst and what must be done with them if he did not. But at least now he would be spared the ordeal of passing a death sentence on the man who had saved the life of his son.

The only orange kilts available were those that had been taken off corpses that the priests were preparing for burial, and the only one not fouled by the blood of its former owner was absurdly tight around Vixini's hips and at least a handbreadth too short. He felt like an exotic dancer.

The first part of the ferry trip across the River was torment. He could have endured the minstrels by themselves, although there were a dozen of them, all talking at once, but the two Sevenths were there also, dragging all the details out of him, and he couldn't refuse to answer their questions. Yes, he had strangled one of the sorcerers with his bare hand. Which hand? No, only one horse had died under him.

"I am not a light load," he explained.

"The giant youth," they muttered. "Vixini's mighty thews... Godlike stature..."

When they had sucked all they could out of him—and he suspected it was going to be at least eight men he had slaughtered singlehanded at Soo—they started in on Joraskinta. He did not seem to mind. No, dear Goddess, the man reveled in their attention! He lapped up their flattery.

Background? Well, he had once ruled his own realm... Lord Shonsu had sent him forward as an advance party...

Listening between the lines, Vixini gathered that all the swordsmen Nnanji had shed as he withdrew from Arbo to Rea—and indeed, every garrison along that reach—had been frantically waiting for him to return with an army. In the meantime, they had been passing information along the cities of the River, in a way only sorcerers and traders normally did. So Joraskinta had not long passed Rea when he learned that Shonsu's plan was known and Pollex was fortifying the bank at Cross Plo. Some high-numbered sutra or other allowed a swordsman to depart from his orders when conditions changed, and this Joraskinta had proceeded to do. When he received word that the counter-tryst was assembling, he prepared to attack it in the rear, hoping that Lord Shonsu would arrive on its other side as planned. Without the rebellion Vixini had inspired, his force would almost certainly have been slaughtered to a man. What right had he to preen in front of the minstrels?

In truth, it had been Ozimshello who had saved the day, but he refused to discuss his part, and the minstrels seemed to find Joraskinta not quite up to their heroic requirements. Vixini had a sickening premonition that they were going to declare him the singlehanded winner of the whole shameful mess.

CHAPTER 4

THE WIND WAS FITFUL, AND IT WAS AN HOUR after noon before the ship drew near to Plo. Plo was the biggest city Vixini had ever seen, and the most beautiful, gleaming with many-colored marble walls and shining metal roofs. The commercial docks were busy, and the captain headed for the less-used temple area. The temple, also, was the largest and finest Vixini had ever seen. He said so to Lord Ozimshello.

The reeve of Fex nodded proudly. "Second only to holy Hann. But they seem to have heard the news already. Hear the bells? See the flags? They are celebrating."

Joraskinta bristled. "How could they have heard? I gave strict orders that no ships were to leave before this one. And why would they celebrate? Hundreds of their menfolk have died. The city should be in deepest mourning."

The city obviously wasn't.

The Sevenths had agreed that the king should hear the news first. A nimble Second was sent off to the city barracks to fetch horses, and no one else was allowed to disembark. The shore was low near the temple, giving the puzzled passengers a good view across the plaza as crowds came pouring out and lined up there, waiting for something.

Soon the action was explained as Priest-king Arganari XIV the Merciful emerged, leaning heavily on two companions. He was assisted into an open carriage and the other two climbed in beside him. Then it was drawn away by eight snow-white horses, following an escort of swordsmen on black horses, while the crowds applauded louder than ever.

"The king?" Ozimshello exclaimed. "I do not understand. The last I heard, they jeered the old coot every time he left the palace. Now he has lost a war, sacrificing hundreds of lives just to save his own scrawny neck—and he is being cheered?"

The road from the temple ran straight to the River, for the River was the Goddess, before veering sharply away along the shore. The swordsmen's ferry was not moored as close as it could have been, but Vixini had borrowed the captain's telescope. He could guess that the jewel-encrusted woman beside the king must be his daughter or granddaughter, and he thought he knew the boy with them.

He just couldn't believe his eyes.

Once the horses arrived, the two Sevenths set off for the palace to report, and they took Vixini with them, because Joraskinta, too, had recognized Addis. As he acidly remarked, Vixini might have hunted through the city a long time for his lost protégé had the Goddess not arranged that "fortunate" glimpse of him. Ozimshello was looking happier, for the gossip brought back from the barracks was that yesterday he had been appointed acting reeve, replacing the dismissed Pollex. Pollex's departure explained at least some of the cheering.

Joraskinta might have forbidden anyone to tell anyone anything, but that wouldn't stop the men of the city garrison reporting everything to their chief, the acting reeve, so Master Alacrimo was at the palace gate to greet the visiting Sevenths as they dismounted. He happily confirmed that Lord Ozimshello was to replace Lord Pollex, although of course the actual transfer of power must wait until the king accepted his oath.

The palace flunkies were flustered and hence obstructive. After letting the noble lords cool their heels to the boiling point, they returned to say that his Majesty was fatigued by the service of thanksgiving, and they would be received by Prince Arganari. At that news both Sevenths turned very icy towards Adept Vixini, as if this were all his fault.

Wasn't it possible that they were being deceived by an incredible likeness? No it wasn't, because Acting Reeve Ozimshello insisted that his Majesty had only ever had one son, who had died years ago. Now he was apparently alive again. Master Alacrimo refused to discuss the royal family, but he seemed suspiciously amused about something.

After a full day as heir-elect, Addis was starting to enjoy himself. Being prayed for personally by several thousand worshipers was terrifying, but being cheered by hysterical crowds could easily become addictive. Swaggering around with a treasure like Chioxin's fourth on his back definitely was. When the king tottered off to lie down, telling him to take charge for a while, he asked the lord chamberlain what he would have to do and was told nothing.

So he settled down for a quiet luncheon with Princess Argair and told her everything that had happened at the temple. She was undoubtedly a cute child, but she seemed to have no friends of her own age, and Addis thought he would have to do something about that. She was also a little scatterbrained and more than a little greedy. She dearly wanted—'needed' was the word she used—a snow-white pony, a bodyguard of at least four handsome swordsmen, and rubies like mama's.

"You don't need rubies to make you beautiful," Addis said truthfully—at her age she would look absurd. "I certainly will not let you have any swordsmen as handsome as me, because they would all fall in love with you and I would have to fly into a jealous rage and put them to death. But your mother wants us to have a betrothal ceremony soon, so why don't I give you a white pony as an engagement present, and you can give me—" He was about to suggest a coal-black stallion and decided that would be more romantic than safe, given his modest equestrian skills. "A white horse? Then we could ride back from the temple together while the crowds cheer us."

Argair grew very excited at that and announced that he could kiss her.

Fortunately, the lord chamberlain intervened then. The lord chamberlain was a dignified, historical personage, draped in a silver chain of office and robes of a shiny blue so pale as to be almost white. With an angular face, floury complexion, and silver hair, he resembled a human icicle.

"Your Highness, the new reeve has arrived and ought to be sworn in right away."

"Can't it wait until his—I mean my royal father, feels up to it?"

"That would not be advisable, your Highness," the icicle said frostily. "Also, he is accompanied by a certain Lord Joraskinta, swordsman of the seventh rank and councilor of the Tryst of Casr, who is anxious to speak with his Majesty, but might be persuaded to report to your noble self in his stead."

That certainly spoiled the mood. Addis had a horrible premonition that Joraskinta might spoil his party completely, but it had been a wonderful dream while it lasted.

"My beloved princess," he said, "state business requires me to fly, but I look forward eagerly to our next few precious moments together."

Argair blushed furiously and simpered at the same time. Addis let the lord chamberlain escort him back to the throne room, where the sun dimmed, the temperature dropped, and grim-faced palace officials gathered around like storm clouds.

On no account must he do anything they had not advised him to do, they said. He must not vary one word from the script they were about to give him. Results could be catastrophic. His Majesty would be enraged. Addis knew roughly what his real father would retort at that point, but he wasn't Dad, so he didn't dare. He was escorted to the throne itself by a dozen grandees in shimmering robes and chains of office, sporting facemarks whose like he had never seen

before. He would sit there. The reeve-elect would approach
and give him the salute to a superior and he would—

"*Never!*" Addis said. "That is absolutely absurd. He is a
Seventh and I am a First. I am not the king yet." He hoped
that his apprenticeship would last many years, so he could
learn how the job properly. "I am only his representative.
But I am the son of Liege Nnanji and I have watched him
and Lord Shonsu perform in public thousands of times. I
will not sit on the throne. I will stand right here, beside it.
Now don't keep the noble lord waiting any longer. Go!"

They all started to argue at once.

"Stop! If you don't, then I shall walk along to the door
and greet him there."

Teeth bared and tails down, they stepped back and
signaled to the waiting heralds.

Two blue kilts appeared at the far end of the hall. As they
marched closer, Addis confirmed that the second was indeed
Joraskinta, which was a surprise and not a very welcome
one. They halted.

Before there could be any mix-ups over precedence, Addis
whipped out his glorious sword, and gave the new reeve the
salute to a superior: "I am Arganari, swordsman of the first
rank, heir to the king of Plo and Fex, and it is my deepest
and most humble wish that the Goddess Herself will see fit
to grant you long life and happiness and to induce you to
accept my modest and willing service in any way in which I
may advance any of your noble purposes."

Puzzled, the reeve-elect hesitated, then gave him the
response to an equal: "I am Ozimshello, swordsman of the
seventh rank, reeve of Fex; I am honored by your courtesy
and do most humbly extend the same felicitations to your
noble self."

Addis smiled his thanks then turned his attention to
Joraskinta. "I am Arganari, swordsman of the first rank,
heir to— *Vixi! You're alive!*"

He had registered that the tall swordsman who had
followed them in was a Fourth, and only now had noticed
his face looming over them. He barely restrained himself

from throwing himself at Vixi and embracing him. Might give people the wrong idea...

All four swordsman exploded in laughter. The palace flunkies shuddered.

"I'm alive, protégé," Vixi said in his giant-sized voice. "And so are you, I see."

"And you've been promoted!"

"So have you!"

"Slightly," Addis admitted, sheathing his sword. He tried what he hoped was a winning smile. "My lords, forgive me for bungling the formalities. I am new to this job. His Majesty is very fatigued, and told me to receive you, Lord Ozimshello, and to accept your oath in your new post as acting reeve of Plo."

Looking decidedly bleak, the Seventh drew his sword again and swore obedience and fidelity to the First. Addis accepted on behalf of the king.

"Lord Joraskinta," he said. "I am happy to see you arrive safely. Have you news of Lord Shonsu?"

"Lord Shonsu is well, so far as we know, but delayed at Soo. We do bring news, both good and bad. There was a great battle yesterday at Cross Plo. Lord Ozimshello declared that he could no longer honorably support the sorcerers and Lord Pollex, who thereupon denounced him as a traitor. For a while it seemed like the Fex contingent would be defeated, but I led in Tryst forces and we carried the day. Pollex was among the slain, as were about eight hundred others, many of them from this city. Forty-nine sorcerers were identified this morning masquerading as other crafts, and were taken prisoner. Lord Ozimshello has formally sworn loyalty to the Tryst of Casr on behalf of the swordsmen of Plo and Fex. The war is over."

Addis gulped. Great Goddess! The realm had just been turned upside down and Boy Wonder was supposed to know how to deal with this? The flunkies were aghast and probably about to explode with advice. He made a couple of fast decisions.

"Lord Reeve, your appointment as acting reeve of Plo is

effective immediately. Please see that the heralds proclaim the news around the city. We'll leave the details up to you. Keep the people calm. His Majesty will announce, um, the proper religious observances shortly. You must have many duties. We... I, I mean... I will excuse you if you wish to go and attend to them.

"Lord Joraskinta, his Majesty must be informed of the details. He will be both happy and deeply saddened. Let me take you to the queen, who can then break the news to him in private. Adept Vixini, you may accompany us. Lord Chaplain, please prepare a schedule of prayer and observances for the high priest's approval. Lord Chancellor, I will be in my quarters if you need me for anything."

The human icicle managed to bow without cracking. "I will keep your Highness informed." That probably meant that he would not disturb the king without Addis's permission. The fact that he was not raising a hundred objections might mean that he quite approved of the way the upstart was performing.

It was the work of a few minutes to turn Joraskinta over to Queen Daimea, so that she could be brought up to date and then advise her husband. Pray to the Goddess that the shock didn't kill him on the spot.

Then Addis threw open a door, ushered his mentor inside, and shut it firmly against the world.

"*I thought you must be dead, you great ox!*"

"I thought you might need help, you sleazy imposter!"

Then they did embrace, roaring with joy, pummeling each other, and dancing around the hall.

"For gods' sakes, what happened, Vixi? I know we went to buy boots for me and the next thing I remember, I was upchucking in a fishing boat. Let's go upstairs and have some wine. I've got some of the best swill here you ever tasted." He led the way to a grand staircase, leading up to a balcony. The roof was several times as high.

Vixi was gaping open-mouthed, all around and also up.

"Nice billet you've got. You could keep eagles in here, or giraffes."

"Oh, it's not all real. The gold pillars aren't solid, just gilt, peeling a bit at the edges. There's moths in the tapestries. It's all been shut up for fifteen years, see. I slept on a couch last night, my bed chamber's through here."

"You mean these are all just *your* quarters?"

"The heir's quarters. They're working on cleaning it up for me. This is my reception hall. I can either receive the unwashed down here, or make a pompous entrance down these stairs, or I can run down with hands out to greet friends informally, or I can sit on a throne up here and make them crawl up to me on their hands and knees. There's also a ballroom, a private skittles alley, and a few other things. Look here." He opened one of several doors and led the way into a room furnished with a rack of foils, a full-length mirror, and several exercise contraptions. It was obviously a gym.

"This is sad. The dead prince was a novice swordsman, like me, and this was to be his fencing room, but he never saw it completed."

Vixi demanded to inspect the topaz sword. He marveled at its beauty, its balance, the fineness of the engraving.

"I think I like it better than the sapphire," Addis said offhandedly. "I expect old Chioxin was getting past it by the time he got around to making Dad's."

"My dad's!" Vixi said, reopening a childhood argument. "The demigod gave it to my dad, and he just loaned it to yours."

"Through here is my private withdrawing room. I use it for heavy drinking and indecent parties..."

Next on the tour was the prince's bathroom, including a marble tub big enough to float a horse. "Nice, huh? Seats six."

"Hot water too?" Vixi said. "Oh, I could use that! It's been weeks."

"I can tell. You want it now, or wine and talk first?"

"All three now."

"Fine. I'll join you. Haven't had time to try it myself yet."

Addis opened the door to his bedchamber and peered in. A team of cleaners looked around in alarm. He ordered the bathtub filled. Then he took Vixi back to his private sitting room, where they could sit and sip wine and make coherent conversation. The time had come to explain to his friend and mentor a miracle he was only just starting to understand himself.

"He's a fine old boy, really. He reigned well for a very long time, but as his strength failed and his blindness closed in, he become too reliant on a corrupt reeve. He's in constant pain. He wanted no change, refused to trust advice from anyone else, couldn't understand why he'd become so unpopular. Pollex and Grand Wizard Krandrak were the ones with reason to fear the coming of the Tryst, and they poisoned his mind against it. He was obsessed by the coming failure of his line. He foresaw his orphaned daughter being forced into marriage by some ruthless swordsman. With Pollex as a model for swordsmen, that was not unreasonable. He may even have been serious about putting me to death because Dad Returned the prince. So I was fetched. He couldn't see me, but he heard my voice."

"Always a nasty shock."

"Shut up, commoner. Then I produced Angie's hairclip... As a priest, he convinced himself that his son had been returned to him by a miracle. As a king, thinking dynastically, he could marry his daughter to the son of the most powerful man in the World and the kingdom would be protected. Under the circumstances, his 'son' can marry his daughter and solve all his problems at a stroke. My Uncle Katanji always says if you can find out a person's dearest wish, then you've got them by the short hairs."

"Which you obviously did. Technically, you need my permission to adopt new parents or even marry."

"But you'll give it," Addis said happily, "or I'll have your head chopped off. Where was I? Yes, this morning he dragged me out to a roof terrace overlooking half the World and proudly showed me 'our' ancestors—Arganari the

Benevolent, Arganari the Just, and the rest of the gang. He even pointed out his own future location, and mine beyond it. That's Arganari XIV the Merciful and Arganari XV the Fraudulent. How did you wangle that orange kilt?"

"I cut off the grand wizard's head."

"*Swoosh?* Just like that?"

"He pissed me off. I've queered your promise to your dad, though. You swore to avenge what happened to him, but Krandrak was behind it all and I got to him first."

Addis drained his silver goblet and reached for the bottle. "I'll forgive you; just don't do it again. I'm thinking of hiring a reeve for my personal bodyguard. Care to be interviewed? You seem very young to be an adept, adept. What experience..."

CHAPTER 5

TWO DAYS LATER, THE SAME TWO YOUNG MEN met in that same private room with an older man, Lord Shonsu. This, too, was a happy reunion, but it had somber undertones. The king had taken badly to news of the battle and had taken to his bed. Addis was deathly worried. He was also much annoyed that the queen had taken well to Lord Joraskinta and had taken him to her bed, although Princess Argair had told him not to worry about it, because everyone knew of Daimea's shortcomings and the king didn't mind. Besides, the queen was a strong Addis supporter, seeing him as a guarantor of her daughter's future.

Addis had formally welcomed his oath uncle to the kingdom. After his meeting with Quarlaino, Wallie had sent word back to Yoningu at Soo to pay off the army and send everybody home. He had completed his ride over the hills to Cross Plo, where he had spent a day interviewing sorcerer prisoners and giving orders about the captured guns and ammunition. He had then sailed across to the city and prepared to take the weight of the World on his shoulders again. Meanwhile it was family reunion time.

On a handsome chalcedony table the same height as an earthly coffee table, lay the fourth and seventh swords of Chioxin, while three swordsman admired them.

"The first time they have been reunited in eight hundred years?" Vixini said.

"We don't know they have ever been together before," his father said. "But I suspect they have. According to the legend, Chioxin won seven more years of life from the Goddess to make the set. You've seen the fragment in the lodge, of course?"

"My lord," Addis said, "I am told that no one ever challenges a First. Is that a sutra?"

Wallie thought for a moment. "I don't recall it being totally forbidden anywhere, but to kill a First to win his sword would be a major breach of honor. You're worried about wearing this?"

"Mm?" Vixini said thoughtfully. "A First can't own anything. Maybe it's my sword?"

"It belongs to the kingdom," Addis said. "I just wear it. Provided I have some bodyguards around, I should be safe from challenge, yes?"

"Only as long as you remain a First," Wallie said.

Addis looked at him appraisingly. "Why can't I stay a First all my life? Kingship is not a craft. A king is superior to everyone by definition. Arganari XV, the First."

That was rank heresy, making Wallie wonder if his own un-Worldly thinking had infected these natural-born leaders of the next generation. The coming of the Tryst was already changing the People, and would do so much more as the industrial revolution gathered speed. But why not? It was often a good thing to break the mold, and the young were always the first to do so.

"That is very ingenious. You know the Tryst doesn't allow swordsmen to be rulers, but we could make an exception for a novice swordsman, because Firsts aren't bound by the third oath."

Vixini looked shocked. "You going to trust this smart-ass yearling to rule a kingdom, Dad?"

"What has he done wrong so far?" Wallie asked, confident that the answer would be 'nothing'.

"Nothing," Vixini admitted, and pretended not to see his protégé's leer of triumph.

Now Wallie understood why he had been prompted to

bring these two young wonders along to the war. Between
them, they had won it for him. That he had been made
to seem an idiot in the process did not bother him in the
slightest. The gods were within their rights when they played
jokes on mortals. And he *had* been an idiot, in that he had
taken so long to see what his real mission was.

"Of course he will need a first-class bodyguard. A king
must surround himself with good councilors, Addis, and
listen to them, but he must not let himself get boxed in, not
by them, nor by priests and palace officials. If you recruit
some hotshot youngsters for your guard from among the
locals, they can provide you with, not just protection, but
also an independent source of information about your
people."

Addis was nodding. "I think the present king honestly
hadn't realized that Pollex was the source of his unpopularity.
I was the first person to tell him so."

"Brave of you!"

"Just ignorant. And lucky."

"To lead your guard you'll need a respected swordsman,
a man they'll be proud to serve under. How would you feel
about Valorous Giant of Mighty Thews Vixini?"

Addis grinned wickedly. "He'd do, if I could be certain his
knowledge of the sutras was adequate. Test him on Number
981, will you?"

"Dad," said the valorous giant, "I know a mere adept
shouldn't threaten a Seventh, but if you keep throwing those
crazy epics at me, I may start trying to live up to them!"

"Mercy, mercy! I promise never to mention them again
for the next ten minutes. I shall appoint a first-class reeve
for Plo, and of course Addis will listen to his advice also…
Won't you, your Highness?"

"I pray that XIV the Merciful will live another ten years."

"How about Joraskinta? He was a king himself until your
father walked in on him."

Addis pulled a face, which did not surprise Wallie.

"You have someone else in mind, Dad?" Vixini asked
suspiciously. He did know his stepfather very well.

"Possibly me," Wallie said and two young faces flashed from incredulity to delight.

"You?" they cried in unison.

"Well, I am thinking of sending for Jja and the kids to come and join me, and staying on in Plo, although probably not as reeve. Jja was born here, you know. The Tryst has grown too big to govern from Casr alone. We need at least two centers. Casr in the north and Plo in the south would be a good match. Or perhaps Kra."

The bantering mood vanished. "What will you do about Kra, my lord?" Addis asked.

"Joraskinta has already moved about five hundred men there, so no one is getting in or out. Tomorrow I'll ride over there. Either it surrenders or we sack it."

"Can I come?" asked two voices together.

The answer, of course, was, "No." The gods had now assigned the kids their lives' work. Their campaigning days were over already.

CHAPTER 6

WALLIE TOOK REEVE OZIMSHELLO WITH HIM to Kra, because he had local knowledge and any Seventh in the Tryst was a member of the council. The only swordsmen who had ever visited a coven and lived to tell of it were Nnanji and Thana, who had described Vul as a single vast, tentacled building of black stone. Wallie would not have been surprised to find only smoking ruins at Kra. Even yet, the obsessive secrecy of the sorcerers' craft might lead them to choose suicide over surrender.

What he saw when he arrived within sight of the sorcerers' lair, just after midday, was a sheltered, fertile valley and a sprawling walled complex of black stone buildings, reminiscent of a fortified medieval monastery. It had several towers of various heights, which he inspected with his telescope. He was especially interested in the tallest.

In front of Kra stood the tents of the army, and behind it the peaks of RegiKra. Joraskinta and three companions rode forward to meet him.

"They agree to a parley, my lord," he said. "We can meet whenever you wish."

"As soon as you like, and wherever you like, as long as there can be no hidden marksmen within at least two hundred paces." Wally was acutely aware that the sorcerers knew how special he was, in that he understood more of their arcane arts than they did. He was the greatest danger they faced. A nice suit of Kevlar body armor might come in handy about now.

The parley took place under an awning that the swordsmen had erected on their side of the little river that watered the valley. As proof that the World had not yet fully adopted the ways of literacy, the only furniture was a pair of hard wooden benches, without a table. The three lords of the council rode there with a Second, who led the horses away. Two persons emerged from the gates of Kra, and when they drew close it was clear that one was only a child. The adult, in a blue gown, dismounted stiffly. The girl took both horses away, back to the gates.

The woman who came limping across the little stone bridge had pushed her hood back to reveal a strong, intelligent face and silver-streaked hair. The two embassies faced each other across the benches for a moment, and then she made the equal's salute to Wallie, giving her name as Uzdrawun.

He responded, and presented Ozimshello, the elder of his two companions.

She smiled sourly. "The turncoat." It was an old sorcerers' trick to display superior knowledge, but how had she learned details of the battle? Easily, because anyone in Plo could be a sorcerer agent, and the swordsmen's siege line would not keep out pigeons.

"And another member of our council, Lord Joraskinta."

Another sneer. "The weakling who gave up a throne at sword point."

Wallie was reminded of his long-ago negotiations with Rotanxi, sorcerer of the seventh rank. He had been a grouch too, but together they had hammered out the Treaty of Casr. It was too early to give up hope.

"Please be seated, my lady." He sat opposite her, flanked by his companions. "I understood that sorcerer covens were always governed by councils of thirteen."

"You were correctly informed. Nine of our members were at Cross Plo and are presumed dead. The other three are too old and infirm to attend, but they have granted me plenipotentiary powers. State your terms, swordsman."

Not so fast!

"Lord Krandrak is dead, but we took forty-nine prisoners at Cross Plo, persons whose facemarks did not pass close inspection. They refuse to give their names or ranks."

"That is decreed by our sutras."

"We must change that. I have been studying your buildings through a telescope. That was a sorcerer discovery, although I taught Vul how to turn the image the right way up. I notice that you are now using lightning conductors. That was another secret I taught Vul."

She shrugged, giving away nothing.

"Tell me, what are those wires on the roof of that tallest tower?" he asked.

"Perching wires for birds. You know how we use pigeons to send messages. It was you who gave that secret away to the World."

"But pigeons do not perch on wires! They walk on the ground." Just as crows usually did.

"We hold all birds sacred, as you can see from our facemarks."

"Perhaps you do, but now you have better ways of sending messages. There are wires like that on the sorcerer tower in Casr. I have seen them a thousand times and failed to recognize them for what they are, but now I know. I inquired of the Plo garrison just when Lord Pollex began making preparations on the far bank, and they confirmed that your knowledge of my movements has been far too detailed to have been spooned out in pigeon droppings. That would have needed thousands of pigeons. Now you talk at a distance with those wires. What is your name for that device, Lady Uzdrawun?"

Her face was a rock. "I have no idea what you are talking about."

Joraskinta and Ozimshello must be wondering if he'd lost his mind. He did not take his eyes off the hard-bitten old sorceress.

"Yes you do. Well, let us go on to the terms. First, my lady, let me say that I am a man of peace, surprised as you may be to hear that statement from a swordsman. But you started this war. You struck down thirty men at Cross Zek, and murdered two heralds. You began the war and you lost it. Kra has fallen. My word rules. Tampering with facemarks is a capital offense among the People, as you well know, so either you surrender Kra to me unconditionally, or I shall put all our forty-nine prisoners to death and every adult I catch in those buildings. Every single one! And when I have done that, I shall move against the other covens, for they have obviously been supporting you. I know they aided the assassins Kra sent against myself and Lord Nnanji. Lord Rotanxi of Vul and I tried to prevent an all-out war between swordsmen and sorcerers, and for many years our treaty held. As far as I am concerned, the sorcerers have broken it, not the swordsmen. I ask you again, what is the name of your long-distance way of talking through the air?"

She sneered. "Kra never signed your treaty. You are planning to destroy the sorcerers' craft, which, like all crafts, was established by the Goddess Herself."

Wallie kept a firmer grip on his temper. He was frightened now that he had gone too far and she was going to call his bluff by telling him to begin the massacre, which he never could.

"I am going to transform it. I am going to make sorcerers into teachers—not teachers of children, for that craft exists already, but teachers of adults, adults of any craft. Your discovery of writing has already brought great blessings to the People. Traders, apothecaries, priests... almost every craft can benefit from writing, and yet you hoarded it for centuries. Telescopes, soap, lightning conductors—all of these are valuable to the People. I will see Kra opened as a great school, where adults can come and learn your wisdom."

Now he thought he saw a flicker of interest in her eyes, and realized that it was a first spark of hope in a stygian darkness of despair. Perhaps she had been expecting the massacre.

"You will teach the People, for example, how to take a container of glass or ceramic and fill it with plates of two kinds of metal, such as copper and lead; how to connect the similar plates together with wire; how to top it up with acid. What sort of acid do you use? Not vinegar. I know you have much stronger acids than that."

She bit her lip. "The higher volcanic acid. Dilute, of course."

She probably meant sulfuric, and sulfurous acid would be "lower volcanic". Wallie had a whole new language to learn and he couldn't wait to get started.

"And what do you call this device?"

Her name for a battery was *god box*. Electricity was *god spark*, and radio telegraphy—which she now admitted to having—was *god speech*. It would all make sense to worshippers of the Fire God, much more sense than Wallie's terms, which were mostly based on the Latin name for amber, *electrum*.

"Those are my dictates, my lady. You will open Kra to the World and reveal your secrets. You will make your wisdom available to benefit all the People. But I promise that I will give you other secrets, just as I gave Vul the lightning conductor and the hot air balloon. I will swear that there will be no reprisals or trials, no blame for starting the war. We shall write out this agreement and bind our two crafts to observe its terms forever, and it will be known as the Treaty of Kra."

She thought for a moment, fists clenched. She glanced at the other two unfriendly swordsman faces, then back to Wallie.

"I have no choice, do I?"

"Not really," he said. "Starting a war and then losing it is a very good road to disaster. But I think you will find the future is better than the past. I can show you much better ways of making god spark than a god box."

For the first time she smiled. "Bribery! Very well, my lord, I must agree."

Three things Wallie insisted on being shown right away: the telegraph office, the foundry where gun barrels were cast, and especially the places where thunder powder was made and stored, because he wanted to put those under guard. He took Joraskinta with him and sent Ozimshello back to the camp as insurance against treachery. Uzdrawun acted as guide.

The armory and magazine seemed genuine, but were almost empty. According to Uzdrawun, all the weapons and ammunition had fallen into the hands of the Tryst at the Battle of Cross Plo. If she was telling the truth, the sorcerers in Kra did not have enough gunpowder left to blow up anything significant.

The foundry impressed Wallie, although he knew little about casting. The furnaces were cold that day and the only person he met there was an elderly supervisor of the fifth rank. Wallie explained what a piston was and asked if he could make one tight enough to compress air, but slick enough to move. He outlined how a steam engine worked, with a boiler, a cylinder, and a condenser.

"A device like that," he said, "could drive ships against wind and current both. Can you imagine that? Think how easy travel would be then. Such a device plying the waters of the River would be a true marriage of your Fire God and the Goddess."

He left the old man open-mouthed, but he thought Uzdrawun was starting to believe in him.

The telegraph office was located on the uppermost room of the tower where he had seen the aerials. It was an untidy jumble, as if a packrat's workshop, a laboratory, and a library had all been run through a blender together, but it was a glorious treasure house for him. He could have spent days there. Amid this spider's nightmare of wires, few of which seemed to be insulated, he recognized equipment he had seen in museums: Leyden jar capacitors, acid batteries the size of washtubs, and the brass rods of a spark-gap transmitter. The tiny glass tube of the coherer fascinated him, because it proved that the sorcerers could create vacuums. They were further advanced than he had thought.

A single male Third sat at a table, sorting pieces of paper. He looked up in alarm when he saw two swordsmen gazing down at him.

"I am Shonsu," Wallie said, "the monster himself. I am not going to draw my sword in here, nor even wave my hands around, so let us forget formal saluting. Your name?"

"Zzamb, my lord." He touched his forehead in the sorcerers' salute.

"We do not use formal gestures within the coven," Uzdrawun said.

"Good. Tell me how god speech works, Sorcerer Zzamb."

The Third looked in fright to the Sixth.

"Do as Lord Shonsu says."

It was much as Wallie had guessed: a spark-gap transmitter, an aerial, and a receiver using the iron-filings coherer. "I can show you how to make one much, much better. How far can you reach? Can you send a message directly to Casr?"

"Certainly not at this time of day, my lord. After dark I have done so, sometimes. Just now I would direct the message to Ulk, with instructions to send it on, by way of Zan. If Zan or even Casr, managed to receive it clearly, they would cancel the repeat."

"And if Honorable Uzdrawun wished to send such a message, could she dictate it to you, or would she have to write it down?"

Again Zzamb hesitated and again the Sixth told him to answer.

"Regulations are to write it down, my lord, but I could send from dictation, if she spoke slowly."

"I will write one out for you."

Wallie sat down and wrote on the slate provided, "SHONSU, LIEGE OF TRYST, TO WOGGAN, WIZARD OF CASR STOP KRA HAS FALLEN STOP MY WORD IS LAW STOP INFORM LORD BOARIYI WAR IS WON STOP INFORM LADY JJA HER

SON GREAT HERO PROMOTED ADEPT STOP INFORM LADY
THANA HER SON BETROTHED PRINCESS NOW HEIR TO PLO
KINGDOM STOP NOT JOKING STOP ASK RECIPIENTS TO REPLY
STOP MESSAGE ENDS"

Zzamb had been fussing around, making his equipment
ready, turning switches, connecting wires. When he was
ready, he pulled a face at the length of the text, while he
stuffed his ears with felt plugs. Then he reached for a brass
key the size of a car jack, and began.

Blue fire exploded between the brass rods with a clap of
thunder that made Wallie jump. The noise was incredible,
going on and on, but in recognizable dots and dashes. Soon
the air reeked of ozone. Zzamb stopped, unplugged one ear,
and put it close to a box the size of a hockey puck supported
on two slender rods. Wallie decided that a set of headphones
might be a good first improvement. Of course a better
way of generating radio waves would help, too—either an
alternator, or a thermionic tube.

Zzamb's frown suddenly became a broad smile. "I have
Ult responding already, my lord!"

He replaced the plug in his ear and the spark machine
began its terrible racket again. Wallie gestured to his
companions that it was time to go, and led them down the
stairs. Now he understood the noises he had heard in the
Casr tower.

Even at ground level, it was possible to hear that Kra was
still transmitting. God speech was well named. The larger
alphabet would make any Morse-type code less efficient,
and each dot and dash took far longer than should be
necessary. It might take an hour to spell out the message
to Ult, and twice as long again to reach Casr, but even a
Neolithic-quality radio still beat pigeons. Wallie chuckled,
thinking that he would know when the message had been
received when he heard Thana's screams of joy. She would
probably come to Plo for the coronation.

"That is very impressive," he told Uzdrawun. "But I can
show you how to make it a hundred times better. That little
river... Does it flow year-round?"

She nodded, bewildered by the apparent change of subject.

"And does it flow through a narrow gap, anywhere? Could it be dammed, I mean?"

"I have no idea, my lord." Evidently senior sorcerers did not go mountain climbing.

"Never mind just now, then. We shall make your god speech so clear that Zan can talk to Kra and Ult at the same time, or even have the palace in Plo speak directly to the palace in Casr. We shall put stations in every city in the World and charge people to send messages. Please let me know when you receive acknowledgment or replies." *Damn!* "But I forgot to ask after Lord Nnanji. Have you heard news of his health recently?"

"We received a report on Lord Nnanji yesterday, my lord. He left Casr about six weeks ago and should arrive in Plo no later than Midwives' Day. Extraordinarily fast travel!"

So the Nnanji express was running again. Wallie discovered that he was not surprised by the news. He had played out the stand-in role he had been given and was now expected to return the seventh sword to Nnanji so he could continue his life's work of building the Tryst into a world-wide regime of law enforcement. Wallie's job had always been to kick-start an industrial revolution, and clearly he had not been progressing fast enough to satisfy the Goddess.

But he also felt a huge surge of relief that Nnanji had been spared. The Tryst had dodged the bullet this time. It could not always be as lucky.

CHAPTER 7

THE SHIP JUST TYING UP AT PLO WAS FLYING Nnanji's flag. He must have learned in the last few days that the war was over, but he had a sizable crowd of swordsmen on board with him, so he had been prepared to fight. Wallie was waiting on the wharf with an honor guard.

Typically Nnanji did not wait for the port official's clearance, but came running down the gangplank as soon as it was in place, red ponytail flapping. Fifteen years ago he would have vaulted over the rail, but he was in his thirties now and even Nnanji had to start slowing down eventually. Yet he had changed very little in those years, even retaining most of his youthful slimness. And now he seemed none the worse for his recent narrow escape, except that he might be wearing the waistband of his kilt a fraction lower than was normal, thus exposing the edge of his scar. Amazingly, after all those years of frequent mortal combats, that was still almost the only scar he had. Grinning mightily, he strode over to Wallie and pulled his sword in salute. His eyes gleamed when he saw the seventh sword making the response.

"Not now, brother," Wallie said. "When we get to the palace."

Barely visible eyebrows rose. "Not the barracks?"

"No, you and I to the palace. May I present Reeve Ozimshello..."

As soon as a minimum of formalities were over, the two liege lords mounted and rode off, leaving the reeve to deal with the rest of the visitors.

"You won the war, I hear. I feel cheated."

"I did not. I made an idiot of myself. I stood up before the assembly and promised all kinds of things and did none of them. I was outwitted by a sorcerer, can you imagine that?"

Nnanji looked impressed, if not quite convinced that he was hearing the truth. "Well, what did happen?"

"I sent Vixini against them. He did it. It's quite a story."

"Later, then. This is quite a town. And if that's where we're headed, that's quite a palace. What's the hurry?"

"A couple of things you should know. One is that the old king is failing. His heir may have to take over almost any day now. His heir is another Arganari."

"He had two sons named that, or he sired a replacement?" Nnanji never forgot anything.

"He adopted a likely lad and gave him that name. He'll succeed as Arganari XV."

Nnanji shrugged. "We'll keep him honest. What's the second thing?"

"That the heir is so desperately eager to meet you that I almost had to tie him to the throne to stop him from rushing down to the port with me, and royalty mustn't do that."

The familiar pale eyes narrowed in a sideways grin. "You're keeping something from me, brother."

"The heir's original name was Addis."

It was very rare to see Lord Nnanji surprised, but he gulped and rode on in silence for about half a minute as the horses plodded up a steep part of the hill. "Is this your doing?"

"Not a bit of it. The old fellow is almost blind, but he thought he recognized his son's voice, and you'd given him the hairclip. Why did you give him the hairclip?"

"I have no idea. I don't remember giving him the hairclip, although Thana swears I did." Had Nnanji ever had to make that sort of admission before?

"Well, the king realized that Addis was Arganari reborn, and adopted him."

"You say 'realized'? You believe that?"

"I've sort of known it since before he was born," Wallie said. "The last time I saw the demigod he hinted at it. The prince was killed just after you and Thana had exchanged your marriage vows, remember, and the god told me that you conceived a son that night. He said that Arganari's was one of the great souls, and they are always needed for important lives." Nnanji himself was another, the god had said, but Wallie wasn't about to tell him so. His ego needed no additional support.

Nnanji whistled and took another look at the palace looming over them. "The gods have done him proud, haven't they! My son a king? He's very young...". ."

"He's doing wonderfully already. Vixini's been watching the palace officials coming around to the idea. At first they thought they'd run the brat, then they were outraged that he wouldn't march to their beat, and now they're starting to believe the old king's dictum that the Goddess has sent them a miracle. I guessed something like this was in the wind on the day Addis was sworn. The assembly cheered him because he was the son of Nnanji. He hadn't even had time to sheath his sword, but he saluted them with it, and they loved it. It was perfect! Now Plo has taken him to their heart. If the son of Nnanji marries their princess, then the ferocious Nnanji the Barbarian won't sack their city."

Nnanji might not have heard that. Often he seemed superhuman, but just then his face had taken on a very goofy proud-father expression. His parents had been rug makers, and his son was to rule one of the World's greatest kingdoms.

"The Goddess moves in strange ways, sometimes," he said at last. "You had to fight and win a war just to get Addis to Plo?"

"I didn't win it, brother. I told you, Vixini won the war. You should hear what the minstrels are singing about him."

"Good for him," his oath brother said coolly. Nnanji loved heroic epics, especially epics about Nnanji. Epics about swordsmen of the next generation would take some getting used to. "So who started this war? Who killed all my men at Gor and Arbo?"

"A grossly corrupt reeve, Pollex, who knew his reign would end as soon as you hit town, and a reactionary grand wizard, Krandrak. Once they'd killed some of your men, war was certain, which let Pollex swear his men by the blood oath."

"They're both dead now?"

"Very. Oh, by the way, you must have made a very fast recovery after we shipped out."

"I don't like lying around in bed doing nothing."

Wallie laughed aloud. "Oh, I know that! You never do. What I was about to say is that your wife tells me she is expecting your fourth child. Congratulations."

By the time he had explained as much about god speech as Nnanji would ever want to know, they were riding into the palace courtyard. Wallie did not mention his plans to turn Kra into a university. The language had no word for that, and Nnanji wouldn't be interested anyway. Nor did he mention his idea of opening a branch office of the Tryst here in Plo. There would be time aplenty to talk about that.

A band was playing, the palace guard was lined up outside the great door.

"Is this for me or the holiday?" Nnanji asked as he dropped to the cobbles.

This was Midwives' Day, start of a new year. That felt nicely symbolic.

"Both."

Only after the formal salutes and responses were the liege lords ushered into the great hall. Prince Arganari seemed very small at the far end, standing by the throne, and Vixini behind him not a great deal bigger.

"Wait!" Wallie said, drawing the seventh sword. "Take this now. We can say the words later if you want. He's only a prince yet, so he will salute you. But he's got the fourth, so you'd better have this for your response."

And then, not even waiting for the heralds to announce them, the two proud fathers marched forward, side by side, hastening to greet their spectacular sons.

EPILOGUE:

THE DEATH OF NNANJI

THE SUMMONS CAME JUST AFTER DAWN: A quiet tap on the door, a voice outside.

"Coming!" Wallie called, and pulled himself awake. He sat up, rubbed his face, ran fingers through his hair. Then he put his feet on the floor and dressed. It didn't take long, although a robe was slower than a kilt. He gathered his hair into his ponytail—a thinner ponytail now, far more salt than pepper. He fumbled with his harness.

"You go ahead," Jja said from the far side of the bed. "I'll follow as soon as I can."

"Whenever you're ready, love. I'm sure it'll be a while yet."

The corridor outside was empty. As he strode along it, he reflected that an epoch was ending. He thought briefly of that gangling, awkward teenager he had met on a beach, a Second so hopelessly cursed by the Goddess that he could no longer fence. He thought of the man that boy had become and what he had achieved, transforming a world. Then he nodded to the heralds and guards on the door, crossed the antechamber, and arrived finally at the bedchamber beyond.

Thana was there—bent, now, and silver-haired. She rose as Wallie entered, and he embraced her briefly. She had probably been there all night. The healer was a nervous little man, strangely unimpressive for his high reputation, but perhaps he was merely awed at having to preside over such an epochal passing. Wallie raised eyebrows in a question, the healer nodded, mouthing the word, "Soon."

And Nnanji. Bright red hair had long since faded to a dowdy fawn, lean features had become gaunt. He had recognized Wallie and the others when they first arrived, two days ago; he had smiled but not spoken. Now his eyes were closed and his breathing was very shallow. The door opened to admit Lord Tomisolaan. He went first to Thana, as Wallie had, and then to stand over the dying man. He glanced at the healer and then Wallie, both of whom nodded that the time had come.

Tomisolaan, swordsman of the seventh rank, took up the seventh sword of Chioxin from the table beside the bed, and placed it on the coverlet, laying his father's hand on the hilt: *Live by this; wield it in her service; die holding it.* No swordsman could ever have obeyed those commands any better than Nnanji had. And this son looked very like him. His hair was as red, and his mastery of a sword almost as impressive. His eldest, another Nnanji, had been sworn in as a novice just a year ago.

Three more family members entered to join the vigil: Queen Argair, King Arganari XV the Blessed, and Tomisolaan's wife, whose name Wallie never could remember. Jja arrived, closely followed by her second son, Lord Jjon, who went to stand with his parents. Voices murmured outside, in the antechamber, and more family members entered.

The last were Lord Vixini, reeve of Plo, and his wife Nnadaro. Theirs had been the fastest romance in the history of the World. Nnadaro had accompanied her parents to her brother's wedding in Plo, and lightning had struck the moment she and Vixini set eyes on each other. Childhood friendship had blossomed into marriage fast enough to use up the leftover wedding cake—so Addis had said. Nnadaro put an arm around Thana.

So Nnanji was dying at last, but dying in the best way possible: at peace, in his own bed, in the care of his loved ones, not bleeding to death on some distant street with his bowels in his hands, a fate he had risked innumerable times. And in a sense his world was already dead, murdered by the sorcerers and Wallie, who had taught them. Swordsmen often carried guns now, and the juniors bragged as much about their marksmanship as their fencing. An industrial revolution was what the Goddess had wanted, with the Tryst to keep order and fairness and avert the worst of the calamities that beset that transition on other worlds. Wallie had delivered the first, and Nnanji the second.

None of the youngsters present, Wallie reflected, could really appreciate what a great miracle it was that the family contingent from Plo was able to be there at all. The telegrams had arrived only two weeks ago. He had at once sent word to Addis that the gunboat *Chioxin* was at his disposal, and would have steam up within two hours.

Exactly two hours later they had departed, leaving Prince Argie to take care of the kingdom—plus, of course, his own children, including the future Arganari XVII the Tyrannical. Addis had been unsympathetic to his son's misgivings, pointing out that he had been a lot younger when the kingdom had been dropped on him.

In their race from Plo to Casr they had traveled on three more steam boats and four trains, timing their transfers to the minute. Public newscasts had followed their progress. Not all the Tryst's gunboats were as speedy as *Chioxin*, which was screw-driven, but in general they were the fastest things on the River. Now that even trader ships could have radio, the Tryst was at last managing to clean up the pirates who had ravaged honest commerce for centuries.

News of Nnanji's impending demise had flashed around the World within hours, and toward the end of their journey it seemed that half the stern-wheelers and paddle boats in the World were racing to Quo with Sevenths aboard.

The room was very quiet now.

The healer went to the bed and produced a stethoscope. Kra still made the best stethoscopes. After a moment he closed Nnanji's eyes and stepped back. Nnadaro put both arms around her mother.

Then it was Wallie's turn. After allowing a long moment for reflection, he went to the bed and retrieved the seventh sword, musing that this must surely be the last time he would ever touch it. He made the salute to a hero. He glanced around at each of the swordsmen present, then led them out through the antechamber, all except Addis, for he was still only a First.

At the top of the grand staircase, he motioned for them to precede him. The great hall below was packed with Sevenths. More than four hundred had been present at the council meeting yesterday, and others had arrived on the evening train from Quo. When Tomisolaan, Vixini, and Jjon reached the bottom, Wallie started down after them. A peculiarity of the grand staircase was that it included a seemingly useless landing about five steps up. Now he understood its purpose and wondered what genius had designed it. He stopped there, where he was in clear view of everyone.

"Lord Nnanji has been called to the Goddess," he said, "and She will cherish him dearly, for the great services he has rendered in this life. I can no longer fulfill my duties as they should be fulfilled, so we need a new liege." At least fifty of the Sevenths present would consider themselves qualified to succeed, and no doubt several of them were, but one was doubly qualified, for he had the right of inheritance on his side. Yesterday's council had agreed on that, seeing that any other decision would risk a bloodbath or civil war. He was also an honorable and honest man, which in Wallie's own opinion, was the most important factor of all.

"I give the Chioxin sword to his son, Lord Tomisolaan, commanding all of you to swear to him the third oath as you swore it to his father."

As he knelt to Tomisolaan, he recalled the prophecy of the demigod: *He will be Nnanji the Great, founder of the first dynasty. For almost a thousand years the symbol of his house will be the sapphire sword.*

When the brief ceremony was over, Wallie rose, which was no longer the effortless process it had once been. As Jjon prostrated himself before his brother to swear the blood oath, Wallie went slowly back up the stairs to join the rest of the family.

ABOUT THE AUTHOR

Dave Duncan, born in Scotland in 1933, is a Canadian citizen. He received his diploma from Dundee High School and got his college education at the University of Saint Andrews. He moved to Canada in 1955, where he still lives with his wife. He has three grown children and four grandchildren. He spent thirty years as a petroleum geologist. He has had dozens of fantasy and science fiction novels published, among them *A Rose-Red City, Magic Casement,* and *The Reaver Road,* as well as a highly praised historical novel, *Daughter of Troy,* published, for commercial reasons, under the pseudonym Sarah B. Franklin. He also published the Longdirk series of novels, *Demon Sword, Demon Knight,* and *Demon Rider,* under the name Ken Hood.

In the fall of 2007, Duncan's 2006 novel, *Children of Chaos,* published by Tor Books, was nominated for both the Prix Aurora Award and the Endeavour Award. In May 2013, Duncan, a 1989 founding member of SFCanada, was honored by election as a lifetime member by his fellow writers, editors, and academics. His website is www.daveduncan.com.

OPEN ROAD
INTEGRATED MEDIA

Open Road Integrated Media is a digital publisher and multimedia content company. Open Road creates connections between authors and their audiences by marketing its ebooks through a new proprietary online platform, which uses premium video content and social media.

www.ingramcontent.com/pod-product-compliance
Lightning Source LLC
Chambersburg PA
CBHW020426030726
47495CB00006B/1671